LAWS OF YOU SERIES

WHEN I'M WITH YOU

SAMANTHA BRINN

To everyone who ever told me I was either "too much" or "not enough."

Fuck off.

Prologue
Asher

Five Months Ago

Cameras flash and reporters yell out my name as I get out of the backseat of my SUV in front of the Fairmont Hotel in downtown Pittsburgh. I grin and wave, well used to the fanfare that comes with arriving at an event in this city. As the veteran quarterback of the Renegades, Pittsburgh's much beloved NFL team, I attend a lot of events, but there is no event quite like the Kids Play annual gala. Started by a retired hockey player, Kids Play is a powerful foundation in the sports world that funds sports equipment for kids and sponsors scholarships for teams and leagues at all levels of sport.

After almost nine years as a professional athlete, you would think it would get old. I know there are guys who have been in the league as long as I have who would rather sit in a two-hour ice bath than show up at one more event, but that's never been me. I live for this. I have always been fascinated by the razzle-dazzle of a big, fancy event. Charmed by the well-dressed athletes and city movers and shakers gathered together to raise money for a cause. The hum of energy from the crowd is a welcome shock to the system. It buzzes through me as I make my way towards the green carpet stretched along the sidewalk in front of the hotel.

"Excuse me, can you take our picture?"

The voice, rich and smooth and commanding even in its question, stops me in my tracks. I turn, ready to smile at the sexy voice that has me thinking about laying, limbs tangled with its owner, in a darkened bedroom in the middle of the night. But when I get my first look at her, my smile freezes, and I feel like I've been hit by lightning. She is standing with three other girls, but she holds every ounce of my attention. She's tall, with curves for days poured into a floor length black dress that leaves her shoulders bare and shows a flash of well-toned leg out of a slit stretching to mid-thigh. Her blonde hair tumbles in waves down her back, and her cobalt blue eyes arrow straight through me. She exudes purpose and an aura of something unnamable that is sexy as fuck. She is tapping her phone against her palm in a gesture of anxiety and impatience so incongruous to the confident way she carries herself that I am instantly intrigued. Realizing I may have been staring at the gorgeous stranger for an uncomfortable amount of time, I grab her phone and motion the four girls together.

"You ladies look stunning," I say, and I inwardly cringe because *for fuck's sake, Asher. Do better.*

I snap a bunch of pictures and hand the phone back to the blonde stranger whose gaze is making my insides go haywire. My fingers graze hers, and the electricity of the touch shoots up my arm. I have never reacted like this to another person in my life, and I have the sudden urge to grab her hand and pull her away so we can be alone. But I still have some chill, so I take a step back and flash all four girls a grin.

"Enjoy the party." I go to turn towards the hotel entrance before I think, *what the hell*. Looking straight at the blonde, I say "save me a dance Blondie." Her cheeks instantly flush and I love it. Forcing myself to walk away from her when all I want to do is stand there and stare like a super fucking creeper, I shoot her a wink and head towards the hotel.

"Come meet my friends," Jeremy says, gesturing towards a table on the edge of the dance floor. Jeremy is the founder and executive director of Kids Play. We have crossed paths on and off over the years I have been in the league, and he is an excellent guy. I love what he has done with his foundation and have been looking around for ways to get involved. When I mentioned that to him, he immediately gave me his number and told me to call him next week to talk about it.

"Hey best pals." Jeremy starts talking as we approach. The only guy sitting at the table starts talking to Jeremy, but I don't hear anything he says because the blonde from outside is occupying one of the chairs, and all I can see is her.

"Have you guys met Asher Hansley? He's going to be doing some work with the foundation."

Hearing my name snaps me back to reality and I find my words. "I met these lovely ladies outside earlier." I shoot a smile right at the blonde. "They drafted me to be their photographer."

"Great, well, Ash, this is Emma, Molly, Hallie, and Julie."

With the last name, he points to the blonde, and I finally have a name. *Julie.* Then he gestures to the guy, who has his gaze firmly pinned on Hallie, the pretty brunette sitting next to Julie.

"This is Ben, one of my best friends. And wait, where's Jordan?"

"Having sex," Julie and Molly say together.

I grin at that, liking them already. "I think you all are my people."

I chat with them for a few more minutes. But when the music, which has been loud and upbeat, changes to something slower, I take it as a sign and hold my hand out to Julie.

"Want to dance Blondie?"

She pauses for a minute before shrugging. "What the hell?" She takes my hand and lets me pull her up.

"Well, if we're dancing now, I'm going to hunt me down an athlete." Molly grins and stands. She has this magnetic energy about her that I like instantly. I point a couple of tables away.

"Take a walk past table twelve. Rookie table."

I wink at her and then lead Julie to the dance floor. When we reach it, I turn her around, sliding my hand around her waist and bringing our joint hands up between us. The movement has a dull, familiar pain shooting through my right shoulder, but I ignore it. No time for that right now. Not when Julie wraps her hand around my neck, fitting herself perfectly against me. In her heels, she is the perfect height for me to rest my cheek against her temple. The rightness of her body against mine is sudden and startling and has my heart pounding against my chest in a way that I hope she can't feel. I wrack my brain for something to say, but like the first time I saw her earlier in the night, words escape me.

Get your shit together Asher. Gorgeous, intriguing woman in your arms. Conversation. Make conversation.

"You look gorgeous tonight."

Fucking hell. Stunning earlier and gorgeous now. Get some new material.

She looks unimpressed. "Really? That's what you're going with? That tired line?"

I shrug at her. "Just because it's a line doesn't make it any less true. You're gorgeous."

"I know." She smirks at me, and the look goes straight to my dick, which I keep in line through sheer force of will.

My arm tightens around her waist, and I turn us gently to the music. "Have you been to this gala before?"

"I have. Every year since it started, actually. Jeremy and my brother Ben have been best friends since college."

"I've been every year too. First one was the year I joined the league. I wish I had seen you here. We could have met before tonight." *What the fuck is wrong with you?* I inwardly cringe again at the cheesy as shit line, hoping she'll just let it sail by.

No such luck. She smirks at me again.

"You're just full of lines tonight. Guess I should expect it. Football player and all."

"Hey now, I'm not just a football player. I'm a quarterback."

She snorts out a laugh, and fuck if I don't find it sexy as hell.

"Oh, a quarterback, he says, as if I should be impressed by that."

"Well, aren't you?"

She laughs again. "Um, no. Look around. Jeremy is my twin brother's best friend. I've been surrounded by professional athletes most of my adult life. I am a lot of things, but impressed is not one of them."

Fuck if I'm not completely turned on by her nonchalance bordering on complete disinterest. Something is definitely wrong with me. "Tell me about all those other things. What else are you?"

"A lawyer, for one. A busy one." An anxious look crosses

her face at that, and I feel a tremor in the hand wrapped around my neck. Like the phone tapping earlier tonight, it seems so out of character for the sharp-tongued, has her shit together, ball-buster in my arms that it makes me want to unravel her completely.

The hand I have around her waist drops lower to sit right at the curve of her ass, and I pull her tighter against me. She lets me. The move brings our faces closer together, and her gaze drops to my lips. Something intense passes between us. Forgetting where we are, I move closer to her. My entire world shrinks to the distance between us, my focus wholly centered on laying my lips on hers. Our mouths are centimeters apart when the music changes suddenly, turning loud and upbeat.

Julie jerks away from me and takes a step back. She glances around the dance floor and back at me, and I panic for a second that she is about to walk away, and I'll never see her again.

"Can I get your number?" I blurt it out louder than I mean to. My chill has apparently escaped me completely. "I'd like to see you again."

She looks at me for a second, considering.

Just when I think she's about to cave, she smiles wickedly and says, "I don't think so. But thanks for the dance. See you around, Hot Shot."

Then she turns and walks back to her table. I stand there alone on the crowded dance floor, staring after her, wondering what the fuck just happened and when I can make it happen again.

Chapter One
Julie

I jerk awake at the sound of a door slamming, my heart pounding out of my chest. Weak winter light filters through the room as I rub my bleary eyes, trying to get my bearings. As quickly as my aching neck allows, I survey my surroundings. Bookshelf. Expensive couch I never sit on. Peppermint Hershey Kiss wrappers—my favorite candy that I hoard in December like the world is ending—scattered all over my desk. Mug still half full of the coffee I made last night in an unsuccessful attempt to stay awake. Kessler file stacked on the floor. Kessler draft last will and testament now a crumpled mess from serving as a pillow for my impromptu nap. And is that...yep. A puddle of drool right on the disposition of tangible personal property clause.

Classy, Julie. How super law partner who definitely has her shit together of you.

The giggling from downstairs snaps me to attention. I would know that giggle anywhere. My life-long best friend Hallie was never a giggler until she and my twin brother Ben got together, but now the two of them walk around with perma-grins on their faces. And Hallie giggles. Ben was, evidently, in love with her for eleven years before he worked up the nerve to tell her this past summer. They got engaged a few days ago and I don't know how I missed his pining for all those years. I never miss anything—especially not when it comes to the people closest to me, and no one is closer to me than Ben. But his love for her caught me completely off guard, and there is nothing I hate more than being caught off guard.

The footsteps on the stairs snap me to action. I swipe all the candy wrappers into the trash before flying to my feet, one hand swiping down my face and the other plunging into my top desk drawer for my emergency makeup bag. I whip a brush through my hair and reach for my lip gloss.

The footsteps pause before they reach the top of the stair-case outside my office, and I don't have to see it to know that Ben has Hallie pressed against the wall, probably kissing her senseless. Those two can barely go ten minutes without having their mouths attached together. I love them both madly but good lord, that is a lot of kissing.

Although this morning, I'm grateful for it because it gives me a couple extra minutes to pull myself together. I tug on the sweater hanging on the back of my chair, swipe on some lip gloss, and pinch my cheeks to add some color. By the time my office door opens, I've shoved the Kessler will into a drawer and erased all other signs that I just napped on my desk like a college student cramming for finals.

When Hallie strolls in with Ben following close behind, I paste what I hope is a serene smile on my face and start randomly typing on my keyboard, hoping I look busy and put together and not at all the twisted-up hot mess I am on the inside.

The story of my fucking life.

"Seriously, Jules, it's eight-thirty on a Saturday morning," Hallie says, handing me a take-out coffee cup—bless her—and dropping down on my office couch. She is bright-eyed and glowing, everything about her giving off the kind of contentment that comes from a rock-solid relationship and the soul deep love coming off her in waves. An involuntary rush of jealousy settles in my stomach, and I immediately hate myself for it.

"Didn't you leave your mega law firm so you didn't have to work at stupid o'clock on the weekend?" Ben asks, sprawling out next to Hallie. He wraps an arm around her and tugs her closer, as if the six inches of distance between them is too much for him to bear. "What time did you even get here this morning?"

"Oh, you know, a while ago," I say vaguely, taking a sip of the latte Hallie brought me and hoping they'll drop it. Telling them I'm here because I never left last night and that the last thing I remember before hearing the door slam five minutes ago was idly wondering if I could get an Uber at four in the morning is a complete nonstarter. I will take the secret of my middle of the night desk naps to my grave. Smart, sophisticated, have-it-all-together owners of their own law firm do not take four-hour naps with their heads pillowed on estate planning documents.

And that's what I am. A partner in a law firm that Hallie and I started with our best friends Emma and Molly. We have been planning this in one way or another since Hallie and I met Emma and Molly during our first year of law school. We officially opened for business a month ago but left our jobs this past summer to start putting our plans into action. We started off as a firm focused solely on estate planning, but last summer Hallie made a big career change and switched her practice to family law with a focus on adoption, transitioning the bulk of her estate planning clients to me.

Ben is right that we started this firm to give ourselves the kind of balance that doesn't usually exist in the big law firm world. But our firm is new and there is always something to do, and I like Saturdays at the office. I can plow through a whole pile of work without email notifications and ringing phones and my friends constantly coming in and out. No one is ever here on Saturdays. Come to think of it...

"What are you two even doing here anyway?"

"We came to tell you about our plans for the football game," Hallie says, pulling off her jacket and making herself more comfortable on the couch.

I scratch the inside of my left wrist, my fingers itching to pull the Kessler estate planning documents out of my drawer and get back to work. "You couldn't just text me?"

"We tried, but none of our texts were delivered and your phone kept going straight to voicemail. I figured you were here, so I tried calling the office line, but I kept getting a busy signal, so we came in person."

I reach for my phone and try to turn it on. Dead. Glancing over at my office phone, I see the receiver sitting on my desk, not in the cradle where it should be. I must have knocked it off while I was asleep. *Fuck.* My stomach clenches, and my heart pounds at the thought of being totally unreachable to my clients. I hang up my desk phone and hastily plug my cell into the charging station on my desk. I take a deep breath once my phone boots up, and when I see the only missed messages are the ones from Hallie and Ben, my heartrate returns to normal.

"So you'll come, right?"

It's only then I realize Hallie is still talking, oblivious to my panic.

"Sorry, what did you say? I spaced for a second." I wince inwardly, hating having to ask her to repeat herself.

"The football game, Jules. Playoffs? The clients your dad was supposed to take to the game got snowed in and can't make it, and your mom said the only place she's going today is to the kitchen for snacks, so we're taking the tickets."

"Seriously, Hal? It's freezing outside and I have a ton of work to do." I love a football game, especially when we get to sit in my dad's corporate seats in the third row right on the fifty-yard line, but I do not love a football game in January. And I definitely don't love a football game when I have a ten-mile-long to-do list.

"Come on, Jules," Ben pipes in. "Molly and Emma are coming too. Jeremy even got passes to the friends and family room after the game, and Allie and Jordan are both off today. We're going early and drinking in the parking lot. Jeremy is bartending. How often do we all get to hang out together? Come with us and eat eleven a.m. hot dogs that we'll definitely regret and day drink like we're twenty-one again."

Jeremy and Jordan are Ben's college best friends and, along with Jordan's fiancée Allie, round out our friend group. Jeremy is also Ben's partner in Fireside, the bar they own. He is a former NHL player and, in addition to the bar, runs a foundation that gives him connections all over the sports world, so it's not surprising that he could score friends and family room passes.

"Please come, Jules. It's been weeks since we've done something together that's not work related. I miss us."

It's Hallie's *I miss us* that weakens my resolve to hole up in my office for the rest of the day. Because I miss us too. The breakneck speed of Hallie and Ben's relationship gave me whiplash. The two people closest to me in the world are building a life together, and I don't know where I fit in. If I fit in.

I shake away that thought as quickly as it comes. My fingers sneak towards my wrist again, but I pull them back before they can start scratching. I can have today with my best friend and my brother. I need today. Decision made, I press my hands to my desk and push myself up to standing.

"Okay, let's go to the football game."

Chapter Two
Asher

I'm out of eggs. I consider this irritating fact while staring into my refrigerator as if a dozen eggs will somehow magically appear from its depths. I don't know how this happened. But, like, in the metaphorical sense. I definitely know realistically how it happened, and I blame my sister Kyla. She lives across the street from our parents and sent me a picture yesterday morning of the cookies my mom made and brought over to Kyla's house.

It was a real younger sister move. An *if you lived in Boulder like the rest of us mom would drop cookies off at your house too* taunt. So, then I had to bake cookies and send her back an *actually I'm just fine in Pittsburgh when the rest of my family is thirteen hundred miles away and I can make my own cookies thank you very much* picture.

Except I added too much flour to the first batch, so I had to start again, and now I have three dozen cookies I didn't want but no eggs in my fridge for my game day breakfast. When I cracked my last egg yesterday, I made a mental note to run out to the store before bed. But then *Goodfellas* was on TV last night, and I am one hundred percent that guy who needs to watch *Goodfellas* when it's on TV. So of course, I forgot to go to the store. Like I said, I blame Kyla. It's a big family thing. And with two younger sisters and two older ones, all married and half with kids, my family is borderline ridiculous levels of big.

I sigh and shut the fridge door, grabbing my phone to order an omelet from the diner down the street because my game day breakfast is sacrosanct. The day I'm playing in the divisional round of the playoffs is not a good day to tempt the football gods. Ordering in isn't as good as making it myself, but it'll do in an emergency, and waking up to an eggless refrigerator on the morning of a playoff game is an emergency.

It's not that I'm superstitious. It's just that I like to do things a certain way on game days. Like wake up at the same time. And eat the same breakfast that my mom used to make for me before game days when I was in high school. And put my pads and uniform on in the same order. Okay fine, I'm superstitious as fuck, but show me a professional athlete who isn't.

After I eat breakfast, I head upstairs to my room to pack my game day bag. My house is probably too big for just me, but when I was drafted to Pittsburgh after playing four years of college football ten minutes from my parent's house, the idea of living permanently in the soulless downtown condo I stayed in for a few months before training camp didn't appeal to me.

With my signing bonus, I bought a big old house on one of the tree-lined Squirrel Hill streets that reminds me of my neighborhood in Boulder. It has plenty of bedrooms for my family to come visit, and I love every inch of it. The only thing that would make it better is if my family actually lived close by. My sisters make me crazy half the time, but I miss the shit out of all of them during the season. I'm just reaching the top of the staircase when my phone pings.

MOM

> Kyla showed me the picture you sent her
> yesterday. I can't believe you made cookies
> just to spite her, you little shit.

Snorting out a laugh I walk the rest of the way to my room before dropping down on my bed to have this conversation.

ME

> If it makes you feel better, I used up all my
> eggs in the cookies and forgot to get more so
> I had to order my game day breakfast.

MOM

> You deserve a subpar breakfast for
> antagonizing your sister.

> Miss you. I hate that we can't be there for you
> today.

> I miss you too. But you need to be there for
> the girls.

My family would usually make the trip for a playoff game, but my older sisters Charlie and Annie are pregnant, and both are due in the next two weeks. They both have other kids so it's a logistical nightmare, and I insisted that everyone stay put. Kyla is pregnant, too, and due a little later this winter. It's about to be baby o'clock in the Hansley family.

MOM

> I know, but I hate that you won't have family
> at the game—win or lose.

I hate it too, especially as I sit in my silent house. With four sisters, my life has never been silent. Even after living here alone for almost nine years, I've never been able to get used to it. But I would also hate if one of my sisters had a baby this weekend and my parents weren't there for it.

ME

> Don't worry about it. And one way or another,
> I'll see you all soon.

At the Super Bowl, hopefully. It's not superstitious to be confident, right? But if not, I take a road trip back to Boulder at the end of every season and spend most of my off-season with my family.

MOM

> Okay, we'll be watching. Call us after. Love
> you, hon.

ME

> Love you too. Kiss the girls for me.

I toss the phone on my bed and pack my bag before going to the bathroom for my least favorite part of my game-day ritual. Opening the bottom drawer of the bathroom vanity, I grab the black zipper pouch. I unzip it and take out the syringe and the vial of liquid. Prepping the syringe, I pull down the waistband of my joggers, swipe an alcohol wipe over my hip, and administer the painkiller injection. It should take effect just in time for warm-ups and last the whole game, leaving me with a pain free throwing shoulder. I hate this, but it's a necessary evil if I want to play.

It started during the first game of my fourth NFL season, when I took a bad sack and dislocated my shoulder. I rehabbed it, but the pain lagged longer than any of the trainers expected. With physical therapy and cortisone shots, I managed to play the second half of the season and stopped mentioning the pain to anyone associated with the team. As far as anyone knows, I rehabbed more over that offseason and came back stronger than ever. They don't know that a very quiet evaluation from a family friend who practices sports medicine led to a diagnosis of post-traumatic arthritis. And they don't know that, before every game, I inject myself with anti-inflammatory painkillers I buy from a guy I know from my offseason gym. And during this season, sometimes when there isn't a game.

I stare at myself in the mirror, rolling my shoulder and feeling the familiar dull ache that is as much a part of me as the color of my eyes. I'm not an idiot. I know medicating myself isn't great, even if the painkiller is the same one the trainers use in the locker room before, during, and after every game. I know my shoulder is getting worse. And I know that throwing a football with an arthritic shoulder that I keep a secret, masking pain with injections no one knows about, could cause long-term, permanent damage. I know all this, and yet I do it because if I didn't play football, I don't have any idea what I would do. Or who I would be.

I'm Asher Hansley, NFL quarterback. I've always been a quarterback. I'm not the biggest or the most innately talented, but I am the hardest worker on the football field. And since I was eight years old, that field has been my home. Even thinking about hanging up my helmet has dread pooling in my stomach. I'm not ready, and this isn't the season.

My phone pings again, breaking me out of my reverie.

LUCY

[pic attached] Good luck today, Ash! We miss you!

I grin at the text from my youngest sister, even as my heart gives a tug of longing. In the picture, my entire family is piled in my parents' living room. All fifteen of them are wearing my jersey. I love those idiots. Every last one of them. For a split second I have the crazy thought that if this is my final season, I could move back to Boulder and never have to miss another family gathering. But as quickly as the thought comes, I shake it away because I'm a quarterback and it's the playoffs. I live for this shit.

And I have a game to win.

Chapter Three
Julie

"Your drinks, ladies."

Ever the bar owner, Jeremy hands each of us a margarita where we sit in a circle of camping chairs in the parking lot of the stadium. With his photographic memory for drink orders, I didn't even have to tell him what I wanted, and that's the kind of efficiency I can get behind. He hands Emma hers last and hovers by her chair an extra few seconds before going back to his makeshift bar in the trunk of Ben's SUV. Leaning on the side of the car, his gaze lingers on Emma, and Emma turns the shade of red that I only ever see when Jeremy's attention is focused on her.

Emma is the youngest of our group, and she's the quietest of the four of us. She avoids social situations if at all possible and rarely speaks unless absolutely necessary, unless she is with us or one of her clients. She is our calm voice of reason, and I think she sees more than any of us give her credit for. She and Jeremy have had a glaringly obvious attraction to each other for years. Whenever they get their act together and finally give in to it, watching the quiet introvert and the gregarious former NHL star figure each other out is going to be so much fun.

"Well, if we have to go to a football game in a frozen tundra, this is definitely the way to do it." Molly leans back in her chair and sips from her margarita. I laugh at the picture she makes. With jeans tucked into furry boots, a puffy pink jacket, purple gloves, and giant black sunglasses—peach margarita in hand— she's giving Real Housewives of Winter, and it is so Molly. She's the most outgoing and colorful of the four of us, which never fails to fascinate me because she is also the most brilliant, working in an area of estate planning with the most complex and intricate tax planning that I could only dream of under- standing. With her brilliant mind and artist's soul, she and I butt heads in a way that I'm sure drives everyone insane, but I prefer looking at it as the way we show our love for each other.

"I'll take the frozen tundra if it means we can all be together outside of the office," Hallie says, setting her drink down on the floor and reaching into her pocket, tossing each of us a couple of tiny packets. "Hand warmers. Just shake them and stick them in your gloves and your hands should stay warm for the game."

I do what she says, and warmth immediately rushes into my frozen fingers. "Hallie is the smart one today," I say, with a wink in her direction.

She grins at me and picks her drink back up. "So, gossip. I need it from everyone, and I need it now. No work talk allowed."

Molly opens her mouth, but Emma beats her to it. "Don't even think about it, Mol."

Molly looks at Emma with false hurt written all over her face. "What?"

"You know what," Emma says, pointing at her. "You were about to say something about how Julie doesn't have any gossip because she spends all her time in the office, and girl, that's just not it today."

I smile at Emma even as my stomach twists and my fingers sneak towards my wrist before I remember I'm wearing gloves and pull back. It's not that I don't appreciate Emma intervening. She has a sixth sense for when Molly and I are about to get into it and has a weirdly clairvoyant way of knowing when to intervene and when to let it go. Sometimes I wish she just wouldn't, though, because every time she does, I know I'm due for a round of *Julie and her perfectionist workaholic ways.*

I wonder how long it's going to be before they all realize that I may be a perfectionist on the outside, but on the inside, I'm dark and twisty and anxious and scared. I don't like it—I just don't know how to be any other way. Or whether anyone would still want me around if they knew what a mess I actually was.

"We're here! Jeremy, you better have my drink ready!" Allie's voice pulls me out of my thoughts as she and Jordan make their way towards us. Allie is engaged to Jordan—the third in the Ben, Jeremy, Jordan college best friend trio. She is a badass pediatric cardiothoracic surgeon and met Jordan when she started as an attending at the same hospital where he was a pediatric surgery resident. Their love story is the stuff of legends, and they are amazing together. Allie is funny, sarcastic, brilliant, and fits in perfectly with our group. Because of her insane work schedule, we don't see her much—she and Jordan tend to stick close to home when their days off match up—but I love it when she's around.

"You know it, my sweet." Jeremy comes over and hands Allie a drink, pressing a kiss to the top of her head.

"Don't be hitting on my girl, hockey star," Jordan calls from the group of chairs next to us where he parked himself next to

Ben, beer already in hand. Jeremy just shoots him a grin then kisses Allie's head again before making his way back to his bar.

"Don't worry, hon," Allie calls out. "You know you're the only man for me."

"Fucking right I am. As soon as we get home tonight, I'll remind you exactly why."

"I just bet you will," Allie mutters, turning back to us. I look over at Jordan and see that his eyes are plastered to the back of Allie's head, swirling with a mixture of heat and desire. Like it did this morning when Hallie and Ben came to my office, jealousy settles in my stomach as I wonder what it would feel like to have someone so devoted to you that he can't keep his eyes off you.

I want that. The thought is as involuntary as it is unwelcome. I have too much going on for a relationship, and besides, there is no man on earth who would want to get tangled up with a perfectionist workaholic who falls asleep at her desk during a marathon Friday night work session. Unwilling to let my mind wander down that road, I turn my attention back to the girls.

"So, what did I miss?" Allie asks, sipping her drink and settling into her chair.

"Nothing yet," Hallie answers. "We were just about to get to the gossip portion of this tailgate. No work talk allowed."

"I love no work talk allowed. You wouldn't believe the stupid shit my residents got up to this week. Anyway, Jules, is this the first football game you've been to this season?"

Allie's mind works in mysterious ways that are sometimes Bond-villain levels of sneaky. With such a random question, my mind looks for the trap. Not able to spot it, I answer her. "Yeah, I haven't had much time for games this season. I haven't even really caught any on TV. Work has been so insane."

"Thought so. I'm just wondering how you feel about seeing him in person again."

I look at her quizzically. "Seeing who?"

"Asher Hansley. You know, the quarterback whose hands were practically plastered to your ass at the gala over the summer?"

I mentally kick myself for not seeing that this was where she was going. You would think they would all forget about the one single dance I had with Asher Hansley at Jeremy's foundation gala last summer, but no such luck. I don't know why they make such a big deal out of it. Yeah, he's sexy as sin and charming as fuck, but he is also a playboy athlete who collects women and is probably allergic to the word commitment.

And okay, maybe we did have a *moment* on the dance floor where I thought he might kiss me and I considered letting him, but cooler heads prevailed. And maybe he asked for my number, but it's not like he would have used it, so really, I saved myself a whole bunch of angst and phone watching by refusing to give it to him.

"I barely remember. I was too busy watching Ben try not to spill his Very Big Feelings all over our unsuspecting Hallie during that spin around the dance floor."

Hallie just grins and turns toward Ben who, predictably, already has his eyes on her. He winks at her, and she turns back around, blushing, because apparently that's another thing Hallie does now that she and Ben are *Hallie and Ben.*

"I still think a tumble in the sheets with a mega-hot athlete would be good for your mental health," Molly says, finishing off the last of her drink. "It would give you something to focus on other than your work. And our work. And all the other work."

"Damn straight it would," says Allie, grinning slyly at me as I mentally wish her a spilled beer all over her jacket during the game as payback for this can of worms she opened at my expense.

"I mean, they're not wrong, Jules." I just gape at Emma. If anyone was going to be on my side here, I figured it would be her. She just smiles and shrugs, looking at me in that way she does, where she knows something about you that you don't know yet.

"We're going to the friends and family room after the game," Hallie reminds us. "I'm sure he'll be there. And even though you pretend not to remember that dance, I know you do, and I bet he does too. You looked hot the night of the gala and you are totally unforgettable, Jules."

I groan. "I love you all, but no thank you. I have work and I have you guys, and I have a drawer full of fully charged vibrators. I don't need to add an NFL quarterback to the mix."

Chapter Four

Asher

The game is tied.

Sweat pours down my face, my shoulder aches, I'm exhausted, and it's fourth and long with twenty seconds left in the game and the ball on the fifty-yard line. The game we should be winning. That we would be winning if I hadn't thrown an interception in the second and fumbled in the third.

I can't blame anyone but myself. I threw the interception because my shoulder locked up as I started my forward motion on the throw, completely jacking the pass. I fumbled the ball when an unexpected shot of pain in my shoulder made my fingers lose their grip on the football before I even dropped back. I never have two turnovers in a single game. Especially ones that, from the outside, look like stupid rookie-level mistakes. Coach is pissed, and the offensive coordinator looks so angry I'm shocked his head doesn't just explode all over the sidelines.

Fucking hell. This is not how today was supposed to go. We

were supposed to cruise to a win and ride our way into the AFC Championship next week, not be trying desperately to avoid overtime on a fourth and long with twenty seconds left in the game.

This isn't the first time I've had shoulder pain during a game. Post-traumatic arthritis is degenerative, and anti-inflammatory injections aren't foolproof. Pain occasionally bleeds through the numbing effect of the medicine, but I've always been able to play through it.

This feels different. It's never affected my game this way.

I shake my head, shoving that thought away as quickly as it comes.

I force my head back in the game as I huddle up with my offensive line, rolling my shoulder as I duck my head.

"You okay A?" Drew Johnson, my wide receiver and closest friend on the team, has concern written all over his face.

"I'm fine," I snap, inwardly wincing at the flash of hurt I see on his face.

I close my eyes and take a deep, steadying breath before looking each of my teammates in the eye. "Fuck field goal range. Drew, it's to you. We're taking it to the endzone." I call the play and break the huddle.

Walking back to take my place behind the offensive line, I scan the stands like I sometimes do when I need a mid-game boost. I draw energy from a crowd, and there is no crowd more energetic than Pittsburgh Renegades football fans during a playoff game. I fucking live for this. For the signs and the painted faces and the fans twirling yellow towels and kids with their hopeful expressions and the love for the city and the game. I want this win for me, but I want it for all of them too.

As I turn back to the line, a flash of long blonde hair in the stands has goosebumps that have nothing to do with the subzero air temperature racing up my arms. I blink and look again, sure my mind is playing tricks on me. But nope. There she is, standing right in the third row surrounded by her friends. Just like the night of the Kids Play Gala back in July, she commands my entire focus.

Julie Parker.

The gorgeous blonde in the black dress. The ball-busting lawyer who refused to give me her number after an almost kiss on the dance floor. The girl with steel in her voice and a nervous tremor in her hand—a curious juxtaposition that made me want to unravel her on the spot and discover all of her layers. Six months after the gala, I can still remember how she felt against me while we danced. For six months, her sultry voice, cobalt eyes, and honey vanilla scent have invaded my dreams.

She's laughing with her friends, but almost as if she senses me, she turns her head in my direction. Improbably, our eyes meet. The noise of the stadium drops away as our gazes lock and hold. It must just be a second or two, but it feels like an eternity as electricity hums in my veins. I have never felt this kind of attraction to another person, and as the smile leaves her face, I wonder if she feels it too.

Drew slaps me on the shoulder, and the jolt of pain reminds me where I am and what I need to be doing right now. Julie's eyes are still on me and, unable to resist, I give her a wink and blow her a kiss. Even with the distance between us, I swear I can see the flush crawl up her face. The sportscasters are going to speculate wildly about who I was blowing that kiss to, and I chuckle, knowing exactly how much she is going to hate that.

She makes me want to throw her off her game. Destabilize her perfectly organized world. But to do that, I'd have to have her number first. I could find her work number on her firm's website, but something about her makes me think she would balk at me taking the easy road. A girl like Julie Parker deserves a man who puts in the time to figure her out.

The play clock is winding down, so I push Julie out of my mind for the time being, lining up in shotgun formation, ready to make the long pass downfield to Drew for the touchdown.

"Blue forty-two, blue forty-two. Set, hut!"

The center snaps the ball, and my hand settles into the position that is as familiar to me as breathing. I drop back in the pocket, relying on my linemen for protection as I search for Drew. He is exactly where he's supposed to be, flying down the middle of the field with his trademark speed, turning back towards me, ready to receive the pass.

With my eyes on Drew and my arm drawn back ready to launch the ball, I don't see the sack coming until two hundred and fifty pounds of linebacker barrels straight into me. Without any time to control my fall, I land directly on my right shoulder.

The pain steals my breath, and my arm goes limp, the ball coming loose from my hand and rolling away. Before I can react, the other team's defensive back scoops up the ball and takes the fumble recovery all the way to the end zone. With two seconds left in the game, there is no coming back from this.

We lost. The season's over. And it's my fault.

I roll onto my back, holding my right arm tightly across my body to keep my shoulder steady, my left hand coming up to grip my facemask. The trainers and coaches are already making their way onto the field to assess my injuries, but before they reach me, I roll my head to the left.

I thought she would have started making her way out of the stadium already, but she's still there. Julie's friends are all talking around her, but she is looking straight at me. Our eyes lock again, and despite the throbbing in my shoulder and the weight of the loss bearing down on me, with her eyes on mine, everything inside me settles.

A second later, team staff surround me, blocking my view of Julie. By the time they help me up and I start walking off the field, she's already gone, taking all my calm with her.

Chapter Five
Julie

People and conversation fill the Renegades friends and family room. Kids chase each other around and steal cookies off the well-stocked buffet tables, supervised by exhausted-looking moms in bedazzled jerseys emblazoned with their husbands' names and numbers.

Jordan and Allie had to leave early since they both have a night shift at the hospital, but everyone else is occupied. Jeremy knows practically everyone in the room and is carrying on what looks like four conversations at once. Ben is curled up with Hallie on a couch, whispering something in her ear. Emma is leaning against a wall like she's trying to disappear into it, and Molly is surrounded by a group of what looks like rookie players who are hanging on her every word.

Every time the door to the room opens, my anxiety spikes. I'm not even sure Asher's coming, and I don't know whether the anxiety is because he's not here yet or because I hope he never shows. I've been replaying the moment our eyes met on the field over and over for the last hour and a half. He was at least two hundred feet away from me, but the distance didn't dull the zing of awareness in my blood as his sky-blue eyes locked on mine. Or the full body flush when he winked and blew me that kiss.

I hate myself for it—the idea that a wink and a kiss from a football player stirred me up like I'm a fucking cleat-chaser or something. My only saving grace is that no one seemed to notice the kiss was directed to me, thank fucking god.

And I hate myself even more that when he took the hit on the final play of the game, my feet glued themselves to the stadium floor. God herself couldn't have made me leave my spot. When he rolled his head towards me, and our eyes met again, I could practically see the pain swimming in his gaze, and all I could think was how much he probably hates being vulnerable like that, displaying his pain to the world. I know I would. Hating my soft thoughts towards him, as soon as I saw him sit up and shake out his shoulder, I ran out of our section like my ass was on fire, muttering to Hallie about needing the bathroom.

The chatter around the room is that he tweaked his shoulder when he fell on it, but nothing is torn or broken. Since this was the last game of the season, no one seems particularly worried about it. My relief is embarrassing.

"I saw it, you know."

Thoughts broken, I whirl around to find Molly standing in front of me, a satisfied smirk on her face.

"Saw what?"

"That it was you he was blowing that kiss to."

Fucking hell. Deflect, Jules.

"It really wasn't. He was too far away. It could have been to anyone."

"It could have been, but it wasn't. That was some intense eye contact. I was sure one of you was going to spontaneously combust."

"Keep your voice down," I hiss at her, glancing around the room for eavesdroppers. Not only do I not want anyone to hear this conversation because, embarrassing, but I'm part owner of a brand-new law firm, and no one wants their estate planning attorney to be gushing about some professional athlete.

"Calm down, Jules. No one is paying attention to you now and they weren't paying attention to you then."

Relief shudders through me. "No one else saw?"

Molly grins triumphantly. "So, you admit it was you he was looking at."

"I admit nothing."

"Okay, sure. We'll go with that. But that man was hot as fuck in July and he's even hotter now. The football season has been kind to him. Did you see his ass in those uniform pants?"

Yeah I did. I bite the inside of my cheek to keep from responding.

"I thought you should fuck him back then and I still think it now. No one needs professional athlete sex more than you do. You need a better hobby than ordering us around the office and coming in on Saturday morning to work."

I get a flash of Asher and me rolling around, tangled in my sheets, but shake it away before it can materialize any further. "No thanks. I didn't have time in my life for an athlete six months ago, and I definitely don't have time for one now."

"Jules, everyone has time for athlete sex. And if you don't have time, you should make time."

With that, she flounces away, heading towards Emma to, I'm sure, try and coax her away from the wall. I would rather die than admit it to her, but Molly is the best at knowing what we all need, even if I sometimes hate her a little for it. She's not wrong that I could use a night of no strings athlete sex in theory, but in reality, I'm exhausted even thinking about it. All the performing and worrying about what I'm wearing and what

I smell like and whether my body is angled right and if he's enjoying himself and trying to make sure I fake it well because if I don't, I'll have to deal with a manchild sized bruised ego. I'd rather just use a vibrator. It never cares what I look like, and it always gets me off.

Unwilling to let my thoughts drift any farther down that road, I glance around, my mind turning to all the potential clients in this room and the opportunities I'm missing by just standing here. I should walk around, introduce myself to people. My right hand scratches just above my watch as dread pools in my stomach. I didn't consider that this room would be ripe for networking opportunities, so I didn't prepare any talking points. Without them, I could say the wrong thing. Do the wrong thing. My fingers scratch harder.

"Stop thinking so hard, Blondie."

The voice in my ear is low and deep, and the rasp in it has chills running down my spine. I spin around and come face-to-face with Asher. He's standing closer to me than I expected, and even though he's almost a head taller than I am, I can see every gold fleck in his sky-blue eyes. His brown hair is perfectly tousled, and he must have shaved the playoff beard he was sporting during the game because his square jaw is on full display. It should be illegal to look that good. The warmth of his body and his spicy scent wash over me, and for a split second I want desperately to wrap myself in it like a blanket.

Like earlier when I saw him lying on the field, my feet are glued to the floor, and with a mind of their own, my eyes drift down to his lips before I realize what I'm doing and jerk my gaze back up, taking a giant step back. The way he smirks at me, as if he can see every thought in my head, has me slipping into my badass lawyer persona like a suit of armor.

"Hey Hot Shot, glad to see you back on two legs."

Lawyer mode activated.

His grin is wide and dazzling. "You know us quarterbacks. Nothing can keep us down."

He rolls his shoulder in what looks like an involuntary motion. The grimace on his face is so slight and so quick that if I wasn't looking right at him I would have missed it, and I wonder if his injury is really as minor as everyone is saying it is.

"So, how's your shoulder really doing?"

He just shrugs. With his left shoulder. "It'll be fine. I'm far more interested in knowing how I got lucky enough that Julie Parker herself not only came to my game, but waited for me afterwards. Am I finally going to get your phone number after all these months?"

"Not a chance. And don't flatter yourself. I came to the game with my friends because my dad wasn't using his company tickets and my brother and his fiancé, also known as my best friend, ganged up on me and forced me out of my office. I'm still here because they're my ride and they are currently wrapped up in each other, unaware that the rest of the world exists, and the other passenger in our car is deep in conversation with your head coach."

"Well, good thing I'm here to keep you occupied while you wait for them." He winks at me and the warmth that settles in my belly has my hackles rising.

"What makes you think I'm just going to stand here and talk to you?"

He shrugs again. "Luck and unwavering persistence?"

"I'll show you what to do with your luck and unwavering persistence, big guy."

I start to turn away, but as I look around the room with my back to Asher, I don't know where to go. Allie and Jordan are long gone, and I don't see Molly or Emma anywhere. I feel like a third wheel interrupting whatever Hallie and Ben have going on, and Jeremy is still talking to the coach. I feel deeply, unexpectedly alone. My stomach twists. My left hand starts drumming a rhythm on my thigh, and I clench my fist to keep from scratching at my wrist.

"I can just stand here with you," Asher says quietly into my ear. "We don't even have to talk."

I turn back around, and our eyes meet. His are filled with an understanding I don't like, and I have the sudden, uncomfortable feeling that he sees too damn much. Before I can respond, Ben strolls over.

"Jules, you ready to go? Jeremy's almost done with the coach, and we're all going to the bar for drinks and food." He sticks his hand out to shake Asher's. "Sorry about the game, man. How's your shoulder?"

Asher shrugs his left shoulder again and gives Ben a smile more muted than the grin he gave me earlier. "Nothing a few days of rest won't take care of."

"Glad to hear it. I'm sure you have family and teammates you want to hang with, but we're all going to mine and Jeremy's bar. You're welcome to join."

Please say no, I mentally chant. *Please say you're going out to drown your sorrows with your teammates.*

"Actually, my family couldn't make the trip. I'd love to come."

Goddamn Ben for being so friendly.

"Happy to have you. It's Fireside on the South Side."

"Thanks, Ben. I just have to grab a couple things from the locker room, and I'll head out."

"Sounds great, we're driving over now, so we'll see you there."

"Looking forward to it." Asher turns to leave and then spins back around, winking at me. "See you there, Blondie." As he saunters out of the room, heat rushes to my face again and I honest to God can't tell at this point if it's fury, embarrassment, or arousal.

Hallie links arms with me. "What the hell was that? I think you have some explaining to do in the car."

"You have no idea," I mumble to myself, and follow everyone out the door, wondering how easy it will be to ignore Asher for the rest of the night.

Chapter Six
Asher

Julie's ignoring me. I briefly consider how fucked up I must be for that to both amuse me and turn me on. She's standing by the bar with her friends, her back to me and her head facing aggressively forward. She's trying her hardest not to turn in my direction. I keep replaying the way she looked when she turned away from me in the friends and family room. Her haunted eyes and drumming fingers giving away her anxiety at searching the room for a friendly face and coming up empty.

Even now, as she laughs and talks with her friends, nervous energy cascades off her in a wave but no one seems to notice except for me. I barely know her, but it's like I *know her*, and that's not a feeling I've had before. I don't understand it, but I sure as fuck want to explore it. She feels differently for now, and that's fine by me. I'm a patient guy.

Beer in hand, I drop into a chair at one of the tables Ben saved at the back of the bar, my legs no longer interested in holding me up after four grueling quarters of football. A second injection after the game, this one administered by the team doctor, has kept me from the inferno levels of shoulder pain I felt when I took the hit, but the pain is always lurking, waiting for its trigger. It feels wrong to be relieved that we lost—even though the loss was on me—but the idea of playing another game this season on my shoulder is unbearable. I have the whole offseason to work out my shit. I'll be good as new in time for training camp in July.

I have to be.

Unconsciously, I roll my shoulder.

"How's the shoulder?" Jeremy takes the seat across from me, his own beer in hand.

I shrug, resisting the urge to roll it again. "It'll be fine."

Jeremy looks at me, understanding written all over his face. "I've definitely said those words before." His hand drifts down to his right knee in a move that seems more habitual than conscious. Jeremy was an NHL superstar who was forced to retire early. He knows something about brutal injuries and for a second, I consider telling him everything. I have a moment of anticipatory relief, thinking of sharing the burden with someone who understands. Sanity prevails before I can open my mouth. No one can know.

I change the subject before he can ask me anything else. "So, how are things at the foundation?"

Jeremy leans back in his chair and lets out a groan. "God, it's been nonstop since we launched the campaign for the camps at the gala. I want these camps, but man, I underestimated how much work it was going to be."

Jeremy's foundation has always paid for kids to go to training camps for different sports, but at the gala he launched a campaign to support the foundation running camps of its own in partnership with local sports teams. He's planning to start with hockey and football and then branch out into other sports over the next few years.

"Well, like I said at the gala, I've been thinking a lot about focusing my charity work more heavily on kids, and I'm game to help plan for the football camp in the offseason."

"I was hoping you would say that. I've got a planning meeting next week. Interested in joining?"

"Definitely. I'm around for the next two weeks, and then I'm heading home to Boulder for a month or so. I can cut the trip short though if you need me here in person."

"Nah, go see your family. All our work for the next six or so months is meetings and strategy sessions and phone calls. If you're up for it, you can work with us remotely."

"I'm definitely up for it. Just tell me what you need and I'm all in."

I'm relieved I don't have to cut my trip short, but I would have if Jeremy asked me to. Even though I don't know him all that well, I liked him immediately when we formally met back in July. He was dealt a bad hand with his injury at the start of what would likely have been a record-setting career but took that hand and turned it into one of the most powerful and successful foundations in the sporting world. He made enough money during his three years in hockey to do whatever he wanted to do, but he chose to stay in the city that gave him his career, doing charitable work and opening a bar with his best friend. I don't have a lot of friends, but I'd really like him to be one. It's fucking weird trying to make a new friend at thirty-one years old, but I figure it's worth a shot.

"What are we talking about over here?" Ben drops into the seat next to Jeremy.

"Oh, so you finally decided to peel yourself away from Hallie to come have some guy talk?"

Ben backhands Jeremy on the arm. "I've been behind the bar, fuck you very much. Someone has to keep this place running while you sit around drinking all our beer."

Jeremy just smiles, unbothered by the brotherly ribbing. Just like Hallie and Julie are sisters in all but blood, it's easy to see that Ben and Jeremy are brothers. The same tug of longing I felt when Lucy sent me the family picture before the game hits me again. It's on me that I haven't made good friends here in the years I've been playing, but watching Ben and Jeremy together, I consider that maybe I should have tried harder.

"Sorry about the game, Ash; it was a tough loss, but you had a great season." Ben tips his beer bottle towards me in a silent toast.

"Thanks, man, it was a rough one. I'm ready for the offseason though."

"Got any plans?" Ben asks. "Hallie and I are planning some ski weekends over the next couple months up at our family's lake house in Western Maryland." He points to Jeremy. "This asshole will be there even though he can't ski with his knee. Jordan and Allie and the rest of the girls will probably come too. You're welcome to join us if you're around."

I consider the offer and my brain floods with images of Julie and all the things we could get up to in a lake house in the middle of the winter. I simultaneously think *hell yes* and *pump the brakes Asher*.

"Sounds great. I'll be with my family in Boulder for a while, but maybe when I'm back."

"Works for me. Give me your number, and I'll let you know when we decide to go."

I give Ben my number and he texts me from his phone. Julie's brother could not be more different from her. With their fair hair and blue eyes, the physical resemblance is striking, but that's where the similarities end. Where Julie is all depth and complexity hidden by her tough lawyer girl persona, Ben is a what you see is what you get kind of guy. The hometown boy running a local bar, who invites veritable strangers to ski weekends at his lake house and is head over heels in love with his lifelong best friend.

I glance over at Julie, still standing by the bar with her friends. I wonder how she feels about the change in Hallie and Ben's relationship, almost certain that it had to have been hard for her. Julie doesn't seem like the kind of person to handle it well when life doesn't go according to her plans. Perhaps sensing my gaze on her, she turns. A beat after our eyes meet, she turns back around but I keep staring at the back of her head, my heart speeding up in my chest. Jesus fucking Christ I have to get a grip. If this is what attraction feels like, I've been doing it wrong this whole time.

"Well, this is an interesting development."

The smirk in Jeremy's voice has me turning back around.

"That was way more than friendly eye contact, pal of mine."

Not interested in hiding anything, even from Julie's own brother, I just grin and shrug a shoulder. "My feelings are more than friendly."

Jeremy leans forward, propping an elbow on the table and resting his chin on his hand. "Wouldn't have figured her for you. You're all happy and sunshiney and Jules is...not that."

His tone has my protective instinct humming. "There's nothing wrong with her. She's fine how she is."

Jeremy stares at me. It's Ben who speaks next.

"It's you," he says, a considering expression on his face.

"What's me?" I ask, confused.

"You're what it's going to take."

"Dude, what the fuck are you talking about? Are you drunk or something?" Jeremy takes the words right out of my head.

I let out a chuckle. "I was about to ask you if he's always cryptic and weird like this."

"Our Ben has *layers*. How else could he keep his feelings

for Hallie a secret for eleven years? He just pined away for her silently and none of us was the wiser."

Ben just grins. "Got her now, don't I?" He holds his hand out to me. "Give me your phone."

"I already have your number; you texted me, remember?"

"Not for my number. Hand it over."

I unlock my phone and give it to him. He inputs a number and hands it back. I look down at the new entry in my contacts. *Julie Parker*.

With a smile, I look back up at him. "I was prepared to work for this number."

"I just bet you were. Hal told me Jules turned you down when you asked for it in July. Figured I would give you a leg up. Welcome to the group, man. I think you'll fit in just fine."

"Fuck yeah, you will." Jeremy grins at me. "We need another guy around. Shame Jordan had to work tonight. He's missing all the fun. Fucking doctors."

He says it with affection, his love for his friends evident in every word. I lean back, enjoying them, and this night, more than I have any right to, considering the playoff loss and the ever-present ache in my shoulder.

I think Ben is right. I am going to fit in fine. I smile to myself, knowing how much Julie will hate that. Already loving the challenge it's going to be to change her mind.

Chapter Seven
Julie

I stare out the passenger side window of Asher's Range Rover.

How the fuck did I get here?

It was all very confusing, and I'm not someone who gets confused. Something about Ben and Hallie staying at the loft above the bar instead of going home. Then Emma volunteered to take Jeremy home which is weird, considering Emma tries her hardest to avoid any close encounters with Jeremy. Molly was riding with Emma since they're neighbors but I couldn't ride with them because...something about a trip to the grocery store?

My tipsy brain that only slept four hours last night on a pile of legal documents instead of in a bed was too tired to make sense of it all, and before I knew it, Asher was tossing an arm around my shoulders and leading me toward his car, asking me for my address so he could drive me home.

The hum of attraction when he put his arm around me was irritating and unwelcome, and I silently cursed my friends for putting me in this position. I'm already concocting the appropriate punishment and it looks something like the three of them spending next weekend organizing our online client relationship management system. I grin at the thought.

"You look like you're plotting your friends' demise."

I turn and stare at him.

He glances over at me and then back at the road. "You had your evil face on."

"How do you know it's my evil face?

He looks at me again, just long enough to have my anxiety spiking that his eyes have been off the road for too long and my fingers drumming a beat on my leg. He looks back at the road and then back at me, smirking as if he can tell exactly what's going on in my head.

"It's the same face you had on when you refused to give me your number after we danced at the gala."

I hate that he can read me so easily. Anxiety over what else he can see has me snapping back, "You could ask for my number every day for the next year and I still wouldn't give it to you."

"Blondie, I won't be asking for your number ever again."

The tug of disappointment is swift and startling, but I work to school my face into a neutral expression.

Apparently, I don't do a good enough job because he tosses me a grin, and the smug look on his face makes me want to scream.

"You want me to have your number, don't you? You just don't want to give it to me yourself."

I turn back to the window, gritting my teeth and wondering how badly hurt I'll get if I open the door and jump.

"Don't worry, Blondie; your brother saved you the trouble."

I whip around to face him. "He did what?"

"Ben gave me your number back at the bar. He was under

the impression that I wanted it, and you refused to give it to me." He gestures to me, one side of his mouth quirking up. "And, well, he's obviously right."

A rush of warmth that Ben thought of me when he's still so deeply in his *Hallie and Ben* bubble wars with my frustration that Asher can now contact me whenever he wants to. Not that he couldn't before; my law firm number is on the goddamn internet. But having my cell is something else entirely. He can call me whenever he wants. He can text. He can Facetime, Jesus Christ. He'll see things. He'll discover things about me. He already sees too much, and this is the first day I'm seeing him since our single dance at the gala five months ago.

He'll find out you're a mess and then he won't want you at all.

My fingers scratch at my wrist as I try to shove down the rising panic. And I remind myself I don't want him anyway, so why does it even matter?

With one hand still on the wheel, Asher reaches over, laying his other hand over both of mine. I take a deep breath in, fighting the urge to close my eyes, lean my head back on the seat, and let his warm hand calm me.

I'm about to give in when the car glides to a stop. Looking up, I realize we're parked in front of my house. Needing to get out of this car as fast as possible, I unhook my seatbelt and shove the door open, stepping out into the frigid January night. I'm heading up the front walk when a car door slams behind me. I turn and see Asher following me up to my house.

Oh no. No way. I need distance from this man immediately.

"What are you doing?"

I idly wonder how many pairs of girls' underwear have melted straight off their bodies at the sight of Asher Hansley's grin.

"I don't know how you grew up, but my mom taught me that when you take a girl home, you walk her to the door."

I open my mouth to tell him I'm a grown woman who can find her own front door, but then I think of my own mom and know it's futile. I bet Ben has walked every single girl he's ever taken out in his life to her door. He probably walks Hallie from the bedroom to the fucking living room. Fucking well-raised men and their good manners. In this moment, I want to hurl them all straight into the sun.

"Okay, well, walk fast. It's cold."

He does the opposite of that. He saunters up the walk. *Fucking saunters.*

Climbing the four steps onto my front porch, I dig around in my purse until I find my keys. I unlock the door, but my partner-in-a-law-firm manners won't let me go in without thanking him for the ride.

Keys in hand, I turn and practically stumble back, sucking in a breath at his proximity. Like earlier at the stadium, he's just inside my personal space. He reaches out an arm to steady me, and sparks ignite where his hand grasps my arm, even through the thick material of my winter coat. There are only inches between us as our eyes lock and hold. His spicy scent surrounds me, and I am at war with myself, wanting both to run into my house and lock the door to get away from this man who sees far too much, and also burrow into the comfort of his big, warm body and never let go.

Where the fuck did that thought come from? I burrow into no one. I need no one.

"I can see the wheels turning in your head," he murmurs to me. "What is this? Where could this possibly go? I don't have time for this. This would be chaotic. It would be messy. And Julie Parker doesn't do chaotic and messy. She definitely doesn't do the unknown."

One hand still holding onto my arm, he reaches his other hand up and glides his fingers over my cheekbone before pushing a lock of hair behind my ear. His hand drifts down the side of my face, his thumb tracing the line of my jaw before he grasps my chin between his thumb and forefinger, his eyes still locked on mine.

"But lucky for you, I'm a quarterback. I thrive in chaos. I like a mess. And the unknown is my specialty."

I like a mess. I don't know why, but I latch on to those words and grasp them like a lifeline. It's those words that have me moving without thinking, leaning forward and laying my lips on his.

Asher

Fuck. Me.

Julie's lips are full and soft and the second our mouths touch, I suck in a breath. This is not where I thought we would end up tonight, but I am not mad about it. And her kissing me? Sexy as fuck. I reach up, cupping her face in both of my hands. Tilting her head, I glide my tongue over her lips.

She opens for me, and the second our tongues meet, my entire body ignites. Heat sears through me, and my cock has never gotten so hard, so fast. My brain empties of every thought other than how good her lips feel against mine. She feels it too —I know she does because she lets out an honest to god whimper and there's something heady about having this strong, impressive, independent woman whimpering in my arms.

I never want to let her go.

I move one hand to the back of her neck and slide the other down the side of her body to grip her denim-clad hip just below the waist of her coat. I pull her as close to my body as I can get her so she can feel exactly how much this kiss is affecting me. But it's not close enough. Walking her backwards, I press her against her front door and lean my hips into her, and my tongue tangles with hers. She responds immediately, grinding against me, and I go lightheaded. One of her legs hooks around my calf, and I reach down and grasp the back of her thigh, pulling her leg up and griding my dick right against her center. Pleasure rushes my system. She pushes her hips forward against me and moans against my mouth as she reaches up to wrap her arms around my neck.

The sound of her keys hitting the wooden floorboards barely registers in my lust-addled brain, but it's as good as a bucket of water tossed in her face. She straightens instantly, one of her hands flying to her hair and the other reaching down to straighten her jacket then back up to her face to wipe around her mouth, cleaning up any lipstick smears. It would be fascinating to watch her snap back into Julie Parker mode if the anxiety covering her face while she does it didn't make my chest ache. When the fingers of her right hand start scratching at the inside of her left wrist, I reach out and gently take both of her hands in mine. She yanks them back.

"Sorry. That was...I don't...I can't...Yeah..." Before I have a chance to say a word, she bends down and swipes her keys off the porch, shoving open the door and going inside before slamming it right in my face.

I stand there staring at the door, wondering what the fuck just happened. I'm torn between wanting to give her the space she clearly needs and not wanting to leave her alone in an anxiety spiral.

Then I hear it. A thump from inside the house, as if she

dropped her head back against the front door, and a whisper. "Holy hell, that man can kiss."

I grin at that. Fuck yes, I can. And so can she. My still hard-as-stone cock is proof. Satisfied that she is okay for tonight, I turn and walk back to my car, whistling to myself, already plotting for the next time I can rattle the great Julie Parker.

Chapter Eight
Julie

Muttering to myself, I stomp up the stairs to Ben's loft.

I am full of irritation this morning, and Asher fucking Hansley is to blame. Oh, and Ben, the brother I used to like but no longer do. The text that appeared on my phone this morning before I even opened my eyes is squarely on him since he, you know, gave the man my goddamn phone number.

UNKNOWN NUMBER

Morning Blondie. Sleep well?

No, I didn't add his name to my contacts and no, I fucking didn't sleep well and it's his fucking fault. And Ben's. I tossed and turned all night long thinking of Asher pressing my back against my front door and being so close to the edge that if my keys hadn't fallen and startled me out of whatever lust-trance Asher put me in, I am one-hundred percent sure I would have come right against that door. The only orgasms I've ever had have been the ones I've given myself, and Asher had me ten seconds from begging on my front porch, fully clothed, in the middle of the winter.

Julie Parker doesn't beg.

Julie Parker also doesn't make the first move.

I shove the thought from my head, not interested in reliving that particular humiliation. The one where he told me that he likes a mess, and I leaned in and kissed him like I had taken leave of my faculties. That comment shouldn't have made me want to kiss him. It should have freaked me the fuck out because Asher sees too damn much. He sees things I have kept hidden for my whole life. People see what I want them to see. The poised, put-together woman. The successful, has her entire life planned lawyer. The present friend, daughter, and sister.

No one knows how much work it takes to maintain the façade. How much anxiety. How many sleepless nights. How much worry and stress and preparation. No one ever sees it, but after one dance five months ago and a few hours last night, I'm almost positive that Asher can, and that scares the shit out of me. But instead of running, I fucking kissed him. Then just before the good part, I panicked and slammed the door in his face.

What is wrong with me?

I still haven't responded to his text.

Fingers scratching at my wrist, I climb the last two stairs and knock on the door. Not long ago, I would have just walked in, but things are...different now.

Before he and Hallie got together, Ben lived in the big loft apartment above his bar full-time. Last summer, he moved into Hallie's house a few streets away from me, but since he and Jeremy own the building, Ben ended up leaving the loft as is. He and Hallie occasionally crash here when they're at the bar late.

Ben opens the door, shirtless, with a dishtowel slung over his shoulder. I bet he's making breakfast. It's a Parker family tradition for the men to make breakfast. My dad made breakfast for all of us every morning while I was growing up and still makes breakfast for my mom. I love that Ben carries on the tradition with Hallie. I also have the sudden urge to turn and run back down the stairs, so I don't intrude on a morning routine clearly meant for two.

I hesitate a second too long.

"Jules!" Ben's eyes light up when he sees me, and he pulls me into a hug. A real one, where he wraps both of his arms around me and holds on. Ben is so much like my dad that it makes me smile against his shoulder. When family is around, the Parker men are gooey.

"Did I hear Jules?"

Hallie's voice has me pulling away from Ben and turning towards the kitchen where she's perched on a barstool at the counter wearing an old University of Pittsburgh t-shirt that must be Ben's, her hair piled on top of her head.

"Yep. Hey, Hal."

I slide onto the barstool next to her while Ben busies himself at the counter.

"What are you doing here? Did you eat? Ben's making breakfast, so you're just in time."

I realize suddenly I have no idea what to tell her. *Oh, I'm here because I kissed Asher Hansley last night and have no idea what to do about it* isn't an option. In my rush to get out of my house and away from my thoughts, I didn't plan what to say. I always plan. My mind races to conjure a believable lie.

"Oh, well, I was just in the neighborhood, so I thought I would stop by and say hi."

Weak Jules.

She looks at me strangely. "Why were you on the South Side?"

Shit. I'm at the loft on the South Side where the bar is and not Hallie's house which is in my neighborhood where it would be logical for me to be at nine o'clock on a Sunday morning.

"There's a new coffee place I wanted to try." Not my best lie but believable. I really need to get better at thinking on my feet.

Hallie looks skeptical but seems to forget about it when Ben puts a coffee mug in front of her. She glances down at it before looking back up at him with a big smile.

"Exactly what I wanted."

Ben gives her a wink and then puts a latte in front me before turning back to the stove. Hallie's eyes are still glued to his back, the love on her face so strong and undeniable that I'm uncomfortable—like I'm intruding on a moment meant to be theirs alone. There are a lot of those moments lately.

Ten minutes later, we're all sitting with breakfast plates in front of us. I mostly push food around my plate, my mind preoccupied with thoughts of last night and my left hand tapping out a pattern on my thigh. I smile at the right times and join the conversation when it would be weird not to, but in my mind, I'm a million miles away. I'm thinking about Hallie and Ben. How they practically exist as a single person—always turned towards each other, always touching each other in some way like they would die without that tiny, constant connection. How in sync they are. How well they know each other, all the way down.

No one knows me like that. Not my friends or my parents or my brother. I've never let anyone see below my Perfect Jules shield, and the shield is impenetrable enough that it's never occurred to anyone to look.

Not until Asher.

Improbably, he seems to like what he sees. It's unbelievable, considering I don't even like what I see most days. But I think about our almost kiss at the gala five months ago. His wink at the football game. His quiet offer to stand with me in the friends and family room so I wouldn't be alone. The way he laid his big hand over both of mine in the car. The feel of his hands on my face. The way he pressed me against the door.

I feel my shield drop just the tiniest amount.

As soon as I get in the car after leaving Ben and Hallie to their Sunday, I pull out my phone and save Asher's number.

ASHER

Morning Blondie. Sleep well?

ME

I did. Thanks for asking.

Chapter Nine
Julie

I'm sitting at my desk with my second latte of the day, a handful of peppermint Hershey Kisses, and a complex trust I'm drafting open on my computer screen when the text comes in. Out of habit, I glance at the clock before reaching for my phone. Seven fifty-five a.m. Right on schedule.

ASHER

[pic attached]

Morning Blondie. I met my cutest fan this morning. His name is Simon. I've decided dogs should always wear snow boots.

I open the picture of a grinning Asher, wearing running clothes and a knit beanie, crouching in the snow next to a golden retriever puppy. Fitting, since Asher is basically a golden retriever puppy in human form. The dog is clad in snow boots with the Renegades logo on them.

ME

Simmer down Hot Shot. Are you sure he's a fan of yours, specifically? Not everyone likes a quarterback, you know.

ASHER

Everyone likes this quarterback.

I don't.

Tell it to someone who believes you. I bet my entire salary next year that you're smiling right now.

Well, fuck.

I haven't seen Asher in the two weeks since we kissed on my front porch like the world was ending, but he texts me after his morning runs. Like clockwork, my phone has pinged every morning a little before eight for the past two weeks. Sometimes he just says good morning. Sometimes he texts a picture of the latte art the barista at his coffee shop made for him. Sometimes he tells me about a cookie recipe he found that he wants to try—yes, the man bakes, Jesus take the wheel. Twice it was a picture of an hours old baby—apparently, he has two sisters who had babies within days of each other. And sometimes, like today, it's a picture of something ridiculous he sees while he's on his run.

I would rather give up spreadsheets and wear mismatched clothes every day for the rest of my life than admit I look forward to his texts. There's something about knowing he's thinking of me every day while he runs. That he takes the time to consider what to text me. That he takes the time to get in the pictures. I glance at the photo again and smile (again) before I catch myself. The warmth that swirls in my belly every time my phone pings is unsettling. I hate it. Except when I don't. My phone pings again.

ASHER

I'll be at your office later today. Can I take you to lunch?

Startled, I drop my phone and sit back in my chair, scratching at my wrist as my mind searches out his motive. Asher has been texting every day for two weeks, but in all that time he hasn't asked to see me once. It's confusing as hell. After our kiss, I expected him to be relentless. I expected him to ask me out a million times and for me to have to find creative ways to turn him down.

He's not what I expected, and I don't like that at all. I always know what to expect.

I consider ignoring his text, but wonder whether that will just encourage him. Do I want to encourage him? No. I definitely don't. Absolutely not. I don't have time to be playing mind games with professional athletes. Also, why the fuck is he coming to my office?

ME

Why are you coming to my office?

ASHER

Wouldn't you like to know?

I would, actually. I own the firm.

I have a meeting with Emma, but never mind about that.

Lunch later?

I'm busy later.

I didn't tell you when later.

I'm busy all of later.

That's really too bad. Catch you later, Blondie.

Well, okay then. I guess that takes care of that. That's not disappointment I feel that he didn't press harder to see me. It's relief that I can focus on my work for the rest of the day. Definitely relief. Picking up the phone, I dial Emma's extension.

"You know you can just walk down the hall, right?" Emma says, with no preamble. Work mode Emma always makes me smile.

"I could, but then I would have to get up, and I'm busy." More like I knew if I asked her what I'm about to ask her in person she would read me like a fucking book. No one knows about the kiss or the texting, and I'd rather it stay that way.

"Well, you're not the only one. What's up?"

"Why is Asher Hansley coming in to see you today?"

Emma pauses for so long I check to see if the call dropped.

"So that's the reason you're calling instead of walking ten feet down the hall."

Fucking hell. She's spooky sometimes.

"Just tell me Em."

"How do you even know that he's coming here?"

Shit.

"He told me, okay? He's been texting me a little. He told me he would be here but didn't tell me why."

"I just bet that's making you crazy."

"Yes," I mumble, not sure if she's referring to the texting or the not telling me why he's coming. Either way, the answer is yes.

"He's coming in with Jeremy. I'm helping Jeremy with the capital campaign and funding structure for his sports camps. Asher is working with him during the offseason." Emma's practice focuses on non-profit organizations. Despite not being able to say two words to Jeremy when we're in a social setting without her face turning bright red, she seems to have no problem communicating with him professionally.

"So...Jeremy's coming in too. How do you feel about that?" I can't help but needle her about it a little. I love her and I love Jeremy. If they would just do something about their obvious feelings for each other, they would be great together.

"Oh, sorry, my other line is ringing; gotta go, bye."

The line goes dead before I can say goodbye.

A few hours later I'm typing out an email to a client transmitting the draft of the trust I worked on all morning when my office phone rings.

"Julie Parker."

"Julie dear, it's Cindy Erikson."

"Hi, Mrs. Erikson, what can I do for you?"

The Eriksons are longtime clients of mine. I did their estate planning at my old firm, and they followed me here. They are friends of my parents, so I updated all their planning as a favor before we officially opened, and I'm glad I did because Bob Erikson died in November.

"I met with our financial advisor this morning to start consolidating and streamlining some of our accounts. He asked about the status of Bob's probate so we could consolidate the brokerage account in Bob's name with mine, and I didn't know anything about that, so I told him I would call you."

"No problem, Mrs. Erikson, but your financial advisor is mistaken. When I updated your planning, we transferred that account into the revocable trust I set up for Bob. Once Bob died, you became the trustee, so you have authority to manage the account. No probate is necessary because the account isn't in Bob's individual name."

"Well, that's just the thing. Our financial advisor says the account was never transferred to the trust."

A pit forms in my stomach. That can't be possible. I did the paperwork myself to transfer the account to the trust. The account worth millions of dollars. The account we specifically did not want to go through the probate process. My hands start to shake as sweat beads on my forehead.

Keeping my voice as steady as I can, I speak into the phone. "Mrs. Erikson, I'm sure this is a mistake. I'm going to go through my files and reach out to your financial advisor person-ally, and I'll call you back."

"Thanks, honey, you always know just what to do."

I manage a polite goodbye. It takes me three tries to get the phone back in the cradle. Breathing heavily, I turn to my computer and click on the Erikson's email folder. My clammy fingers slip on the scrolling wheel and my heart pounds. When I find what I'm looking for, it takes an extra minute for my eyes to focus on the words.

```
From: jvance@vancefinancial.com
To: jparker@eplj.com
Date: November 17, 2023
Re: Erikson Account Documents


Ms. Parker,


This email is to confirm receipt of the
scanned executed transfer documents to
transfer account #767-458-9760 to "The Bob
Erikson Living Trust u/a/d November 3, 2023."
Please send the originals by mail. Once we
```

receive the originals, we can effectuate the
transfer.

All the best,
James Vance, CFP

I stand up so fast my chair goes flying backwards and clatters to the floor. Opening my cabinets, I find the Erikson file. Still standing, I slap the file down on my desk and flip through it. My fingers are numb as I try to turn the pages and my arms weigh a thousand pounds each. My teeth are clenched together so tightly my jaw aches. I sent those documents. I know I did. Any second now I'm going to find the FedEx receipt with the tracking number.

Except I don't find it. What I find is so much worse.

With numb and shaking fingers, I hold up the original account documents. The ones that the financial advisor needed to finalize Bob's transfer. They're here in my office, which means the account was never transferred to the trust. And it's too late to make the transfer without going to court because Bob is dead.

Think Julie.

Except I can't think. There is nothing to think about. There is only what I know.

I made a mistake. An enormous, unconscionable mistake. A mistake so stupid that even a baby lawyer wouldn't make it.

My heart beats so fast I get lightheaded, and my teeth start to chatter so violently my already aching jaw clenches tighter to try and make it stop. My breaths are fast and shallow, and black spots race across my vision. I try and grip the desk, but my numb fingers just drag along the glass surface, knocking the Erikson file to the floor and scattering papers everywhere.

What the fuck is happening to me?

I lean over and put my hands on my knees, attempting to take a full breath, but the vise around my chest tightens. The harder I try to breathe, the tighter it gets.

I'm dying.

The thought has my legs buckling. I sink to the floor on my hands and knees in the sea of paper that used to be the Erikson file. Blood rushes in my ears, and my chest heaves in a futile attempt to take in oxygen.

Breathe Julie. Take a fucking breath.

Except I can't. All I can do is gasp for air as darkness seeps into the edges of my vision.

Chapter Ten
Asher

"So, between the gala fundraising and the volume of donations you have received in the almost six months since, you have two years of operating expenses covered if you run the football and hockey camps at full capacity."

I look at Jeremy sitting in the seat next to me. His elbow is on the chair's armrest, his chin resting on his palm. Eyebrows drawn together, he's clearly deep in thought. We're sitting in Emma's office as she goes over the financials for the sports camps Kids Play is establishing. She specializes in nonprofit law and is the foundation's outside counsel. Handling financials for the camps seems like something an accountant would do, but when I asked about it, Jeremy's glare practically melted the skin off my face.

Message received.

I don't know why I have to be here for this, but when Jeremy texted last night to be at the law firm at three, I didn't argue. I want to help where I can this offseason, and the thought of stopping by Julie's office after the meeting to get in her way has had me grinning all day.

It's been more than two weeks since I've laid eyes and... other parts of me on her, and that's two weeks too long. My dick is probably two minutes from falling off with the number of times I've jerked off to the thought of Julie's leg wrapped around me, her hips pushing forward, grinding into mine while our mouths danced. Fuck, it was hot. I shift in my chair, trying to counteract the blood suddenly rushing south. A hard on right now would be inconvenient.

Not the time, Asher.

I might not have seen Julie in the two weeks since the kiss, but I've been texting her every morning. Sometimes she responds and sometimes she doesn't, but she reads them all and that's fine with me. Until this morning, I hadn't asked to see her. I want to see her. I'm dying to see her. To be in her orbit. I'm not stupid—Julie Parker, of the fierce competence and fiery attitude and brilliant mind, is the kind of woman men fall for. The kind of woman men ask to see and take to dinner and a movie and home to their place for a night rolling around in the sheets. The men who see what's on the surface and think they know all of her.

They don't. I know that with as much certainty as I know the feel of a football in my hands.

I'm starting to understand what's beneath her armor. She has so many sides. The successful attorney. The dedicated friend and sister. The girl after the football game with the deer in headlights expression as she stood alone, trying, and failing, to find a familiar face. I want to know all of her. I want all of her to be mine.

I get the sense no one has ever taken enough time with Julie to really get to know her all the way through, which is weird considering she has such close friends and what seems like a tightknit family. What I do know is that Julie is too smart to fall for the expected, which is why I've been texting. Letting her see me through tiny snippets of my day, funny stories, the strange and the mundane. I even sent her pictures of my new nieces on the days last week they were born. I want to keep her a little off-balance. I want to take my time.

And I want to woo the fuck out of her.

"Okay, so how much additional funding do we need if we add girls' lacrosse and volleyball in year one? Do we have the funds to run all four camps the first year? We can always worry about year two and beyond later."

Jeremy's response to Emma has me tuning back in to the conversation.

Emma gives him an exasperated look that has me thinking this isn't the first time he has suggested a big change.

"That wasn't the plan, Jeremy. Ten months ago, you came to me and said you wanted to fundraise for hockey and football camps, so I gave you a plan for that. We *executed* the plan for that. I have no idea how much it would cost to run lacrosse or volleyball camps because *you didn't ask me to run those numbers*. But you know what I do know? Exactly how much it costs to run your football and hockey camps for two years. So do that and stop trying to change the plan."

I stare at Emma, fascinated that this is the same woman who didn't say a single word to me the first time we met and turns bright red and stammers every time Jeremy talks to her in a social setting.

"We can't even give it a try?" Jeremy looks like someone kicked his puppy, and I wonder what his deal is. Two camps seem like a lot to take on when the foundation hasn't done anything like this before. Why would he want to add two more?

Emma closes her eyes and takes a deep breath, as if willing

herself to be patient. She opens her eyes and talks to him like he's a child refusing to brush his teeth.

"Jeremy. I know these camps mean a lot to you. I know you want to go big. But you hired me to help you be *successful*. You hired me to make this work and I'm telling you, adding two additional sports on top of the two we planned for is going to overextend the foundation, and you'll run the very real risk of all four camps failing. You know hockey. Asher knows football and is here to help all winter. Start with those two and I promise, I can help you grow."

Jeremy blows out a breath and leans forward, elbows on his knees. "Fine. We'll do it your way Ems. I don't like it, but I'll do it."

Emma's smile is both smug and satisfied. "Good. Glad you see things my way. Now, you both know what you need to do, and I have another client coming in half an hour so it's time for you to go." She stands, straightening her skirt and walking around her desk.

Jeremy practically shoves me out of the way to get to her. He tosses an arm around her shoulders and as they walk toward her office door I hear him murmur, "I love when you talk lawyer to me."

I cough to cover a laugh when I see Emma duck out from under Jeremy's arm, her face bright red and her eyes a little wild; she's now a far cry from the poised, competent attorney who just handled the six-foot three former hockey star like she deals with stubborn athletes every day of the week.

Standing in the hallway outside Emma's office after she practically shoved us out the door and slammed it shut before we had even crossed the threshold, I glance up and down the hall, wondering which closed door is Julie's.

"It's the one at the end of the hall." I turn as Jeremy gestures to the last door on the right.

"What is?"

Jeremy smirks at me. "I'm not stupid. You were wondering which door belongs to a certain female Parker twin."

I shrug. "Thought I would go see if she wanted to have lunch." She may have said no when we were texting, but I'm willing to bet that was a knee-jerk reaction. Besides, I do my best work in person.

"It's a little late for lunch, buddy."

"Coffee then. Or dessert. Whatever she wants."

Jeremy laughs. "Damn, you've got it bad. Good luck, dude. In all the years I've known Julie, I've never seen her date anyone. Not seriously anyway. I think she scares them all away."

It makes me happier than I have any right to be that Julie doesn't date, so I let the "scares them all away" comment go even though I want to tell him that's not what she's doing. She pushes them away before they get the chance to see her. She's afraid if they do see her, they'll walk away themselves.

"I'm not anyone, and I don't scare easily. You're one to talk about having it bad. 'I love when you talk lawyer to me'? How long have you had a thing for Emma?"

"Too fucking long," he mumbles under his breath. "But I fucked it up," he says, staring at her door. "You know what? I just remembered something I forgot to tell her. You okay to leave on your own?"

I smile at him because he's ass over tits for the freckled, redheaded conundrum who just unceremoniously kicked us out of her office. "Yeah man, I'm good."

He turns and knocks on the door, and I head straight for Julie's office.

I knock twice and wait, but there's no answer. I knock again, disappointed I missed her and already thinking about what I can do later to get under her skin. I wonder if Ben will give me her address so I can send her something ridiculous.

I'm just about to head out when I hear what sounds like a faint gasp from inside the office. I knock again.

"Hey Blondie, you in there?"

I hear the gasp again, louder this time, and then another one.

"Julie?"

No answer. The gasp again.

Dread pools in my stomach. Instincts honed from years of reading defenses scream that something isn't right.

Mind made up, I call "Blondie, I'm coming in," and push open the door.

Chapter Eleven
Asher

I see her the second I open the door. She's sitting on the floor in a black pantsuit and heels, surrounded by a sea of paper. Her knees are drawn up to her chest, arms wrapped tightly around her legs, fingers drumming out a beat on her thigh. Her long blonde hair is tangled around her face, and I can hear her breath coming in short gasps, back heaving as she tries to take in air. Seeing the strong and extraordinarily capable Julie Parker making herself as small as she can while struggling to breathe shatters my heart into a million pieces and has me snapping into action.

I gently close the door, knowing Julie wouldn't want anyone to see her like this. Then I'm beside her in two strides, dropping down to the floor.

"Hey, Blondie, what's going on?"

Not wanting to startle her, I keep my voice light as I lay a hand on her back, rubbing in circles. Her body jerks like she didn't realize someone else was in the office, but her breathing doesn't slow. If anything, it speeds up, coming in rapid pants.

"Asher," she manages. "I can't...I don't...I can't breathe," she finally whispers. "I think I'm dying. Am I dying?" Her voice is ragged and laced with panic and confusion, her face as white as the paper scattered all around her on the floor and filled with terror.

I've seen this before. I know what this is.

As gently as I can, I pull her between my legs, so her back is pressed against my chest and my legs bracket hers. I wrap both my arms around her and hold tight. Her heart thunders violently against my arms, and her entire body is shaking.

"You're not dying, Julie," I say into her ear. "I know it feels like you are, but you're not. I promise. You're having a panic attack, but you're going to be fine. Sweetheart, I want you to breathe now. We'll do it together. Feel me breathing and do it with me, okay?"

She lets out a jerky nod. Tightening my arms around her, I feel a throb of pain in my shoulder—the injection I gave myself this morning is wearing off, but I ignore it. Nothing else matters but getting Julie to breathe. I take deep, slow breaths until I feel her breathing start to slow ever so slightly. I drop a kiss on her shoulder and start to talk quietly.

"You're doing such a good job. Keep breathing with me, Blondie. Look around. Can you tell me some of the things you see?"

She takes in a shaky breath and looks around. When she speaks, it's like she's forcing the words out. "The couch."

"Sure looks like a comfortable couch. The kind you could take a good nap on. What else?"

"My diplomas on the swall."

I glance up at them, surprised by the name written in ornate cursive.

"Juliette?"

"My great-grandmother's name, but no one calls me that."

I turn the name over in my head. "It suits you." And somehow, it does. It's both soft and powerful, just like the woman in my arms. "What else do you see?"

"The window. Is that...is it snowing?" Her voice is steadier, stronger. I press a kiss to her hair and lean my forehead against the back of her head. She's coming back to me.

"Sure is. It started about an hour ago. It's not heavy, but it's not flurries either. It's..."

"The perfect snowfall," she whispers.

"The perfect snowfall," I agree.

"I love the snow," she murmurs.

The wonder in her voice as she says it has my heart squeezing in my chest. Almost like it's been years since she's taken the time to look at the snow and she's seeing it again for the first time. It makes me want to say a prayer to the weather gods to make it snow every day this winter, so Julie gets to see it over and over again, anytime she wants.

Her body relaxes back against me as she stares out the window, her breathing steadying, her heart starting to slow. I loosen my hold on her, shifting to run a hand up and down her arm as I keep talking.

"Snow is magic. Even growing up in Boulder where it snows all the time, I never get sick of it. It's my favorite thing. Now, when I go back to visit my family, I get to play in the snow with my nieces and make it magic for them."

I keep talking to her until her head drops back onto my shoulder, her breathing even and her heartbeat slowed to a normal rhythm. Feeling that her panic has subsided, I keep my voice gentle and ask, "Do you want to talk about it?"

Julie sighs, leaning more heavily against me. "Talk about what?"

"About what brought on the panic attack you were having when I walked in here."

I don't know what post-panic attack universe she was living

in, but I feel the exact second she snaps back to reality. Her entire body goes rigid, and she jerks away from me, shooting up to her feet and looking wildly at the papers scattered on her office floor. She bends to gather them up, muttering to herself. I catch the words "mistake" and "account" and "probate" but not much else. When I see her hands start to shake again, I stand, putting myself right in front of her and circling her wrists gently with my hands. Her eyes meet mine and they are filled with fear and a muted version of the panic I saw earlier.

"Talk to me, Blondie. What's going on?"

I see the hesitance on her face. The reluctance to talk. But it's mixed with something else that looks a lot like...longing maybe? Like she wants to share but she's afraid of what will happen if she does. I know just what to do.

"You know, I do stupid shit all the time. Sometimes it's intentionally stupid, like when I decided to bake cookies the day before the game a couple of weeks ago to prove to my younger sister that she's not better than I am just because my mom brings her homemade cookies. I wanted to show her that I could make my own, you know? And other times it's a real mistake, like when I threw an interception straight into a defensive back's hands like I thought he was on my team or something and then he scored, and we lost."

Like I intended it to, my rambling has the corner of her mouth lifting slightly.

I gather the papers from her hands and stack them on her desk before taking both of her hands in mine. "I promise that whatever is going on, it's going to be okay. Whatever happened to make you panic can be fixed. You're Julie Parker. There's fucking nothing that you can't do. But it's also okay to ask for help."

She's staring at the floor, so I let go of one of her hands and cup the side of her face, tilting her head up until her eyes meet mine. "Let me help you, Blondie. I think you might be the strongest, most capable person I know. Asking for help doesn't make that any less true."

She takes a deep breath and lets it out slowly. "I made a really big mistake, Asher."

I keep my gaze locked on hers. "Tell me."

Shockingly, she does. She sits in her chair, and I lean a hip on her desk while she tells me every detail about a dead client and an account that was supposed to be transferred to a trust before he died but wasn't. About how it's much more complicated to make that transfer after someone dies. About realizing the mistake because of a call she got from the client's widow and a search through the file that led to the panic attack. It all comes out in a frantic rush of words, as if she isn't used to sharing and wants to get it over with as quickly as possible. When she's finished, she blows out a breath and shrugs.

"That's all of it."

Treading carefully, knowing she abhors showcasing her vulnerability like this, I say, "So how are you going to fix it?"

It's exactly the right thing to say. I see her strength seep back in. She stands up taller, and her shoulders square. She straightens her sweater and pushes her hair back behind her shoulders, leaving her gorgeous face unframed. Expression determined, she walks me through her plan. I don't understand all the legal jargon, and there is a lot of talk about court and filing deadlines and something about a pour-over will, whatever that is, but her intelligence and her competence is sexy as fuck. Every single thing about this woman turns me right on.

Right now, I'm regretting my decision to leave for Boulder, because what I really want is to stick as close to Julie as possible, and warm her up to the idea of dating me. I'm not above begging.

But that's not the only reason I'm regretting it. Thinking

about Boulder has the wheels turning in my head. I'm supposed to leave tomorrow afternoon and be gone for a few weeks, but the thought of leaving her after what I just witnessed has me uneasy. I don't like thinking about her being alone. Having to deal with another panic attack by herself. I know from my sister Kyla that once you have one, there's a strong chance you'll have more.

"So, you're going to tell your friends what happened, right? And Ben?"

Her head shoots up from the pile of documents she's sifting through.

"Why would I do that?"

"You had a panic attack."

She just shrugs. "I know. I was there. I'm fine now though. You were here. You helped me. I know what I need to do to fix everything. No one else has to know."

Like hell. The image of her curled into herself on the floor gasping for air is seared into my brain. The idea of that happening again and her having to deal with it alone is more than I can bear. I don't want her to have to deal with anything alone ever again. But if it's up to her, that would be her default. Alone, in her office, buried in work, drowning in anxiety, without anyone to tell her that every part of her is magnificent.

I want to show her there's a different way. That she can work hard and also have fun. That she can be exactly who she is, all the way through. That she can tell her people exactly who she is, and they'll love her for it. I also want to attach myself to her side and never leave her because I'm already in deep.

Without warning, an idea slams into my head. A wild, hair-brained idea I suddenly need to follow through on more than I need to take my next breath. A wicked grin slides over my face.

"Hey Blondie, want to take a road trip?"

Chapter Twelve
Julie

I toss the last couple sweaters into my suitcase in a heap and slam the lid shut with a little more force than necessary. I pause.

I can leave them like that.

I'm fine.

This is fine.

I absolutely can't leave them like that.

Cursing under my breath, I open the suitcase back up and fold the sweaters into perfect squares before closing the lid and zipping it shut.

Muffled laughter has me turning towards the bathroom where Molly is standing in the doorway with a hand over her mouth, very clearly laughing hysterically.

I side-eye her. "I could have left them like that."

Molly just laughs harder. "Jules, I love you, but there is no universe where you leave sweaters in an unfolded tangle and close the suitcase. I don't know what possessed you to take this road trip with the sexy quarterback, but you're still you, even though you taking two weeks off means I'm a little worried you were temporarily abducted by aliens who did experiments on your brain."

"What Molly said." Hallie comes strolling into my room, a bag of peppermint Hershey Kisses in hand, Emma following closely behind.

"Come on, Hal, that's my last bag—you couldn't pick a different snack?"

The stash from my December supermarket sweep usually lasts until Easter, but since my kiss with a certain football player, I've been stress eating.

She just shrugs, hopping up to sit on my dresser in a move she knows drives me insane. "I like them too."

Emma reaches her hand into the bag and grabs a couple. "Same. Anyway, you're leaving for two weeks, so you won't be needing them. Why are you leaving for two weeks again?"

"What Emma said." Molly flops on my bed, rolling over onto her stomach. Resting her chin in her hands, she kicks her legs up behind her. With her pink leggings and striped socks, she looks like a teenager at a slumber party.

"You've been changing the subject every time we bring it up for the last week. Not that I'm opposed to some alone time for you and the hot quarterback, but leaving town for two weeks with a guy you barely know is so unlike you, it's not even in the same universe as you."

All three of my friends, plus Ben, and even my parents, have taken turns asking me why I'm leaving with Asher for two weeks, and I haven't given anyone a concrete answer. I can't even summon a decent lie. They don't know about the kiss or the text messages, and they definitely don't know about the panic attack. To them, this is coming out of nowhere. As far as they know, Asher stopped by my office last week after he met with Jeremy and Emma and asked me if I wanted to go with him. They're not wrong, but they're not exactly right either.

It's been a week since I agreed to go with Asher on his off-season road trip to Boulder. And I use the term agree very, *very* loosely. It was just a panic attack. No one died. I got through it. There's no reason for him to be making such a big deal over it. I ignore the voice in my head telling me there was nothing *just* about that panic attack. That, for what seemed like hours but was probably only minutes, I actually did think I was going to die, and the only reason I got through it is because Asher wrapped his big, strong quarterback arms around me and talked me through it.

The voice in my head is an asshole.

Once it was over, Asher wanted me to tell my friends and I refused. Then he told me to call Ben, and I refused that even harder. When he asked me if I wanted to take a road trip, I just laughed and turned back to the papers I was sorting through. But Asher didn't move from where he was sitting on the edge of my desk before casually dropping his bomb.

Come with me on my road trip to Boulder, or I'm telling Ben about your panic attack.

His habitually cheerful face was deadly serious, and that departure from his norm had me sitting up straighter. It was his quarterback face. The face that leads a team of men to victory on the football field week after week. The face that got me to agree to a week in the car with him and a week at his parents' house when I have only spent a grand total of five hours, two weeks' worth of text messages, and one afternoon mid-panic attack with him in my entire life.

I'd be lying to myself if I said it was just the quarterback face that got me to agree.

I'm worried about you.

I don't want you to be alone.

You don't have to be alone.

Let me help you, Blondie.

In my life, no one has ever offered to help me. I'm the one who does the helping. I help and plan and lead and organize everyone and everything and no one offers to help because everyone knows I would never accept it. But Asher either doesn't know me well enough to know that, or he understands me so well, he knew exactly how to ask. I'm not naive enough to think it's the former.

We'll take a week to drive there and make some fun stops along the way.

I can't wait to show you everything there is to do in Boulder.

Just pack a suitcase and leave everything else to me. I'll take care of all the plans.

I think Asher offering to take care of everything melted my brain because I found myself saying yes, spending a week clearing my calendar and getting Molly and Emma to cover whatever I couldn't cancel or reschedule.

Molly is right that this is unlike me. But with my suitcases packed and my friends crowding my space, I admit something to myself. Something that has been hovering in the background of my mind all week, since I agreed to Asher's insane idea. That the relief of saying yes to Asher, of clearing my calendar and getting away from it all for the first time in my life, was so overwhelming that it almost brought me to my knees. And that's fucking scary because if I'm not the go-getter who always wants to be in the office, the attorney who thrives on the pressure, the has it all together law firm partner, then who the hell am I?

The doorbell interrupts my thought spiral.

"Tacos!" Molly jumps off the bed and runs down the stairs to answer the door with Emma close behind her, leaving Hallie and me in my room.

"I'm proud of you, you know," Hallie says from her perch on top of my dresser.

I just scoff at that. "Proud of me for what? And can you get off my dresser? You know I hate when you do that."

She smirks at me but doesn't move. "I know. I'm proud of you for going on this trip and for taking the time away. You deserve it, Jules. I won't ask you again why you're going because I know you have your reasons, but I just want you to know I think it's a good thing."

"You don't think it's crazy? A two-week road trip with a guy I barely know?"

Hallie grins at me. "Oh, it's definitely crazy, but the good kind of crazy. Asher is a good guy, Jules. He and Ben have a miles long text chain and are basically besties. Jeremy wants him to come work for the foundation full time, and you know how protective Jeremy is over who gets close to his baby. And did you know he went to the gym with Ben, Jeremy, and Jordan yesterday?"

I did, in fact, know that because Asher texted me a selfie they took and fuck if his smiling face next to some of the most important people in my life didn't hit me right in the feels. And...other places. I really need to get a handle on myself before I get into his car tomorrow morning.

"It's nice that he's making friends with them. It seems like he doesn't have close friends here which is weird because he's played for the Renegades for eight seasons."

Hallie looks at me strangely. I realize my mistake almost immediately and start talking before she can question how I know anything about Asher's friend situation.

"Anyway, it'll probably be weird and if it gets too awkward to be stuck in a car with him and I have to escape and fly home from some tiny town in the middle of nowhere, can you come pick me up at the airport?"

Hallie hops off my dresser and wraps an arm around my

waist, squeezing me in a side hug. "Literally anytime, day or night."

Both the hug and the reassurance go a long way towards calming my nerves about the next two weeks. Things may be different now that Hallie and Ben are together, but moments like these remind me that we're still Jules and Hallie, even if she's also part of Hallie and Ben.

"Thanks, Hal. We better get down there before Molly and Emma eat all the good tacos."

As if on cue, Molly yells from downstairs. "Jules, Hal, get your asses down here. I'm already pouring my second margarita, and Emma's eating all the chicken tacos."

"Don't listen to her," Emma calls up. "She's actually pouring her third marg."

Hallie and I both dissolve into giggles and head downstairs. I spend the next few hours sitting on my living room floor with my best friends, laughing and eating too many tacos and getting a little drunk on margaritas, and trying not to think about the gorgeous man with the strong arms and the sky-blue eyes who somehow sees the parts of me I bury deep and why I don't hate that nearly as much as I want to.

Chapter Thirteen
Asher

"Good morning, ladies," I say as I slam the driver's side door and circle around the car to the sidewalk in front of Julie's house.

"Quieter, Asher. Much, much quieter," Hallie mutters.

"What she said," Emma hisses through gritted teeth.

"What happened to you guys?" I ask, already knowing the answer but wanting to see what they'll say, mostly for my own amusement. It's the little brother in me.

"Tequila," moans Molly. "So. Much. Tequila."

"Shut the fuck up, Molly. Your voice is an ice pick to my brain." I grin at that, and Julie turns her glare on me. If the daggers shooting out of her eyes were real, I would be extremely dead. Fuck, she's sexy in the morning all hungover and claws out.

The four women sitting on Julie's front stoop are an intimidating bunch. Or, they would be, if they didn't all look a little worse for the wear. I swallow down a laugh at the sight of them; the experience of having four sisters tells me that laughing in this moment would be a guaranteed way to have my dick permanently removed from my body.

Emma has what looks like yesterday's makeup smeared under her eyes, her red hair in a haphazard bun leaning messily to one side. Hallie's eyes are half closed, a coffee mug gripped in her hand. Molly's head is covered in a hat with a purple pompom on it, her curly hair wild beneath it, and her eyes are shielded by enormous sunglasses.

Julie is leaning on the railing as if she would topple over without its support, her face just a little green and set in a grimace. She's wearing leggings and a hoodie with a puffy hip-length jacket tossed over it. Black tie dress at the gala Julie stopped me in my tracks. Football jersey and jeans at the playoff game Julie made me forget my own name. Professional Julie mid-panic attack had all my protective instinct roaring. And casually dressed, hungover Julie? Well, I just want to bundle her up and snuggle her, green face and all. I almost do it, just to see how she'd react, but we're about to get in the car and drive five hours so I put a pin in that. Lots of opportunities to snuggle the shit out of her while we're on the road. Hopefully. I'm manifesting.

"So, anyone want coffee?"

"Asher, if you are toying with me, I will actually kill you right now." Molly slips her sunglasses down and eyes me warily.

Chuckling, I turn to open my passenger door and grab the take-out coffee tray on the floor. Ben texted me this morning to tell me the girls had a sleepover last night that included bottomless margaritas, so if I wanted to live though picking Julie up, I should bring coffee. Then he texted me everyone's regular coffee orders.

I lift the first cup and give it to Molly. "Peppermint mocha for you, my lovely."

I hear Julie suck in a breath at the "my lovely" and I light right up. Jealous looks good on her.

"Bless you, quarterback. You are my favorite person today."

"Just over here doing the lord's work. French vanilla with regular milk," I say, handing the next cup to Emma.

"Hallie, Ben said to tell you he assumed you already had your first cup of coffee, and to get you an iced coffee. I told him he was insane since it's twenty degrees out, but he insisted. It has milk and one Splenda."

I hand her the cup and assume Ben got it right, because I can practically see the hearts shooting out of her eyes.

I lift the last cup and give it to Julie with a wink.

"Juliette. Latte for you. Caffeinate while I put your bags in the car."

"That's not my name," she grumbles. I grin at her, more excited than I have any right to be at the prospect of being alone in the car with her.

While she takes the first sips of her coffee, I grab her bags where they sit at the bottom of the steps. Opening the trunk, I swing the bigger suitcase inside first and as I do, a white-hot bolt of pain lances through my shoulder. Hissing out a breath, I drop the suitcase into the car harder than I mean to, and it lands with a loud thud. I wrap my right arm across my body to hold it steady and with my other hand flat in the trunk, I lean into my left side, dropping my head down and closing my eyes while I wait for the pain to pass.

My shoulder has been aching since I woke up this morning. It's been aching every morning since I took the hit in the last game. In a mild panic thinking of spending the entire road trip with Julie in pain, I called the guy I buy the meds from, thinking I should stock up. I lost my nerve and hung up before he could answer. I've been able to justify the anti-inflammatory injections during the season as a necessary evil to help me play, but if I start using them in the offseason too, what does that make me? I shove that thought from my mind, not ready to go down that route. I'm both anxious and relieved thinking of the black zipper pouch I tucked into my suitcase this morning. *Just in case.*

Once the pain ebbs, I take a deep breath and push myself up off the car. Turning back to the girls, I see Hallie, Emma, and Molly chatting away, clearly feeling better after a hit of caffeine. But Julie isn't talking to them. Instead, she's looking at me. Her eyes are narrowed, and her face is set in thoughtful lines like she's trying to work something out, and fuck. I wonder how much of that she just saw.

Sauntering over to them, I stop at the bottom of the stairs and look up at Julie.

Shit, she's pretty. The kind of pretty that has my heart pounding my chest and my dick wondering about the next time I can get my hands on her.

"Ready to go, Juliette?"

"You're seriously going to call me that?"

"I like it. It suits you."

"It was my great-grandmother's name, and it's prim and proper and stupid and doesn't suit anyone under the age of eighty. No one calls me that. Not even my parents."

"I love that he calls you that," Molly says. "Pretty swoony, quarterback." She flashes me a grin.

"Shut the fuck up, Molly," she hisses again, pinning Molly with a death-glare that is almost entirely offset by the fact that Julie's cheeks are also flushing red.

Looks like someone likes their new nickname after all.

"I like it too," says Hallie. "It's like something out of a romance novel."

"Okay." Julie speaks a little louder than absolutely necessary. "Time to go."

She pushes herself to her feet, and the rest of the girls follow. She hugs Hallie first, and I hear Hallie whisper, "Remember, literally anytime, day or night." I don't know what that means but it makes Julie smile, and I love anything that makes Julie smile.

Emma is next, and I don't hear what she says but the hug is long, and she whispers in Julie's ear the whole time. When they break apart, they hold eye contact for a second before Emma leans in and whispers one last thing that has Julie nodding. Between this little scene and the meeting in Emma's office the other day, I'm fascinated by the only sometimes quiet redhead and am curious about her story.

Molly is last to hug Julie and doesn't bother to whisper when she says, "Please just fuck the hot quarterback."

Julie's face flushes hot again, and I grin, charmed by these women and the obvious and open affection they have for each other. They remind me of the way my sisters are together, and it feels a lot like home.

The girls walk Julie to the car, and I open the door for her. With one last round of goodbyes, Julie slides in, and I shut the door behind her.

"Take care of our girl, Asher."

I turn and face Emma. She's standing on the sidewalk with Hallie and Molly right behind her. I consider my response for a second before saying the most honest thing I can think of.

"There is literally nothing in my life I want to do more."

Satisfied, Emma smiles and steps back, standing shoulder-to-shoulder with the other two girls.

I round the car and hop into the passenger seat. Turning to Julie, I flash her a grin.

"Ready for an adventure, Blondie?"

"Definitely not," she mumbles.

I don't know what it says about me, but her grumpy mood

really gets me going. I'm practically kicking my heels at the thought of a week in the car with her and of all the stops I have planned along the way. She's going to hate at least half of them —of that, I'm sure. Julie Parker has no idea what's coming for her.

"Well, ready or not, here we go."

I reach out and lay a hand over hers where she's tapping out a beat on her thigh. Then I lean over and kiss her cheek, making her face flush again. The anxious tapping and flushed face tell me that she doesn't hate our close proximity, and I kind of love it.

Then I slip on a pair of aviators, set the GPS, and pull out into the street, noticing suddenly that my hand is still on hers, and she hasn't done a single thing to move it away.

Chapter Fourteen
Julie

Tingles race up my leg from the spot where Asher's hand rests. His touch makes me antsy and also calms my anxiety in a way I'm not quite sure I'm ready to explore. I can't decide whether I want to shove his hand away or press it deeper into my leg and beg him to never stop touching me. That thought scares me shitless enough that I pick up his hand, placing it onto the wheel.

"Two hands on the wheel," I mumble. I couldn't give a fuck whether he has two hands on the wheel, but if he has two hands on the wheel, that's one less hand that's touching me in a way that makes my insides go haywire.

He looks at me with a smirk on his face, as if he can read my chaotic thoughts. I'm starting to think it's possible he actually can.

"There are snacks in the back for when you get hungry."

When he said he was taking care of everything for this trip, evidently he meant more than just hotels and activities along the way. He texted me yesterday that he was buying road trip snacks, and when I asked if he needed a list, he told me he already knew what I wanted. Unused to someone else taking the reins like this, I spent more time than I'll admit feeling anxious about his snack choices. Snack choices, for the love of god.

I need to get a grip.

I have no idea how to get a grip.

Wanting to see what he brought, and a little desperate for something to do with my hands, I turn to grab the bag. But what I see when I peer into the back seat is actually three reusable shopping bags and a cooler.

Turning back to him, I say, "So when you said you were getting snacks, you weren't kidding around."

He just winks at me. "I wanted to make sure you had everything you liked."

I narrow my eyes at him. "How do you know what I like if you didn't ask me?"

He just shrugs and smiles. "Psychic."

His face is his usual mix of calm and happy, but I didn't miss the wince that crossed his face when he shrugged just now, or the way he rolls his right shoulder like the muscles are tight. He also looked like he was in pain when he was putting my suitcases in the car, and I wonder what that's all about.

"Is your shoulder okay? It seems like it's bothering you."

His smile vanishes. "It's fine, just a little tight. Bruised it in the last game."

He says all that a little too fast, and it's been long enough since the game that a bruised shoulder shouldn't still be bothering him. I'm immediately curious, but I don't press him because if anyone knows a thing or two about hiding vulnerability, it's me. You could probably hack my arm off, and I would just go about my day, insisting I was fine. It tracks that a professional athlete would have similar instincts.

I want his smile back, though.

Asher should always be smiling.

I reach into the back and pull out one of the grocery bags. I set it on my lap and when I open it, my jaw drops. Inside are peppermint Hershey Kisses. But not just one bag; there must be at least twenty in there. I look at him in disbelief.

"It's the end of January."

He gestures toward the dashboard. "I know the date, Juliette. It's right there on the screen."

I let that snark and the use of my full name sail by because I have more important things to focus on. "Stores stop selling peppermint Hershey Kisses before New Years. I have never, in my entire life, seen a bag of this candy in a store in January. I look every time I go. How did you get these?"

He grins. "One of my teammates knows a guy who works for Hershey. He hooked me up."

"And how did you even know I liked these?"

His grin widens. "I called Hallie. She told me you're, and I quote, *fucking obsessed with them*. I told you I wanted to take care of everything. That included getting you everything you might need or want without having to ask. Asking you what you want gives you more work because then you have to make me a list. I figured out another way."

Well, shit. I stare at him, my brain unable to form words, entirely unused to anyone attempting to take some of the mental load off my plate. I bear my mental load, and everyone else's too. I like it that way. I always have. Doing all the things helps me feel in control, and I need to be in control. Always. Except I can't deny how good it feels to have just shown up with a packed suitcase and nothing else, even if what's in my suitcase might be all wrong because he wouldn't tell me what we were doing along the way.

"You okay there, Juliette? You went quiet."

I clear my throat and shake off my thoughts. "That's still

not my name. But I'm good. Thanks for these. Hallie ate my last bag last night, so I thought I was out of luck until December."

"Anything for you. Check out the rest of the bags."

The second bag I open is filled with gummy candy. Gummy worms, sour gummy worms, gummy bears, gummy peaches, and that's just what I can see on top. Asher glances over.

"That's my bag."

"Just yours?"

"I mean, I'll share if you ask nicely, but I really like gummy candy."

"Between this and your soda all your teeth are going to fall out."

I gesture to his Big Gulp of Dr. Pepper in the cupholder next to my latte. Apparently, the man doesn't drink coffee. Instead, he starts every day with a fountain soda the size of his head.

"Haven't yet." He winks at me and turns back to the road.

"So do you go out and get a fountain soda every morning?"

He grins at me as if he is just tickled pink at me asking him a personal question.

"Nope. I have a soda fountain in my house."

"You...seriously? With Dr. Pepper in it?"

"Yep. There's room for a second soda, so if you tell me what your favorite is, I'll add it in."

"What makes you think I'll be at your house?"

"Luck and unwavering persistence, Juliette."

The same words he said to me in the friends and family room after the game.

"You really think you're that lucky?"

"You're sitting in my car right now, aren't you? So that

makes me the luckiest fucking guy on the planet. So, what's your favorite soda?"

"Diet Pepsi," I mumble.

"See now, I'm a Coke man myself, when I'm not drinking Dr. Pepper. But since it's you, I'll allow it. Consider it done. Check the rest of the bags."

I do and discover a veritable cornucopia of my favorite snack foods, including my top three, salt and vinegar potato chips, Peanut Butter Oreos, and caramel corn. Lifting the lid on the cooler, I spot lime seltzer in my favorite brand, a couple bottles of water, and assorted other drinks.

"Hallie really did give you the full list, huh?"

Instead of responding, Asher gently guides the car over to the shoulder, and stops right there on the side of I-70. Putting the car in park, he takes off his sunglasses, tosses them on the dash, and turns to me. Expression serious, he picks up one of my hands and holds it in both of his, locking eyes with me.

"Hallie gave me the list because I asked her to, and she loves you. I wanted you to be comfortable with me, and I wanted you to have everything you might want or need without you having to ask. I know you think you don't know me very well, but all you need to know right now is that I take care of my people. And Juliette, I think you are going to be my most important person."

He draws my hand to his lips and brushes a kiss over my knuckles, sky blue eyes holding mine. My stomach erupts in butterflies and my heart takes off at a gallop. Startled, I yank my hand away from him, my right hand coming down to scratch at my wrist. Asher just reaches over and lays one of his enormous quarterback hands over both of mine, halting my anxious scratching.

His eyes bore into mine, and for a minute, and I get lost in the deep pools of blue. I have the crazy thought that I could drown in him, give myself over to his comfort and steadiness and never worry about another thing as long as I live. My brain rejects that thought as quickly as it comes. I give myself over to no one.

"You're safe with me, Juliette," he says, his voice low and sure.

Then he puts the car in drive, slides his sunglasses back on, and pulls back onto the highway, leaving me sitting in the passenger seat gaping at him, sure that I have never felt quite so unsafe in all my life.

Chapter Fifteen
Julie

"Juliette, wake up sweetheart; we're here."

Asher's voice filters through my subconscious and I jerk awake, shooting up in my seat, heart pounding out of my chest and my breathing sharp and fast.

"Hey, it's okay. It's just me." Asher reaches out and cups the side of my face with one hand, his thumb sweeping over my cheekbone, eyes filled with concern as he takes me in. "Take a few deep breaths, okay?"

With his eyes on mine and his warm hand on my face, my breathing evens out and my heart slows.

"That must have been some dream."

I look at him, confused. "What do you mean?"

"The way you woke up just now. I figured you were having a bad dream."

I scoff. "Definitely not a dream. I wake up like that every morning."

He stares at me. "Every morning? You wake up every morning like you're escaping a bear?"

I shrug. "Yeah, so?" I don't see what the big deal is. I've woken up that way for as long as I can remember. It helps me get out of bed and get shit done.

"Okay, well, we're going to work on that."

I roll my eyes. "Hot Shot, I've been waking up like that for years. One week in the car with you and a week hanging out at your childhood home isn't going to change it."

His eyes narrow in response, and he holds out his hand to me. "Bet?"

Damn my competitive streak. "What are we betting? And where are we anyway?"

"We're in Columbus, Ohio. And the bet is, if you're waking up like a normal human being by the end of this trip, you have to let me take you on a date when we get back to Pittsburgh."

"A date? Seriously? That's what you want? Isn't this whole insane road trip you proposed and forced me on one big date? That seems like weak sauce to me."

A wicked grin takes over his face. "First of all, I didn't make you do anything. I merely suggested that you come with me, or we could tell your brother and your friends about your panic attack."

"In some cultures, that's considered blackmail."

"I can see how you would think that, but really, I had your best interests at heart. What if you had one and I wasn't around? What if you were all alone? Who would ask you about all the things you see? Who would make sure you keep on breathing? You're too pretty not to breathe."

I do my best to smother a smile because there have been very few people who can keep up with me and the ones who can are almost all related to me or might as well be. I forgot how much fun it is to banter with someone on my level.

"I would have managed. And what about the bet? Are you

sure you want to go with a date? I'll give you a pass if you want to change your mind."

"Juliette, I can promise you that no date with me would ever be weak sauce. And this road trip isn't a date. It's fun."

"And a date with you wouldn't be fun?"

His eyes darken and do a slow sweep down my body and back up again. "Oh, it would be fun alright. And...other things."

The way his voice drops an octave at the *other things* has my entire body heating. Suddenly there isn't nearly enough air in this car. Releasing my seatbelt, I shove open the car door and jump out into a large parking lot, taking a deep breath of frigid winter air.

Asher climbs out on the other side, chuckling at my obvious discomfort in a way that makes me want to throttle him and also heightens all my senses. That must be why it's at that moment I notice the car.

"Hey, did you get a new car?"

He looks at me, confused. "What do you mean?"

"This is a blue Range Rover. Your car used to be black." What I don't say is I'll never forget the black car he was driving the night of the kiss we are no longer discussing. The kiss that makes my cheeks heat every time I think about it.

As always, Asher seems to know exactly what's going through my mind because he smirks as he rounds the car to stand next to me. "This is a rental. Usually, I drive my own car to Boulder, but I wanted to be able to fly home with you if you wanted company. Getting my car back to Pittsburgh is a pain in the ass, so I rented one I can return in Boulder."

"You didn't have to do that. I've been flying by myself for years." What I don't mention is how much I hate flying, especially by myself. How much I loathe having my schedule entirely at the mercy of flight delays and cancellations, and how hard it is for me to relax since I'm not the one flying the plane, especially when I don't have anything to distract me.

Asher bends down to zip up my jacket for me. "Yeah, but why should you have to?" Then he tugs a black beanie with the Renegades' logo on it onto my head and kisses my cheek. Tossing an arm around my shoulders, he steers me through the parking lot.

The casual way he says that surprises me, but I guess at this point it shouldn't. I don't understand how he can see me so clearly where people I have known my entire life can't, but I also can't lie and say there's not a part of me that likes it.

As we get to the end of the parking lot, it occurs to me that I never even asked Asher where we were making our first stop. It's a new experience for me, giving up this kind of control over my day to another person, but at least for today, it's not as bad as I thought it would be. Looking up, I see a big sign that says Franklin Park Conservatory and Botanical Gardens.

I glance over at Asher walking next to me, his arm still slung over my shoulders. "A botanical garden? That's a surprising choice."

"Is it? It's too cold for all the outside stuff, but inside the conservatory they have different biomes, so we get to see all these different ecosystems, all in one place. We can go to a rainforest, a desert, and the Himalayan mountains, all without leaving Ohio. It's fucking cool is what it is."

It does sound cool, but I'll be damned if I tell him that. "You sound like my mom talking about her plants."

"She gardens?"

"She's an interior designer, but every spring she does the gardens at our lake house in Maryland. She's deadly serious about it, and every year the whole thing gets bigger. My dad offers to hire a gardener at least once a summer, but she refuses.

I think I've heard her mention this place. She lives for a botanical garden."

Asher reaches into his pocket and pulls out his phone. "Go stand by the sign."

"What?"

"The sign. I'll take your picture and you can send it to your mom. If she's anything like my mom, she'll want to hear from you at least once a day to make sure you're still alive."

"Yeah, that sounds about right. But I could just text her without a picture."

"Come on, Juliette, live a little. Let's start documenting our trip. We can do a shared album that we can both add pictures to."

I turn to him. "What makes you think I'll want pictures of this trip?"

"You will."

He winks at me and pulls me over to the sign, pushing me next to it and ordering me to smile. Once he snaps the picture, he comes over to me and tosses his arm around my shoulder again, holding the camera out in front of us, but at the last second before he clicks the shutter, he turns his head, kissing me on the cheek.

"That's going to be my new lock screen picture."

"There's no way that's a good picture! You surprised me. I probably look insane."

He swipes through the pictures before attaching them to a text message and hitting send. "See for yourself."

My phone vibrates in my bag, and I pull it out, unlocking the screen and looking though the pictures Asher sent me and... well, shit. The one of us isn't just a good picture, it's a fucking great picture. My hair is a little windblown and my cheeks red either from the cold or from Asher pressing his lips to them. But I look happy in a way I'm not used to seeing on myself. Not that I'm never happy, but my happy always seems to be a little muted by whatever it is that makes me need to plan and schedule and control everything.

As we reach the conservatory, I open my text thread with my mom and attach the picture Asher took just of me. I'm keeping the one of the two of us close to the vest until I figure out a way to explain to all the people in my life what the fuck I'm doing on this road trip.

ME

Proof of life.

MOM

The Franklin Park Conservatory? I've always wanted to go there! That football player of yours has good taste in road trip stops.

Also, hi my baby, I'm glad you're alive, and I'm also very confused about why you are on a road trip with a professional football player. Please advise.

Well, Rachel Parker is nothing if not predictable.

Don't worry about it, it's just something I'm doing.

You should know better than that. I'm your mom, and I will worry about you until the end of time. It's part of the job.

Sorry, I must have forgotten.

Lucky you have me to remind you. Be safe, Jules. Text me every day. And when you get home, we're having a talk and you are going to tell me everything I want to know.

"Don't hold your breath," I mutter.

"What's that?" Asher asks.

"Nothing, just my mom being my mom."

He puts his arm back around me. "Let me guess. She's happy you're alive, but she's wondering what the hell you're doing on a road trip with me?"

"In a nutshell. I haven't told her, or anyone else, the real reason why I'm here, and there's nothing Rachel Parker hates more than when she's out of the loop on something that has to do with her children." What I don't say is that my mom is out of the loop on all kinds of things that she doesn't even know about.

"I think Rachel Parker and Susan Hansley would get along. But let me ask you something." He drops his arms from my shoulders and turns me to face him.

"How do you feel?"

"What do you mean?"

"I mean, how do you feel? Right now. Right this minute, standing in this parking lot with me, with work miles away and two weeks of adventure ahead of you. How does that make you feel?"

I think about his question. My immediate reaction is to say that I feel like I should be working, or I wish I was back in my office. But something about the way he asks the question makes me want to give it serious consideration. So, I think about the last week. The mistake and the panic attack and how Asher brought me out of it. How he made me come on this trip instead of taking what would probably have been the easier path and calling my brother because I asked him not to. Asher getting me my favorite snacks and planning an entire road trip itinerary and asking nothing of me but that I show up.

I look at him then, his face wide open, waiting patiently for me to respond to his question. My answer hits me then, and it doesn't even occur to me to hold it in.

"Relieved. I feel relieved."

I let out a whoosh of breath at what is possibly that most

honest thing I have ever said, and it's not lost on me that Asher is the one I said it to.

He just smiles at me and nods, "Then that's all that matters."

Then he slides his arm around my waist, pulling me close.

"Come on, Juliette. Let's go see some ecosystems."

Chapter Sixteen

Asher

"The Amazon Rainforest biome was for sure the coolest."

We're sitting in a Mexican restaurant with a table full of tacos. Hallie gave me a list of Julie's favorite foods, and I spent some time seeking out restaurants in all the cities that we're passing through on our way to Boulder. The way Julie's eyes lit up when we walked into the run-down restaurant on a forgotten side street in Columbus told me Hallie was spot on, and we are sitting in front of a truly impressive array of tacos that we're plowing our way through.

"No way." Julie gestures at me with her taco. "It has to be the Himalayan Mountain one. All those plants that have adapted to such harsh conditions and thrived? Now that's cool."

That those would be her favorite plants makes me want to slide in next to her and cuddle her right up. I wonder if that's what she's thinking about herself. That she thrived despite the harsh conditions of the anxiety and mile-wide perfectionist streak she clearly struggles with. I wonder if it's been this way her whole life. I wonder if her parents or anyone she's close to suspects that while she is frighteningly competent, organizes everyone and everything, and rarely puts a foot wrong on the outside, Julie Parker is oceans deep beneath the surface.

"Okay, I see where you're coming from, and I can concede that all those mountain vines were fascinating. But that canopy bridge? Definitely my favorite. Makes me want to go visit a rainforest."

"We're just going to have to agree to disagree on this, Hot Shot." She gives me a considering look. "Do you ever travel during the offseason?"

I gesture around us. "We're traveling right now."

She makes a face. "Not like this. Driving to see your family doesn't count. I mean to somewhere exotic or tropical or interesting."

"First of all, driving to see my family absolutely does count. And honestly, it never really occurred to me to do anything but this in the offseason." I shrug, picking up my glass and taking a sip of water.

"I'm close to my family, and it's harder than I expected to live so far away from them. Whenever I have the chance to see them, I take it. My first couple years in the league we would take a big trip all together every winter, but then my sisters started having babies, which made travel harder and very not vacation-like for them. So, for the past six years I've gone home for a few weeks once the season is over. I get to cuddle the babies and torture all my sisters and let my mom hover since she's never happy unless she's hovering over one of us."

"Wait, all your sisters? How many do you have? More than the two who just had babies?"

I love that she remembers two of my sisters just had babies. She may play aloof, but Julie is paying attention, and I love that for me.

"Four."

Julie chokes on the sip of water she was taking, and it takes her a second to pull herself together.

"You have four sisters?"

"Yep. Charlie is the oldest and the baby she just had is her fourth. Annie is next, and she just had her third. Kyla is just thirteen months younger than I am, and we were basically raised as twins, so I'm closest to her. She's pregnant with her first baby and due next week."

Excitement shimmers through me at the thought of being there when Kyla has her baby. I've missed a lot of births with my job, so I really hope that baby waits to be born until we get to Boulder. "Lucy is the youngest; she got married last winter."

Julie starts laughing then. Like, tears rolling down her cheeks, hysterical laughter. The way it lights up her entire face punches me right in the heart. I'm mesmerized by this grinning, carefree, cackles in a taco joint side of her. There is so much of her to learn. I want to know everything.

"What's so funny?"

"You're the middle child with four sisters. That makes you, like, the most middle child ever. You make so much more sense to me now."

"I might make even more sense when I tell you Charlie and Annie have seven kids between them, and they're all girls. Kyla didn't want to find out what she's having, but it'll obviously be a girl."

"Jesus, that's a shitload of female energy."

"Bet your beautiful ass it is. You'll fit right in."

Julie takes the last bite of her taco and sits back in her seat. For the first time since we sat down, her face takes on an uncertain expression.

"Your family doesn't think it's weird that you're bringing home some random girl for a week?"

"Juliette, you are anything but random."

I see her left hand creep over to scratch at her right wrist the way she does when she's anxious. I knew eventually her anxiety over meeting my family would surface, and I'm glad it's happening here instead of in the car so I can give her my full attention. Thinking fast, I slide out of my side of the booth and take the seat next to her. Turning to face her, I use one of my hands to cover both of hers, and with my other hand, I slide two fingers under her chin and guide her face up so she's looking at me.

"It's okay to feel anxious to meet my family. They're new, and there are a lot of them, but the Hansleys are a welcoming bunch. I promise, they are going to adore you."

I feel her hands clench under mine, so I tighten my grip a little to ground her.

"How can you be so sure? They don't even know me. I'm not that likable."

It breaks my heart a little that she thinks that and makes me even more determined to change her mind. To show her how incredible she is. That she is, without a doubt, the most spectacular woman I have ever laid eyes on.

"You're definitely wrong about that. And they know everything I've told them about you."

"You told them about me?"

"I did. I told them I danced with a girl in July who made my heart race and turned me into an idiot who said things like, 'you look gorgeous tonight,' and then she refused to give me her number even after I practically begged for it."

She laughs a little at that.

"And I told them I saw you again at my game and got to spend some time with you afterwards and finally got your number. I told them you needed a break from work, and I asked you to come with me to Boulder. I told them you are important to me, and that's all they needed to hear. You're important to me, so you'll be important to them too."

Julie's eyes glaze over a little at that so I release her hands and reach over to wrap her in a hug. She stiffens for a second before she melts into it, laying her head on my shoulder and fitting against me so perfectly there is no way in this world or any other that she wasn't made just for me to hold.

Slow your roll, Asher.

She hangs on for another minute before letting go and sitting up, an embarrassed expression on her face. "Sorry about that. I don't...love meeting new people." She says the last part so quietly I barely hear her.

Knowing how much it cost her to reveal that little piece of herself, I lean forward and kiss her forehead, then cup her face in both of my hands. "You never have to be sorry for anything you feel. I want you to tell me every single thought and feeling in that gorgeous, brilliant brain of yours. You're safe with me, Juliette."

Her whole body relaxes at that, and she closes her eyes and takes a deep breath. When she opens them again, they're clear, and she smiles. Pulling back from me she says, "If I eat another taco I'm going to explode, so what's next, Hot Shot?"

I grin, grabbing her hand and pulling her up from the table. "Come on, you're going to love it."

Chapter Seventeen
Julie

"We're going to what?" I can't possibly have heard him right.

"Howl, Juliette. We're going to howl."

His grinning face makes it almost impossible to scowl at him, but I try my very best anyway. I feel myself slipping into warmth and amusement more and more the longer I'm around him, and I don't know what to do with those feelings. Irritation I can handle. So, I try to be irritated.

"I'm going to need more information."

It was a three-hour drive from Columbus to where we are now, about an hour outside of Indianapolis. Three hours during which Asher and I took down an entire bag of peppermint Hershey Kisses and I lost a game of *who can spot the most state license plates in thirty minutes*. As his prize, he got to pick the music and proceeded to throw himself a little Taylor Swift concert.

I'd be lying if I said Asher Hansley wearing aviators and driving his big burly car while singing along to Taylor wasn't hot as fuck. Like, jolt to the clit, wish I had my vibrator and twenty minutes alone hot. I tried to sneak a picture of him but, of course, he saw what I was doing, and just beamed at me.

I swear, I have never met a more cheerful man in all my life.

Five minutes ago, we pulled up in front of what looks almost like a zoo but isn't. The sign at the front says Wolf Park and Asher is now trying to explain to me exactly what we're doing.

"It's called Howl Night. This is a wolf conservation center. We're taking a tour to see the wolves in their natural habitat and learn how they communicate. Then, we get to howl with them. We're howling at the moon like werewolves. Fun, right?"

"It's something," I mutter. And so completely something Asher would pick to do.

"Come on." He pulls me towards the sign and snaps a selfie of us and then taps at his phone. I feel my phone vibrate with the notification that he added it to the shared album he set up earlier today. I pull my phone out to look and of course, we look great. He, particularly, looks fantastic. When we got out of the car, he zipped a navy-blue puffy jacket over the jeans and thermal henley he's wearing and tugged a black beanie down over his tousled light brown hair before tossing me the same hat I was wearing earlier and zipping up my jacket for me again. When I told him I've been zipping my own jacket since I was five years old, he kissed my forehead and said he "wanted to be sure I didn't get cold."

And the fucking butterflies flapped their wings.

Asher grabs my hand and pulls me through the entrance to where a small group of people is gathered. I don't miss him rolling his right shoulder as we walk, a slight wince on his face. He's done it a bunch of times today, but I still haven't asked him about it. I figure if he wanted me to know, he would tell me. Asher is not a man who holds back, but he's holding back this. I'm at peak curiosity.

As we approach the group, a woman dressed in a modified park ranger uniform is just starting to talk. Asher laces his fingers through mine and holds on. Electricity sparks up my arm from the spot our hands are connected, and the way my body reacts to him is both thrilling and confusing. No one has ever had this effect on me; it's the kind of thing that I didn't think actually existed—like something out of a romance novel.

The guide claps her hands to get everyone's attention.

"Welcome to Howl Night everyone! I'm so happy you all braved the cold to be here with us tonight. I hope you're ready for quite the show. For the next ninety minutes, you are going to, hopefully, see some wolves and learn how they communicate with each other and with us. Before we start the program, you are free to stroll along our walking path. It's about that time of night when the wolves will be appearing, so keep your eyes peeled."

The crowd disperses to walk along the path, lined on one side by a fence to, I assume, keep the wolves away from the people. Asher and I walk together, my hand still clasped in his. As we walk, he rattles off facts about wolves. How they mate for life. How they are family animals and apex predators and need lots of space and share ninety-nine point eight percent of their DNA with dogs.

"How do you know all this?"

"You're not the only one in this relationship who knows how to do research, Juliette."

"We're not in a relationship."

He smirks at me. "That's what you think."

I open my mouth to respond, but before I can get any words out, a sleek, silver wolf slinks out from behind a tree, and whatever words I was about to say die in my throat. Its eyes are such a clear blue they are practically glowing as night falls. As we watch, another wolf approaches and they stand together, tall and proud against the darkening sky.

"Wow," I say under my breath, unable to look away from the gorgeous, powerful animals.

"You can say that again." Asher shifts behind me, laying his hands on the fence on either side of me, caging me in. He's barely touching me, but I am aware of every inch of him as we watch the wolves together.

It's full dark by the time they call us over to start the program. I could have watched those wolves all day, so we are last to get to the bleachers. There are no spots left, so we stand side by side against the fence and listen to the guide talk about the communication habits of wolves. I zone out, distracted by Asher's shoulder against mine. Warmth radiates off his body, and his spicy scent wraps around me. I've been attracted to men before, but no man has ever invaded my senses the way Asher does. His proximity makes me light-headed. My heart pounds.

"Now, let's all give it a try!"

The guide lets out a howl that snaps me back to attention.

"Come on everyone, join me. Let's howl."

Slowly, the group on the bleachers starts to howl. Literally howl. I feel Asher shift next to me and I turn to him.

"Don't fucking howl."

He folds his arms and narrows his eyes at me. "Why not?"

"Because this isn't *Twilight*."

"Would be cool if it was. Jacob really got the raw end of the deal."

I stare at him. He grins and shrugs. "What? I have four sisters. You think I've never seen *Twilight*? Read the books too."

"Seriously?"

"You bet. Kyla read them when we were younger, and I was making fun of her for reading girl books. When my mom heard, she took away my phone and all my video games and wouldn't give them back until I read the first book. Obviously, I got hooked and tore through the whole series. They're fucking great."

Asher lights up when he talks about his family; love radiates from him. It makes me miss Ben so acutely I feel it like a living, breathing thing. I've been missing him since the summer when he and Hallie got together. I wonder if I'm going to miss him for the rest of my life. And then I feel terrible because I should be happy for them. A better sister would be happy for them. A better friend would be happy for them. A better person would talk this out with them instead of shoving everything down and covering it with caffeine and productivity.

"Hey." Asher's gentle voice interrupts my train of thought. He tips my chin up and my eyes meet his. "Where did you go?"

For a minute, I consider telling him. Just letting it out and laying all the deepest, darkest, twistiest pieces of myself on him. I rarely feel safe with anyone, but he makes me feel like I could be safe with him. But here in the dark, surrounded by wolves and howling strangers, isn't the place.

"Just thinking."

His eyes follow mine. "Those are some heavy thoughts. You know what helps with heavy thoughts?"

"Let me guess. Howling?"

"You know it. Howl with me Juliette."

Without warning, he tosses back his head and lets loose a screeching howl. When he's finished, his face is flushed and shining with a contagious delight that has warmth seeping past the cold to burrow into my bones.

"Come on, you know you want to."

Then he does it again.

The thing is, I kind of do want to. But I think about how

stupid I'll look. I'm an Ivy League educated lawyer. I don't howl.

But why?

The voice in my head is gentle but authoritative and sounds a whole lot like the man standing in front of me currently howling at the moon for the third time. And suddenly, I'm so fucking sick of myself. Sick of being so perfect all the time. Sick of burying pieces of myself because I'm afraid of who I'll be if I'm not who I've always been. What everyone will think if I'm not that person anymore.

And without giving it another thought, I toss my head back, and I *fucking howl.*

I howl long and loud and fiercely. For the first time in my life, the knot that lives permanently in my chest loosens, and I'm so light I could float away. I'm elated and wild and free.

I feel free.

I want to keep howling forever.

Eventually I run out of air, and I come back to earth, breath fast and heart thumping with the kind of exertion that is everything good. Then I see Asher's face, and my heart speeds up for an entirely different reason.

It's his eyes that pull me in first. They are dark blue with desire, and he's looking at me like he wants to devour me whole, and I want to let him. Our bodies are opposing magnets drawing closer, and suddenly we are rising chest to rising chest, the only thing between us the question of who will close the distance first.

He answers the question with one arm around my waist and one hand cupping my face to bring my lips to his. His kiss is gentle at first, until I reach up and wrap my arms around his neck and it takes on a darker edge. His tongue swipes against my lips and I open for him, forgetting entirely that we are in a public place surrounded by people. I only feel him. He lets out a low groan as his tongue swipes over mine. He tastes like the peppermint Hershey Kisses we ate in the car, and my entire body buzzes with energy. He slides the hand cupping my face around to the back of my head to tangle in my hair, gripping the strands like they are his last tether to earth as his mouth moves against mine.

I know the feeling.

The arm around my waist tightens, pulling me impossibly closer to him. I feel him hard against my hip and in that moment, I need him with a ferocity that swamps me. I am entirely certain he feels exactly the same way, and the knowledge shakes me. I am not the person who needs someone else. Giving someone that kind of control scares me, and I don't know how to sit in that feeling. The buoyancy from before is replaced with a stomach-twisting anxiety, and my heartbeat speeds up in a way that has nothing to do with the kiss. And I don't know how, but he seems to understand where my mind went because he gently pulls away and rests his forehead against mine, a hand on either side of my neck and his eyes on mine. His calloused thumbs trace back and forth over my cheekbones in a calming rhythm, and my heartbeat slows.

"Asher," I whisper, not even sure what else I was planning to say. *Sorry I was halfway to an anxiety attack in the middle of kissing you? Sorry my brain can't fucking relax and enjoy a kiss like every other person in the world?*

"I know," he whispers, pressing a kiss to my forehead and lingering there before his eyes return to mine.

"It's okay, Juliette. You're safe with me."

This time, when he says it, I believe him.

Two hours later, we roll our suitcases down the long hallway of our hotel for the night. It's the first night of our trip and I had no idea what to expect and, per usual, was anxious about it. But it shouldn't surprise me at this point that Asher did exactly the right thing and booked me my own room.

We stop in front of our neighboring rooms, and as we face each other, I'm filled with uncertainty. I can still feel our kiss from before, and I am wide open and as vulnerable as I have ever been. I try to summon Lawyer Mode, but for the first time in my adult life it has abandoned me. My head is a mess. It's only been sixteen hours since we left Pittsburgh, but I feel like an entirely different person from the one sitting hungover on my front stoop this morning. I am now a person who howls in public and kisses a sweet, sexy football player and likes it, and I need to think about all that. I need to be alone. The hotel room in front of me is a refuge. My instinct is to shove my key in the lock and slam the door in his face, but we're long past that now.

As always, Asher knows exactly what to do. Letting his suitcase go, he wraps his arms around me and pulls me against him. My arms go around his waist, and I hold tight. I feel him inhale, like he's breathing me in, and he dips his head, kissing the sensitive skin behind my ear, and tingles race across my skin. Then he pulls away and takes my room key from my hand, unlocking the door for me and rolling my bag inside.

He guides me inside my room and cups my neck, kissing my forehead and then my temple.

"Goodnight, Juliette. Sleep well."

With a grin and a wink, he leaves, closing the door behind him.

Chapter Eighteen
Julie

Whatever you say.

I love it when you're spicy in the morning. I'll get your latte and make it extra hot. Your throat is probably sore from all the howling.

I hate you.

You don't, Juliette. You really, really don't.

Parker Core Four

MOM CHANGED THE NAME OF THE GROUP TO PARKER CORE FOUR

BEN

Parker Core Four mom? Seriously?

MOM

Yes, Benjamin. I don't want you to forget where you came from.

ME

We talk in this group chat every single day. We all live in the same city. I don't think we would forget where we came from.

MOM

It amused me.

DAD

Me too.

MOM

See? It amused dad too.

DAD

Everything you do amuses me, Rachel my love.

BEN

You guys know this is a group chat, right?

MOM

If you're weirded out by that then I have completely failed as a parent.

ME

Is there a point to this chat?

MOM

You mean besides me telling my children how much I miss them?

BEN

Mom, I saw you yesterday and Hallie and I are coming over for dinner tonight. How much could you possibly miss me?

MOM

Well, now I don't miss you at all. Your sister on the other hand…where in the world are you, Jules?

ME

Indianapolis.

MOM

Well obviously you know I need more than that.

ME

A hotel in downtown Indianapolis, but we're leaving soon and driving to St. Louis today.

MOM

And how are "we"? Are "we" having fun?

ME

It's fine, I guess.

When I'm With You

DAD

That doesn't sound very enthusiastic, Jules.

ME

It's eight in the morning and I'm undercaffeinated. Ask me again later. Actually, don't. I'll tell you about it when I get home.

MOM

That's probably for the best. I need to hear all about this in person so I can see your face when you talk. Just like your brother, you have a very expressive face.

ME

Can I evict myself from this group chat?

MOM

You can certainly try. Best of luck.

DAD

She means no. Your stuck with us, Jules.

BEN

You okay, Jules?

ME

I mean, I could use some coffee but otherwise, I'm fine.

You sure? You know you can talk to me about anything.

I know. I really am fine.

Okay, I'm always here if you need me. Just call.

I will, I promise. Hug Hallie for me.

Will do, baby sis.

Four minutes Ben.

Yes, but I learned a lot during those four minutes. Those are four very important minutes.

Fuck off.

Love you too.

MOLLY

Please tell me you are climbing that man like a tree Jules.

EMMA

Molly, locate your tact.

MOLLY

Like you guys haven't been thinking it.

HALLIE

I mean, yeah, but I wasn't going to ask or anything.

ME

Hallie is my favorite today.

MOLLY

I'm never your favorite.

ME

And there's a reason for that.

When I'm With You

MOLLY

Well, I will be your favorite when you check the outside pocket of your bigger suitcase. I snuck in all your good underwear *just in case*

HALLIE

I really think Molly should be your favorite now. I can't believe I didn't think to do that. I've failed as a best friend.

ME

I mean, I wasn't going to say it but...

Thanks for the underwear save, but I won't be needing it. This trip is a friends thing. Not even a friends thing. An acquaintance thing.

MOLLY

I'm sure you could probably convince someone of that, but that someone would not be me.

HALLIE

Or me.

EMMA

Definitely not me.

ME

Can I leave this group chat?

MOLLY

No dice bestie. You're stuck with us forevs.

ME

Why does everyone want me to stay in their group chats? I don't think I'm a group chat kind of girl.

EMMA

If I have to stay, you have to stay too.

HALLIE

EVERYONE HAS TO STAY.

EMMA

So where did you guys stay last night? Indiana right? And St. Louis tonight?

ME

How did you know that? I didn't even know we were going to St. Louis today until ten minutes ago.

Asher gave me your itinerary.

Seriously? Why?

He said he wanted every day to be a surprise, but he was afraid he wouldn't know if the surprises were getting too stressful for you. He knew I would know, so he gave me the itinerary so I could tell you where you were going if you needed me to.

How would you be able to tell?

I just would.

Asher

Hansley Girls

KYLA CHANGED THE NAME OF THE GROUP TO HANSLEY GIRLS

When I'm With You

ME

I've always wanted to be a Hansley girl.

KYLA

You wish you could get on our level.

How's it going with the girl of your dreams?

CHARLIE

I've been drowning in diapers so I'm going to need to get all the way caught up.

ANNIE

What she said.

KYLA

Long story short. Asher likes a girl. He somehow convinced this girl to take a road trip with him from Pittsburgh to Boulder. They'll be here in like five days and they're staying for a week.

LUCY

He more than likes her.

ME

I more than like her.

ANNIE

squeal

CHARLIE

Our baby is all grown up and bringing home a girl! I could cry.

ME

I've brought home girls before.

CHARLIE

Not like this.

ME

No. Not like this.

KYLA

I'M SCREAMING. Is she there with you right now? Can we Facetime? I need to meet her. Five days is way too long.

ME

Slow your roll, Ky. She's not here. We're still at the hotel. She has her own room.

LUCY

What's the fun in that?

ME

The fun is taking it slow, so she knows I'm all in. She's worth whatever time it takes.

CHARLIE

SWOON ASH. Fuck, you're like a man written by a woman.

MOM

How are you doing, my baby?

ME

All good here. We're still on schedule to be in Boulder on Saturday.

I can't wait to see you and meet Julie. Can you ask her what her favorite cookie is?

You don't have to bake, mom. You've never baked for a girl I've brought home.

You've never brought home a girl like this before.

How do you know everything?

It's a gift. And I think you bringing Julie home means exactly what I think it means.

It does. She's the one, Mom. I know it for sure. I've never felt like this before.

Well then, she definitely needs cookies.

ME

What's your favorite cookie?

JULIETTE

Why do you want to know?

It's a whole thing. Humor me, Juliette.

Peanut butter chocolate chip.

Excellent choice.

Chapter Nineteen

Asher

"Waffles really are the superior breakfast food, especially when you eat them for dinner."

Julie swirls her finger through the pile of whipped cream on top of her waffle and sucks her finger into her mouth, licking the whipped cream off.

I close my eyes for a hot second to collect myself.

Keep your shit together, Asher. Get your dick under control. There are kids in the room.

When I open them, Julie is smirking at me, like she knows exactly what she was doing.

"You did that on purpose."

She shrugs. "Could be."

Definitely did.

I don't hate it.

We're at the Goody Goody diner, a St. Louis landmark. I had planned a different kind of dinner, but when she mentioned earlier today that her second favorite kind of food is breakfast, I made an abrupt change of plans. Her face lit up just like it did when we had tacos yesterday, so I knew I was on the right track. I want to do whatever I can to keep the happy on her face. It is now my only mission in life.

It's less than a five-hour drive from Indianapolis to here, but we had a few stops to make along the way. We went to Terre Haute, Indiana to check out America's second largest brewery in operation, which was incredibly cool. Then we stopped in Casey, Illinois, which is now my favorite city of all time. The small town is home to lots of big things, including, among others, the world's largest golf tee and driver, the world's largest pitchfork, the world's largest rocking chair, and my personal favorite, the world's largest barbershop pole. At first the small town caught my eye because oversize things are funny, but when I realized there was a sixteen-foot taco, I was sold.

We spent hours in the town, making our way from big thing to big thing, and with each stop, I swear I could see a little more of Julie's anxiety and icy exterior melt away. Because honestly, who could be anxious when you're standing in front of a thirty-two-foot pencil? And when we got to the taco, she burst out laughing, and laughed so hard tears streamed down her face. Then she grabbed my face in both of her hands and kissed me hard, taking me completely by surprise and, well, anything that makes Julie do that is my new favorite thing.

"Asher?"

"What?" My head snaps up, and I realize I've been zoning out for who knows how long.

"Where did you go?"

She smiles as she gives me back my words from last night. She's been smiling a lot today. Fuck she looks good. When we got to our hotel, she changed into jeans that might as well be painted on and a blue sweater that makes her eyes glow. Her long blonde hair is loose and falls halfway down her back. And her face. God, her face. I could look at it all day.

I think quickly, not wanting to divulge that I was thinking about her. That I'm always thinking about her.

"I was thinking about the..."

"Let me guess. You were thinking about the barbershop pole?"

I point at her. "You bet I was. There's so much to think about. How was it made? Whose idea was it? Who is the person who woke up one morning and thought, 'you know what this town needs? A fourteen-foot barbershop pole' because I would very much like to meet that person and ask him some questions."

She takes the last bite of her waffle and leans back on her side of the booth. "You know what? I think I would too."

"Damn straight you would. Everyone would."

"So now that we've eaten breakfast at eight p.m.—inspired choice by the way—what's next?"

"What makes you think anything is next? Maybe I'm tired."

"Oh. Yeah, no, I'm sure you're tired. Same. Long day, right?" Julie's shoulders fall a little and she seems to shrink into herself as she looks away and starts tapping her fingers on her thigh. I see the same look on her face that I saw when she glanced around the friends and family room a few weeks ago and didn't see anyone familiar. It's her anxious and uncertain look. Like she's waiting to be rejected. Told she's not good enough to be around. Expecting it, even.

I reach across the table and capture her free hand.

"Juliette, look at me." It takes her a few seconds, but she raises her eyes to mine.

"I was kidding, sweetheart. Of course we're doing something next. I want to do all the things with you, all the time. I want to spend every minute of every day of this trip with you, and all the days that come after."

She takes a deep breath. "Sometimes it feels like people

don't. Like maybe I'm...too much. Or not enough? I've never been quite sure which. I think maybe if I let people see the mess I actually am, they won't want me anymore."

Her voice goes quiet on that last sentence, and I give her hand a squeeze, wanting more connection. Like yesterday at the restaurant, I understand what it takes for her to give me these pieces of herself. The ones she keeps hidden. I want her to know she can give them all to me. That I'll hold them gently.

"There's nothing about you that's too much, and you are exactly enough. I like every single part of you—the ones you've shown me and the ones you haven't yet that I hope you'll feel safe enough to share with me one day. You're safe with me, Juliette."

She goes quiet then, looking down at our tangled hands and then back up at me, and she seems to be considering her words carefully. Finally, she speaks.

"You make me feel safe enough to share. Safer than I've ever felt with anyone else, at least."

My chest tightens at her admission. This feels monumental. Julie has parts of herself she keeps locked away behind high, impenetrable walls. That she feels safe enough with me to let those walls down, even a little bit, is all I want for her. For us. Julie starts chewing on her lip, and I get the sense that she feels uncomfortable with what she put out there, so I tuck this conversation away like a gift to take out and examine later, and I change the subject.

"So, since we've established that all my moments belong to you, I have an idea for what we can do with some of them."

Like I thought she would, she brightens, relieved to put the heaviness away.

"What do you have in mind, Hot Shot?"

"How do you feel about video games?"

"You have to be kidding me!"

Julie cackles as her ball lands in the one-hundred hole again and tickets come shooting out of her machine. After dinner, we drove to an adult arcade in downtown St. Louis. As soon as we walked in, Julie made a beeline for the skee ball machine in the back and proceeded to kick my ass. Multiple times.

"Face it, Ash. Skee ball is just not your game."

Her shortening my name for the first time does something to me. More accurately, it does something to my dick which, between the nickname and Julie smoking me at skee-ball six times in a row, is now just permanently hard. I wouldn't be surprised if it's sporting an imprint of my jeans zipper by the end of the night.

"I'm a professional athlete, Juliette. Every game is my game."

She just laughs again. "I could totally tell that by the way you've lost every single game we've played tonight."

"Okay, I think we need a drink break."

Julie slides me a sly grin. "Do we need a drink break, or are you tired of losing?"

"Juliette, if it makes you smile like that, I would be happy never to win another game we play for the rest of our lives."

"The rest of our lives, huh?"

"I'm manifesting, baby."

"Are you ever not cheerful? You're like a fucking ray of sunshine."

Unconsciously I roll my shoulder, feeling the familiar dull ache. She's right that I'm a happy guy, until I feel that ache and think about what it means for my football career. I shove that thought right out of my head because tonight isn't about that. Julie's looking at me in a way that makes me certain she didn't miss my shoulder roll. Hasn't missed any of them in the last two days, but she hasn't said anything. I'm grateful for that. I don't want to lie to her. I won't lie to her. But I don't know how I would tell her the truth either.

"What's not to be happy about? We're here together, we're having fun, there are about to be drinks. It's a good night."

She stares at me, as if she's trying to figure me out. "It's really that simple for you?"

My stomach sinks a little because no, it's really not that simple, but I tell her the truest thing I can.

"I hope it can be."

Then I grab her hand and pull her towards the bar. "Come on Juliette—there are boozy milkshakes and a round of air hockey calling our name."

"You know I'll beat you at that too, right?"

"I'm counting on it. You're radiant when you're kicking my ass at arcade games."

"Well then, Hot Shot, lead the way."

Chapter Twenty
Asher

"The last milkshake might have been a mistake," Julie says, as she stumbles into the lobby of our hotel. "I can't feel my toes."

I wrap my arm around her waist to steady her and grin, utterly charmed by drunk Julie, with her cheerful disposition and mile wide smile and her willingness to cling to me so she stays upright. "That's the perfect amount of drunk."

As we walk across the lobby to the elevator, she looks up at me with a considering expression on her face. "How do you figure?"

"Well, any less drunk and you would just have a stomachache from too many milkshakes. Any more drunk and you'd spend some time with your head in the toilet, and you'd have a killer hangover tomorrow. You are exactly in the middle, and on the drunk/sober continuum, that is the perfect place to be."

"Continuum is a good word," she says absently. While we wait for the elevator, she leans her head against my shoulder and rolls her neck so she's looking up at me. "You know, you're pretty smart for a football player."

"Quarterback, Juliette. I'm a quarterback."

"A hot ass quarterback," she mumbles under her breath.

My grin widens. "Hot ass, huh? Tell me more."

She reaches up and pokes me in the cheek. "Nuh uh, Hot Shot. I'm not that drunk, just the perfect amount, remember?"

The elevator dings with its arrival and when the doors slide open, we walk inside. Leaning up against the back wall, I kiss the top of her head, breathing in her honey vanilla scent. "Everything about you is the perfect amount, Juliette."

"I think you might be perfect for me, Asher," she whispers, resting her head back on my shoulder and closing her eyes.

I close my own eyes at that and take a few deep breaths. I try and remind myself that this is drunk Julie who has no filter and will likely regret saying this in the morning, but it's no use. Hearing her say that twists up my insides because I want to be perfect for her with a fierceness that, until Julie, has been reserved for football and football alone. But for the first time ever, I can see what my life might look like one day after football is over, and it looks just like her.

Too fast, Asher. Way too fast.

But it's no use. This train has already left the station.

The elevator opens onto our floor, and with my arm around her waist, we walk down the hall. The hotel didn't have any separate room available, so I booked adjoining rooms, which I'm grateful for now so I can hear Julie in case she gets sick in the middle of the night. Standing in front of our rooms, I dig around in my pocket and find her key, holding it against the door until I hear the lock disengage.

"Come on, Juliette. Time to get you into bed."

"Good idea." She walks into the room, and with a dramatic sigh, flops down on the bed and collapses backwards, her feet hanging off the side. I drop to one knee and take off the Converse she wore out tonight. You would think high-top

Converse would be out of character for Julie, but somehow, they make perfect sense. Everything about her makes perfect sense to me. Setting aside her shoes I ask, "Where are your pajamas?"

She cracks open an eye and hits me with a sexy smirk. "You going to undress me, Asher?"

Lord give me strength.

"Not tonight, Juliette. Tonight, I'm going to get you your pajamas and make sure you're hydrated before I tuck you into bed. So where are they?"

"Over there." She gestures towards the big suitcase sitting on the luggage rack in the corner. On my way to the suitcase, I flip the lock and open the adjoining door. Then I unzip the suitcase and right on top is a matching pajama set—pants and a long-sleeve shirt covered in tiny pink hearts. I smile at them because she really does contain multitudes. I want to unravel every single one of her layers.

I grab one of her hands and pull her into a sitting position, handing her the pajamas. "Do you think you can get dressed by yourself?"

"I'm not that drunk. Just the right amount, right?" Without warning, she tears her shirt over her head, revealing a black lacy bra. It stands out against her creamy skin, and I can see the shadows of her nipples beneath the thin material. Julie. Half-naked. On a bed. Black lace.

Jesus take the wheel.

"Let me help you there." As fast as I can, I grab the shirt and tug it over her head. Once she has her arms in, she reaches back and unhooks her bra, and in the sexiest fucking move I have ever seen, she somehow manages to pull it off her shoulders and slide it through one of the arms of her pajama shirt. Women really should be ruling the world.

I have to get out of this room and calm the hell down before she takes her pants off or it really might end me.

"Juliette, you okay to get your pants? I'm going to run to my room and grab you a bottle of water."

"I'm a grown ass woman, pal. I can take my own pants off. But I really wish you would do it for me." She mumbles that last part under her breath. I stifle a groan and run next door like my ass is on fire.

I grab the bottle of water I stashed in my backpack earlier today and take a few deep breaths to steady myself before unlocking the adjoining door on my side and walking back into her room. She's already in bed, comforter pulled up to her chin and blonde hair spread out all over the pillow. She looks so cozy that my arms literally ache with the need to wrap her up and hold onto her all night. Approaching the bed, I sit on the side and look down at her. She gives me half a grin.

"You think you can sit up and drink some water? In the morning you'll be glad you did."

"You got it, Hot Shot."

She sits up and downs half the bottle in one go before handing it back to me. Then, before I even have a chance to set the bottle on the nightstand, she leans forward and wraps her arms around my neck. Surprised by the move, it takes me a second before I respond by wrapping her up just like I wanted and pulling her close. She feels so good against me, and my insides are a tangle of emotion and arousal.

"Thanks, Asher," she whispers into my ear.

"Thanks for what?"

"For tonight. It was fun. I never drink too much with anyone except for Hallie, Molly, and Emma, and sometimes Ben and his friends. I never feel comfortable being out of control. But I feel comfortable with you. Safe."

I tighten my arms around her waist. I am steeped in

warmth and emotion and fierce gratitude for whatever power made it so that I get to live on this earth at the same time as Julie Parker. That I was lucky enough to cross paths with her. To be here right now, in this moment, with her.

I drop my head and kiss the spot where her shoulder meets her neck.

"You're always safe with me, Juliette."

"I know," she whispers back. And the fact that she does, that she gets it, feels like the biggest gift she could give me.

Untangling myself from her, I gently push her back until her head lays on the pillows.

"Sure you don't want to join me here Hot Shot? It's a really big bed."

I stroke my hand over her hair, pushing it back from her face. "I want that more than anything, but the first time we share a bed, you're going to choose it without drinking first, and you're going to be clearheaded enough to remember every second of it."

"Is that a promise?"

"You know it, Juliette. Now, where's your phone? I'll plug it in for you, so it's charged in the morning."

"In my bag." She points to the bag she dropped on the floor before she hit the bed. I grab it and root around, not seeing a phone.

"You sure? I don't see it."

She grabs the bag and rifles through it before her head pops up. "Oh my god. I think I left it at the arcade. Remember I took it out when we were playing air hockey so I could have photographic evidence that I beat you again? I think I put it on the air hockey table before we played the last game and must have left it there."

"No problem. It's just a block away. I can run back and get it for you."

"You sure?"

"Absolutely sure."

"You're a good guy, Asher Hansley."

"You make me want to be the best guy." I lean down and kiss her forehead, pulling the covers up over her.

"That's all I get?" She actually pouts, and if I didn't want to lean over and kiss her so fiercely I would laugh.

"That's it, baby. Like I said, the next time my lips are on yours, you're going to choose it with a clear head."

"That's not the only thing I'm going to choose," she mutters, snuggling further into the pillow.

I look at her for another few seconds and then hightail it back through the adjoining door, thinking that a cold shower might just be in order before I go get Julie's phone.

Chapter Twenty-One
Julie

My head feels light as air, and the spot on my forehead where Asher kissed me buzzes with electricity. All I wanted was his lips on mine, but he had to go and be all *gentlemanly* and *kind* and *fucking perfect*. God. What does a girl have to do to get a little action around here?

I want to Do. Him.

In a moment of clarity in my tipsy state, I remember I packed my vibrator for just this kind of moment. I am definitely the smart one. I jump out of bed a little faster than my still partially drunken state will allow and trip over the shoes Asher lined up neatly on the floor. They go flying, and I would too, but at the last minute I slap a hand against the wall to break my fall.

Rushing over to my second suitcase that sits on the floor, I unzip it and root around, looking for the small toy I buried in there. Not able to find it, I toss open the top, expecting to find the jeans and sweaters that usually live in there. But instead, I find myself looking at a pile of boxer briefs. Calvin Klein boxer briefs to be exact. It takes my alcohol-soaked brain a couple extra seconds to catch up to what my eyes are seeing and realize what happened. I flip the top closed to confirm. This is Asher's suitcase. When they brought up the luggage, they must have switched one of our bags.

Knowing that Asher is still out getting my phone, I march to the connecting door between our rooms and fling it open, happy he had the foresight to leave it unlocked. My eyes immediately fall on my suitcase sitting on his luggage rack. It's only when I'm halfway across the room that my brain registers the noises coming from behind me.

Running water. A low groan. I whirl around and *Holy Jesus Christ*.

The bathroom door is wide open, and a very naked Asher stands in the shower, water cascading down his body. His muscled back is to me, the highest, tightest ass I have ever seen on full display. His left hand is splayed out on the wall, and his right hand is in front of him. I can't see it, but with the way his arm is moving I know he's stroking his cock, and my eyes practically burn with the need to see what it looks like.

With each slow stroke, his muscles bunch and twist, and I don't know how it's possible with the noise of the shower filling the hotel room, but I can hear his heavy breathing as if he is breathing right into my ear, and my entire body shivers, my nipples pebbling against my pajama top.

I should turn and walk away; I know I should. It's wrong to stand here and watch him, but I'm rooted to the spot; I can't get the message from my brain to my feet to *get fucking moving*. It seems like my entire body agrees that we are staying right here and watching the show.

Asher lets out a gasp as his strokes speed up, and it's a light-ning bolt to my clit. I must make some noise then, or maybe he just senses me, because he turns slowly, his right hand still gripping his cock. Our eyes meet, and if he's surprised to see me there, he doesn't let on. His face darkens with an emotion I can't name and don't understand. Neither of us speak, and I still don't move.

My eyes travel down his chest to his muscled torso and words I can't make out tattooed across his ribs and the deep v that points straight down. His body is a work of art, and I want to run my hands over every inch of him.

Then my eyes drop down and take in his erection, and I swallow audibly. It's long and thick and I haven't seen that many cocks in my life, but I know I'm looking at a prime specimen. My hands twitch at my sides, desperate to touch him, but still, I don't move.

My gaze trails back up his body and when my eyes meet his, he starts stroking again, slowly moving his hand up and down his length, groaning with each twist of his hand over the head. The unfiltered pleasure and raw lust on his face have my entire body heating to intolerable levels, and I wonder what he's thinking about as he strokes himself. For one crazy, lust filled second, I hope it's me, and only me, on his mind.

Our eyes stay locked as his strokes speed up and his hips start to rock, fucking into his fist as if just his hand isn't enough anymore. My nipples could cut glass and my clit throbs, and for a minute I wonder if it's possible to come from visual stimulation alone. In this moment, watching Asher take his own pleasure while locked in a stare-off, it feels possible.

Hand never slowing, he smirks at me then, as if he knows what I'm thinking. But as quickly as it comes, the smirk disappears, and a sound comes from him, something between a groan and a gasp. He rocks faster and faster, and our eyes never break contact as he slaps his free hand to the shower door and his hips start to lose their rhythm. They jerk forward, thrusting his cock into his fist hard and fast as a groan rumbles out of his chest, long and low, and I watch as he comes, ropes of cum erupting from his cock and covering his hand and the shower door in front of him. It's so fucking hot I'm shocked I don't combust on the spot.

His hips slow, riding out the last of his orgasm, and he drops his head down as he leans into the hand on the shower door, his chest rising and falling rapidly and his knees locking with the effort of staying upright. He takes another minute to recover as I stand there, still unable to move. Then he lifts his head, his eyes meeting mine again.

"Juliette."

My name from his lips is what shocks me back into consciousness. Suddenly, all too aware of what just happened, what I just watched happen, I spin around and run back through the adjoining doors, slamming my side shut and leaning back against it. My breaths come fast and hard, and my entire body vibrates with a mixture of embarrassment, lust, and raw, unfiltered need. As scenes of Asher jerking off filter through my brain, I admit to myself the thing that I have been pushing to the back of my brain since I first met him last summer.

I want him. All of him. Badly. As soon as possible.

Chapter Twenty-Two
Asher

Well, that happened.

I jog the block or so back to the bar quickly, as if I'm trying to outrun the memory of what just happened. But it's an exercise in futility because I am going to remember the look on Julie's face as she watched me fuck my own fist in the shower until the day I die. I have no idea what possessed me to keep going when I realized she was standing in my room watching me, but my hand took on a life of its own.

I didn't mean to jerk off in the shower, but after watching Julie tear off her shirt in front of me and everything she said? I was hard as steel and the cold shower didn't do shit, and, well, I'm only human. Being watched has never been a kink of mine, but being watched by Julie? Yes please. Every drop of blood in my body rushed to my dick so fast that I was harder than I have ever been in my life, and I also had no brain cells left to tell me to stop.

So...okay. It happened, and we'll just have to deal with it. And I saw her eyes. And her face. That was not the look of someone who was unaffected by the show. And yeah, I know what I look like. I've been an athlete for my entire life. But that was more than just a woman appreciating a man with muscles. That was curiosity and lust and something...else. Something deeper and a little darker that has my stomach swooping just thinking about it.

It was so damn hot, and the only thing that would have made it hotter would have been if I had been fucking her instead of my hand. Having her watch me made one thing crystal clear. I have never wanted another woman in my life the way I want Julie. And not just in a sexual way. In an absolutely everything, hop a plane to Vegas right now and find a chapel, 'till death do us part kind of way.

But this isn't about me. It's about her. It's about making sure she's comfortable with me even though I know she's going to hate how much she liked it.

She'll try and clam up on me in the morning, but I won't let her. I'm going to annoy the fuck out of her until she takes some swipes at me because if she's swiping at me, she'll forget to be anxious about what happened and what it all means. I'm a little brother; I've been training for an *annoy the fuck out of someone* moment for my entire life.

When I get to the arcade, I go straight back to the air hockey table we used, but Julie's phone isn't there. Heading to the bar, I get the bartender's attention quickly.

"What can I get you?" he asks.

"Did anyone find a phone by the air hockey tables? Purple case?"

"It's your lucky day." He reaches under the bar and pulls out Julie's phone, handing it to me.

"Thanks, man." I take the phone from him and dig a twenty out of my pocket, dropping it in the tip jar. "Have a good night."

He salutes me. "You bet."

As I leave the arcade, the phone vibrates in my hand and, out of habit, I look at the pop-up notification on the screen.

MOLLY

Jules, it's not a friends thing and everyone knows it. Have all the sex with him, Jules. Then tell me all about it. We'll do a virtual sexy breakfast story. With donuts.

I snort out a laugh, not sure what a sexy breakfast story is and why donuts are involved, but glad that Julie is staying in touch with her friends while she's away since I know they mean a lot to her. And I'm even happier that they all seem to be on my side. Or, at least Molly is, and she seems like a woman who could convince anyone of anything.

When I get back to the hotel, I slip into Julie's room using her key since I'm betting she shoved that lock back onto the adjoining door as hard as she could. Julie is sound asleep, so working as quietly as possible, I fish the charger I saw earlier out of her bag and plug her phone in on the nightstand. Grabbing another bottle of water out of the mini-bar, I set it on the nightstand with two Tylenol I shake out of a bottle I found in her bag.

Satisfied she'll have everything she needs in the morning, I lean down and kiss her forehead, smoothing her hair back from her face and wondering how long I can stand there watching her before it turns creepy. I decide five minutes is the limit and walk back to my room, hoping there will be a night soon when I can stay with her and never leave again.

"Your latte, Juliette."

Julie is standing in the doorway to her room, cheeks bright red as she takes the coffee cup from me without making eye contact. I take a sip from my Big Gulp to hide my smile. I knew she would be feeling some kind of way about last night. She's wearing what has become her road trip uniform. Tight black leggings, a soft sweater—purple today—and shearling lined boots. Her hair is pulled up into a high ponytail, and her face is free of makeup with a fresh, just washed look. She's so pretty it hurts.

"And how are we doing on this fine morning?"

She takes a sip of her coffee and says nothing, eyes still firmly fixed on the floor, the fingers of her free hand tapping out a beat on her thigh.

I grab a handful of peppermint Hershey Kisses out of my jacket pocket and slip them into hers. I accidentally graze her hip as I do, and even though it's through at least two layers of clothing, my fingers tingle at the contact, and I hear her suck in a breath and lean a shoulder heavily against her room door.

"Breakfast of champions. It's not actual breakfast, don't worry. But I figured we would get on the road first—there's a diner I found about an hour out I think you'll love."

She just mumbles something under her breath. She still hasn't looked at me.

The lack of eye contact is making me itchy, so I gently lift her chin with my fingers. When her gaze meets mine, I see it. Anxiety swirling in the deep blue depths. I can practically see her brain working through all the different scenarios of last night and what it means and what she should do about it. She has opened up so much to me over the last couple of days, so the last thing I want is for her to crawl back behind her walls. Not with me. Never with me.

So, I paste a smirk on my face. "See anything good last night?"

Her eyes narrow just a fraction, like she's trying to figure out what I'm doing and react accordingly. "Watch any shows after I left your room? Anything...spicy?"

Come on Julie. Scratch me, baby.

Still nothing.

"Was the temperature in your room okay? Anything make you...hot?"

"For fuck's sake, Asher, do you ever stop talking?" she explodes.

Bingo.

I tear open a bag of gummy worms and toss a couple in my mouth, washing them down with Dr. Pepper. "Nah, not when I have so much to say to you."

"I honestly sometimes wish you would say less," she mutters.

Relieved that she's talking to me again, I grin at her. I want her to feel however she needs to feel about what went down, but I want her to talk to me about it. I want her to talk to me about everything. I want every thought in her head. So...fuck it, I guess. If we dance around it, we won't get anywhere. We might as well just face it and get it all out right here in this hallway before we get in the car.

"Juliette, I know you're feeling some kind of way about what happened last night. And by what happened, I mean, you caught me jerking off in the shower and I didn't stop, and you didn't leave. I think it'll help to say the words."

Face turning red all over again, Julie blows out a breath, sliding down until she's sitting right on the floor of the hotel hallway, her door slamming shut behind her. I join her on the floor, sitting cross legged opposite her so our knees are touching. Electricity flows from that tiny point of contact. The way I react to her is unlike anything I've ever experienced before. It's as if the first time we touched, my body said "Yes, her," and my fate was sealed. Setting my Dr. Pepper down, I reach out and grab her coffee, putting it next to my cup so I can take both of her hands.

"I'm sorry if last night made you uncomfortable. I like to think I know you well enough now to know if you are, but you know your own mind, and if it made you feel uncomfortable or unsafe, you can tell me. I want you to tell me."

She looks back down at the floor. "It didn't," she whispers.

I give an internal fist pump and then squeeze her hands. She squeezes back, holding my hands like they're a lifeline from the tornado of her own thoughts. I find I quite like the idea of being her lifeline.

"Okay, I'm glad it didn't. You're safe with me, Juliette. Always and no matter what. Look, did I want the first time you saw me naked to be when you were fully clothed while I stood ten feet away from you with my dick in my own hand? I did not. But I'm a go with the flow kind of guy. And yeah, I wanted to take things a little slower, but you can't always plan for these things. But I want you to know that just because that happened, it doesn't mean that anything else has to. I would never take anything from you that you didn't want to give me. Ever. And if we're headed where I hope we're headed, we have all the time in the world. So, you take your time baby, because I'm not going anywhere."

As I was talking, her eyes drifted down to the carpet, but once I finish, she raises her head, and her eyes are glassy with unshed tears. Reacting immediately, I swing around so I'm sitting against the wall next to her and pick her up, sitting her right in my lap. The quick movement has pain throbbing through my shoulder, but I ignore it. She curls right into me, laying her head on my chest. I band one arm tightly around her waist and thread my other hand through her hair, holding her against me.

"Talk to me, Juliette."

She lets out a watery laugh. "It's nothing, really."

"I very much doubt that. No thought that's in your head could ever be nothing."

She sighs. "It's just what you said. That you would never take anything from me that I didn't want to give you. I guess, maybe, I needed to hear that? No one has ever said anything like that to me before."

I tighten my arms around her, pulling her as close to me as I can. "I never would," I whisper against the side of her head. "I only want what you're willing to give me. I know the parts of yourself you have already given me are more than you usually give to anyone else, and I need you to know that I see that."

She takes a deep breath and sits up then, twisting around to face me. "How do you get me so well? How do you understand me better than anyone when we've barely known each other a month?"

I take her face in both of my hands and kiss her forehead. "First of all, I've known you ever since you asked me to take your picture at the gala last summer. I heard your voice, and I was a goner."

She scoffs at that. If only she actually knew what went through my head when I first heard her voice. But this isn't the time to get into all that.

"I am deadly serious. But also, when it feels right, when it works, who cares how long it's been? This feels right to me. It feels like it works. I think it feels the same to you."

With my hands still cradling her face, her eyes bounce between mine before she finally answers.

"I think so too."

Then she takes a deep breath and leans forward, laying her

lips on mine, and even though the kiss is short and sweet, my body explodes in heat. I meant it when I told her I started falling from the first time I heard her voice, but it's right here in this hotel hallway, with Julie's face in my hands and her lips on mine that I take the final fall. It's sudden and easy and absolutely inevitable, and I will remember this moment for the rest of my life as the one where I tumbled into love with Julie Parker, and nothing has ever felt as right to me as that.

We break apart and I kiss her forehead again before pulling back and just looking at her, feeling the magnitude and sheer rightness of this moment.

And then the moment is broken by the buzzing of my phone in my pocket.

"You can grab that," Julie says, pushing up to standing. "I need to go get my bags and stuff."

It's like she doesn't even know I just fell face first in love with her. It'll be fun keeping this one close to the vest for a while, so I don't absolutely freak her the fuck out before she's ready.

When Julie disappears into her room, I pull my phone out of my pocket to see who called. I missed the call, but it rings again in my hand. It's a Pittsburgh area code, and the number isn't saved in my phone, but I know who it is. It's Danny—the guy from the gym I buy my painkillers from. He must have seen my missed call from the day before we left and is calling me back. I know late winter is slow for him with no baseball and no football, and I'm a good customer.

My shoulder gives a little throb, as if reminding me what's at stake. Julie learning that I've been buying what essentially amounts to black market anti-inflammatory painkillers for years. Whether I'll even be able to throw a football with this arm when pre-season starts in a few months. What I'll do if I can't. As soon as I miss the second call, the phone starts to ring a third time. I reject the call and shove the phone back into my pocket, pushing my dark thoughts to the very back of my brain just as Julie opens her door.

"Ready to go?" she asks, giving me a bright smile that hits me right in the chest. Fuck, I love her.

"You know it, Juliette. Kansas City awaits."

Chapter Twenty-Three
Julie

"I really think the peach gummies have to go in the number two slot," Asher says, swallowing a mouthful of candy. "It's a hard choice, but they're just a better candy than the gummy cherries. It's the sugar coating I think."

I chew the last of the gummy peach in my mouth, considering. "You know, I hate when anyone who isn't me is right, but I think I have to give this one to you."

He flashes me a grin. "Tell me I'm right again, Juliette. It just does something to me."

"You're an easy man to please."

"I mean, I've got the wide-open road, you in my passenger seat, ten different kinds of gummy candy, and we're eating dinner tonight in an actual igloo. What's not to be pleased about?"

He grins at me, and I get a long, liquid pool low in my belly. With a backwards baseball hat, his aviators, jeans, and a long-sleeved dark green t-shirt that hugs his muscles like it was custom made for him, he is almost unfairly hot. And now that I know exactly what he looks like under all those clothes, my mind has gone to some pretty dirty places. I thought it would be awkward and weird this morning. And for a minute, it was. But then Asher did his thing where he makes something that feels terrible not terrible at all. I don't know how he does it—he might be magic.

After last night's little show, I woke up this morning with my stomach twisting with anxiety, wondering whether I should grab the first flight I could find out of St. Louis and have Hallie pick me up at the airport later today. I couldn't make sense of it all—what it would mean for Asher and me, if it would mean anything, and whether I wanted it to. How he would act and how I would act and whether the rest of the trip would be awkward and weird.

But then he was outside my door with his signature grin and my latte and his giant soda and that irritatingly endearing habit he has of getting me to talk about things that I never talk about with anyone, and before I knew it, I was sitting on the carpet of a hotel hallway in his lap, with his arms tight around me.

I would never take anything from you that you didn't want to give me.

Those words have been playing on a loop in my head since the hotel, and I've been trying to make sense of why they hit me so hard. It's not that anyone has ever taken anything from me that I didn't want to give, exactly. It's more that I give so much, the people in my life don't even realize that they're taking. I need control and I need to take charge because I need every-thing to be perfect, and I always think the only way for it to be perfect is to do it myself. I hand out assignments and I organize everyone to within an inch of their lives and I worry about everyone and everything, and I'm beginning to see that maybe this life hasn't served me so well.

Because what do I have to show for it? The constant thrum

of anxiety in the background. A reputation for being a hardass who never takes a break. Hiding the more vulnerable parts of myself so my friends and family don't realize what a disaster I am underneath my Lawyer Mode shield. I mean, I canceled my entire life for two weeks for a road trip with a man who was basically a stranger rather than tell my brother and my friends —the closest people in the world to me—I had a panic attack. That can't be healthy. And yet. As the days go by, I realize more and more that I don't want to be anywhere else except for right here, with him.

And isn't that a kick in the ass?

I sneak a side glance at Asher, who is bobbing his head to the music we have playing, mouthing the lyrics as he hits the blinker to change lanes. He must have a sixth sense when it comes to me because he glances over and gives me a wink before turning his eyes back to the road.

He sure doesn't feel like a stranger. We've only been on this trip for three days and he might know me better than anyone else in my life. He just gets me. Somehow, this man, who is likely a future hall of fame NFL quarterback, who is constantly named one of the best-looking players in the league, who looks like he just stepped off the pages of a magazine, really looks at me, and he seems to like what he sees.

I like what I see too.

I like the way he constantly searches for fun wherever we go, and when he can't find it, he makes it himself, like deciding this morning when we got in the car that we were going to rank the best gummy candy in his stash. I like the way he lights up when he talks about his family. I like how he's not intimidated by me—how he likes it when I beat him at things, and when I take swipes at him, and when I'm in a crap mood. He doesn't want me to be anything except exactly what I am. I think this is the first time in my life I have experienced that, and part of me wishes this road trip would last forever. That maybe we would last forever.

Forever? Back the truck up, Jules.

Because we might be having fun now, but vacations end, and real life happens, and in real life, the lawyer with awful anxiety and a mile-wide perfectionist streak who can't even give up control and relax enough to have an orgasm with another human does not end up with the gorgeous, happy-go-lucky, golden-boy quarterback. No matter how much she wants to.

"So, what are the final standings?"

Asher's voice yanks me out of my head and back into the car.

"What?"

"The candy. We're ranking the candy, remember? For science, Juliette. Science is counting on us."

I snort out a laugh. "I hated science. If science is counting on me, science is doomed."

Asher's phone rings then. An unknown Pittsburgh area code flashes on the car's LCD screen, and he rejects the call. The phone immediately rings again with the same number, and he rejects that one too.

"You didn't need to get those?"

"Nah, I don't like answering unknown numbers."

He reaches over and tucks a piece of hair that fell out of my ponytail behind my ear, and traces his fingers down my jaw, letting his hand linger an extra second. Tingles explode out from where he touches me, and he smiles like he knows exactly how this contact is affecting me. I swear the man can read my damn mind.

"Good thing for us, I love science."

"You do?"

"I do. Bio major in college."

"Like, biology?"

"Yep."

"You majored in biology?"

"Sure did. With a minor in physics."

"But, why?"

He shrugs. "I wanted to be a doctor."

I stare at the side of his face. "You...huh?"

He chuckles. "You really did think I was just a dumb jock, didn't you?"

I shift, uncomfortably. "I mean, not dumb but...I thought all football players sort of coasted through college, studying just enough so they stayed eligible to play. Why kill yourself if you knew you were going to the NFL?"

"I didn't always know that."

I scoff at that. "Come on. I grew up in Pittsburgh. I'm a life-long football fan. I remember when you were drafted. Phenom quarterback out of the University of Boulder, standout all four years of college, started every game all four seasons, third overall draft pick. There was no way you weren't making it to the NFL."

He lays a hand on my leg and just rests it there. "Please feel free to keep reciting my stats to me. It's hot as fuck, Juliette."

"I would, but I really want to know why you thought you needed such an intense backup plan when your future seemed so clear." I'm practically burning with the need to know this fact. For some reason, it feels like this little piece of information will unlock a piece of Asher that I desperately want to understand.

He sighs, shifting in his seat, his grip tightening on my leg. "My whole life has been football. Ever since the first time I held a ball when I was five or so years old, I've loved it. I loved playing on a team, and I loved throwing a football around with my dad and my sisters in the backyard. The game is a part of me. It always has been. The thing is, football didn't always come naturally to me. I've never been the biggest, or the strongest, or the fastest. But what I was, was the hardest worker. I would get to practice early, leave late, and workout on off days. I studied playbooks when I should have been sleeping and then fell asleep watching tape of our opponents."

This, at least, I completely understand. "You wanted it more than anything, so you worked your ass off to get it. If you didn't get it, it wasn't going to be because you didn't work hard enough."

He nods. "You understand." He says it like a declaration, like he knows he can give me this truth and I'll see him. My heart suddenly feels like it's too big for my chest. I put my hand over his, and he turns his over, lacing our fingers together.

"So, since I had to work so hard for it, I didn't take anything for granted. Not like the guys on my team who were born with a football in their hands and never doubted they would make it. I never looked at the NFL as a certainty, and I wanted to have a plan, in case it didn't work out. But not just a fallback plan, a real second option that I could be as passionate about as I was about football."

"Medicine."

He nods. "Medicine. My dad is a surgeon, and my older sisters Charlie and Annie are both doctors. I love science, and I've always been fascinated by my dad's job. When I was a kid, he would sometimes bring me to the hospital and let me come with him to round on his patients, and those are some of my best memories. Before I realized the NFL might be an option for me, I knew I would go to medical school. I guess I kind of started college with two dreams and wanted to make sure I could make one of them come true."

I'm a little stunned at the thoughtful way he approached his career, but I realize I probably shouldn't be. This is a man who brought me back from a panic attack and took me on a road trip so I could take a break from work I desperately needed but wouldn't ever have taken on my own. A man who has stopped at nothing to make sure that I have everything I could need or want. Who has worked so hard to make sure I'm happy. Who seems to see me without me having to say a word. He is nothing but thoughtful. I get the sudden urge to pepper him with questions; to learn every single thing about this man who is so much deeper and more complex than he lets on. But he is taking his time with me, and he deserves the same in return. So, I start small.

"What kind of doctor did you want to be?"

He grins. "Pediatrician."

"Somehow that makes perfect sense."

"Right? I love kids. They're so fun and funny and they still think everything is magic. I try and volunteer where I can; I make a lot of trips to Children's Hospital, and I'm working with Jeremy a little during the offseason on the camps he's setting up."

"Would you ever think about going to medical school when you retire one day?"

He stiffens a little at that and rolls his right shoulder in a move I've been noticing more and more as the days go by. I'm still curious about it, but don't want to pry too deep, too soon.

"I don't think so. It's a lot of school and training, and I'm already thirty-one, so by the time I retire and start school, I'd be a pretty old doctor. Also, I miss my family and my sisters keep having babies, and if I go to med school, I'll have even less time to see them than I do now. So as much as I would have loved to be a doctor, I'm happy with the path I chose. I don't regret it for a second. All in all, I'm a pretty lucky guy."

"God, how did you get so emotionally healthy? I've never known a guy like you."

He smiles and shrugs. "It's probably the four sisters."

"I can't wait to meet them." I squeeze his hand when I realize this is the absolute truth. I want to know here this man came from. I want to know everything about him.

Asher's phone rings again then, the same number that rang before. He rejects the call and just like last time, it rings again, and he rejects that one too. My stomach does a little flip wondering who might be trying to get in touch with him. Whoever it is, they clearly want to reach him pretty badly, so why doesn't he want to pick up the phone?

"You sure you don't need to get that?"

"Definitely not. It's not important."

"How do you know it's not important if you don't answer the phone?"

He tosses me a grin. "I know everything."

I smile back but unease curls into my stomach. Four missed calls in an hour from the same number when his phone has barely made a sound in the three days we've been on the road unless it's his family or the group chat he has with Ben, Jeremy, and Jordan feels like it might be important.

"Hey, want anything from the gas station convenience store? I need to fill up."

He signals and pulls off the highway, turning into a gas station and pulling up at one of the pumps.

"No, I'm good."

He looks at me strangely. "This is the first time since we stopped that you didn't tell me to get you more caffeine or look for some insane potato chip flavor."

I just shrug, trying to act casually when my mind is starting to race with all the potential explanations for the four phone calls. Like maybe he's seeing someone else. Someone who isn't me. The thought turns my stomach.

"Guess there's a first time for everything."

He holds his gaze on me for a second before opening the car door. "Sit tight, Juliette. I'll be right back."

He doesn't take his phone with him, and as soon as he gets out of the car, it rings again. Same number. And again. And again. With every call, the knot in my stomach tightens. I try and breathe against it and force my brain out of worst-case scenario mode. Because right now, it's trying very hard to go to that place. The place where the things he's been saying to me aren't real. They feel real. God, do they ever feel real. But what if they're not? My fingers scratch at my wrist as my mind races.

His phone buzzes again, this time with a text. I look down at his phone in the cup holder and see the message preview on the screen. As I look, the messages keep coming.

UNKNOWN

Ash, where are you?

Everyone is saying you left town. You didn't want to come see me before you left?

You know I can give you what you need. I always do.

You need me just as much as I need you.

Call me.

Tears prick at my eyes as the messages finally stop coming through. I lean my head back against my seat and will myself to calm down. My breathing to slow. My fingers to stop scratching my wrist. There may be some reasonable explanation for this, but I curse my analytical, lawyer mind for abandoning me in my moment of need.

I can't grab hold of logic. All I can grab on to are images of Asher and some faceless woman who probably has a perfect body and perfect hair and a perfect brain that never gets anxiety and never needs to be calmed down and who never needs to hear things like "you're safe with me" because she never feels unsafe and she can probably have an orgasm on command through penetration alone. I hate her and I try to hate him, but I can't summon it because what I feel for him is the opposite of that, and when the fuck did *that* happen?

Because the hell of it is, I didn't realize just how much I wanted every single part of him—body and mind and soul—until right this minute, when it seems like he's not mine to have.

Chapter Twenty-Four
Asher

"Are you sure you don't want to go to dinner?"

"I'm sure." Julie is curled into a ball against the passenger door, sitting as far away from me as she can get. I don't understand what's going on, and it's freaking me the fuck out. One minute we were talking about my medical career that wasn't, laughing and holding hands. It felt so good to talk to her. To open up in that way. She seemed to understand why it was so important to me to keep my options open, and the way she was looking at me. It was...different. It wasn't fondness for the cheerful quarterback who plans fun road trip games. It was something else. Something deeper. It was a look I have been waiting for. It felt like *more*.

When she asked me about going to medical school after I retired, I had to bite my tongue to keep from telling her everything. About the post-traumatic arthritis and the anti-inflammatory shots and the pain that won't go away even in the offseason and my paralyzing fear that I might not be able to play anymore and who I am if I don't have football.

Every instinct I have is telling me that she is a safe place to lay my truths, but five years is a long time to keep a secret, and silence is a hard habit to break. I will. Just not quite yet. I hope I get the chance.

Because when we stopped for gas, by the time I got back into the car her mood had shifted completely. She turned quiet on me in a way she hasn't been in days. She didn't crack a smile when I handed her a bag of the most bizarrely flavored potato chips I could find and didn't respond when I told her it was her turn to pick the music.

For the past three hours she's been all silence and one-word answers when she wasn't pretending to be asleep. Someone who doesn't know Julie would think she's pissed, but I know better. The anxiety is coming off her in waves, rolling straight towards me. She is scratching at her wrist and drumming her fingers on her thigh and when I laid my hand on hers to stop it, she tossed it off, and the look she gave me was a jagged knife slipped between my ribs. Her eyes were shattered, and I would burn down the world to figure out why, but she's locked up tight, and I can't find the key to open her back up again.

I try one last time, knowing it's futile, but hoping anyway. "But it's an igloo, Juliette. I've always wanted to eat in an igloo. Haven't you?"

She whips around and stares daggers at me.

"Oh, my fucking god, Asher. If you want to eat in an igloo so badly, go eat in an igloo, but I'm not coming. Take me to the hotel."

Then she turns around as far as she can in the seat, staring out the window into the darkness, fingers tapping out a rhythm on her thigh. Weirdly, her outburst makes me feel a little better. Anger is better than total silence and devastated eyes. But I can't help but wonder where my Juliette went and whether I'm going to get her back.

"Here's your key."

I hand Julie her room key and she mumbles thanks under her breath before making a beeline for the elevators, leaving me staring at her back for a second before I take off after her. She doesn't look at me as we wait for the elevator, and we make the ride up to the fifth floor in silence, her eyes firmly fixed on the floor while her hands tremble on the handle of her suitcase.

It feels wrong not to reach out to her. Not to lay my hands on hers and gather her up and tell her that whatever is going on, we can work through it together. I feel myself leaning towards her, all of me reaching out to be whatever she needs me to be right now. This distance feels so wrong. Julie and I aren't meant to be this far apart.

When the elevator reaches our floor, she gets out first, and by the time I catch up with her outside our doors, she is fumbling with her room key, shoving it into the slot while it beeps and flashes red. Her breathing is fast, her hand still shaking, and I know she's about to fall apart. I don't understand why, and she's not going to let me help her when all I want to do is take whatever it is that is weighing on her and carry it myself.

Not able to watch her struggle for a second longer, I reach out and take her hands, gently pulling them away from the door. She stiffens but doesn't protest when I take the key from her and fit it into the lock, pushing the door open.

I hand her the key and she turns to go into the room. Before she can make it all the way in, I capture her wrist gently in my hand, pulling her back and spinning her to face me. Letting her wrist go, I cup her face in both of my hands, thumbs stroking her cheekbones as I lift her head to look at me. My heart lurches in my chest at the look on her face. She looks exhausted. She looks sad. I try one last time.

"Talk to me, Juliette."

"I can't," she whispers, eyes glassy. "I just...I can't."

I lean in and kiss her forehead, and she lets out a shuddery breath, her eyes dropping closed.

"You can. You can tell me anything. I'll be right next door if you need me. You're safe with me, Juliette."

At that, her breath hitches and she spins away from me into her room, shoving the door closed behind her. Letting her go when every instinct I have is screaming that she doesn't really want to be alone is the most counter-intuitive thing I have ever done, but without much of a choice, I let myself into the adjoining room. Stripping out of my clothes as I walk, I grab all the blankets and pillows off the bed and pile them up on the floor. Then I sit and lean my back against the door adjoining our two rooms hoping that if she won't let me in, I'll at least be able to hear her if she needs me.

Julie

The tears are already falling when the door to my hotel room closes behind me. I can't even make it to the bed. I just sit right down on the floor, wrapping my arms around my legs and laying my head on my knees as I let them come. I sit there for what feels like hours as tears pour down my face. Every time they slow, I think about the string of texts on Asher's phone, the way his hand feels when he lays it over mine, and I find a new well of unshed tears to cry.

I should be appalled at myself for crying over a man. RBG would never. Hillary would never. Gloria would definitely never. But Julie Parker, it seems, does. Because maybe, when the man is thoughtful and kind and sees you and makes you feel safe and takes you to do things like howl with the wolves because he thinks you'll like it and it turns out you do, he's worth crying over a little. Or a lot. A whole lot.

When I'm all cried out, I drag myself to the bathroom. I wince when I look at myself in the mirror. My eyes are puffy and red-rimmed, my skin blotchy. I splash water on my face, and without the energy to do anything else, I take off my clothes and fall into bed.

I realize suddenly that I'm not used to being alone. Even though I've slept by myself every night we've been on this trip, with Asher in the next room, and knowing that I'd see him in the morning, I never really felt alone. But now, with my brain screaming at me that something isn't right, and unable to let go of what I saw on Asher's phone, I think maybe I have never felt so lonely. Suddenly desperate for some sort of connection, I reach for my phone on the nightstand.

ME

Hey, Hal.

HALLIE

Jules! How's the open road?

I consider telling her that everything is fine. But everything is very not fine, and I don't have the energy to pretend it is.

ME

Not so great.

HALLIE

Seriously? What happened? Are you okay?

I think this whole thing might have been a mistake.

What did he do? Do you want to come home? I'll pick you up at the airport and then I'll kill him. Actually, I'll have Jeremy kill him. He can be kind of scary when he's not staring at Em like she's about to disappear.

I chuckle despite my general misery because she's right about that.

ME

I'm surprised you didn't say you'd make Ben kill him.

HALLIE

Have you met your brother? He's more of a, try to reason with him and when it doesn't work, swiftly cut him out of your life guy. If you want to exact violence, Ben is not your man. And if Asher hurt you, we are exacting all the violence.

So, are we? Exacting all the violence? What happened?

It's nothing. I just...don't think Asher is the guy I thought he was.

And here I thought you didn't think anything about Asher. Didn't you say it was just "a friends thing?"

Shut up.

Jules, it's Ben. I just wanted to tell you that Asher is one of the best guys I know.

I suck in a breath at that and let it out slowly. That may

seem like a normal thing to say for some people, but I know my brother doesn't open up his circle for just anyone, and he rarely does acquaintances. Jeremy and Jordan are his brothers, Hallie is the love of his life, and I'm his sister. Molly and Emma come with Hallie and me, and Allie comes with Jordan, and we are his people. No one else. If he says Asher is one of the best guys he knows, it's not hyperbole. Asher is one of his people now.

HALLIE

> Okay sorry, it's me again. Listen Jules, I don't know why you're on that road trip or what's going on between you and Asher, but I know this. In the three days you've been gone, you haven't checked in on work once. You haven't called or texted or made sure we're handling all your clients the way we said we would. That's not like you, in a good way, and I think you have to consider what that means.

Fuck, she's right. How is it possible I haven't checked in on work once and didn't even notice? I know the answer and I hate it because if Asher isn't the person he has shown me over the past few days, then maybe I'm not either, and I like the person I am when I'm with him. The one who howls with wolves and doesn't check in at work every twenty minutes. I take a deep breath and for the first time, maybe ever, I tell my best friend what's really on my mind.

ME

> I like him, Hal. I really, really like him. And that scares the shit out of me because what if he's not who I think he is?

HALLIE

> But what if he is?

I toss my phone down and bury my face in a pillow as my stomach churns and my mind races. I resign myself to a long, lonely night of no sleep and unrelenting intrusive thoughts of Asher and whatever woman was on the other end of his phone today. God, I hate that bitch. And I hate myself for opening up enough that I care.

"Juliette?"

I sit straight up at the sound of Asher's voice through our connecting door. It doesn't sound like he's standing at the door though. The sound is coming from lower down, like maybe he's sitting? And my eyes fill again at the thought of Asher sitting on the other side of the door, as close to me as I'll let him be right now.

"Juliette, I know you don't want to talk, and that's okay. I don't know what's going on, but I want you to know that I'm right here. You're not alone. You never have to be alone. I'm not going anywhere. You're safe with me."

You're safe with me.

I wish I was. I wish I could be. I probably even am. But my anxious brain that gives up control for no one and nothing has decided for me that Asher can't be mine, even though every other part of me wants nothing more than to be his.

Chapter Twenty-Five
Asher

"Shit," I mutter, turning up the windshield wipers as high as they'll go.

It's only five-thirty p.m., but it's pitch-black outside. The snow started an hour ago. At first it was the good kind of snow. The perfect snow that we saw out of Julie's office window the day of her panic attack. But the closer we get to Wichita, the worse it gets, and now, about forty-five minutes outside the city, it's a full-blown blizzard.

Ordinarily, I would make light of this. The Range Rover can drive through anything, and I have a full tank of gas and plenty of snacks, and my favorite girl is in the passenger seat. But Julie is still barely speaking to me, and my nerves are shot.

I had plans for today. We were going to stop in Leavenworth, Kansas to see a museum full of carousels. And then when Julie had her fill of the whimsical and insane, we were going to drive to Topeka to the Brown v. Board of Education National Historical Park because Emma told me that Julie's favorite classes in law school were Constitutional Law and

Education Policy, and I thought she would like it. Instead, Julie texted me early this morning that she had to do some work, and would it be okay to leave later than we planned and drive straight to Wichita without stopping. If she really had to work, of course I wouldn't care, but she didn't.

I glance over at the passenger seat where she is curled up against the door again, this time with earbuds in her ears. Her eyes are closed, her hair falling in her face.

She has effectively shut me out in every way possible, ducking back down behind the walls that she has slowly been lowering to me. I want to tear my hair out of my head.

With my mind wandering, I don't see the car in front of me start to spin until it's too late. It's a small sedan that has no business driving in this weather, and with the road snow covered and slippery, its back wheels lose traction quickly and it careens into a full spin, heading straight for us.

Julie gasps, her hand flinging out and clamping onto my leg. I grew up driving in Boulder in all kinds of inclement weather, so I react on instinct. I tap the brakes and steer the SUV as gently as I can into the next lane, thanking whatever higher power is out there that the road is relatively empty. Miraculously, the car in front of us recovers from the spin unscathed and continues on its way in the storm.

I should be shaken by the near miss, but I'm distracted by the feel of Julie's hand. It's the first time she's touched me in twenty-four hours. It's just a hand on my leg, but with the way my heart knocks against my ribs, it might as well be a hand right on my dick. All too soon she seems to realize what she's doing and pulls her hand away like my leg burned her. Saying nothing, she starts scratching at her wrist. I know she won't let me help her, and suddenly my giant car is too small and there isn't enough air and I need to get the fuck out of here.

I steer the car over to the shoulder and throw it into park.

Pulling out my phone, I open a browser and search "hotels near me."

"What are you doing?" They're her first words to me in hours.

"The snow is getting bad, so I think we should stop for the night." I turn to look at her. "Are you okay with that?"

She just shrugs. Okay then. I turn back to my phone and the first listing is for Roses and Lace Inn four minutes away. I do a quick scroll through the pictures and it looks nice enough, so I pull the car back onto the road and take the next exit.

The inn sits at the end of a long, winding driveway with a canopy of leafless trees that sway in the swirling snow. The whole effect is reminiscent of a nineteen-sixties horror movie and is creepy as hell. Julie is staring out her window, her fingers tapping on her thigh, and I can only hope that the inn doesn't match whatever is going on with this endless driveway or we're in for a long night.

When we finally reach the end of the driveway, I breath a sigh of relief. The inn is an old but well-maintained Victorian style mansion. It's light blue with scalloped wood siding, tall, narrow windows, and a giant wrap-around porch.

Pulling up into one of the parking spots in front that is as cleared as it could possibly be in the middle of the blizzard, I get out of the car and go around to Julie's side to open her door, but she is already out of the car by the time I get there. In silence, we go to the trunk, and I pull out the suitcases we need for the night, wincing a little at the throb in my shoulder. I start to head to the porch and out of the snow when Julie tries to pull her suitcase away from me. I turn towards her.

"What are you doing?"

"Taking my suitcase." She tries to pull it away again, but I don't let her.

"I've got it."

She attempts a glare, but her eyes aren't angry. They're sad. Resigned. I wish she would tell me what the fuck is going on. "You don't got it. I saw the face you made back there. Carrying both is hurting you."

My stomach drops a little at her acknowledgement of my pain. "Julie, just let me carry the suitcase. And let's get out of the snow, okay?"

Her breath hitches and her eyes glass over. Yanking her hand from her suitcase, she turns and stomps up the stairs and disappears inside.

Motherfucker.

I follow her inside where it's warm and bright and smells like apples and cinnamon. The woman sitting at the carved wooden desk that serves as the reception area has silver, curly hair and is wearing a red dress covered in gingerbread men. When she sees us, her eyes light up, and with her plump, flushed cheeks, she looks like a bed and breakfast owner straight out of central casting.

"Terrible weather out there," she says with a smile at us. "Welcome to Roses and Lace. I'm Shirley. How can I help you tonight?"

"Do you by any chance have a couple of rooms for the night? We were supposed to go to Wichita, but the weather got too bad to keep driving."

"Oh, I'm so glad you found your way here. It's way too dangerous to keep driving out there. Unfortunately, you're not the only people who have decided to stop for the night to get out of the weather, so I just have one room available."

I can hear Julie's sharp inhale from across the room where she's studying the pictures lining the wall. I know she hates the idea of one room with whatever is going on in her head, but she's going to have to deal with it and with me.

"That would be fine; thank you so much." I hand her my

credit card, and she runs it through a machine that looks as old as I am and gives me back the card.

"Wonderful. Here's the key." She hands me an actual brass key on a keychain in the shape of a flower. "You'll be in room eight. It's straight up the stairs, last door on the right. Breakfast starts at six-thirty."

"Thank you so much. We appreciate it."

I turn to grab the suitcases and find Julie right behind me reaching her hand out.

"Don't even think about it, Blondie." I grab the suitcases and carry them upstairs, with her following closely behind me. When I unlock the door and push it open, I see three things immediately. The most garish red floral wallpaper that has ever existed. A fireplace almost as tall as I am. And one bed. One. Fucking. Bed. I don't even realize that I'm stopped in the doorway until Julie pushes past me into the room. The second she sees the bed she freezes.

"Oh no. No way. Definitely not. Not happening." She spins to face me. "Not. Fucking. Happening." She punctuates each word with a finger to my chest then crosses her arms, glaring at the bed as if she can make it split in two through sheer force of will.

I'm suddenly exhausted right into my bones.

"It's fine, Julie. We're adults. We can share a bed. And if sharing a bed with me is so terrible, I'll sleep on the floor, okay?"

"I can't."

"You can."

"No. You don't understand. I can't. I just...can't."

Her breath hitches on the last word, and she looks around the room a little wildly. Her fingers scratch at her wrist and her breath comes fast and sharp. I can tell she's on the verge of a full blown panic attack, and I take one step towards her, hating to see her struggle. Wanting so badly to help her. For her to let me help her. To tell me what the problem is so I can fix it. But before I can reach her, she throws a hand out to stop me then spins on her heel, running out of the room and thundering down the stairs.

It takes my brain a second to engage, and she's fast when she's panicking. By the time I catch up with her, she's flying out the front door of the inn. I find her in the parking lot, standing in the falling snow, bent over with her hands on her knees, her back rising and falling rapidly. I reach her in two strides. I place a hand on her back and she jerks at my touch, her breathing so fast I'm afraid she's actually about to hyperventilate.

I can't watch her struggle anymore. I don't have it in me.

"Fuck this." I wrap my arms around her from behind. She struggles against me for a second before giving in, melting into me and fitting so perfectly against me it's like she was made just for me. I tighten my arms, whispering into her ear.

"Breathe, Blondie. You're okay. Feel me breathe and do what I do. We've done this before. In and out, okay?" I keep holding her, taking deep, exaggerated breaths until I feel her breathing match mine. "You're doing great; just keep breathing. Stay with me."

I don't know how long we stand there like that, the snow falling around us, but as I feel her breathing return to normal, I just can't take it anymore. The last twenty-four hours have been an eternity.

"What's going on, Julie? Why are you so sad? Talk to me, baby. I miss the sound of your voice."

"I can't."

"You can. You're safe with me. I swear it."

At that, she pulls out of my arms, whirling around to face me, her face a mask of pain.

"Am I, Asher? Am I safe with you? Because I don't feel all that safe."

Nothing she could say would possibly cut any deeper than that.

"If I did something to make you feel like you weren't safe with me, then tell me so I can make it better. Just...tell me."

"I saw the texts on your phone," she explodes.

"The...huh? I have no idea what you're talking about."

She scoffs. "Really? *You know I can give you what you need? You need me just as much as I need you?* Come on, Asher. I'm not an idiot. If this whole road trip is just a fun way for you to pass the time, that's fine—I just need to know. If you're seeing other people, just tell me. I mean, you're not even seeing me, so I don't know what I'm getting so upset about. But still. Just tell me. I'm a big girl and I can handle it. I'm not going to fall in love with you over some wolves and a giant taco and a bag full of peppermint Hershey Kisses."

Well, fuck me. She saw the texts from Danny. It kills me that she has spent the last day worrying that there might be another woman. And I know it's time to tell her. Everything. It occurs to me for the first time that if this conversation goes badly—if she doesn't understand me self-medicating so I can play football—I could lose her for good. I've been so preoccupied with losing her for some unknown reason that I forgot there is an actual, tangible reason she may not want to be with me, and that thought is a punch straight to the gut.

I could spend a minute pondering the irony of the fact that I finally found something that would hurt more to lose than football and now I might lose them both, but I can't dwell on that for too long or I'll go insane. I didn't have *tell my biggest secret and potentially lose the love of my life during a blizzard at a roadside bed and breakfast in rural Kansas* on my bingo card, but I guess you can't always plan the major crossroads in your life. Whatever the outcome, this conversation has to happen, and it has to happen tonight. But first thing's first.

I step towards her, cupping her face in both of my hands so our eyes meet. I lean forward, pressing my lips to her forehead before locking eyes with her again. I can feel the intensity blazing in my gaze and I hope she sees it. "There is no one else. I haven't so much as looked at a single other woman since we danced together almost seven months ago. I only want to see you. I don't want to see anyone but you ever again. Ever, Juliette."

She closes her eyes, and a single tear slips down her cheek. I catch it with my thumb, wiping it away.

"You called me Juliette." Her voice is small, and I hate it. Her voice should never be small.

"I always call you Juliette."

"Earlier you didn't. In the parking lot. And in the room. And just now, when you were telling me to breathe. I don't..." She stops, taking a shaky breath. "I don't want you to call me anything else. I like that I'm Juliette to you. I like who I am when I'm with you."

I lower my forehead to hers, breathing her in, my heart expanding with love for her, knowing how monumental it is for her to say those words. "I'll never call you anything else, ever again," I murmur.

"Thank you," she whispers. She pulls away a bit then, leaning her head back so she can look at me. "But the texts. The phone calls. Asher, I really need to know what they're all about because my mind is going to some pretty bad places."

I take a deep breath, because here goes nothing. "It has to do with football, and it's a long story. I want to tell you. I want to tell you everything. Will you come upstairs with me, out of the snow, so we can talk?"

She smiles.

Fuck I've missed her smiles.

Then she steps into me and puts her arms around my waist, leaning her head on my shoulder. I wrap myself around her, holding on and letting out a breath I feel like I've been holding since yesterday as the snow falls all around us.

"Let's go upstairs. Tell me everything."

Chapter Twenty-Six
Julie

Our room is warm when we get back. Shirley must have seen us go outside and assumed we would be freezing because a fire is roaring in the giant fireplace and even with the god-awful wallpaper, the room is inviting.

Asher closes the door behind us before unzipping my suitcase and handing me the pajamas he somehow knows are always on top. "Go warm up in the shower. We can talk afterwards." He kisses my forehead again and pushes me gently towards the bathroom. I sense he needs a minute to gather his thoughts, and now that I know whatever is going on is career related, I'm happy to give him whatever time he needs.

I come out of the bathroom to a bare mattress and a nest of pillows and blankets on the floor in front of the fire. Asher is sitting in the middle of the pile, wearing gray joggers and a navy hoodie. His light brown hair is disheveled, like he has spent the last ten minutes running his hands through it, and he looks so cozy I want to curl myself into him and never let go.

I take a seat across from him, cross-legged so our knees are touching, and he immediately takes both of my hands in his, holding them tighter than necessary, like he needs a touchstone for whatever conversation we're about to have. His face, normally so open and cheerful, is tense, and his sky-blue eyes look troubled and anxious. I'm suddenly almost desperate to put him at ease. To calm him the way he has done for me so many times over the last few weeks. I pull one of my hands out of his and lay it on his cheek. He leans into my touch immediately.

"Asher. Whatever it is, you can tell me."

"I'm a little afraid of this conversation." His admission comes in a raspy whisper.

"Tell me why."

"I'm afraid you'll walk away once you hear what I have to say."

"I won't." I'm starting to think there is nothing on earth that would make me walk away from this man. He could tell me he killed someone, and I would grab a shovel to help bury the body, law license be damned. "I swear I won't. You're safe with me too, you know. We can be safe with each other." I feel the truth of those words more deeply than I have felt anything in my life. I want to be his safe place, because he is absolutely, undoubtedly mine.

He leans into my hand for another minute before he recaptures it with his and starts to talk.

"Okay, so it started about five years ago. It was the first home game of my fourth season on the team, and I dislocated my shoulder in the third quarter."

I narrow my eyes, thinking back. "I was at that game. It was a bad sack, right?"

"Yeah. You were really there?"

"I go to a lot of home games. My dad's company has a bunch of tickets, and when he's not using them for business, he gives them to us. Ben and Hallie and everyone were there too. I remember when you went down." And I do. I remember him laying on the turf, holding his arm close to his body so it stayed immobile, and I remember thinking I could see the pain in his eyes as the trainers helped him off the field. Weird to have such a vivid memory of a single football game from years ago.

"So, you might remember that I didn't come back to the game. Not that day and not for eight more weeks. It was my first real football injury, and I didn't need surgery, so everyone expected a quick recovery. They kept saying I would be back to practice in a month and then back to the game after six weeks. But that didn't happen. Instead, I missed more than half the season. For some reason, the pain wouldn't go away, and no one could figure out why. I did intense physical therapy and got cortisone shots that let me play the second half of the season. I was never pain free, but I got good at hiding it. As far as the coaches and trainers knew, I was healed. But I wasn't."

He stops then, taking a breath. He looks at me, as if he's asking for permission to keep going. To tell me whatever comes next. I say nothing, just squeeze his hand and give him what I hope is a reassuring smile. It must work, because he continues.

"I was worried enough about the pain that when I was in Boulder that offseason, I went to see a close family friend who is an orthopedic surgeon specializing in sports medicine. He did an MRI and diagnosed me with post-traumatic arthritis. He couldn't tell me why it happened—it was mostly just bad luck. He kept the appointment completely off the books as a favor, and no one ever found out. As far as anyone else knew, I healed fine, and the injury was forgotten."

The pain in his eyes when he took the hit in the playoff game. The way he rolls his shoulder. His discomfort when I mentioned his post-football plans yesterday. My logical brain slots these pieces right into place to form the whole picture.

"But you didn't forget about it." It's not a question. Asher clearly lives with at least some pain, and the thought of this sweet, strong, confident man being in any kind of discomfort kills me.

"I didn't. Post-traumatic arthritis can be temporary, but my job literally requires the near-constant use of my shoulder, so it wasn't temporary for me. That first season after my injury, I was in pain all the time for the first few weeks. I could get through the games, but practice was excruciating, and off-days were terrible. But I still didn't want to tell anyone because I didn't want them to pull me from the game."

He stops then, taking his hands from mine and running them down his face before he continues.

"I belong to a gym near my house. Sometimes on off days, I like to get a break from the team gym. I could work out at my house, but I like being around other people, and sometimes I take a spin class. Or yoga." He gives me a wry grin, and the thought of Asher in a yoga class makes me giggle. Actually giggle like a fucking teenager.

"Anyway, one day this guy at my gym came up to me and said he had something that could help me. I had no clue what he was talking about, but he told me he had been watching me and noticed I was having shoulder issues. It freaked me the fuck out because I had been able to hide it from the team trainers who are literally paid to notice shit like this, but a stranger saw it right away. But I guess when your income depends on selling things that help people not feel pain, you get pretty good at noticing who's in pain."

Asher stops speaking again. He runs his hands through his hair a couple of times and tugs at the cuffs of his sweatshirt. I can feel the anxiety pouring off of him. It's a strange dynamic shift, but the more anxious he gets, the calmer I get. Almost like I was put here in this moment to help carry whatever is weighing him down. I want this burden, I realize. I want to be the keeper of his secrets.

Like he does for me, I take both his hands in mine, and wait until he looks at me. "It's okay. Whatever it is. I swear, it's going to be okay. I'm not going anywhere."

He takes another deep breath before he starts talking again. "His name is Danny, and for the last four or so years I've been buying anti-inflammatory injections from him that I use before every game. They aren't narcotics or anything, and it's the same painkiller the trainers use on players every day. It has worked pretty well, except this season it isn't, and I've needed the injections before practice too. It was Danny who called and texted yesterday. I called him before we left but hung up before he answered because I don't want to be the guy who can't get through the day without injecting painkillers into his body. The pain isn't terrible, but it's always there lately—a kind of dull ache in the background. The thing is, I've never really had pain in the offseason before. I think it was already starting to get worse, and then with the hit I took in the playoff game..."

His voice trails off then. I can hear what he's thinking as if he's saying it right out loud, and my heart aches for him.

"You're afraid of what this means for your career."

His eyes fill with gratitude, that I said the words, so he doesn't have to.

"I know how terrible it is. I know all about the possibility of long-term permanent damage. You must think I'm such an idiot for doing this, and trust me, I do too. But I do it anyway because football is my entire life. I have no idea who I am without it, and I think losing it would kill me."

Asher's voice breaks a little on the last word, and before I can even think, I'm moving towards him, straddling his lap and wrapping my arms around him. I feel his arms go around me and hold tight. He buries his face in my neck, his breathing harsh. I hold him until his breaths even out, and when I go to move off his lap, he grabs my hips and holds me in place.

"Can you stay here? I like you close to me."

"Anything." And I mean it. I like everything about cheerful, upbeat, howls with wolves, loves gummy candy and Dr. Pepper, and is fascinated by giant barbershop poles Asher. But it's vulnerable, uncertain Asher that has my heart leaping out of my chest and straight into his hands. It's not nearly as scary as I thought it would be.

I lean in and kiss his forehead, letting my lips linger there. My habitual instinct to fix the problem in front of me is nowhere to be found. Instead, all I want to do is offer comfort and a safe landing spot. To be whatever he needs me to be in this moment. He lets out a shuddering breath and lays his hands on my cheeks, bringing our foreheads together. We stay like that for a few minutes, breathing each other in, before I hear him whisper.

"Thank you."

I lean back so I can look him in the eye. "For what? I didn't do anything."

"For listening. For not judging me for this. I know it's pretty stupid."

I shrug. "Ill-advised maybe, but not stupid. Look Asher, there is no one on earth who understands hiding vulnerability better than I do. I would rather eat dirt than show anyone my hurts. And for you, when your entire career and sense of self depends on you being physically able to throw a football better than anyone else? You did what you needed to do. I am the last person who would judge you for choosing your career."

He doesn't answer, just stares at me with a look in his eyes I can't decipher. When he brings his hand up and tucks a strand of hair back behind my ear, gliding his thumb down my jaw before resting his hand on the side of my neck, warmth floods me and butterflies explode in my stomach. When he finally speaks, his tone is low and deadly serious.

"Juliette, you are my favorite person."

"Because I didn't run away when you told me something hard? That seems like the very least a person could do. Not nearly enough for favorite person status."

"No. Because you're you."

He doesn't give me a chance to answer, just grips my hip with one hand and with the other still on my neck, he brings my lips to his.

Chapter Twenty-Seven
Asher

The kiss is meant to be one of relief and gratitude, but in two seconds flat it takes a turn right to *not that*.

Having my lips on Julie's is a shot straight to the dick, and I know she feels it too because I've barely glided my tongue along her lips before she opens for me, tangling our tongues together as I sweep mine inside her mouth to taste her. She lets out a moan that I feel all the way through my body. She moves her hands up my chest as I devour her mouth, my body straining to get as close to her as possible. When she wraps her arms around my neck, my hands start to explore, gliding down her ribcage, my thumbs grazing the sides of her tits. At the contact, Julie lets out a full body shiver and whimpers against my mouth.

The sound of this gorgeous, formidable woman *fucking whimpering* makes me feral. Sliding my hands further down her body, I palm her ass through her leggings, yanking her closer so she can feel every inch of how she affects me.

"Asher," she whimpers, rocking her hips against mine. And I suddenly hate every layer between us. I want to strip her down, lay her out on these blankets, and catalogue every inch of her body so I see it every time I close my eyes for the rest of my life, but every instinct I have is screaming at me to take this slowly. Dragging my mouth from hers, I skim my lips over her jaw and down her neck, closing my mouth over her pulse and sucking gently. Her body jolts, her hands flying from my neck to my hips to grip on, her thumbs skimming under my sweatshirt to graze my bare skin.

"Can you...take it off?" she whispers, her voice quiet and a little uncertain. I want to wipe that uncertainty right from her consciousness.

"Take it off, huh?" I pull back slightly and flash her a cocky grin. "You want to see all of me, Juliette?"

"I've seen all of you, remember?" she says, her face heating as her eyes drift down to my very obvious erection. My cock jumps behind my sweatpants at her gaze, and she sucks in a breath.

"That was an accident. This is on purpose. You want to see me on purpose, baby?"

Her eyes come back to mine. "So, so much."

Lust whips through me as I grab the hem of my hoodie and tear it over my head, tossing it somewhere behind me. Julie's eyes drop to my torso, her gaze fiery as she takes me in.

When she traces my abs with a single finger, my cock hardens even more and my stomach muscles flex. She trails her fingers down the tattoo on my ribs, leaning closer to read the words. "Your sisters' names right? And your nieces?"

"Yeah. I love watching my sisters as moms, and I just adore all those little girls. I can't always be with them because of my job, so this felt like a way to keep them close."

"How are you even real?" she mutters,

"I could ask you the same thing," I say, curling my fingers in the hem of her t-shirt.

"Can I?" I ask

She nods.

"Words, Juliette. Use your words."

"Yes," she whispers. "I want you to."

I pull her shirt over her head and toss it on top of my sweat-shirt before roving my eyes over her. My hands move before my brain engages, coming up to palm her perfect tits, rubbing my thumbs over her black lace covered nipples. She takes a sharp breath, a low moan coming from her throat.

"Gorgeous," I murmur, skimming my hands down her sides, over her hips and her legs until I reach her knees. Gliding my hands back up her thighs, I dip down and graze one finger along her pussy, feeling the heat of her through her leggings. I am desperate to sink inside her, to feel all that heat wrapped around my cock as she moans my name into my ear. I press my finger a little harder, circling it over her clit, and without warning her entire body stiffens. As if I tossed a bucket of ice-cold water all over her, she jerks backwards off my lap, landing on her ass on the blankets. Staring at the ground, she crosses her arms across her chest, clearly uncomfortable being so exposed.

Wanting to understand what the fuck just happened, I grab my sweatshirt from the floor and tug it over her head. She slips her arms into it and seems to relax slightly once she's covered up. With a hand on her face, I guide her head up until she's looking at me.

"Talk to me, Juliette. What happened just now?"

Her eyes dart around the room, avoiding eye contact with me as best she can.

"It's embarrassing."

"You don't ever have to be embarrassed with me. You're safe with me, Juliette, remember? We're safe with each other."

She takes a deep breath. "I've never told anyone this before;

I guess tonight is the night for big confessions. I've never, um. You know. With another person."

I try and decipher what it is she's telling me. "You've never had sex before?"

She rears back. "What the fuck, Asher? I'm thirty years old. Of course I've had sex before. Having sex has never been the problem. It's finishing that's the problem."

"You've never had an orgasm during sex before." It's a statement, not a question. I'm starting to understand what's going on here.

She huffs out a breath, hand coming up to scratch at her wrist, but I cover her hands with mine before she can. "No, you don't, Juliette. You don't need to be anxious about this. Not with me. We're going to talk about it, and then we're going to fix it." I flash her a grin. "I'm really, really good at sex."

She smiles, but it doesn't reach her eyes. "I just bet you are, but it won't matter. I'm, like, defective or something."

I hate that she thinks that, but she won't for long. "You're not defective, baby. I promise you're not. You can have an orgasm on your own, right?"

"Of course I can. I'm great at making myself come and I have enough toys to open my own sex shop. But when I'm with another person, I can't turn my brain off enough to enjoy it. I worry about everything. How I look, how I smell, what sounds I'm making. Literally everything. Then I worry that it's taking too long and he's going to get annoyed, so I end up faking it just to make it stop." She drops her head back and groans. "Fucking hell, I can't believe I just told you all that. What the fuck is it about you that makes me tell you everything?"

I smirk at her. "My mom says I have a very trustworthy face."

She snorts out a laugh, and it baffles me that I think she's the cutest person alive and I also want to fuck her right into this floor. Turns out, it's an irresistible combination.

"We'll get back to all the toys because, so awesome. But I'll just say this. It sounds like you've been with assholes who didn't care about your pleasure. But I'm not an asshole and literally all I care about it making you feel good, so if you're up for it, I have an idea."

She just shrugs. "I mean, nothing has worked before, so do your worst."

"You liked watching me the other night. In the shower."

She scoffs. "I mean yeah. Have you *seen* you?"

"I think I'd like to watch you too."

Her eyes snap up to mine. I thought maybe I would see anxiety in them, but I don't. Instead, it's curiosity and heat, and I want to make this good for her more than I want to take my next breath.

"You like the thought of that, Juliette? You want to touch yourself while I watch? Sink a finger inside that tight pussy and rub your clit until you come with my eyes on you? I bet you look beautiful when you come. I can't wait to see it."

Heat floods her face and slowly, she locks eyes with me and nods.

"Words, baby."

"Yes," she says, confidently. "Watch me. But I want to watch you too."

"Again. You want to watch me again."

Her eyes narrow and she lifts her chin. "Take off your pants, Asher."

She's a fucking queen.

I wink at her. "I'll show you mine if you show me yours."

Without hesitating, she whips my sweatshirt up and off her body before reaching back and unclasping her bra, letting it slide off her shoulders and onto the floor. I swallow thickly because she is, without a doubt, the most stunning thing I have ever laid eyes on. My gaze travels from her face down to her bare chest. I have to clench my fists to keep from reaching out and palming her perfect tits, taking her dusky pink nipples into my mouth and sucking on them until she is writhing and crying out my name.

She must like whatever she sees on my face, because I see a flash of confidence cross hers. She drifts her fingers up her torso and skims them over her tits, using her thumbs to circle her nipples, a low moan falling from her mouth when she pinches them between her thumb and forefinger. Looking up, she gives me a knowing grin.

"Now you."

She could ask me to rob a bank for her right now and I would do it without a second thought. Lifting my hips, I drag off my sweatpants and briefs in one motion and toss them away. I'm already hard as steel. Fisting my cock, I give it one long, slow stroke, hissing out a breath at the contact and at the look of pure lust on Julie's face as she watches my hand.

"See this, Juliette? See how hard I am right now? It's all for you. I want you so fucking much. I've never wanted anyone the way I want you."

Staring at my hand slowly stroking myself, she takes a deep breath and when she speaks, it's quiet.

"No one has ever wanted me the way you do."

"Well then everyone else was stupid, but I'm glad they were because it means I get to be here with you. Can I see you now? I want to see all of you. Will you show me?"

With her eyes on mine, she gets on her knees and slowly peels her leggings down her thighs and fuck me, she's not wearing anything under them. Sitting back down, she rolls the leggings down the rest of the way and kicks them off, drawing her knees up to her chest. For a split second I think she's trying to cover herself, but then she drops her knees to the blankets, and I see all of her, her pussy already glistening with arousal. With the way my heart pounds in my chest, I consider for a second that I might not survive this night.

"Fuck, Juliette. Look at you, already dripping. Does thinking about me watching you make you wet?"

She strokes a hand from her knee to midthigh. "Thinking anything about you turns me on."

Jesus Christ. "Every inch of you is gorgeous. I can't wait to get my hands all over you. But right now, will you touch yourself for me? Show me how you make yourself feel good, so I know what to do when it's my turn."

Saying nothing, she slides a hand up her thigh and through her slit, collecting her wetness and using it to circle her clit lightly with one finger, breathing in sharply when her fingers make contact with her tight bundle of nerves. When she adds a finger, alternating between pinching her clit and swirling her fingers around it, I can't hold myself back anymore. Tightening my grip, I speed up my strokes, rolling my hand over my tip, collecting the precum pooling there.

Heat is already sizzling in my spine, and when Julie slides two fingers inside herself, breathing heavily as she pushes them in deeper, I have to grip the base of my cock to keep from coming on the spot.

"Talk to me, Juliette. Tell me how you're feeling."

"Shit, Asher," she gasps, her hips rising up to meet her fingers as she pumps them in and out, her other hand still circling her clit. "It feels so fucking good."

"Me too, baby. Watching you touch yourself is the hottest thing I've ever seen. The image of you with your fingers stuffed inside yourself while you rub your clit is going to live in my head forever." I keep my strokes slow and steady, not able to stop touching myself but needing her to come first.

"Were you...thinking of me the other night? In the shower?" Julie's voice is breathy, catching on the last word.

I smile, wondering if she's been stewing over that. Absolutely sure she has been. "Juliette every time I've stroked my dick since July I've thought about you. Your voice. Your face. What it would feel like to have your thighs wrapped around me while I licked your clit."

At that, her hips shoot up off the blankets and her fingers speed up, her breath coming in fast pants.

"You like the sound of that? You want me on my knees for you? Your legs thrown over my shoulders? My tongue on your clit, inside of you? I bet you taste amazing. I'll give you anything you want. Fucking anything. Look at me, Juliette. Eyes on me while you come, baby."

"Fuck, Asher," she gasps, as she adds a third finger and begins thrusting them faster. Knowing she's about to come, I speed up my strokes, lifting my hips to fuck up into my hand. A red flush crawls up her chest to her face, and her fingers fly over her clit as she comes on a loud moan, her pulse fluttering in her throat and her eyes never leaving mine.

Watching her work herself through her orgasm, I drop my free hand to my balls, rolling them in my hand as I tighten my grip.

"Watch me, Juliette. Watch me come for you." Thrusting up harder into my hand and with my gaze locked on Julie's, my release barrels up my spine, pleasure erupting through every limb as I come hard, all over my hand and my stomach. Chest heaving, heart hammering, I slow my strokes as I come down. I use my sweatpants to clean off, and I've barely tossed them aside again before a very naked Julie is throwing herself at me, wrapping her arms around my neck.

"Thank you," she says into my ear.

I grab one of the blankets from the floor and wrap it around both of us before I settle her onto my lap and hold tight, stroking her hair and breathing her in, more content than I have any right to be, considering the conversation we had earlier.

"You did so well, baby. Watching the way you came for me was the sexiest fucking thing I've ever seen. I'm so proud of you; I know that wasn't easy for you."

"That's where you're wrong. I thought it would be hard, but it wasn't. It was good. So, so good. You made it easy. You make a lot of things easy."

She burrows deeper into me, and I hold her close, staring at the fire, thinking that being with her makes a lot of things easy for me too.

Chapter Twenty-Eight
Julie

Weak winter light filters in through the blinds as I blink awake, confused. I lay still, cataloguing my surroundings. Horrible floral wallpaper, a giant fireplace with embers still glowing. A heavy arm banded tightly around my waist and a wall of hard muscle against my back. I'm lying on the floor in a nest of pillows and blankets, and I'm almost positive I'm naked.

And then I remember. Asher's confession. Freaking out like a complete lunatic when he touched me. The way he took it totally in stride. Feeling comfortable and powerful taking my clothes off in front of him, touching myself. Watching him. How tightly he held me afterwards, whispering praise and comfort. The way we shared a pillow and whispered secrets in the dark while we drifted off to sleep.

"You owe me a date." Asher's voice is low and gruff with sleep, his breath fluttering against the shell of my ear, sending shivers up my spine.

"And why is that?" I yawn and turn in his arms so I'm facing him, my head pillowed on his bicep. Hot damn, he looks good in the morning, eyes heavy with sleep, golden brown hair disheveled, and scruff covering his jaw.

He leans in and captures my mouth with his, his hand coming up to wrap around the back of my neck while his tongue curls around mine. When we break apart, he grins at me, sky-blue eyes sparkling. He is, undoubtedly, the most beautiful man I've ever seen, and for some reason, he wants me. I want to scream into a pillow and kick my heels and text my friends like a teenager to tell them the football quarterback wants *me*.

"Now that's a way to wake up."

"If you're finished, why do I suddenly owe you a date?"

He kisses my nose. "Because you woke up like a normal person and not like you were running the last quarter mile of a marathon."

I sit straight up, staring at him, because shit, he's completely right. I haven't woken up calmly since I was a teenager. I consider whether one night with him has turned me into a completely different person. There's a non-zero chance that it did and a non-zero chance that I don't hate it.

"Are you magic?"

He winks at me. "I don't know if I'm magic, Juliette, but this morning might be."

I huff out a breath and lay back down. He immediately curls his arm around my back and pulls me close, and I am suddenly acutely aware that another part of him is wide awake, too, and pressing urgently into my hip. I shift against him, and he gives me a sheepish smile.

"I'd like to say I just woke up like that, and I kind of did, but also you just sat up and the blanket fell off and, well, look at you. You're beautiful all warm and naked in the morning."

He makes me feel beautiful. With an uncharacteristic rush of confidence brought on by his words and the quiet winter morning and the warm, cozy bubble of this blanket fort on the floor in a bed and breakfast in the middle of nowhere, I lean in and kiss his neck, trailing my lips down and across his collar bone, smiling at his sharp intake of breath.

"Let's see if I can take care of that for you."

In one motion, he rolls us, so I'm sprawled on top of him, and he trails his hands down my back and up my sides, his fingertips grazing the sides of my breasts, causing goosebumps to break out across my skin. It should feel ridiculous that we're doing this on the floor when there's a perfectly good bed two feet away, but it doesn't. It feels cozy and sexy and perfect.

"You first, Juliette. I've got plans for you."

I feel a flutter of nerves, wondering what he means. Before I have time to think too hard, he tells me exactly what he wants.

"I want you to sit that gorgeous cunt right on my face so I can get my first taste of you."

His eyes hold mine as I consider that. I get a flash of last night. Of him telling me he wanted my legs wrapped around his head. How that image had me hurling over the edge into the most intense orgasm of my life. But then my nerves flare. I've never let anyone do that. Could never relax enough to be that vulnerable with another person. What if he doesn't like it?

"No way." Asher grabs my face in both of his hands, leaning up to kiss my forehead. "Get right out of your stunning head," he murmurs. "If you say no, the answer is no, and that's that. But if you're worried that I won't like it, toss that thought straight in the fire because baby, I'll love it."

God, I want it. I want it so damn much. And this is Asher. I'm safe with him.

I lean down so my forehead rests against his. "Yes."

His eyes are a little fierce as he runs a hand down my side and between my legs, swiping his fingers against my pussy where I am already hot and wet for him. He brings his hand back up and sticks his fingers in his mouth, licking them clean, groaning a little at the taste. When he presses his lips to mine, sweeping his tongue inside my mouth so I can taste myself, it's so raw and filthy that I almost come on the spot.

"I love the way you smell. The taste of you drives me wild. I want to spend every second of every day with my face between your legs and my tongue inside your sweet pussy, drinking up every last drop of you. So do it, Juliette. Sit on my face. Right. Fucking. Now."

He grabs my hips and hauls me up his body, so I'm kneeling on the floor, straddling his face. When he leans up and swipes his tongue through my slit, my hands fly out and grab onto the footboard of the bed so I don't topple over.

I look down and lock eyes with Asher, his dark and filled with arousal. "I said sit, Juliette. All the way." He grips my hips tighter and pulls me down, burying his tongue inside me in one motion that has a moan ripping out of my throat. He eats me like a man possessed, keeping his grip tight on my hips while he fucks me with his tongue. And when he moves his tongue up to circle my clit, I grind down on him on instinct, looking for more, harder, faster.

"That's it, baby," Asher grunts. "Fuck my face. You look so goddamn sexy up there, taking what you need."

He moves one of his hands from my hip around to my ass, trailing down until he finds my entrance, pushing two fingers deep inside me. He curls them up and I gasp, rolling my hips against his mouth and grinding back on his fingers, the dual stimulation making my head spin and my orgasm build faster than I thought possible. I let go of the headboard and palm my breasts, pinching my nipples as he alternates between fucking me with his tongue and circling it around my clit.

"Asher," I whimper. "I need…" I don't even know what I need. I just *need*.

But he seems to know. In one motion, he curls his fingers up again, pumping them in and out of me while he sucks my clit into his mouth, flicking his tongue over it once, twice, three times, and I detonate around him. My orgasm hits me so hard and fast that my vision blurs. The noise I make is low and feral, and I don't even have it in me to care as waves of pleasure pummel me. Asher sticks with me until the pleasure ebbs, and I slide bonelessly down to his chest. I bury my face in the crook of his neck, breathing hard, my heart pounding. His spicy scent surrounds me as I breathe him in, letting my heart rate return to normal.

"Jesus Christ," he mumbles into my ear as he strokes his hands up and down my back. "You are perfect."

"No, you are," I say, a little breathlessly.

He laughs, and the sound of it warms me to my core as he wraps his arms around me, holding me tight.

"We'll have to agree to disagree, here. Seeing you above me, pinching your nipples while you rode my face? That was the hottest moment of my entire life."

I smile against his shoulder, suddenly overcome with the urgent need to give him back some of what he gave to me.

I lift my head so I can see him. "I want to taste you too."

"You don't have to, you know."

I scoff at him. "Don't be stupid, Asher. I know that."

"Well, okay then. You want to get on your knees for me, baby? Wrap those gorgeous lips around my cock? Suck me off until I come down your throat?"

A curl of lust snakes down my spine at his words. No one has ever talked to me like this, and I love it. Every fucking word. I say nothing, climbing off him and standing, pulling him up with me and turning us so his back is to the bed. I grab his chin with my hand and lock eyes with him.

"Julie Parker gets on her knees for no man. But Juliette would really like to get on her knees for you."

Before he can say anything, I drop down to my knees and wrap my hand around his cock. He is long and so thick that my hand doesn't quite fit all the way around him. I stroke from base to tip, rubbing my thumb over the precum leaking out of his slit. When I look up, Asher's eyes dilate until they are practically black. His nostrils flare and his chest rises and falls rapidly.

"Juliette," he says, his voice a little shaky. "This is...you are...fuck."

He seems to give up on words, closing his eyes and shaking his head while I run my fist up and down his length, my other hand gripping the back of his thigh. Watching this beautiful, powerful man crumble a little while I'm the one on my knees makes me feel like I could run the world. I lean forward and run my tongue along the underside, tracing the thick vein and flicking my tongue into the sensitive groove below his tip. His chest rumbles with a growl, and when I take him into my mouth, sliding down to take as much of him as I can, his hands fly back to the footboard, gripping so tightly his fingers turn white.

I slide my mouth back up to his tip, circling my tongue around before diving back down, taking him so far that he bumps the back of my throat. When I swallow around him, he lets out a moan and closes his eyes again, his face screwed up in concentration like he's trying not to come too fast, and, well, that's not going to work for me. I replace my mouth with my hand, gripping him hard.

"Open your eyes." My voice is a little raspy from having his cock in my throat, and I like the way it sounds. He does what I ask. His eyes are glazed with pleasure.

"Don't hold back," I order. Then I give him back the words

he gave me last night. "Look at me, Ash. Eyes on me while you come."

His eyes flash and I dive back on his cock, keeping my gaze locked with his while I bob up and down on his length, speeding up when I hear his breath start to catch. Like I saw him do last night, I grasp his balls, rolling them in my hand while I swallow him down. He gasps out a breath and I know he's close when he cups my cheek with one of his hands and tries to pull away, but I grab his ass with my other hand, keeping him in my mouth.

"Juliette. I can't...I'm going to...shit, baby I'm gonnna come." His legs start to shake, and I slide my mouth up, sucking hard on his tip. He comes in a full body shudder, groaning as his release fills my mouth and slides down my throat. I stay with him until he gives me everything he has. Then I let him slip out of my mouth, my gaze still on his as I swipe my thumb over the side of my lips, catching a drop of his cum and sucking my thumb into my mouth.

I think that might do him in because he reaches down and hauls me up, lifting me straight up into his arms, covering my mouth with his, and toppling us both back onto the bare mattress. He kisses me breathless before ripping his mouth from mine and sucking in oxygen.

"Holy fuck, Juliette. You know how to suck a cock. You sucked my soul right out of my body."

I grin and shrug. "You know how I hate to be bad at anything."

He laughs, breathlessly. "A-plus. Gold star. Gold medal. Best head of my life."

Then he hugs me tightly, raining kisses all over my face while I giggle, and I love every damn thing about this morning.

Chapter Twenty-Nine
Julie

"Do you ever think about just chucking it all and moving to the middle of nowhere? Settling in a place like this, far away from everything?"

We're sitting outside in rockers on the inn's front porch, dressed in our winter gear and drinking hot chocolate, looking out at the snow-covered landscape. The blizzard was over by the time we woke up this morning, but the roads out here hadn't been plowed yet, so we're staying put for now. The cold and snow called to us both, and sitting here bundled up side-by-side next to a fire pit, hot drinks in hand, and breathing in the crisp winter air makes for the very best morning.

He reaches over and covers my gloved hand with his. The question has been on my mind since we woke up this morning and looked out over an endless blanket of undisturbed snow. Actually, it's probably been on my mind since we left Pittsburgh. This whole trip has made me think about living in a different way. Not jolting awake every morning, working eighteen hours a day, and surviving on anxiety and caffeine. Enjoying things like a cold winter morning.

"It's beautiful here, but I'm pretty happy where I am. I sometimes think about Boulder, though. I miss my family a lot during the season."

My stomach bottoms out at the thought of him leaving Pittsburgh. Leaving me. *I don't want him to go anywhere.* The thought is immediate and crystal clear. The old Julie might have kept it in and worried over it, but the me who takes spontaneous road trips with NFL quarterbacks and howls with wolves asks the question on my mind.

"You think you'll move back there one day? When you're done playing?"

"Not anymore."

The answer surprises me, so I ask the second question. "What changed?"

He puts his cup down on the floor and turns his chair so he's facing me, then reaches out to spin my chair around too.

"I met you. My plan was to go back to Boulder when I retired. But then I danced with a brilliant, gorgeous, smart-mouthed lawyer who refused to give me her number when I asked for it, and I've thought of her every damn day since. And now that I have her? I never want to let her go. Boulder used to be my favorite place. But now? My favorite place is wherever you are."

His answer has tears pricking my eyes, but I blink them back. I don't want anything blurring my view of the man sitting in front of me. I don't know how I got this lucky, but I've always thought winter mornings have a way of making wishes come true.

"You would really stay in Pittsburgh for me, even when you don't have to be there?"

"Of course I would. Pittsburgh is your place. The business you built is there. Your family is there. Your whole life. You need to be there, and I need to be with you. Everything else will work itself out."

A little stunned by his answer, I say nothing. Instead, I put my cup down on the porch and climb out of my chair, right into his lap, curling myself into him and resting my head on his shoulder. He slides his arms around my waist, kissing my forehead, leaning his head against mine.

"I can't imagine a day without you in my life. Is that weird? It hasn't been very long."

He just chuckles, probably at the way my analytical mind tries to make sense of the nonsensical. "I told you, Juliette. All I had to do was hear your voice. You asked me to take your picture outside the gala and I was a goner before I even turned around and saw your face. I can't explain it. I just know what I know. You were it for me then and you're it for me now."

"I've never been good with things I can't enter into a spreadsheet, but I think I'm just fine with that."

He presses a kiss to the top of my head. "I'm just fine with that too."

I let out a little sigh and snuggle deeper into him, as close as our puffy winter jackets allow, and speak another truth. "I wish we didn't have to leave later this afternoon. I like it here."

"We don't have to leave. Let's stay here again tonight and drive straight to Denver tomorrow. We'll still get a night in Denver so I can show you my favorite places, and we'll make it to Boulder on time."

She sits up to look at me. "But the Eisenhower Presidential Library. The Underground Salt Museum. There are so many things you want to do between here and Denver."

Asher runs a hand over my hair and down my back. "Part of being on a road trip is being spontaneous. Be spontaneous with me, Juliette. You like it here? As long as Shirley has space, let's stay another night."

"Oh, Shirley definitely has room." We both turn around to find Shirley grinning at us from the front door. "I couldn't help but hear the end of your conversation and honey, you hang on to that man of yours. He's one of the good ones."

Asher smirks and nudges me. "You hear that, Juliette? I'm one of the good ones. Better hang on to me."

I snort out a laugh. "I'll be so sure to do exactly that."

"Anyway," Shirley says. "I just came out to see if you two had any interest in ice skating. There's a frozen pond at the back of the property that's great for skating, and we just got the path cleared. We have skates in a bunch of sizes. No one else wants to go down, so you'd have it to yourselves."

I smile inwardly. "I don't know," I say, hoping I sound unsure. "I'm not the best skater."

"Well lucky for you, I grew up in Boulder and was practically skating before I could walk. I'll make sure you don't fall."

I just barely resist the urge to cackle. Men, even the very best ones, are sometimes so utterly predictable. I'll play this chivalrous, *protect my woman at all costs* boy like a fiddle.

I shrug. "Okay, sure, I guess. But no laughing."

Asher stands up, taking me with him. "I would never. Shirley, lead the way."

Ten minutes later, we're sitting on a bench on the very edge of a giant frozen pond lacing up our skates. Asher finishes first, standing and holding out his hand to me. "Come on, Juliette. We'll take it slow."

I tilt my head, studying him. "You know Asher, there are some things in life that just aren't meant to be taken slow."

His expression is confused. "Like what?"

"Like ice skating." I pop up from the bench and leap onto the pond, landing steadily on one foot. "Catch me if you can, Hot Shot!" Then I take off without looking back.

The frosty wind slaps at my cheeks as I fly down the ice

and it feels amazing. Halfway down the pond I push off with my back foot and launch myself into a two-foot spin, raising my arms above my head and whipping around so fast my hair flies behind me and the pond and surrounding trees are a blur of color and motion. I come out of the spin breathing hard, facing Asher, who is standing motionless on the edge of the pond, staring at me, jaw slack and mouth partway open.

I skate back over and come to a stop right in front of him.

"That was...you were...huh?" He looks a little dazed, and I laugh out loud and smack a kiss to his cold cheek, delighted with him and this day.

"Surprised?"

He blows out a breath and runs a hand down his face. "Turned on, more like," he mumbles. "You can skate."

I laugh again. "Little bit. Twelve years of figure skating, ages six to eighteen."

"But, like, you can really, really skate. Did you compete?"

I decide to give him another little piece of myself, one I haven't even given my family. "I never wanted to compete. I love winter, and I love skating. Learning tricks and spins was fun, but really, being on the ice made me feel free. I stopped when I went to college and my life became one achievement after another. Magna cum laude from college. Summa cum laude from law school, getting the best job, being at the top of my associate class so I could stay on partner track, starting my own firm and, well, you know the rest. But now I think I should have kept up with it. I forget how much I miss skating until I do it, and I don't do it nearly enough. Skating makes my brain quiet in a way that nothing ever has until..." I trail off, realizing something for the first time.

Asher cups my cheek and tips my face up so my eyes meet his. "Until what, Juliette?"

I swallow hard. "Until you. When I'm with you my brain is

quiet, when in the rest of my life it is so, so loud. You make me feel like it's okay to be whoever I need to be. You make me feel free."

"Juliette," he says quietly, eyes swirling with emotion. He looks at me for another few seconds, gliding his thumb over my bottom lip before leaning forward and kissing me deeply, his free hand sliding around my waist to pull me flush against him as his tongue strokes over mine. Every move of his mouth stokes the fire in my belly, and I press closer, needing to feel every inch of him against me. His arm tugs me even tighter against him, and I grind my hips to his, feeling his hard cock so close to my core it makes me dizzy.

Still kissing me senseless, he reaches down and hikes one of my legs up over his hip. His cock settles right against my clit, and I roll my hips, licks of pleasure sparking out my limbs. *I could come just like this.* Fully clothed, wearing ice skates, on the edge of a frozen pond right out in the open where anyone could walk by. I don't hate that nearly as much as I should, and it's that thought that has me breaking the kiss. I pull back just enough to look Asher in the eye and give him the only thought currently in my head.

"Ash. We need to go inside. I want you to fuck me. I *need* you to fuck me. Now. Right now."

Asher's gaze turns molten. In two seconds flat he has my ass on the bench, pulling the skates from my feet and replacing them with my boots, which he ties himself. He deals with his own skates, then grabs both pairs with one hand and wraps his other arm around my waist, tossing me a wink that has me contemplating dropping to my knees in front of him right there in the snow.

"How fast can you walk, Juliette?"

Asher closes the door to our room and tosses the winter gear we stripped off on our run up the stairs onto the floor. We kick off our boots, and he presses me back against the door with his hips, reaching behind me to flip the lock. He doesn't kiss me, just hovers his lips over mine.

"You were gorgeous skating on that pond, Juliette. Nothing has ever turned me on more than watching you fly around the ice. If I wasn't afraid my dick would freeze, I would have stripped you down and fucked you right there."

"I would have let you," I gasp out, as he leans down and licks a stripe from my collar bone to my ear, taking my earlobe between his teeth and biting gently, before soothing the spot with his tongue and grazing his teeth along the sensitive skin behind my ear. I press my thighs together needing something, anything, to relieve the ache between my legs.

When he speaks, his lips graze my ear, sending a shiver down my spine.

"I just bet you would have. Julie Parker on the outside, the brilliant, put together lawyer who never makes a mistake and never makes a mess. And Juliette on the inside, wild, free, a little dirty. Rides my face and sucks my cock like a dream; wants me to slide inside her and fuck her until she's screaming my name. And I'm the only one who gets to have both parts of you. All of you. Every single beautiful inch of you is mine. Is that what you want, Juliette? You want to be mine?"

He slides his hands down my hips and around to cup my ass, yanking me against him so I feel every inch of his hard body against mine. My head falls back and knocks against the door as my entire body thrums for him.

"I'm already yours," I choke out. "I'll never be anyone's except for yours."

"Good answer."

He grabs the hem of my sweater and pulls it up and over my head, throwing it on the floor. My bra follows, and then he's palming both of my breasts, leaning down and circling one of my nipples with his tongue before sucking it into his mouth while he rolls the other one between his thumb and forefinger. I gasp, grabbing onto his hips as sensations pummel me. He lifts his head and looks at me.

"Tell me what you want, Juliette. You want me to lick that sweet pussy again before I slide inside you? Or do you want to ride my fingers until you come all over my hand?"

But even as I let out a low moan, I feel my brain start to race at his questions and my stomach sinks. I thought after last night and this morning, this wouldn't happen. Not with him. Asher has seen every inch of me, and he obviously likes what he sees, so why can't I shut my brain off and enjoy this? I feel so safe with Asher. I want this. I just don't want to fucking think, for once. Then I have an idea.

I slide my hands up to tangle in the hair at the back of his neck. "Do you think you can do something for me?"

"Literally anything. Just ask."

I take a deep breath. "Can you...take control? Like, total control. Don't ask me any questions. Don't ask me to make any decisions. Just tell me what to do." I cringe a little, frustrated with myself for not being able to say this more coherently, but I hope he understands.

I think he does when he takes my mouth in a deep fever of kiss before pulling away.

"You want me to boss you around a little, Juliette?"

"That's exactly what I want you to do. I told you last night it's hard for me to turn my brain off during sex. Last night and this morning you helped me do it. I never feel safe enough to give up control to anyone, which is why I never stop thinking. But I feel safe with you. I trust you, Asher. I want this with you. More than I've ever wanted it with anyone."

He leans his forehead against mine and takes a deep breath, as if gathering the tattered pieces of his control.

"Okay."

Chapter Thirty

Asher

"But if we're doing this, you need a safe word."

Julie scoffs. "Seriously Asher? This isn't hardcore kink. I can tell you what I like and don't like."

"Seriously, Juliette. If you're giving me control, you need to have a way to take it back if you're not feeling safe."

She just rolls her eyes. "I'm a grown woman. I'm perfectly capable of saying no. Or stop."

I grip her chin and force her to keep her eyes on me. "Baby, I want to toss you onto that bed over there and play with your pussy until you beg. Then I want to slide inside you and fuck you until you come so hard you don't remember your name. I want to wring so many orgasms out of your body that you're begging me to stop. Before this night is over, you're going to *fucking beg.*"

I see the pulse flutter in her throat and my own words have me as hard as a rock—right on the edge and I've barely even touched her. "I want to do all of those things more than I want to take my next breath. But to do that, I need you to have a way to tell me when you've had enough. I would die before I hurt you or make you feel unsafe. Pick a safe word."

She huffs out a breath. "Fine. Gavel."

I give her a wry look.

"What? I've always wanted to be a judge."

She puts a hand on her waist and pops out a hip, her blonde waves streaming over her naked breasts. The image is so hot I almost have to grip my cock to get it to calm the fuck down.

"So now that I have a safe word, should I call you daddy?"

Her sass has me snorting out a laugh. Sex—or almost sex I guess—has never been this fun with anyone before.

"Nah, but you can call me Ash. It does something to me when you do."

She grins at me. "Good to know. Can we get on with it now?"

"Oh, we most definitely can."

I reach behind me and drag off my shirt, tossing it onto the growing pile of clothes. Julie runs her fingers over my tattoo, and I let her for a few seconds before I pick her up. She lets out a little gasp as I stalk over to the dresser and drop her on top of it. Then I dig into my suitcase and find the box of condoms I stashed there and toss it onto the bed so I don't have to go looking for it later.

"What made you think you would get so lucky you would need a whole box of condoms?"

I turn and Julie is grinning at me from her perch on the dresser. With her naked tits and long blonde waves, she looks like some kind of erotic mermaid. I walk slowly back to stand in front of her. Running a hand over her shoulder, down her sternum between her breasts, I let it linger low on her stomach.

"Like I told you before. A little luck and unwavering persistence. And look where that's gotten me. I'm the luckiest fucking guy in the world."

I kiss her hard and then, moving fast, I curl my fingers into the waistband of her leggings, dragging them down. Pressing a hand down on the dresser, she lifts her hips, and I pull them all the way off, dropping them on the floor. With a hand on each knee, I push her legs apart and run a single finger lightly over the thin fabric covering her pussy. She sucks in a breath and tilts her hips, trying to get closer.

Keeping my eyes locked on hers, I strip off her thong, pushing her legs even wider apart so I can stand between them. I grip her chin with one hand and run my other hand up and down her inner thigh.

"Fuck. Touch me. Please," she gasps out.

"Uh uh, Juliette. I'm in charge, remember? You'll take what I give you."

I wrap one hand around the back of her neck and pull her mouth to mine. She opens for me immediately. She tastes like the hot chocolate we drank on the porch and something that is so completely Julie that it makes my head spin. With our mouths locked together, I slowly run a hand up her inner thigh one last time, swiping through her slit and pushing one finger inside. I use my thumb to circle her clit and she moans against my mouth, lifting her hips to meet my fingers. I keep rubbing my thumb around her clit, and when I feel her tightening around me, I pull my hand away and she lets out a whimper, chasing my hand with her hips.

She hasn't seen anything yet.

I drop to my knees in front of her. Curling my arms around her thighs, I slide her closer to the edge of the dresser, and I put a foot on each of my shoulders so she is completely bared to me. Staring down at me, she deliberately takes the foot off my right shoulder and props it on the dresser instead. And that wordless care for my injured shoulder has my chest tightening with love for her, even as she is spread out for me to devour.

Dipping my head, I give her one long lick from asshole to clit, and she lets out a low moan that has me leaking inside my boxer briefs. Then I dive in, flattening my tongue and laying it over her clit, swiping back and forth while I slide two fingers inside her, pumping them in and out, curling them to hit the spot that I know will have her seeing stars. And I know I get it right when her hips shoot up to meet my thrusts. I lay my free arm across her hips, holding her down while I feast on her, knowing that not being able to move against me is going to frustrate the shit out of her. Sucking her clit into my mouth, I flick my tongue over it as I tap that spot inside her.

"Shit, Ash," she moans. "That feels so good. Don't stop."

When I add a third finger, she moans so loudly that I would worry about other guests hearing her if I cared about that. But I don't. Let them all hear her. Let them all hear how she falls apart for me. Only me.

"Look at me, Juliette."

She glances down at me, her eyes hazy with pleasure. I hold eye contact while I suck her clit, hard, and push my fingers in as deep as I can. Her inner walls start to tighten up on my fingers almost immediately. I give it another second until she's just about to fall over the edge before I pull away from her.

She sobs out a breath. "No, fuck. I was so close."

I smirk at her. "I know."

Rising to my feet, I lift her off the dresser and sit her on the bed. Taking her face in both of my hands I kiss her, letting her taste herself. And I know she likes it when she licks into my mouth, groaning against me, her hips lifting to fuck the air, searching for friction.

Her hand sneaks down between her legs and I clasp it in one of mine before she can touch herself.

"Don't you fucking dare, Juliette. I'm the only one who is making you come tonight."

"Well then fucking do it."

I grab her face in both of my hands, bringing our foreheads together. "Oh, I will. But you're going to do something for me too."

She grips my forearms in both hands.

"And what's that?"

"You're going to suck my cock while I eat your pussy until you come so hard every person in this house hears you screaming my name. Then I'm going to suck your clit until you come again. And afterwards I'll slide into you and fuck you until you soak my cock and I come so deep inside you that you'll feel me for days."

She inhales sharply, and I watch her carefully for any sign that this makes her uncomfortable, but all I see is a mixture of curiosity and lust that has my cock jerking in my briefs.

"On your back, Juliette. Hang your head off the bed."

She does what I ask, and I shove my boxer briefs down, my dick springing out, long and hard. I lean down so my head is level with hers. "If it gets to be too much, tap my leg twice, okay? I'll stop right away." She nods.

"Good. Now open that mouth so I can feed you this cock and watch it disappear between those pretty lips." She does what I ask, and I slide the tip of my cock into her mouth, almost coming at the pleasure that shoots up my spine and the image of my dick disappearing between her lips while her head hangs upside down. "You're doing so well, Juliette. Swallow me down, baby, while I get my mouth on you."

Locking my knees to keep them from shaking at how good it feels to have her tongue swirling around the head of my cock, I lean over and pull her legs up so they're bent. Wrapping my arms around her thighs, I cover her entire pussy with my mouth, fucking my tongue into her before latching onto her clit and sucking hard, flicking in steady strokes. She moans around my dick, and the vibrations almost have me combusting. I won't last much longer, but I'm not coming anywhere but inside her.

With my mouth still around her clit, I slide three fingers inside her, curling them at the same time as I suck, and she comes, hard. Her moan is low and long, her muscles contracting as she soaks my face and fingers. While I slow my strokes and lick up her release, she takes my cock into her throat, gagging around me, and the pressure is so intense that I feel a low tingle of my impending orgasm at the base on my spine. I stand straight up, pulling my cock out of Julie's mouth and spinning her around on the bed, dropping to my knees again in front of her.

"You're going to give me one more."

Julie's entire body is flushed from her orgasm, her chest heaving. I can't even believe she's real and she's mine. "I can't. I've never come more than once. Until you I've never even come once. There's no way."

"You can and you will."

I don't let her answer, just dive back down between her legs, sucking her clit right into my mouth and shoving two fingers back inside her. I don't edge her this time. When she falls back on her elbows and her hips jolt up to grind herself on my face, I let her take her pleasure. When she reaches down and tangles her fingers in my hair, yanking my face closer to her, I groan against her clit, and I know she feels it because she arches her back while she moans and lets out a string of unintelligible words. And when she gasps out, "Ash, I'm so close. Please don't stop," I alternate between flicking her clit with my tongue and sucking it between my lips, and that shoves her over the edge. She comes on a scream, and it's my name that falls from her lips while she simultaneously pulls her sensitive clit away from my mouth and grinds closer to ride out her orgasm.

When she slides back onto the bed, spent, I grab a condom

from the box I tossed there earlier and tear it open with my teeth, rolling it on before settling between Julie's legs. I slide my cock against her center, nudging her clit with my tip and she gasps, lifting her hips to meet me. I do it again and again until her chest is heaving, her breath coming out in sobs.

"Please, Ash."

"Please what?"

"Inside me. Please get inside me."

"Eyes on me, Juliette. Look at me while I make you mine."

She locks eyes with me. "I already am yours."

My heart rolls over inside my chest. "Once I slide inside you, there's no going back."

She grabs my hair with both of her hands, holding my head in place. "There never was."

I drop my head, kissing her deeply as I hitch one of her legs up over my hip, and she wraps her arms around my neck. Notching my cock at her entrance, I slowly slide inside her, and our moans mingle together. She's drenched from her back-to-back orgasms, but she is still so tight around me that I have to grit my teeth to keep from blowing too early. Julie cants her hips up, taking me even deeper as my lips travel from her mouth to her cheek, down her jaw to graze at the sensitive skin at her throat. When our hips press firmly together, I pause, needing a second to get a grip on my frayed control.

Julie wraps both her legs around me, lifting her hips, grinding her clit against my pelvis, and even that little move has me right on the edge.

"Move, Asher. I need you to move. Now."

I pull out almost to the tip and then slide back in, angling my stroke so it hits her in all the right places. The noise she makes is a mixture between a moan and a groan, and it's so damn hot watching her unravel for me.

"Fuck, Juliette, you feel so good. Nothing has ever felt as

good as your tight pussy squeezing my cock. We fit perfectly. It's like you were made just for me."

"I think maybe I was," she whispers, lifting her head to kiss me. Deepening the kiss, I start to move, keeping my strokes slow and steady. Julie's hips rise to meet me thrust for thrust. The sounds she makes will play on repeat in my head for the rest of my life. A bead of sweat rolls down her collarbone, and I lean down to lick it up, trailing my tongue up her neck and nipping at her earlobe, sucking it into my mouth to sooth the bite.

"Oh god, Asher. Oh fuck. It's so good. I'm going to come again. I'm so close."

"You want to come, Juliette? You need it?"

"Yes. Please. God," she moans out as I grind myself against her clit.

"Then Let. Me. Hear. You. Beg." I punctuate each word with a quick thrust of my hips, and Julie whimpers and writhes underneath me, locking her ankles behind my back and pressing her heels into me while she tightens her arms around my neck.

"Please, Ash," she sobs out. "It's too much. I can't...I need...*fuck*. Fuck me, please. Fast. Hard. Please, please let me come."

"It would be my pleasure, Juliette."

I speed up my strokes. My vision is starting to blur, the pleasure overwhelming. Knowing I won't last much longer, wanting to give her what she needs, I take one of her hands from around my neck, lacing my fingers with hers and pressing our joined hands into the bed over her head. I sweep my other arm under her back, holding her firmly against me as I thrust once, twice, three times before she convulses wildly underneath me, screaming out my name as she comes. My hips jerking out of rhythm, I pound into her twice more before I come, dropping my head to Julie's neck and groaning as I pour into the condom.

I slow my hips until we both come down before lifting my head and sealing my mouth over Julie's, letting my kiss say all the things that I can't say out loud. It says I love you and I need you and please and forever and always, and never have I wanted to say words more in my life, but right now isn't about me. It's about her.

And she has gone quiet on me.

Gathering her close, I pull out and lift her into my arms, carrying her straight to the bathroom. I don't put her down as I get rid of the condom and flip on the shower. When the water warms up, I step in with her, only putting her down once we're under the hot spray. I pull her into my arms, wrapping one arm around her waist and tangling the other hand in the back of her hair, holding her against me and murmuring into her ear.

"You did so well, baby. You're amazing. I'm so fucking proud of you. Thank you for letting go for me. I know that's not easy for you."

As I continue to talk quietly to her, I feel her start to shake, and when I look down, tears are streaming down her face. My heart clenches, watching her fall apart under the cascading water, and I wrap her up even tighter, gliding my hand up and down her back as she presses her face to my shoulder.

"Let it all out, Juliette. It's okay. You're safe with me. Always and no matter what. You can talk to me about it or not talk. Either way, I'm here and I'm not going anywhere."

When her tears slow, she stands back, and I spin us so she's under the warm water. "I'm sorry...that was so weird. Like, who cries after sex, right? Especially amazing, best I ever had sex."

I take one of her hands in mine and lift it to my mouth, kissing her knuckles. "It's the adrenaline leaving your body.

That was intense for you. I knew it would be. That's why I gave you a safe word, in case it got to be too much."

"I wish I could use that safe word right now," she mutters.

I laugh, relieved she seems to be back.

"Amazing, best you ever had sex, huh?"

"Tamp down that ego, Hot Shot. It's not like I have so much to compare it to."

"And you never will," I shoot back.

She stares and me and starts to laugh.

"What?"

"You just got all growly."

"I did not." *Shit, did I?*

"You did, but it's okay. It was kind of sexy. I didn't know you could also be possessive Asher."

I never have been before, but Julie brings out a whole side of me I didn't know existed.

"Only for you, Juliette. Now let's get clean and get into bed," I say, reaching for the shampoo and lathering up her hair.

Chapter Thirty-One
Julie

We had sex and I cried. *I cried.* God, how embarrassing.

Except Asher didn't make me feel embarrassed.

He just held on to me and whispered into my ear and then he washed my hair. He washed my fucking hair for me, and my heart jumped out of my chest and straight into his hands. No one has ever taken such careful, deliberate care of me, and I'm struggling to process it. What I do know is that what I feel for Asher is enormous—bigger than anything I have felt before for anyone—and that scares me as much as it thrills me.

After our shower, we dried off and tumbled into bed, naked. We're tangled up under the covers, his arm tight around me and my head on his shoulder. In our little winter bubble in this out of the way town, our silence is comfortable. But tomorrow, it'll be time to rejoin the world.

"Can you tell me more about your family?"

Asher shifts so he's laying on his side facing me and we're sharing the same pillow, and he is so gorgeous I almost can't believe he's real. His hair is disheveled, and with his gold-flecked eyes on mine, he radiates a contagious sort of contentment.

"I'll tell you anything. What do you want to know?"

"Well, I'm meeting them in two days. So...everything?'

He laughs and presses a kiss to my shoulder. "Okay, well, it's chaos, but the good kind. There are lots of kids and lots of noise and as long as no one is bleeding, we mostly let the chaos reign."

"Okay so I know you have seven nieces, and their names are literally tattooed on you, but I'm going to need a crash course in all their names because I can't exactly lift up your shirt if I forget."

He smirks at me. "Honestly, with this crew, no one would bat an eye, but I'll tell you. Charlie is the oldest, married to Jeff. Their girls are Olivia, Lilah, Harper, and the new baby Cammie. Annie is next, married to Zach. Their girls are Addie, Riley, and the new baby Zoe. I'm next, right in the middle."

I laugh. "That I'll never forget. You have middle child written all over you."

He grins and strokes a hand over my hair, as if he can't go a second without some kind of contact. I kind of love it.

"Kyla is fourth, married to Alex, and Lucy is the baby; she just got married to Noah last summer. Kyla's having a baby any day now. She and I are the closest in age. I'm close to all my sisters, but it's different with Kyla. We've always had an extra special relationship. Kind of like you and Ben, probably."

I just nod, not wanting to get into the complexities of my relationship with my brother.

"Anyway, I'm really glad I'll get to be there to meet her baby when she's born. With football I couldn't always be there for the other girls, so this is really special to me."

His eyes get a little misty, and seeing this big, strong athlete turn into a puddle at the thought of holding his sister's new baby has my heart doing one long slow roll in my chest.

"And your parents?"

He smiles a little, thinking about them. "Tom and Susan Hansley are something else. My dad's a general surgeon, and I don't think anyone in the world loves their job as much he does. Watching him have so much passion for it is what made me want to go to medical school if football didn't work out. But he's also such a good dad. He worked a lot, but he was always present, you know? At my games, at family dinner when he could be. Helping with homework. And the way he is with my mom? I've always wanted what they have. They still love each other so damn much, even after five kids and almost eight grandchildren. Everything I know about how to be a good partner I learned from my dad."

I reach out and lay a hand on Asher's cheek. "I think he taught you pretty damn well."

He lays his hand over mine. "You think?"

"I absolutely do. And it sounds like your dad and mine are cut from the same cloth. What about your mom?"

"She's just the best. She's brilliant and funny and knows everything and loves to bake cookies and pretty much runs all our lives no matter how old we get. She's a lawyer too. Judge actually."

"Seriously? How have we never talked about that?"

He gives me a wry grin. "I mean, you told me about your judicial dreams when you were topless. Telling you about my mom's career wasn't top of my mind."

I chuckle. "Point taken. What kind of judge is she?"

"Family court. Adoptions mostly. It's a tough job, but she's really good at it."

"For real, how have we never talked about this? Hallie is an adoption lawyer."

He looks confused. "I thought she did wills and trusts like you."

"She did, but she also always did some adoption work on the side. Last August she got an opportunity to take over an adoption practice and move it to our firm. It turns out she wasn't happy doing will and trust work anymore, so she transitioned her clients to me, and she took on adoption full time. We made it work." I shrug, like it was no big deal when it was, in fact, a huge fucking deal.

"That must have been hard for you." His eyes bore into mine and like always, he sees under my surface to what lies beneath. My instinct is to brush it off, but I'm so damn tired of doing that. I don't want to hide anything from him.

I take a deep breath and let it out slowly. "It was."

He nods but says nothing, waiting for me to continue.

"Hallie had been thinking about switching practices for a long time, but never said anything to us. When she finally told me in August, we were already deep in preparation to open the firm and I..." I break off, trying to collect my thoughts before I tell him the worst of it. "I didn't handle it well."

I laugh a little, but there's no humor in it. "That's a lie actually. I handled it so terribly that I'm sometimes shocked Hallie is still my friend at all."

Asher reaches out and takes my hand, setting our joined hands on the pillow between us while he waits for me to continue. "We had a huge fight about it. The biggest one we have ever had." I shake my head, trying to find the words to explain this to him. "I still think about it all the time. We talked it out and she forgave me, but the things I said to her? It still keeps me up at night."

"What were you afraid of?"

His question catches me off guard. "What do you mean?"

"Juliette, there isn't a single mean bone in your body. If you lashed out, it's because you were scared. So, what scared you?"

The relief of being seen like this, all the way through, is so enormous that it takes me a minute to answer him. And when I tell him my biggest, most hidden truth, my voice wavers.

"I was afraid of being left behind."

Asher squeezes my hand, and that little gesture gives me the courage to continue.

"Last summer was not the best. In July we closed on our office space. There was so much to do, and we only had six months before we opened. Hallie, Emma, and Molly all did everything they were supposed to do, but it was...different for me. I was so anxious about everything. I took charge when I shouldn't have and was constantly ordering everyone around. My spreadsheets had spreadsheets and I didn't sleep more than a few hours a night for weeks. I tried but my brain wouldn't shut off, and when I was so exhausted I finally passed out, I would be up two or three hours later. And well, you saw how I wake up. It wasn't pleasant. I basically mainlined caffeine and got really good at concealer so I could fake the well-rested, put together lawyer everyone expected me to be. That's pretty much where I was when you met me at the gala."

Asher leans forward and gives me a soft kiss. "I know, baby. I knew there was something on your mind that night beyond champagne and formal wear and a dance with a football player."

"How did you know?"

"When you were waiting for me to take your picture, you were tapping your phone against your palm. And when we were dancing and you mentioned you were a lawyer, your hand shook. I don't know if anyone else noticed it, but I did. I remember thinking that I wanted to unravel you. To see what was beneath the badass attorney."

I stare at him, a little stunned. "You remember all that?"

"I remember everything about you." He shrugs like it's no big deal. It is definitely not no big deal.

"Do you want to hear the rest?"

"Absolutely I do."

"Okay, well the day after the gala, we left for our annual lake trip at my parents' house in Western Maryland. I never told anyone this, but I resented every minute of the forced relaxation because all I could think about was everything we had to do at the firm. While we were at the lake, Hallie and Ben got together. It was so sudden. Our second morning at the lake, I went to wake Hallie up for breakfast and Ben strolled out of her room. He told me that he had been in love with her for eleven years. Eleven fucking years, Asher. He's my twin brother and very best friend, and he never told me his biggest secret. I thought I knew everything about him, and it fucked me up a little when I found out he kept this from me for more than a decade."

"And then you had to adjust to Ben and Hallie being, well, Ben and Hallie."

"Yes," I whisper. "That was the hardest part of all. One day we were all friends, and the next day they were a couple. They got so serious so fast and were deliriously happy and everyone was thrilled, and I had whiplash. It's not that I'm not happy for them. I am."

"Juliette, you have the biggest heart of anyone I know. Of course you're happy for them. But you can feel other things too. So how does it make you feel?"

Tears spring to my eyes, and I blink them back because I need to get this out. "Lonely. It makes me feel lonely. Hallie has been my best friend since we were born. Where it counts, she's my sister, just as much as Ben is my brother. But now they have each other and are building this whole life together that belongs just to the two of them, and I don't know where my place is."

Asher glides his thumb along my cheekbone, wiping away a tear that escaped. "Your feelings are all valid, you know. Your life changed just as much as Hallie and Ben's did when they got together."

I sigh then, and get ready to tell him the worst part. "You asked me what I was afraid of when I lashed out at Hallie? I was afraid of this. Of feeling like the two people closest to me were leaving me behind. I felt like Hallie had already left me for Ben and then she was leaving me at work too, and I felt..."

"Abandoned. You felt abandoned."

"I did. I still do. Sometimes I feel like I don't have a place with anyone anymore."

Asher sits up then, pulling me up to straddle his lap, cupping my face in both of his hands and tangling his fingers in my hair.

"You will always have a place right here with me."

With those words from his mouth and his blue eyes steady on mine, I take the final fall straight into love with Asher Hansley. I know with more certainty than I have ever known anything that he is my endgame. This is forever, and it's not nearly as scary as I thought it would be. I lean forward and kiss him, then wrap my arms around his neck, holding tight.

"Can I make a suggestion?" He asks the question into my ear, and I pull back so I can see his face.

"Sure, why not?"

"Have you ever considered talking to Ben? Telling him some of how you feel?"

"Not really. I never wanted to shit on what he and Hallie have or do anything that could get in the way of their happiness."

"I don't know Ben like you do, but I have been getting to

know him a little, and I know he cares about his people. He would want to know, Juliette. And, sometimes, it just feels good to tell the people you love how you feel. When we get back, maybe do something, just the two of you. I bet he misses you too."

"I'll think about it."

"Okay, I'm going to up the ante, because I think we need this."

I cackle out a laugh. "Up the ante? Are we at a Vegas poker table in the seventies?"

"Nah, but the stakes are just as high. I've been thinking about telling my family about my shoulder."

"Wow, Asher, seriously?"

"I don't know what's going to happen when pre-season starts, or how my shoulder is going to hold up, and in full transparency, that scares the absolute shit out of me. But telling you about it last night lightened the load a little, and I think I want more of that. Need more of that. So, I want to tell them, even if all they do is tell me I'm crazy for still trying to play."

"I'd like to be with you when you tell them, if you want."

"I definitely want. And I want you to do something else for me."

"Let me guess. You talk to your family, and I talk to Ben? Matching high stakes conversations that may or may not devastate the people we love most?"

"You know it. There's no one I'd rather have matching uncomfortable family conversations with than you."

I grin at him, feeling lighter than I expected, considering I just unloaded months worth of emotional baggage.

"You know what, Hot Shot? You have yourself a deal."

A phone rings, yanking me out of a deep sleep and shattering the pre-dawn stillness.

I feel Asher shift behind me, dropping a kiss on my shoulder before reaching for the phone charging on his nightstand.

"Ky?" His voice is rough with exhaustion. A female voice on the other end of the phone is talking fast, and suddenly Asher shoots straight up.

"Now? Really?"

He turns to me, and his broad smile—a stark contrast to his sleepy eyes—hits me right in the chest. "Kyla is in labor! She's going to the hospital now."

His excitement is palpable, and I grin right along with him.

"Okay, we'll be there as soon as we can. Don't fucking have that baby until I get there. Love you."

He ends the call and grabs my face, kissing me deeply. "Let's get a couple more hours of sleep, and then we're going to Boulder."

"A couple more hours of sleep? Asher, we're going now."

"You wouldn't mind?"

"Seriously? No, I don't mind."

He takes a deep breath. "Okay. It's a pretty long drive to Boulder. I was planning on making some stops along the way, but..."

His uncertainty is adorable. I just want to snuggle him. Instead, I snap into lawyer mode.

"Asher, if Ben was having a baby, I'd already be in the car, and I certainly wouldn't care about a little extra time on the road. Get in the shower. I'll pack for both of us. We're leaving in twenty and I'm driving. We'll stop for coffee once we get on the road."

"But...are you sure?"

"Yes, I'm sure. There's no way you're missing this. Come on, Uncle Ash. You've got a baby to meet."

Chapter Thirty-Two
Julie

ME

I fucked the hot quarterback.

MOLLY

OMGGGHHHGJHHGHHFH JULES. PROUD FRIEND ALERT.

Did you wear the underwear I packed for you? I knew they would come in handy.

ME

Let's just say sexy underwear was *unnecessary*

MOLLY

I don't even know what that means and I'm obsessed with it.

EMMA

It means he just wanted to get her naked. There are two kinds of men: lingerie men, and men who think lingerie just gets in the way. Asher strikes me as the latter.

HALLIE

Yeah, I'm going to need details.

ME

No.

HALLIE

JULIE ANNE PARKER YES. Listen, if you were here, I would pry them out of you over donuts and I would be victorious.

EMMA

Don't think you're getting out of a sexy breakfast story with donuts just because you're away. We're calendaring it for when you're back.

ME

I'll be sure to clear my schedule.

MOLLY

Okay but can you just give us one thing right now? One tiny little detail? Consider it payment for dealing with your clients while you're gone.

ME

Fine.

MOLLY

WE'RE WAITING JULES

ME

Give me a minute. There are so many good ones to choose from.

HALLIE

No need to brag

EMMA

Give me a break, Hal. Like your sex life isn't bragworthy. I've heard enough stories about Ben's dirty mouth to last me a lifetime.

Still gets me every damn time.

At one point I had a safe word, and my head was hanging off the bed.

LEGEND.

The first thing I notice when Asher and I get off the elevator on the maternity floor is the noise. So. Much. Noise. Following the signs to the waiting room, we turn a corner and find its source. The waiting room is packed with people, and we're barely through the entrance when a blur of golden-brown hair throws herself at Asher.

"Asher!" She bounces on her toes as she hugs him. "You made it! Kyla is going to be so happy. We missed you, big brother." Asher wraps her right up and she holds on for a minute and then lets go, turning to me. "And you must be Julie."

Every head in the room turns to me. Usually, this kind of attention would spike my anxiety and have me deploying Lawyer Mode, but the woman, who I assume is Lucy, radiates a warm sort of energy that puts me immediately at ease.

Asher slides his arm around my waist, tugging me into his side in a gesture of possession that has my heart pounding.

"That's me. It's really nice to meet you."

"No, girl, it's nice to meet *you*. I've been dying to meet the girl who has Asher even happier than normal."

I slide Asher a grin. "He does have a pretty happy baseline."

He winks back at me. "Look around. What's not to be happy about, Juliette?"

"Oh my god, he calls her Juliette. I absolutely die." Another woman throws her arms around me. "I'm Charlie, and I never knew my brother could be swoony. Like, seriously swoony."

"Hey, what about me?" Asher asks from behind me. "And where are the kids?"

Charlie just waves him away. "I'll get to you later. Jeff and Zach are on kid duty at mom and dad's house. They drew the short straws because, new babies." An evil grin spreads on Charlie's face, I assume at the thought of the two men riding herd on five kids and two newborns.

"Move over Charlie, it's my turn." The third woman shoves Charlie right out of the way to hug me. "Sorry, we're all huggers. You'll get used to it. Or you won't, but we are who we are. I'm Annie, and Asher has told us all about you. You are such a badass and I love you already."

Asher tugs me even closer to him. "Jesus women, give her some space. Sorry for my insane sisters. They don't get out much."

I lean into him. This is all easier than I thought it would be. Asher's sisters remind me so much of my friends, and I love them instantly. "No need to apologize for them, Hot Shot. They're great, and I am a badass."

Charlie grins at me. "Bet your ass. Come sit with us. We have a lot of catching up to do."

Before we can take a seat, a couple walks into the waiting room with cups of coffee in hand. I immediately know who they are. Asher makes a beeline for his parents, hugging them both at once. With his arms around them, he closes his eyes and breathes deeply, and I can actually see his entire body relax. No one has uttered a word, and I know immediately that these people all speak the same language. This is a happy family.

Letting his parents go, he leads them over to me, and I feel a quick frisson of nerves.

"Mom, Dad, this is Julie."

Asher's mom wraps me in a tight hug that screams *mom*. "It's so nice to meet you, Julie. Thank you for making our boy so happy."

I get another hug from his dad, who says, "I'm going to need to know more about the howling." I snort out a laugh and slide my gaze to Asher.

"I see you've been keeping everyone up to date."

He gives me a sheepish smile from where he is standing next to his mom. "What can I say, Juliette? The people needed to know what we..."

Asher stops mid-sentence, and his eyes snap to the waiting room entrance. I follow his gaze to a tall, good-looking blond man standing there. His eyes are tired, but he is absolutely glowing, a giant grin is stretched across his face. This has to be Alex. He has *new dad* written all over him.

Asher is in front of Alex in two strides, the rest of his family hanging back, seeming to understand that Asher needs this moment. "Alex. Is she here? Is Kyla okay? How much does she weigh? What's her name?"

Asher's questions come out in a flood of words, and Alex's smile widens even further.

"His name."

"Huh?" Asher's voice is full of confusion, but it clicks for me right away, and my own grin starts to spread.

"You asked what her name is. That's the wrong question. You should have said, 'what's *his* name?'"

"No fucking way," the guy I'm pretty sure is Lucy's husband, Noah, murmurs, his voice laced with humor.

"It's a boy?" Susan chuckles. "Well, this day is the best kind of surprise."

"But...we don't have boys. I didn't even know any of you guys could make boys. What do we do with a boy?" Asher is adorably baffled. I just want to cuddle him right up.

Charlie pushes through the crowd, radiating serious oldest daughter energy. "For fuck's sake, Asher. Pull yourself together. You literally are a boy." She wraps her arms around Alex. "How's Kyla doing?"

At the question, Alex's eyes fill with tears that he lets run down his face freely. "She wanted a minute to get herself together, but she's amazing. She just..." He breaks off, shaking his head, his face full of awe. "She's perfect."

I feel a rush of affection at the naked love on his face when he talks about his wife.

"As for his name, Kyla made me promise not to tell you. She wants to do it herself."

"Well then what are we waiting for? Let's get in there," Annie says, and the whole family starts moving towards the door. I hang back, not sure what to do, but Charlie grabs my hand. "Come on, Jules. We have a baby to meet."

"Oh, I don't have to. I can just stay here. This is really a family thing."

Charlie gives me a look full of understanding. "I know we can be a lot, but you're family now. You're Asher's, so that means you're ours too."

"Damn straight." Asher comes up and swings an arm around my shoulders, planting a kiss on my cheek. "Follow me, Juliette. This is the fun part."

When we walk into the room, Lucy, Charlie, Annie, and Asher's parents are already crowded around the hospital bed where a stunning brunette sits holding a tiny bundle. Out of all of Asher's sisters, Kyla looks most like him, with her golden-brown hair and blue eyes that look both exhausted and elated. When she sees us walk in, her grin spreads. Tugging me with him, Asher makes a beeline straight for the bed. He leans down and puts his arms around his sister, being careful of the baby she's holding.

"Missed you," I hear him murmur to her.

"Missed you more," she whispers, her eyes filling with tears. She hangs on to him for another minute before her gaze moves to me. She lets go of Asher, her grin returning. "The famous Julie Parker in my hospital room. I love this day."

I don't know what it is about the Hansley sisters, but they are utterly irresistible, just like their brother. "I don't know about famous…"

"Oh, with the way Asher has been keeping us up to date? You definitely are."

"Fuck's sake, Kyla," Asher mutters.

"Oh, has he?" I grin at him, enjoying seeing him embarrassed for once.

"Okay, okay, this is nice and all, but what's the baby's name?" Annie interrupts. "We've never had a boy before; this is a big deal."

"Oh boy, okay." Kyla takes a deep breath. "I assumed it was a girl, so we didn't even pick a boy name. But as soon as I saw him, I knew what it should be, and luckily Alex was happy to let me run with it."

Alex leans down and kisses Kyla's forehead. "It's a really good name."

She glances around the room and her gaze lands on Asher. "His name is Daniel Asher."

Asher sucks in a breath, and his eyes gloss over.

Kyla reaches out and takes his hand. "It was an easy choice.

I thought the first boy should be named after the best man I know."

"Ky," Asher whispers.

"Do you want to hold him?" Kyla asks.

He just nods, and she hands him the tiny bundle. The second the baby is situated in his arms, Asher loses it, his tears spilling over and running down his face. He leans down to hug Kyla again, the baby between them, and watching Asher crumble over the sister he loves so much and her first baby has my own tears falling.

"You love him." Asher's mom speaks quietly from behind me.

It's a statement, not a question, but I find myself wanting to answer. Even though I haven't given Asher the words yet, I turn to Susan.

"Yes."

She gives me a warm smile, her eyes crinkling at the corners.

"Well then, welcome to chaos, Julie Parker. I think you'll fit in just fine."

I really think so too.

Chapter Thirty-Three
Asher

"**S**usan, these are the best cookies I have ever tasted, seriously. If I knew how to bake, I would ask for the recipe because I'm going to need a constant supply."

I grin at Julie, who is sprawled on the living room sofa with my sisters and my mom, three infants in bouncers lined up on the coffee table and plates of cookies everywhere. It's our third day in Boulder, and since Kyla came home from the hospital last night and is officially on maternity leave, my mom, Annie, Charlie, and Lucy took the day off and decided a girls' day was in order. And today, a girls' day means starting with six different cookie flavors and hot chocolate on the couch, while they order me to get them whatever else they might need. Usually, I would balk at being their errand boy, but the contentment radiating from Julie as she sits curled up on the couch, slotting right in with all the most important women in my life as if she has known them forever, means I would do literally anything for any of them right now.

My family's casual acceptance of Julie has put her at ease in a way I haven't experienced with her yet, even in our best moments together. She has held babies, talked law with my mom, asked my dad questions about his surgical practice, read books with my nieces, and displayed a truly impressive knowledge of Disney princesses. That she feels this way in my hometown, sitting with my family, is a feeling almost more intense than I was prepared to handle, and I was prepared for quite a lot when it comes to my feelings for Julie. My love for her is so enormous I'm shocked she can't feel it every time I look at her. The words are right there, ready to spill out every time I open my mouth. I have to tell her soon, otherwise I'm pretty sure I'm going to blurt it out at a really inopportune time.

"Honey, you don't need the recipe. I'll send you cookies anytime you want. Also, Asher can make them for you."

"He can?" Then she turns to me. "You bake?"

"Seriously, Asher? You never told her you bake? That's like a core Asher fact, and also an A-plus way to woo a woman." Kyla stretches her arms above her head and gives me a wicked grin. I step over to the couch and shove her over so I can take the seat next to Julie.

"Shut up, Ky. And anyway, our relationship hasn't exactly been...conventional. I haven't had the chance to wow her with my baking skills yet." I toss an arm around Julie's shoulders and tug her into my side.

"As soon as we get back to Pittsburgh, it's baking o'clock baby."

She leans into me. "I like cinnamon rolls."

"I make a killer yeast dough."

I lean over and kiss her cheek, and I can practically hear all five of the other women in the room sigh.

"Jesus Christ, Hansley women. It's like you've never seen me with a girl before."

"We haven't seen you with a girl before. At least not like

this," Charlie says, while getting up to readjust the blanket covering her baby.

"The only other girl you've brought home since college was that really annoying one during your third year in the league. What was her name again?" Annie looks around the room.

"Alyssa maybe?" Lucy says.

"Yes! Alyssa!" Annie points at Lucy. "She had teeth so white there was no way they weren't veneers, and she called you Ashy, which, gross."

"So gross," Charlie says. "She also had that laugh that made me want to stick my fingers in my ears."

"That laugh was...intense." My mom grimaces and then smiles at me, clearly enjoying this little interlude at my expense.

"Ashy, huh?" Julie pokes my side and grins at me.

"Don't listen to them, Juliette. You're the only girl for me." I haul her into my lap and wrap my arms around her while I tug her back against my chest, and my mom and sisters are the heart eyes emoji personified. They aren't wrong. Because the truth is, while I've brought girls home here and there, or, like, once, this is different. I've never brought *the girl* home. And Julie is most certainly *the girl*. I've dated occasionally during my years in the league, but I sure as shit have never felt like this.

"Anyone home?" The front door opens and closes, and my dad's voice filters into the living room.

"In here, hon," Mom calls. Dad walks into the living room looking a little rough after working for the last twenty-four hours, but his eyes light up when he sees everyone sitting around. "I'm going in to make coffee then I'll be back. Someone better make a space on one of those couches because it was a long night last night."

Now that my dad is home, my mind starts buzzing. With

Kyla in the hospital the first few days we've been here, this is the first time my whole family is in one place, and I'm wondering if I should take this opportunity while the kids are all in school and daycare to tell them about my shoulder. I get a shot of adrenaline every time I think about it, and I've put it off for days, but I'm getting antsy. Julie has brought it up once or twice but doesn't seem to want to push me into anything, which I appreciate, but I think now is the time.

"I think I'm going to tell them now," I say to Julie, just loud enough for her to hear.

She turns sideways on my lap so she can look at me, taking one of my hands in both of hers. "Are you sure?"

My mouth turns up in a half smile that probably looks more like a grimace. "Definitely not, but I need to. It's time."

Her eyes are full of understanding, and she squeezes my hand. "I'm here."

The words are simple, but my gratitude is enormous. I squeeze her hands back, leaning over and pressing a kiss to the side of her head. "I know. I couldn't do it if you weren't."

"What are you two whispering about?"

I turn and see my dad walk back into the room with a giant coffee mug in one hand and two cookies in the other. He leans down to kiss three tiny baby heads and takes a seat on the couch opposite us between Charlie and Annie.

My stomach is a riot of nerves, and I look at Julie. She nods at me encouragingly and slides off my lap to sit next to me, never dropping my hand. I clear my throat.

"I have something I need to tell you all. It's important." I look around the room at my family and everyone is looking at me, their faces open and ready to hear whatever it is that I have to tell them. I hope they still feel that way when I'm done. I'm not sure where to start exactly, so I just open my mouth and words pour out. I tell them everything. About getting hurt in my fourth year, and not getting better, and the secret doctor's visit, and the anti-inflammatory injections, and how after my injury in the playoff game I've been hurting more this offseason than ever before. I don't look at anyone the whole time I speak. My eyes stay fixed on the babies in front of me and Julie's hand tight around mine. But as I finish, I finally look up and meet their eyes.

"I'm so sorry I didn't tell you. That I let you down. I know it was wrong, but all I wanted was to play football. I'm a quarterback. It's been my whole life, and if I don't have it anymore, I don't know…" My voice breaks then, and I close my eyes and take a deep breath to get myself together. "If I don't have football anymore, I have no idea who I am."

The room is silent for ten seconds before Kyla leans over and lays her head on my shoulder, wrapping me in a tight side hug.

"You should have told me, Ash," She whispers. "I never would have judged you for it." Her voice is thick, and I see tears streaming down her face. "I'm so sorry you've been going through this alone for so long."

I lean my head on hers, relief coursing through me at my sister and best friend's easy acceptance of my deepest secret.

My mom gets up from her chair and comes to sit on her knees in front of me. She takes my free hand in one of hers and cups my cheek with her other. "Asher Hansley, I believe I taught you better than to keep secrets like this from us. You can tell us anything; you know that. In this house, none of my children ever get in trouble for telling the truth. I'm going to ignore the fact that you kept this from us for all these years and tell you I'm proud of you for telling us now. This couldn't have been easy for you." She turns to Julie and takes one of her hands too. "I assume you had something to do with him finally telling us the truth?"

"Oh, um, no. I didn't do anything."

"She did. I told her while we were on our trip, and it gave me the courage to tell you too."

"Well then." She leans up and wraps Julie in a hug. "I already loved you for making Asher so happy. Now I love you for making him brave."

Julie returns the hug, looking a little shell-shocked. I let go of her hand and slide my arm around her back.

When Mom releases Julie, she gets up and goes back to her seat but doesn't stop talking.

"Asher, honey, you're a quarterback, but you are also so much more. You are a part of this family. You're a wonderful son and uncle and brother, and you love hard and deeply. There are so many parts of you beyond football quarterback, but I think it's been so long since you thought about those parts that you've forgotten they exist. Take some time and think about it. There's a whole world out there waiting for you when football is over, whenever that might be. You know we'll be with you every step of the way, even when you go back to Pittsburgh. And I have a sneaking suspicion that when you do go back, you won't be alone there, either." She gives Julie a meaningful look.

She smiles and leans into me. "He won't be alone. I swear it. My twin brother Ben and his two best friends have already adopted Asher into their little group. And, well, he has me too. I'm not going anywhere." She shrugs as a blush crawls up her face, and it's the cutest thing I've ever seen.

"Aw, Juliette, does that mean you're my girlfriend now?"

She gives me a bland look. "You mean I wasn't before?"

All four of my sisters start to cackle with laughter, which sets my mom off, and it's exactly what I needed to lighten the mood, even when the laughing wakes up all three babies, who immediately start crying. After a quick shuffle of babies and diapers and bottles, everyone is settled back into their seats. My dad, who has been unnervingly quiet, starts talking.

"Ash, I'm proud of you for coming to us. We're always on your side, no matter what. But you know the injections have to stop, right? From a medical standpoint, the side effects of using these kinds of drugs long-term can be very harmful. And with you constantly masking your pain and never getting evaluated, you have no idea what's actually going on with your shoulder. I am the last person who would ever want to take away something that has given you so much joy, but it's time to see a doctor, on the books, so that you can understand what you're really facing."

I look down for a beat before whispering, "I know." And I do. The thought of not playing football anymore kills me. But the thought of not being able to lift my kids up one day, or hold onto my girl, because my shoulder is so fucked...that's even more devastating.

"I'll make an appointment with the team doctor when I get back."

My dad nods at me and gives me a warm look. "Do what comes next, Ash. One step at a time. And you'll never be alone."

"Never ever," Charlie says from her perch on the couch where she is feeding Cammie.

"You're stuck with us." Annie blows me a kiss.

"Hansley girls forever." Lucy tosses me a grin. "I know how you've always wanted to be a Hansley girl."

Kyla leans over me to talk to Julie. "You're an honorary Hansley girl now, too, you know. We always wanted a fifth sister."

I'm feeling brave, so I decide to test the waters. "One day she'll be an actual Hansley girl, you know. Hopefully sooner rather than later."

Julie smirks at me. "You know me better than that, Hot Shot. Do I seem like a change her name when she gets married kind of girl?"

The whole room erupts in laughter and I pull Julie close, laughing right along with them. I have no idea what will happen next week when I go back to Pittsburgh and the future of my career is uncertain at best. But in this moment, with the weight of the secret off my shoulders and my family and my girl laughing around me, everything feels like it might just be okay.

Chapter Thirty-Four
Julie

"Thanks, honey," Asher's mom says as I hand her the last of the leftover containers to put in the fridge. We're in the kitchen cleaning up after dinner. Susan ordered everyone out but asked me to stay and help her. Asher seemed reluctant to leave me alone and stuck around until his mom kicked him right out, telling him that she's been cleaning up after dinner for far longer than he has been alive, and we would be fine without him. He just shrugged, kissed me on the head, and strolled to the living room where his oldest nieces were engaged in a vicious PlayStation battle. Without any clue as to why she wanted me to stay, my anxiety is firing on all cylinders, my hand tapping out a rhythm on my thigh.

"Cookie?" I jump at Susan's voice and whirl around to where she's standing with a plate of peanut butter chocolate chip cookies. My favorite. Even my own mom has never made a different kind of cookie for every person in her family, and my mom is a capital M Mom.

"Sure, why not?" I grab one and stand there, not sure exactly what to do.

Susan just laughs. "You don't have to be afraid of me, Julie. I'm not that scary."

I wince a little. "You noticed?"

She pats me on the shoulder. "Hard to miss. Your fingers are tapping on your thigh, and you're thinking so hard I bet everyone in the living room can hear it."

I take a deep breath and let it out, expelling some of my nerves. "Asher is a lot like you. He noticed all that right away too."

She motions me to a stool, and we sit side-by-side at the kitchen island. "My boy is perceptive. Some people think it's the quarterback instinct, and maybe that's part of it, but he's been that way since he was a kid. He always seemed to know what one of his sisters needed, even before they did."

I laugh a little, and take a bite of a cookie. They really are excellent. "Story checks out," I mumble. Swallowing the bite, I add, "He understood me from the start. I don't know how, but he got things about me that even the people closest to me never really have. He likes to say he got me through luck and unwavering persistence, but really, it was the way he saw me all the way through and accepted me exactly as I am. That's a first for me," I say quietly.

The understanding in Susan's eyes—the eyes she passed on to Asher—is so strong I almost have to look away. She reaches out and lays a hand over mine. "I bet it is. You're a brilliant, successful lawyer. I bet you've always been at the top of your class, and studied your ass off to get there. When you got into practice, it was working late nights and weekends with partner track in sight, and then you left to start your own firm where you took charge and organized everyone and everything."

I stare at her. "That is...scarily accurate."

Susan laughs a little. "And no one close to you ever knew that, inside, you were an anxious mess, because you never let them see. You covered it all up with spreadsheets and lists and color-coded calendars and really nice shoes."

I have the fleeting thought that maybe I should be insulted by this, but I'm not because what I am is so fucking relieved. I feel like I do every time Asher understands something about me that no one else seems to. "How do you know all this?"

She squeezes my hand. "Because I just described myself too. I'm so happy that you and Asher found each other, and I just want you to know that if you ever need to talk to someone who has been where you are, you can talk to me. Anxiety works for us sometimes. It's probably the reason we're as successful as we are. But when it stops working for you and starts taking you over? That's when things get dicey. You're not alone, Julie. I understand you too."

Emotion from being so well understood and so easily accepted makes my throat tight. "Thank you," I whisper. Then I find my voice. "It's been...hard being perfect all the time. I was exhausted and burned out and I didn't even realize it. Asher did, though. We didn't even know each other that well, but he found me on the floor of my office in the middle of a panic attack, and suddenly I was agreeing to go on a road trip with him, and it wasn't even because he blackmailed me into it, even though I made it seem like it was."

Susan snorts out a laugh and that makes me laugh too. "That sounds like my guy," she says.

"We've only been gone a week, but I feel like an entirely different person. Is that weird?"

Susan shrugs a shoulder in a gesture so much like Asher I have to smile. "You fell in love honey. You are a different person. But at your core, you're still you."

I clear my throat, a little uncomfortable. "I haven't exactly told him about that part yet. The love part."

"I know. You'll tell him when the time is right. He loves you too, you know."

I know it, even though he hasn't said the words. I think it's an honor to be loved by Asher Hansley. Before I can figure out what to say, Susan starts talking again.

"If I could handpick a woman for Asher, it would be you, Julie. I see the way you care for him. The way you understand him too. That's all I've ever wanted for him. I think he's met his match in you."

Tears prick at my eyes, but I blink them back, wanting to see clearly. "He is the best person I have ever known. I would do anything for him."

She nods, with a satisfied look on her face. "I believe you would. I'm glad he has you to stand by him through whatever comes next for him."

At that, I remember something Susan said earlier that got me thinking about Asher's future, and an idea keeps knocking at the back of my mind.

"Susan, did Asher ever do any work with kids while he was in college, or since he's been in the league?"

"He has. A lot, actually. When he was in college, he was a volunteer coach all four years for a youth league here in Boulder. I don't know how he fit it in between practice and games and all his classwork and labs, but he always made it a priority. And since he's been in the league, I know whenever there's an opportunity to work with kids, he takes it. I don't know all the details, but isn't he doing some work with a friend of yours?"

"He is. My brother Ben's best friend runs a foundation focused on kids and sports. Asher is volunteering for him during the offseason. Listen, you can tell me I'm overstepping, but I had this idea, and I need your help to pull it off."

She grins at me. "I love a bit of intrigue. Lay it on me, Jules."

Chapter Thirty-Five
Asher

"But where are we goingggggggg? Tell me, Juliette. Tell me, tell me, tell me."

Stopping the car at a red light, Julie gives me an exasperated look. "Are you five? Have some patience. You'll know when we get there."

We're in the Range Rover and Julie is at the wheel. She woke me up at dark o'clock this morning and insisted I get up and get dressed. When I tugged her back on top of me and slid my hands around to grab her ass and grind up into her, she swatted me away and called me a crazed sex maniac. Then she threw a pair of jeans at my head while she sailed out the door to go make coffee. Spicy morning Julie turns me on even more, so I had to lay in bed waiting for my hard on to deflate, which took a while. Then she came back upstairs all irritated that I wasn't out of bed yet, and, well, spicy Julie, what can I say? I'm not saying I'm irritating her on purpose by asking her where we're going ten thousand times, but I'm also not *not* saying that, if you know what I mean.

"Patience isn't a quality I'm well acquainted with. I'm a professional athlete, baby. We like action."

She reaches over and pats me on the leg, smiling sweetly. "Well, if you ask me where we're going one more time, I can guarantee you that you won't be getting any action anytime soon."

I grin at her then grab the hand she's still resting on my leg and bring it to my mouth, pressing a kiss to her knuckles. "You're my favorite human, Juliette."

"Yeah, yeah," she mumbles. "I kind of like you too."

The reluctance in her voice has me grinning even harder. She may still be a little baffled by us and how quickly this all happened, but that, from her, might as well be a love declaration. Even *thinking* the word love has my heart pounding in my ears and my palms sweating. I've seen the way she's been looking at me and the way she is around my family. She is feeling some kind of way, and I am here for it.

I'm so lost in my own thoughts that I don't realize we're here—wherever here is—until Julie parks the car and turns off the engine. Then I look up and see it.

"What are we doing at my high school?"

She turns to me, her expression solidly *Lawyer Julie on a Mission*. "Okay, hear me out. I've been thinking. A lot. I know you're worried about what your shoulder means for your football career. You took a big step the other day when you told your family, and I know how hard that was for you. How much it cost you to tell them the truth and face what your injury might mean, and how that makes you feel."

I swallow around the lump in my throat as my stomach tightens with nerves. Because she's right. I am worried. Telling my family did cost me something. And thinking about the potential end of my football career is impossible. Talking about it now makes me want to jump out of my skin. Or stick my fingers in my ears and pretend none of this is happening. But Julie obviously has a reason to bring it up, so I force my feelings down and focus on her.

"I think I know you, Asher, just like you know me. And I think you're feeling like the end of your professional career is the worst thing that could ever happen to you. That it means the end of football. And I want to show you it doesn't."

I hear the words she's saying, but they don't really compute. Because if I can't play, then it is the end of football.

I think she really does know me like I know her, because she reads my mind. "I know what you're thinking. If you can't play, it's all over. But it's not. Or, at least, it doesn't have to be. I've seen how excited you get whenever you talk to Jeremy about the sports camps you're helping him with. I know you coached youth football in college. I know how anytime a teammate is doing a philanthropy project that has to do with kids, you're the first one in line to sign up. And I see how you are with your nieces."

I shrug a shoulder. It happens to be my bad shoulder, and it throbs pathetically. I'd laugh if it weren't all so terrifyingly uncertain. "I like kids."

"You more than like kids, Asher. You were born to work with kids. I called your high school coach."

I rear back. Nothing she could have said would surprise me more. "You did what?"

"I called Coach Miller. Your mom gave me his contact information. He was thrilled to hear his best player of all time was in town. He was so excited, in fact, that he called his team together for a special winter practice. And you're going to coach it."

"I'm going to what?"

Julie snorts out a laugh. "Your vocabulary this morning is

particularly impressive. You're coaching a high school football practice."

"But I'm not a coach."

She gives me a look. "Didn't I hear you on the phone with Jeremy yesterday talking about a coaching schedule for his foundation football camp? Your schedule for the football camp that you are going to coach?"

"Okay, yeah, but that's like, just for the offseason."

"And this is just for one single practice in the middle of the winter when there shouldn't even be practice."

Julie leans closer to me and takes both my hands in hers, her gaze steady on mine. "Listen, if you really don't want to do this, I'll turn the car around right now, and we can spend the rest of the afternoon lazing around in the hot tub. But there is a field full of high school boys over there who could probably use a role model like you to teach them how to be a good player and a good person. You're both of those things. You have a gift with kids. Anyone with eyes can see it. Look, we don't know what the team doctor is going to say. He could have a fix for your shoulder that will keep you playing for ten more seasons. But one way or another, someday, your time in the NFL will come to an end. You can use your gift and keep football in your life long after your playing days are over. If you'll let me, I'd like to help you work out how."

Emotion winds its way through me, and I look at Julie, overwhelmed at the thoughtful care she put in to today, without knowing how I would respond to her frank talk about the end of my professional career. It's definitely not my favorite conversation, but somehow, having it with her makes it easier. She makes a lot of things easier. I reach out and pull her closer to me, wrapping my arms around her. It's awkward with the center console, so I pick her up and settle her right on my lap. She lays her head on my shoulder, arms around my neck.

"Thank you," I whisper in her ear.

She leans up and kisses my cheek, trailing kisses along my jaw. "I know none of this is easy, but you're not alone. You have your parents and your sisters, and you have me, for whatever you need."

Pulling away, I frame her face in my hands. "I need you for everything."

Then I bring her mouth to mine, kissing her hard. She lets out a sexy little moan, and her hands pull at my hair as my tongue swipes inside her mouth and glides against hers. The kiss is all passion and a little filthy, and I try and say with lips and teeth and tongues and hands everything I can't say in words. Julie sucks my bottom lip into her mouth, nipping it a little with her teeth, and the tiny bite of pain goes straight to my cock. I almost unzip my pants so I can fuck her right in this car, but then I remember where we are and pull away, resting my forehead against hers. Julie is flushed and panting a little, and when she smirks at me, I wonder for a split second if maybe a quickie in the back seat wouldn't be totally out of the question.

"You were thinking of a way to fuck me in this car, weren't you?"

I laugh, a little breathlessly. "Juliette, I am constantly thinking of ways I can get inside you, wherever we are. It is my most favorite thing. But since I'd rather not get arrested for public indecency and whatever else they can charge you with when you're having sex in a car in broad daylight in a high school parking lot, let's stick a pin in that."

She grins at me. "Come on, Hot Shot. You've got some kids to coach."

"Holy shit, it's Asher Hansley!" When one of the kids on the field says my name, thirty or so heads pop up.

"Language, Brent! Jesus Christ, he's going to think I don't teach you boys anything."

"Sorry, Coach," the kid mumbles, his wide eyes still glued to me as Julie and I approach the group standing in the middle of the field.

I grin at Coach Miller. "Still haven't realized it's an exercise in futility to try and get football players to clean up their language?"

"I'm surprised you even know the word futility."

I chuckle and he grabs me in a bear hug, slapping me on the back. "Good to see you, kid. It's been way too long."

"You too, Coach. It's good to be back." And it's the honest truth. I take a deep breath and look around the field and can see the younger versions of myself everywhere. The me I was before college and fame and the NFL. When I played for the love of the game and nothing else. It's a bittersweet relief to realize that not much has changed since I ran this field. Even when my career hangs in a precarious balance, I still love the game. And I know now Julie is right. I need to keep it in my life, no matter what happens.

"And you must be Julie." Coach Miller reaches a hand out to Julie.

Julie shakes his hand. "I am. Julie Parker. It's nice to meet you in person. Thanks for doing this for our guy."

"It was no big deal. The second I said Asher was in town, the boys couldn't suit up fast enough. Anyway, our guy, huh?" Coach elbows me in the ribs. "How did a guy like you end up with a smart, beautiful woman who does things like this?"

I put my arm around Julie. "Like I always tell her, a little luck and unwavering persistence."

Julie wraps her arm around my waist. "He was so annoyingly persistent that I finally gave in just to shut him up."

"And look at us now." I smile and kiss her temple.

"So," I say, looking around at the kids gathered around. "Anyone want to play some football?"

"That's awesome, Kyle. See how much more accurate your throws are when you lift your elbow like that?"

The freshman third string quarterback grins at me. "Did you see how far that went?"

"Sure did. Go grab some water and take a break. You've been working hard out here."

"Thanks, Coach. Then I'm going to try the quick feet drills you showed me."

Coach. I can't help but get a little thrill when he calls me that. Kyle reminds me a lot of myself as a freshman. Not the fastest, and definitely not the biggest, but he has the purest heart, and he loves the game so much. I can see it every time he touches the football. Watching his face light up when I showed him that small adjustment to his throw had everything inside of me lighting up too.

"Quick feet are going to have to wait until tomorrow, Kyle." Coach strolls over as Kyle tosses me the football. "It's almost noon and it's freezing out here. Time to call it."

I tug my phone out of my pocket and am stunned to see that it is, in fact, almost twelve. We've been out here for four hours but it felt like four minutes.

"Thanks for coming Asher, seriously," Coach says.

"I feel like I should be thanking you. That was the most fun I've had in a long time."

"Look, I don't know what's going on, or why your girlfriend was adamant that you needed to come coach my team for a day, but whatever it is, you should know you've got the touch, Ash. Watching you with the kids—especially with Kyle—was a special kind of magic I don't get to see very often. If you ever want to coach, I think you'd be a natural."

"Thanks, Coach," I say, too thrilled from the day to get into the actual reason I'm here. "It's never too early to start planning for the future."

"Son, I've known you too long to believe that bullshit, but if you ever need a listening ear, or someone to talk to, you've got my number. Don't hesitate to use it. I'm going to head out, but feel free to stay as long as you want. I get the feeling you might need it."

He turns and walks away, stopping to say something to Julie on the way out. I stay where I am and reach out my hand to Julie when she walks up to me. She looks absolutely delicious in leggings, a puffy jacket, and shearling boots. Her electric blue hat with the giant pompom on top makes her cobalt eyes even bluer, and they sparkle when she looks at me. When she takes my hand, I feel the zing of electricity even though our gloves.

"So, how did it go?"

I tug Julie into me, wrapping my arms around her and leaning my head against hers as I survey the field.

"It was actually...kind of great."

"I'm so glad," she says, cuddling into me. She doesn't ask anything else, content to stand in silence as I work out my feelings in my head, and I'm grateful for it. I need some time to sort it all out. But what I do know is that in this moment, with my girl in my arms after spending the last four hours immersed in the sport of my heart, I want to hold on to the joy and fun a little longer. My eyes fall on the bleachers and an idea pops into my head.

"Hey, Juliette?"

"What's up, Hot Shot?"

"You ever make out under the bleachers in high school?"

She chuckles. "No, I can't say I ever experienced that particular high school rite of passage."

I grin, untangling us and grabbing her hand, tugging her towards the sidelines.

"Well then come on, baby. Let me show you how it's done."

Chapter Thirty-Six
Julie

HALLIE

JULES. I wish I was seeing you tomorrow at your parents' house. Seriously, only Steven Parker would bbq in the middle of the winter. I'll be out of town for a case and won't be back until late tomorrow night. But you better be at the office Tuesday morning.

ME

It's like you haven't even met me. Of course I'll be in the office Tuesday morning.

HALLIE

idk, you seem to have turned into a completely different person since you've been away. The kind of person who has lots of sex with a smoking hot athlete and DOESN'T TELL HER FRIENDS ABOUT IT.

MOLLY

I'm bringing the donuts on Tuesday. It's been two weeks Jules, and your girls need DETAILS. You better be prepared to tell us a sexy breakfast story.

EMMA

I need to know all about his sisters. Is four sisters awesome or insane?

ME

So awesome. You guys would love them. They take fierce girl gang to a whole new level.

HALLIE

So what are you doing for your last night in Boulder?

ME

Back deck. Hot tub.

EMMA

We'll be needing those details too.

MOLLY

Fucking right we will. Did you ever check the front pocket of your suitcase?

ME

I thought we established that sexy underwear wasn't necessary. In the way, remember?

MOLLY

I hooked you up with a swim situation too.

ME

"Situation?"

MOLLY

I'm not sure it could accurately be described as a bathing suit.

ME

I packed my own bathing suit.

MOLLY

Not like this one.

When I'm With You

HALLIE

JUST FIND THE BATHING SUIT JULES. Put it on your body.

EMMA

And when you get back tomorrow, tell us all about it.

ME

Why do I like you all again?

EMMA

Even if you don't like us, you're still stuck with us.

HALLIE

Let's put that on a t-shirt.

MOLLY

Just do it, Jules. Asher's eyes will fall out of his head and there's an 80% chance you won't be able to walk tomorrow. But, like, in the good way.

ME

Okay I just found it. Mol, this looks like it was made for a teenager.

MOLLY

It's stretchy. Kind of.

ME

Holy hell. It fits but it's…I'm not sure I even have the words.

HALLIE

Pictures or it didn't happen.

ME

[pic attached]

EMMA

Holy shit Jules.

ME

It's pretty uncomfortable.

HALLIE

I doubt you'll be wearing it for that long.

MOLLY

My work here is done *dusts off shoulder*

The house is silent later that night when we step outside onto the back deck of Asher's house. Dressed in board shorts riding low on his hips and no shirt, Asher pulls the cover off the hot tub built into the corner of the deck and the steam billows out into the frigid air. I untie the belt on my robe and drop it to the deck just as he turns around. When he sees the tiny red bikini with criss-crossing straps I discovered in my suitcase, he says nothing, just swallows hard, a muscle ticking in his jaw. I hum with a deep, dark satisfaction as his eyes travel down my body and back up again.

When our eyes meet, it activates him, and he is in front of me in two strides. One hand goes to my waist, arm wrapping around my back, and the other tangles in my hair as Asher crashes our mouths together. The kiss is hungry and deep, and when his tongue licks into my mouth and dances with mine, desire arrows straight though me, and I grip his hips to steady myself. I have never needed someone the way I need him. The way I feel about Asher is huge and heady and overwhelming in a way that makes me want to wrap myself around him and never let go.

As he assaults my mouth with his, his thumb strokes the bare skin at my waist, and I'm rocked by a full body shiver. Whether it's from pleasure or the cold air I'm not sure, but

Asher reaches down and grabs my thighs, boosting me up and wrapping my legs around him without ever breaking the kiss. In a feat of athleticism that has me melting into a puddle of lust, he climbs up and steps straight into the steaming water. He sits down on the bench with me in his lap, my legs wound around his waist, still never removing his lips from mine.

When he finally does break the kiss, his eyes are deep, dark pools of blue. Both our chests are rising and falling rapidly. Almost involuntarily, I rock against him where he is settled, hot and hard, between my legs. He hisses out a breath and his hands grip my waist, pulling me down even harder on top of him, helping me glide over him. Every time he moves me, his cock hits my clit, sending waves of pleasure through me. He tightens his hands on my hips, grinding me harder against him, and when a moan drops from my lips, Asher speaks for the first time since we walked outside. His voice is low and deep and pure, unfiltered sex.

"Can you feel what you do to me, Juliette? Do you feel how hard I am for you? How badly I want you? I want you every minute of every day. Sometimes I can't breathe for how badly I want you. You're all I think about. All I see."

Asher brings his mouth back to mine, and I'm expecting a wild frenzy of a kiss, but that's not what he gives me. His mouth moves against mine slowly, thoroughly, lips and tongue exploring every inch of me, teeth grazing my bottom lip and then nipping at it before he takes my mouth again. My head spins, and the air around us is electric, the desire and sheer need between us too big for just our bodies to contain. He is holding me so close I don't know where I end and he begins, and suddenly this doesn't feel like a kiss at all. It feels like worship.

Asher breaks the kiss and leans his forehead against mine,

his hands coming up to rest on my face, thumbs stroking my cheekbones and eyes locked on mine.

"Juliette," he whispers, his voice soaked in reverence, his eyes swirling with something I can't name but that makes my heart do a long, slow roll in my chest. Feelings pummel me so hard I can't separate one from the other; I am a tangle of emotion and need. And then there is something else.

It could be the clear night sky above us and the blanket of stars or the swirls of steam rising into the frosty dark or the end of this uncommon, unexpected trip or the gorgeous man looking at me like I am the sun around which he orbits, but everything feels like magic. I pause for a second, not out of fear, but to memorize this moment that I know I will take out and examine again and again for a long time to come. As the words rise up from the deepest depths of me, it feels perfectly right, somehow, that I be the first one to speak them. To give them first to the man who has given so much to me.

"I love you, Ash."

Asher's thumbs stop their stroking, and we are so close I feel the hitch in his breath, the tremble of his body. See his face as he absorbs the words that draw the line between what came before and what comes after. I've never understood why those three words hold so much power, but as I watch Asher's face turn soft with wonder and awe and the tiniest bit of disbelief, as if he can't process the enormity of what is happening, I get it. And I make a silent vow to give him the words, over and over again, for the rest of our days. I tighten my arms around his waist to anchor him to this moment with me. This moment where nothing exists except for the two of us wrapped together, hearts wide open, under the dark night sky.

"I love you too, Juliette. I love you so fucking much. I..." He breaks off, his voice cracking with emotion. I bring one of my hands up to cup his cheek and he leans into my touch, taking a deep breath before speaking again. "I think I started falling for you before I even saw your face. I only had to hear your voice and I was done for. You are the girl of my dreams. Everything is better with you by my side. I never want to spend another day without you. This is always. Forever."

"Forever," I say, before sealing my mouth over his. And this kiss has all the passion and frenzy I was expecting before. Our mouths move together with urgency, Asher angling my head to take the kiss deeper, to swipe his tongue inside my mouth, to tease and taste, and need rises up in me like a tidal wave.

"I need you," Asher says against my lips. His voice a hoarse rasp.

"I'm yours."

Asher slides his hands from my face, reaching around to the tie holding my bathing suit at the back of my neck. With one pull, it comes loose and drops down. While his lips slide down my jaw and his tongue teases the sensitive skin behind my ear, his hands come up to cup my breasts, rubbing his thumbs over my nipples before rolling them between his fingers. I breathe in sharply, the feeling so intense I rock myself over him again.

"You like that, Juliette? You like my hands on you? Tonight, I am going to have my hands on every single inch of you. You're mine, and I can't wait to have you screaming my name."

"Fuck," I gasp as his fingers tighten on my nipples, holding me on the most delicious razor's edge of pleasure and pain. I lift up slightly and slide the hand on his waist around to his stomach, right under the waistband of his board shorts. He is velvet covered steel when I wrap my hand around him, and his stomach muscles tighten, his breath quickening, as I move my hand slowly up and down.

"You think you're the only one who wants to touch what's theirs, Hot Shot? Don't forget you're mine too. Maybe I'll have you screaming my name instead."

He grins at me. "I'm all for equality, baby. But you first."

In one quick move, Asher turns me around on his lap and pulls my back against him, one arm banding around my chest and the other hand sliding down under my bathing suit bottoms. He uses his knees to push my legs farther apart, and his finger finds my clit, slowly circling before dipping down to slide inside me.

I lean my head back against his shoulder, moaning up to the stars and shifting my hips, needing more. Asher's tongue licks a path up my neck to my ear. "You like that, baby? I can feel how wet you are. So tight around my finger and already dripping for me. I can't wait to feel you wrapped around my cock."

He curls his finger up and grinds the heel of his hand against my clit. My hips rise up to meet his hand, and when he pulls away, I let out a noise that sounds perilously close to a whine, but I'm too wound up and needy to care.

Asher chuckles in my ear. "Don't worry, baby. I won't leave you hanging."

"Then fucking touch me," I grind out.

With one arm still holding me against his chest, he unties my bottoms and pulls them off, tossing them onto the deck.

"Oh, I think I can do better than that."

Before I have a chance to work out what he means, he slaps his free hand down on the hot tub controller. In a lightning-fast move, Asher wraps a hand under each of my thighs, and turns us both around, holding my legs open as the warm water gushes out of the jets and straight onto my clit.

"Holy fuck," I gasp out. My first instinct to move away from the all-out assault on my senses is thwarted by Asher's hard chest at my back and his voice in my ear.

"Let it happen, baby. Make all the noise you want. No one can hear you but me."

While the jets pummel my clit, Asher reaches around and

slides two fingers inside me, thrusting them in and out, curling them every time to hit that spot inside me that makes me whimper and clench around him. I am all need and sensation as I hurtle towards the edge.

"Fuck, I'm so close."

"I know you are, baby, I can feel you squeezing my fingers. I can't wait to get inside you."

Asher pushes his fingers deep inside me and curls them up over and over again, and when he moves just a little closer to the jet to increase the pressure on my clit, I fall right over the edge, the pleasure and the heat of the hot tub combining to turn my whole body into a raging inferno.

"Asher, fuck," I moan out as he keeps me angled towards the jets, holding my legs open and milking every last drop of pleasure from my body. When it finally wanes, Asher lets my legs go and I drop my head back onto his shoulder, my chest heaving.

"That was...unexpected," I manage, sucking in oxygen.

"Hot as shit is what that was," Asher says, turning me back around to face him and kissing me, hard and quick. His wet torso shines in the moonlight and desire thunders through me all over again. "I love watching you come apart for me, Juliette. I can't wait to see it again."

He turns and sits us back down on the bench, and I straddle his lap, grinding down on his thick cock. Even though I just came, the move has pleasure licking through me, so I do it again, and then again. Asher sucks in a breath and grips my hips to hold me in place. "If you keep doing that, I won't be able to do what I really want to do, which is to slide inside you and come in that gorgeous pussy of yours."

"Shit," I mutter. The sweetest man in the world with the world's filthiest mouth is the most intoxicating combination. "Do it. Please. Get inside me now."

"Juliette, it would be my fucking pleasure."

I slide my hands down his sides and hook them in the waistband of his board shorts. He lifts his hips and I pull the shorts down and off, throwing them next to my discarded bathing suit, before reaching down and rubbing my thumb over his tip. His cock jerks in my hand, and the way he responds has me feeling a rush of power.

With him in my hand, I rise up on my knees, ready to take him inside me when he stops me with hands on my hips.

"Condom. Fuck. I don't have one out here. We can go inside. We need to go inside. Right now." Arousal has his words jerky, and he starts to rise to his feet when I stop him with a hand on his chest.

"I have an IUD."

The look in his eyes can only be described as feral, but when he speaks, his voice is gentle, his thumbs drawing circles on my hips.

"Are you sure?"

"I am so sure."

"I was serious when I said I haven't looked at a single other woman since the gala. And we get tested before every season, so..."

I cut him off with my mouth on his. "Ash," I say, against his lips. "I trust you."

"I love you," he says, kissing me again, "You are my everything."

My heart turns over in my chest. "I love you, too, Hot Shot. Now get inside me."

"I would love nothing more."

I rise up on my knees again and, with my hands on Asher's shoulder and my eyes locked on his, I sink down slowly. Our moans mingle as he fills every inch of me, hitting spots I didn't even know I had. When I'm fully seated on him, I close my eyes, savoring the feeling of being so full, letting my body adjust to him. Then I rock slowly on his lap, his hands gripping my hips to help guide my movements.

"Look at me, Juliette."

I open my eyes to meet Asher's, and his gaze is dark and intense and full of need, his wet hair falling across his forehead. "When you're riding my dick, your eyes stay on me."

The look in his eyes has me lifting up on my knees and sinking back down on him, rolling my hips so my clit hits his pelvis, and the feeling is so intense that I do it again, grinding down onto his lap and groaning at the building pleasure.

"Juliette. Yes. Fuck. Don't fucking stop," Asher grinds out, his hands leaving my waist and traveling over my body. As I rise and fall over him, Asher covers my breasts with his hands and rolls my nipples, sending a shock straight to my clit. I gasp, lifting up and slamming back down over him. My entire body lights up as Asher lets out a deep moan and starts lifting his hips to meet mine, droplets of water rolling down his torso as he fucks up into me.

"God," I moan out. "You feel so good."

Asher shoots me a grin and snakes a hand between our bodies, his thumb funding my clit and moving in tight little circles as his hips rise, meeting each of my thrusts with his own.

"Give it to me, Juliette. Come for me. Mark me. Come all over my cock and make me yours."

My orgasm builds and builds on itself, and the pleasure is so intense that I'm almost afraid of it. It winds tighter and tighter as Asher moves faster and increases the pressure of his thumb. Then he pinches my clit and angles his hips in just the right way, and I explode around him, crying out his name, my eyes never leaving his.

"Fuck, baby, you are so gorgeous when you come," Asher grinds out, as his hands come back to my hips. Pleasure rolls through me as Asher grips my body, fucking me from below, his thrusts speeding up until they lose their rhythm, his hips jerking as he groans out his orgasm. I feel a rush of warmth as he spills inside me, and I roll my hips against his, riding us both through our releases.

When the pleasure wanes, I melt against him, dropping my head to his shoulder. Asher kisses my temple and runs a hand up and down my back as the water swirls around us.

"Juliette that was...you are..." He huffs out a laugh and seems to give up, leaning his head against mine as our heartrates slow against each other. When our breathing returns to normal, he cups my cheek and guides my head up so our eyes meet. Then he drops his mouth to mine in a long, slow kiss that has my brain fuzzing and sparks lighting behind my eyes.

"Thank you for loving me," he whispers when we break apart. "The best thing that ever happened to me is being loved by you."

Jesus fuck. This man is probably going to kill me with sweetness. In the face of that truth, I give him one of my own.

"You're the best thing that has ever happened to me. I can't do anything but love you."

"Juliette." His voice is thick, and the emotion in his eyes is the twin to what I feel inside of me. No more words are necessary between us. Instead, Asher wraps his arms back around me, and we hold each other close under the night sky.

Chapter Thirty-Seven
Julie

The little voice stops us just as we step off the jetway into the Pittsburgh airport.

"Are you Asher Hansley?"

The little boy is about seven or eight, and he's staring up at Asher with a mixture of awe and disbelief on his face. I smother a laugh at the look on the face of the man standing beside the boy who I assume is his father. Seems no boy of any age is immune to being starstruck by a famous athlete. During our two weeks away, I mostly forgot Asher is mega-famous. Except for a couple fans here and there, being away from Pittsburgh meant he could generally move around incognito. But now that we're back, it seems like that quiet interlude is over. I haven't really considered what it would be like to date someone famous, but I guess I better get used to it, and quick.

Asher immediately crouches down so he's on the boy's level.

"I sure am buddy. What's your name?"

The boy's grin lights up his entire face. "I'm Tommy."

Asher grins right back. "Nice to meet you, Tommy. You like football?"

"Yes! It's my favorite. I play on a team, and I'm a quarterback too."

Asher holds up his fist and Tommy bumps it with his. "Don't tell my wide receivers I said this, but quarterback is the best position on the team."

Tommy nods, eyes wide. "I'll never tell," he says solemnly. "But you're totally right. Can we take a picture together? My friends at school are never going to believe I met you."

"You bet."

Asher puts his arm around the boy, and the dad takes the picture while my heart explodes from cuteness at their twin grins, and my ovaries start screaming at me to have this man's babies. It's a weird flex considering having kids has never been at the top of my to do list, but Asher Hansley has a way of making me consider all kinds of things I never have before.

Asher stands up and shakes the dad's hand then turns back to Tommy. "I know it's awhile from now, but how would you like to come to the home opener when the season starts again? If your dad gives me his phone number, I can have someone from the team call you and set it up."

Tommy's eyes widen again. "Really? Can I? Can we?" He looks up at his dad with a pleading expression on his face.

His dad chuckles. "Sure." Then he turns to Asher. "Thanks for this. You made his day."

"Anytime." Asher high fives Tommy and puts the dad's number in his phone to pass along to the Renegades PR people. When they walk away, he takes my hand and laces his fingers through mine as we follow the signs to the train that will take us to baggage claim.

"So, it turns out you're, like, super famous." I bump my shoulder with his.

He leans over and drops a kiss on my forehead. "Nah, Juliette. I'm just a simple guy from Colorado playing a little game."

I snort out a laugh. "There's nothing simple about getting stopped in airports by awestruck kids and their hero worshipping dads who look at you like you hung the moon. And having half the airport stare at you as you walk? That's celebrity levels of famous, Hot Shot."

He stops walking suddenly, pulling me out of the way of passersby and behind a column next to an empty gate, giving us the illusion of privacy. He spins us so my back is against the column, and he is standing in front of me, one hand planted next to my head, the other on my hip. The look on his face is serious, and his eyes bore into mine.

"We never talked about it...the fact that I'm kind of famous. It was easy to ignore while we were away, but we're not away anymore. It's not always the easiest life. I get stopped a lot and people take my picture and sometimes it ends up online or wherever. My fans are mostly awesome, and I'm used to it by now. But it just occurred to me that you maybe might not be so okay with being in the spotlight. Are you? Okay with it, I mean?"

I open my mouth to answer him, but he just plows on ahead.

"You don't have to answer me right now, and maybe the middle of the airport isn't the best place to have this conversation, but we haven't even been back in Pittsburgh for ten minutes and I already got stopped and I'm thinking about it now, and I didn't want to wait to ask you but now I'm thinking maybe I should have waited. Shit," he mutters, face turning a little red.

Charmed by his uncharacteristic rambling but extremely in character concern for me and my feelings, I grab his face with both hands and kiss him. His other hand immediately moves to my waist. He deepens the kiss, and I pour my whole self into it. It doesn't matter that we're standing in the middle of a crowded airport and he is one of the most recognizable faces in the city. Or that a picture of this kiss will probably land on *Instagram* five minutes from now. This man is mine, and I don't want him thinking for a second that I care about who knows it. My clients will just have to deal with it. Hell, it may even be good for business. When we break apart, Asher looks right and left, where there are at least four people gawking at the site of their beloved quarterback making out with a random girl in the middle of the airport, and then he turns back to me, a slow grin spreading across his face.

"So, I guess you're okay with it?"

I huff out a laugh. "Yeah, Ash, I'm okay with it. This is your life. I love you means I love all of you, even the part that has strangers taking pictures of me in public places and not caring whether they get my good side. Will it take some getting used to? Probably. But I've always been good at figuring shit out."

Asher kisses me again, hard and fast, and it has my entire body buzzing. "Baby, every side of you is your good side. I love you so damn much I think I need a new word for love. So, want to come to my house?" He tangles our fingers back together and looks at me with a hopeful smile.

I consider this. We never really talked about what happens now that we're back. My mind flashes to my house. The one I spent months painstakingly decorating into what I thought the home of a successful lawyer should look like. After a week on the road and then a week in Asher's warm and cozy family home, I suddenly realize I have no attachment to anything inside those walls. It may have only been a couple of weeks, but I think home might mean something different now.

"Sure, Hot Shot. Take me to your house."

Asher

Julie cackles out a laugh when the car I hired to drive us from the airport back into the city pulls up in front of my house.

"What's so funny?"

We climb out of the car, and she points to a house down the block. "I grew up right there."

"No, you didn't."

"Swear to God." She laughs again. "Looks like we can walk to dinner tonight."

I look down the street and then back at her. "Wait, your parents still live there?"

"Sure do. They've lived there since before Ben and I were born. I hope they never sell it. I love that house. This whole street, actually. Come to think of it, this street kind of reminds me of your parents' street in Boulder."

I grab her hand and lavish kisses on it, delighted by her. "Juliette we are so meant to be. I bought this house with my signing bonus before my rookie season. I came to Pittsburgh for training camp that summer and stayed in one of the furnished apartments downtown the team owns. The apartment was white and impersonal, and I was missing my family so much and was totally overwhelmed by how fast my life had changed. One day, one of the veterans had a team dinner, and he lived in this neighborhood. After dinner, I couldn't stand the idea of going back to that condo, so I started walking. These streets reminded me so much of home that for the first time since I moved, I wasn't homesick. I ended up right here in front of this house and there was a for sale sign in the yard. I called the number and bought it the next day."

I look up and down the street, steeped in memories of the me who was so lonely, walking around the neighborhood, wondering what I had just gotten myself into. "It was definitely too big for just me, but something about the house spoke to me. I loved it on sight. Aside from my parents' house in Boulder, it's my favorite place."

Julie leans against me, and I wrap an arm around her, staring up at the house while the driver takes our bags out of the car.

"It's really beautiful," she says.

"Come on, I'll show you inside."

I guide Julie up the front steps and when I fit my key into the lock, the rightness of walking through my front door with her is undeniable. We are barely over the threshold, and I already know the house feels different with her in it. I would almost say the house was waiting for her to come home, if I was someone who believed in that sort of thing.

"Wow, Ash," Julie says, turning slowly to take it all in. "It's gorgeous."

I look around, seeing it through her eyes. The wide foyer, the cozy living room with vaulted ceilings and built in bookshelves, and the dining room I made less formal with a long farmhouse table and an art deco light fixture.

"Whoever decorated for you is brilliant. I should have hired them instead of the painfully expensive company who made my whole house white and boring."

"Charlie and my mom decorated it for me," I say absently, focusing more on the other thing she said. "You don't like your house?"

She pauses for a second before speaking. "I used to like it. Or at least, I thought I did. I was going for perfect, and I guess that's what I got. Except perfect means the furniture looks nice but is mostly uncomfortable, there's no color except white and cream, and I can never relax there. I used to think that's what I wanted but now..."

She trails off, and I feel like this is one of those enormous moments disguised as mundane, so I choose my words carefully.

"What do you think now?"

She looks around again, before turning back to me. "Now, I think maybe perfection is overrated, and I want a comfortable couch I can sink into to do something other than work."

I understand how big of a deal it is for her to admit this, and I tread lightly when what I really want to do is beg her to move in with me and never leave.

"I have a really comfortable couch. You can share it with me."

"I think I'd like that," she says, before wandering down the hall into the kitchen. I trail after her and hear her laugh the second before I step through the kitchen door.

She's grinning when she looks at me. "You really do have a soda fountain."

"Would I lie about something as important as morning caffeine?"

"I just didn't think soda fountains were a thing that people had in their kitchens."

I reach over her head and pull a glass out of the cabinet, filling it with ice from the fridge dispenser and handing it to her. "Check out the left side of the fountain."

She takes the glass and presses it against the dispenser, filling it with soda. When she tastes it, she laughs again, and the sound fills the room in the very best way. I want to make her laugh a million times a day for the rest of our lives.

"It's Diet Pepsi."

"Sure is."

"You filled the second tap with Diet Pepsi. Wait, how did you fill the second tap with Diet Pepsi when we just got back?"

I hop up to sit on the counter, enjoying watching her in my space. "I'm contracted with a concierge company that can do personal assistant type stuff. They sent someone to get the house ready and hired the people to come add your drink."

"Oh, I've had clients with those. They always seem so handy."

I shrug. "They can be. I like doing things for myself, so I've never needed an assistant the way some guys do. But during the season when I'm crazy busy and traveling a lot, it helps to have someone to call to be here when a plumber needs to get in or to stock my fridge when I've been away."

"Or add Diet Pepsi to your soda fountain."

I smile at her. "Or that. Or to track down a six-month supply of peppermint Hershey Kisses in February. Check that drawer." I point to a drawer next to the fridge, and when she opens it, she gasps. It's full of what I know is twenty bags of peppermint Hershey Kisses.

"We ate most of the ones we brought on the trip, so I thought we needed a re-stock."

She looks at me in astonishment. "You are a wonderful man."

"You got me addicted to them too. It was the least I could do after eating half of your stash."

"What about your candy?"

I smirk at her. "Open the drawer below."

She does, and she stares at the vast array of gummy candy filling the drawer. "I think this is my favorite place."

"I'm counting on it being exactly that, Juliette."

"I love your kitchen. I can't cook for shit, but it's the kind of kitchen I would want to cook in, if I could cook."

"Well, lucky for you I can cook, so you can sit your gorgeous ass on this counter and watch me cook for you right in this kitchen anytime you want."

"It's a deal. I'm impressed with your fancy espresso machine, too. I've never even seen you drink coffee."

"I don't, but you do. I bought it for you."

"When?"

"When what?"

"When did you buy that very fancy espresso machine that is sitting on your beautiful kitchen counter?"

"I don't know, like four or five days ago maybe? I put it on the list I gave the concierge." She looks a little baffled, so I reach out and snag her hand, pulling her in between my legs.

"Here's the thing, Juliette. I want to be with you as much as I can. I know you have a house of your own and a big career and a whole life you have built, and we are going to have to figure out how to fit our lives together in a way that works for both of us. I want to do all that work with you, and I don't want to skip any steps when it comes to you and me. I thought a good place to start was making sure I had everything in my house you needed to be comfortable when you're here. Which, selfishly, I hope is a lot because I love you a lot and I want to be wherever you are."

She kisses my cheek and grins. "I would have loved it here no matter what, but I love it even more with Diet Pepsi in the fountain, a drawer full of my favorite candy, and a fancy coffee machine I have no clue how to use on the counter."

I drop a kiss on her nose. "I'm sure it comes with instructions. I'll read them and give you the highlights."

I hope off the counter and swing an arm around her shoulders. "Come on, we have a couple hours before dinner at your parents, and I still have to show you the most important room in the house."

She smirks at me. "Let me guess. Your bedroom?"

"You know it baby. I have a huge bed and the best mattress money can buy, and I can't wait to get my hands all over you."

Julie drops her voice an octave and whispers in my ear. "Well then you better run, Hot Shot. I don't know if a couple of hours will be enough for all the things I want to do to you. And all the things I want you to do to me."

All the blood in my body immediately rushes to my dick, which thickens behind the zipper of my jeans. Without another word, I scoop her up and run for the stairs, with her laughing hysterically all the way.

Chapter Thirty-Eight
Julie

"Julie Parker, you come here and hug me right this second."

The second Asher and I walk in the door of my parents' house, my mom bustles into the foyer, arms wide open. I go to hug her and am immediately surrounded by the floral scent that means *mom* to me more than anything else does. I cling to her for a second, tightening my arms around her, suddenly a little overwhelmed. She pulls away and frames my face with her hands.

"You okay, my girl?"

Rachel Parker misses nothing. And the truth is, I am okay. Better than okay, probably. But I feel like it's possible I'm an entirely different person than I was when I left with Asher two weeks ago, and I don't know how to distill that into an answer that will satisfy my mom. I take a deep breath to pull it together and try.

"I really am, Mom. I'm happy to be home. I missed you." It's the truth, albeit a less complex version of it.

Still holding my face in both hands, she studies me closely

before nodding. "I really think you are. Now, it seems I have someone very important to meet."

She all but shoves me aside to get to Asher, and when she tosses her arms around him, I snort out a laugh. Good thing Asher is used to chaotic family members because my mom never disappoints. He hugs her right back, winking at me over her shoulder. When she pulls away, she takes both of his hands.

"Asher Hansley, it is a pleasure to meet you. Steven's on his way home, so he'll be about half an hour."

Asher grins at my mom. "No problem and, Mrs. Parker, the pleasure is all mine, seriously."

I smile inwardly, knowing exactly what's coming next. "None of that Mrs. Parker bullshit. Mrs. Parker was Steven's mom. She was a stone-cold bitch who never liked me, and I hated her right back. You call me Rachel."

Asher's grin grows. "Rachel, I think you might be my favorite person after Juliette."

My mom slides her gaze to me and then back to Asher, a grin spreading across on her face. "Juliette, huh? Well now, what exactly is our *Juliette* to you?"

"For fuck's sake mom," I mutter.

Asher just shrugs a shoulder. "It's a reasonable question, Juliette."

He turns back to my mom. "She's everything to me. I love her."

Literally nothing stuns my mom silent, but Asher's frank statement seems to have done the job. She just stands there, staring at him, until finally her eyes fill with tears that immediately spill over, and she wraps Asher up in another hug. I roll my eyes at her drama, while on the inside, I'm all lit up at Asher's love declaration in front of one of the most important people in my life.

"Mom, Jesus. No need to cry all over the man."

"Julie Anne Parker you be quiet. When a man comes into my house and tells me he loves my daughter and that she's everything to him, I'm entitled to a few tears."

Asher winks at me again. "This is normal mom stuff. My mom cried all over my brothers-in-law when they first talked about how much they loved my sisters."

My mom unwraps herself from Asher and looks at him curiously. "How many sisters do you have?"

"Four. All married. Three of them have kids."

"And they all live in Boulder? You must miss them." My mom looks at him curiously.

"They do, and I definitely do. It was nice to go back and visit, and I'm happy Juliette got to meet everyone."

"Well, I'm sure it's hard to be so far away, but you have a family here now. You love Julie, so that means you're one of us. If you need anything, you come here."

I know Asher misses his family and doesn't have a lot of people here to lean on, but I don't think I realized just how lonely he's been in Pittsburgh until I see the emotion painted all over his face at my mom's simple declaration that he belongs to us. Every time I think I have reached the absolute depths of my feelings for this man, I find even more. I'm wondering if there is a bottom, or if I'm destined to fall harder and deeper forever. I have never been as grateful for my mom's vast well of love and acceptance as I am in this moment.

"You know Mom, he won't have to go far to come here. He lives pretty close, it turns out."

"Really? Where do you live?"

Asher points in the direction of his house. "About five houses down that way."

My mom grins broadly. "We're practically neighbors. Does that mean I'll have my daughter just down the street soon?"

"I did buy a really good espresso machine," Asher says, as I just shake my head, resigning myself to the fact that my mom is having a no filter on what comes out of her mouth day.

"Jules does love her lattes. And it would be nice to see her in an actual home instead of that showroom she lives in right now."

I look at my mom in astonishment. I've been feeling the same way, but this is the first time she's ever brought up anything like this. It makes me think that I need to have a conversation with my parents. I take stock of my feelings and am surprised to realize that the idea of a good heart-to-heart with my mom makes me feel relief rather than anxiety, and I make a mental note to come back over this week when I have some time. That's not a conversation for tonight.

"Hey, look who's here!" Ben's voice breaks me out of my thoughts as he comes strolling into the foyer from the direction of the kitchen.

"Asher, good to see you, man." They do a one arm man hug kind of thing that has me chuckling. "Now that you're back, will we see you at the gym?"

"Count on it," Asher says with a genuine smile. "I have some stuff with the team I need to deal with this week, but starting next week I'm all in."

"Sounds great. I'll text you our schedule next week."

Then Ben wraps me in a hug. "Missed you, Jules."

"Missed you too," I whisper. Tears prick my eyes as I realize just how true that is. How I've been missing him for longer than just the two weeks I've been away. Out of the corner of my eye I see Asher looking at me with a softness on his face. I remember the promise I made to him to talk to Ben and suddenly, that seems like a conversation I urgently need to have. Asher nods at me and, as if he can read my thoughts, he turns to my mom.

"Rachel, can I help with dinner? I'm pretty good in the kitchen."

My mom is watching Ben and me, and I guess she's a mind reader tonight too. "That would be great. Ben and Jules, why don't you sit and catch up while we deal with dinner?"

Without waiting for a response, she hooks her arm through Asher's and guides him towards the kitchen. He looks back at me and gives me an encouraging nod and a smile before disappearing down the hall.

Ben wanders into the living room, and I follow him. In a habit as old as we are, we take our usual places on the big leather sectional—me curled up in the corner seat and him on the middle cushion, his legs stretched out on the giant square ottoman that doubles as a coffee table.

"Tell me a story, Jules," Ben says, and my breath hitches.

Tell me a story. It's something we said to each other when we were younger and had spent any time apart. It was our way of catching each other up, making sure that we were still part of each other's lives, even when we weren't always together. The familiar phrase has tears pricking my eyes again, and this time I let them come. They fill my eyes and spill down my cheeks, and I do nothing to wipe them away. They feel good. Cleansing, almost. Ben doesn't seem alarmed by the tears. He just slides over and wraps an arm around me, letting me get it all out. I rest my head on his shoulder, and we sit in silence.

"Must be some story," he says, when my tears finally stop.

I let out a watery laugh. "You have no idea."

On instinct, we turn to each other and sit cross-legged, our knees touching like we used to do when we would talk as kids, and the familiar position gives me the courage to jump in.

"I have a confession to make," I start, jumping right in.

"What's that?" Ben asks.

"The past six months since you and Hallie got together have been...hard for me."

Ben doesn't respond, just leans forward a little, watching me, waiting for me to continue. He has always been the best listener I know.

"At the lake last summer, it felt like you two came out of nowhere. And when you told me that your feelings for Hallie were more than a decade old, it shook me hard. It felt like you had kept this massive secret from me when we had never, ever kept secrets before. And I get it, Ben. I really do. I can't imagine how hard it must have been to have such strong feelings for her and not know how all the pieces would shift if you told her. My feelings aren't exactly rational, but there they are anyway. And after the lake, it all happened so fast. It has always been you and me, or me and Hallie, or the three of us together, but once it was you and Hallie, I didn't know where I fit. You are building this whole life together, and god, Ben, it's so beautiful. The two of you are so, so beautiful together."

I look down at my hands, a little embarrassed by this huge confession, not ready yet to see Ben's reaction to the next thing I say.

"But sometimes it makes me feel like maybe I don't fit with you guys anymore. Like maybe I don't fit anywhere anymore."

"Jules," Ben says, his voice soft.

When I finally look up it's not pity in his eyes, but love and maybe even a little...pride?

"Ben, I want you and Hallie to be happy. So, so happy. You are so important to me, sand I love you so damn much. I guess maybe I've just been missing you both."

"I know this wasn't easy for you to tell me, but I'm glad you did."

"You are?"

"Of course I am. Jules, it's been an adjustment for me too.

And for Hallie. You think it's not a little weird for me to tell Hallie something before I tell you? Or for her to do the same? It did happen fast, because it was right, but that doesn't mean we're not all still figuring this out. Why do you think we decided not to worry about setting a wedding date for a while?"

I shrug. "I don't know, I figured Hallie was just busy with her practice and that you'd get around to it eventually, but you should know it's been making me antsy. I had to restrain myself from setting up wedding spreadsheets for her."

Ben chuckles. "Don't you worry, it's coming. But we decided once we moved in together to just stay in this place for a while and enjoy it. To just be together without worrying about jumping to what comes next. To figure out what our lives look like now that we're together. And it's everything I ever wanted. Even better than I could have dreamed of. But Jules, it would be nothing without you. You are our most important person, and you will always have a place with me and a place with Hallie. Always and no matter what. And if Hallie was here, she would tell you the same thing."

Tears spring to my eyes again. I didn't know how badly I needed to hear that until the words came out of Ben's mouth. It's like a giant weight has been lifted off my shoulders. "I love Hallie, but is it selfish of me to say I'm kind of glad she's not here right now? I've missed spending time with just you."

"Me too. Let's try to do more of that, yeah?"

"Definitely."

"Okay good. So, can I ask about your road trip now? Asher Hansley is in the kitchen literally baking a cake with mom, so I assume it went well."

I can't help the smile that spreads over my face. "Yeah Benj, it went well. But that's kind of the other thing I have to tell you. I wasn't exactly honest with everyone about the reason I went on the trip."

Ben smirks at me. "You mean you weren't honest about the absolutely no reason you gave any of us for why you left town for two weeks with a famous NFL quarterback? I'm extremely shocked."

I laugh a little. "The real reason is, right before I left with Asher, I had a massive panic attack."

Ben reaches out and takes one of my hands, saying nothing.

"I made a mistake with one of my clients, and it triggered the panic attack. Asher was at the office meeting with Emma and Jeremy about foundation stuff, and he found me on the floor. I thought I was dying but he talked me down from it. He wanted me to tell you and the girls, but I didn't want to. So, he told me that if I didn't come with him on his road trip he would tell you himself."

"He blackmailed you into getting in a car alone with him for two weeks?" Ben asks darkly.

"Simmer down Ben; your patriarchy is showing. Asher... saw things that no one else has seen. I have anxiety. Bad anxiety, pretty much all the time. I hide it all behind perfection and scary competence, but the truth is, I'm almost always anxious about something, and he saw through me from the very first time I met him at the gala. Him taking me on the trip was his way of getting me away from that part of me for a couple of weeks. And, well, it worked."

Ben blows out a breath. "I'll say. I'm not even going to tell you that you could have told me because it was yours to tell, and you don't owe anyone your feelings. But you look really happy, Jules. Like, happier than I've ever seen you before."

"That's because I am. It seems weird to say because it's only been two weeks, but I feel like a completely different person. Like everything has changed."

"Well, hasn't it?"

"Christ, no wonder Hallie loves you. You're one of the ones who sees everything too."

"Just the people I care about."

"I love him, Benj. I love him so damn much I can barely breathe, and I don't know how to hold the entire feeling inside of me. And I get it now. I totally, completely get it. How you and Hallie could happen so fast and everything could change completely in almost no time at all."

Ben grins at me. "Fucking crazy, isn't it?"

"Sure is. But also, kind of amazing? He sees me, all the way through, and I didn't realize how badly I needed to be seen. The way I love him? I didn't think I was capable of loving like this. I know without one single doubt that I am going to love him for the rest of my life. He's my other half."

"Juliette." I turn at Asher's voice and see him leaning against the doorway to the living room, emotion swimming in his eyes as he looks at me.

"Shit," I mutter. "How much of that did you hear?"

He doesn't answer, just strides towards me and pulls me up off the couch, crashing his mouth to mine and kissing me like we are extremely alone, and probably naked, and not two feet from my brother, with my mom in the kitchen down the hall.

When we break apart, he holds onto me for an extra few seconds, pressing a kiss to my forehead and wrapping an arm around me as we both turn to the couch where Ben is sitting, leg propped on his opposite knee and arms spread over the back of the couch, a shit eating grin on his face.

I point to him. "You shut up. Like I haven't caught you and Hallie making out in every corner of this house."

"We've done a lot more than that in a lot of those corners."

"Fucking gross, Ben. Why would you think I wanted that information?"

"Why would you think I wanted to see you making out with your...what is he exactly? Your boyfriend?"

"You know it," Asher says, giving Ben a grin and a thumbs up. "We're totally official. You can probably even see us kissing in the airport somewhere on the internet."

Ben gives me a quizzical look.

I sigh. "I had to prove to him I don't care about how famous he is and that I'm not going to run away just because some fan sticks a camera in my face, so I kissed him in the airport. Whatever. It's not that big of a deal."

"On the contrary, Juliette. It was a very, very big deal."

"I agree with him," Ben says. "Huge deal."

I look back and forth between them. "I'm not sure I like the two of you being friends."

"Too late, Jules. He's one of us now."

Asher pulls me tighter into his side. "Yeah, Juliette, I'm one of you now."

He sure is, and I don't hate it even a little bit.

Chapter Thirty-Nine
Asher

After dinner, Julie and I walk down the street towards my house hand in hand, in comfortable silence. The sky is clear and the air is cold, and the winter night wraps itself around us, and I'm happy. I'm so fucking happy.

I have always loved this neighborhood, but I'm not sure I had a full grasp on how lonely I've been here until I walked into the Parkers' house and was the opposite of that. Until Rachel hugged me like she's known me forever and we baked a cake together and I chatted with Steven about the plans for a new development his company is building downtown and I made plans with Ben to get together with the guys and Julie was by my side all night. No one asked me about the team or even talked about football.

I was one of them, like Ben said. Important to them because I'm important to Julie, and I have never experienced that kind of easy acceptance, outside of my own family. My phone dings, interrupting my thoughts, and I pull it out of my pocket. The message preview on the screen pierces my bubble of contentment and has my stomach churning.

COACH

Can you be at the stadium tomorrow at 9
a.m.? Doc can see you then.

I take a deep breath and let it out slowly, my breath misting out in the frigid air.

"You okay?" Julie asks, stopping me with a tug on my hand.

"It's my coach." Julie knows I texted him earlier today when we got back, telling him my shoulder had been bothering me since the end of the season and that I wanted to get it checked out. With her encouragement, I left it at that. I felt weird about leaving out the anti-inflammatory injections, but she cut through my attack of conscience in her logical, matter-of-fact way. My shoulder is what it is regardless of how I've been medicating it for the past few years. The injections don't change anything about what an MRI will show today. "He said the team doctor can see me tomorrow morning at nine."

"Don't think yet," Julie says. "Text him back and tell him yes before you think."

ME

Sure, I'll be there.

I pocket my phone with shaky hands. "Done."

"Okay." She takes my other hand and faces me on the sidewalk. "Now, tell me how you feel, if you want to."

"Scared." I give her my most honest truth. "I'm really fucking scared."

Julie nods at my answer. "It's okay to be scared. This is really scary."

I don't know why her saying that out loud eases some of the pressure in my chest, but it does.

"But like I told you when we were in Boulder, you're not alone. You have your family and now you have my family. And my friends—they're all your friends too. And you have me. I'm not going anywhere. Ever. I swear it. Whatever happens, we'll figure it out together."

Steeped in gratitude for her, her brilliant mind, and her unwavering support, I unwind my hands from hers and wrap my arms around her shoulders. She circles my waist and holds on tight.

"Thank you," I whisper.

"Always," she whispers back.

I pull back so I can see her face but keep my arms around her. She is so fucking beautiful I sometimes can't breathe when look at her.

"Well, I probably won't be able to sleep tonight, so want to go to bed and...not sleep with me?"

She gives me a wicked grin and presses her hips forward right into mine, where I was already hard and aching for her. "I would love to go to bed and not sleep with you, Hot Shot."

I lean forward and take her lips with mine, sweeping my tongue inside her mouth to taste her and anchoring one arm around her waist to press her harder into me as our mouths move together. A groan rumbles through my chest when she grinds against me, and her scent surrounds me. I could drown in her.

I pull away slightly, keeping my lips close to hers. "How fast can you walk? I need you naked and moaning my name in the next five minutes."

"Pretty fucking fast."

Three minutes later we crash into my bedroom, mouths locked together. I kick the door shut and press Julie against it, running my hands all over the delicious curves I couldn't feel through the winter coat she shed before we even walked through the front door. Grabbing the hem of her sweater, I pull it up, our mouths only separating so I can get it over her head, and then I tug off my own shirt before we dive back together. Anchoring her to the door with my hips, I slide my hands up her sides and yank down the cups of her bra, palming her breasts and circling her nipples with my thumbs before rolling them between my fingers. Julie lets out a throaty moan and grabs my hair in both hands, tugging as she deepens the kiss.

The sharp edge of pain has me a little wild, and I pull my lips away from hers so I can kiss and suck my way down her neck, grazing my teeth over her pulse and relishing her sharp intake of breath and the way she tugs my hair even harder. I drag my tongue across her collar bone before reaching around and unhooking her bra, tossing it away before I dip my head to suck one of her nipples in my mouth, pinching the other one between my fingers.

"Shit," Julie gasps, dropping her head back against the door. "That feels so good."

Looking up at her, I smirk at her swollen lips and the glazed expression in her eyes. "Baby, you haven't seen anything yet," I say, and I drop to my knees in front of her.

"I've always wanted a big, strong athlete on his knees for me," Julie says, tangling her fingers in my hair again.

"Have you, now?"

"Well, no, but now that I see you down there, it seems like something I should have swanted. I like you down there."

"I will worship you on my knees any chance I get, Juliette. Kneeling in front of you, seeing you look at me like that? It's my every fucking dream come true."

Without breaking eye contact, I unbutton her jeans and slide them down her legs, lifting one foot then the other, to free her from the pants, before slowly smoothing my hands up the outside of her legs, feeling her muscles quiver under my touch. Gripping her hips, I lean in and run my tongue over her belly from hip bone to hip bone, across the top of her underwear and then back again and she gasps, chest starting to rise and fall quickly.

"Asher. Touch me."

Her responsiveness has me leaking inside my boxers and I have to hold myself back from devouring her and burying my face in her cunt, feeling her clench around my fingers while she comes, fast and hard. There is a time for that, but this isn't it.

"Juliette, it's our first night together in my house, and I want to take my time with you. I want to hear every moan and sigh, feel your muscles shake, and watch you unravel for me over and over again. We are going to belong to each other in this room in every way imaginable and we're going to do it slowly because I want to remember every single thing about this night, for as long as I live."

"Fuck me. When did you become a poet?"

"The way I feel about you, Juliette? It is fucking poetry."

Draping one of her legs over my shoulder, I glide my tongue along the skin where her thigh meets her groin, dipping my tongue under the lace covering her pussy, tasting that sweet skin. I do it again and again, watching the wet spot on her underwear grow and breathing in the scent of her arousal, filling my senses with her while she lets out shuddery breaths. Without saying a word, I put her leg on the floor and hook my fingers in the sides of her underwear, sliding them down her legs. She kicks them aside and I put her leg right back on my shoulder. She is spread wide open above me, and I can see every inch of her, pink and glistening. Sliding a single finger through her slit, I circle her clit once, and then again, and she lets out another gasp and a strangled moan when I pull my hand away.

"You are so wet, Juliette. Fucking dripping for me. Should I lick it all up? Make you come on my tongue?"

"God, yes, please. Do that."

Spreading her with my fingers, I give her one long lick from opening to clit, lapping at her with my tongue while I slide a single finger inside her. I thrust my finger in and out while I keep moving my tongue over her clit with enough pressure to make her a little crazy, but not enough to tip her over the edge. I feel her legs start to shake and I smile against her, loving the feel of her coming apart for me.

"Oh my god, Asher, it's so good. You feel so good."

"You are fucking gorgeous, Juliette. Just looking at you makes me so hard. You want more?"

"Yes, please," she says, breathlessly, her eyes locked on mine

Without breaking eye contact, I slide a second finger inside her, rubbing my thumb side to side over her before I dive in, covering her pussy with my mouth and devouring her. She cries out when I suck and lick her clit, moving my fingers in and out of her, thrusting them deeper every time, hitting every inch of her. Julie's chest rises and falls like she can't get enough air and it makes me take her faster, curl my fingers to make her moan louder, shake harder. She grinds against my mouth, and I groan against her, loving the feel of her above me, taking what she needs. Wanting to feel her come apart on my tongue, I graze my teeth over her clit before sucking it into my mouth, pulsing my lips around her.

"Yes, Asher, right there. Don't stop. Please don't stop," she moans out, her eyes dark with pleasure.

"Never, baby," I rasp, sealing my lips back around her clit and swiping it with my tongue while I curl my fingers inside her as deep as I can, holding them there while I suck on her, hard, and that does it. She comes with a gush on my face, groaning out her release as her whole body trembles and her hands tighten on my head to steady herself. Her hips buck against my mouth and I stay with her while she rides wave after wave, licking up everything she gives me like it's my last damn meal.

When I feel her start to collapse against the door, I stand, lifting her with me. She wraps her legs around my waist, and I immediately cover her mouth with mine, kissing her deeply. My head spins, and I am right on the edge already just from making her come and feeling her mouth against mine. Without breaking the kiss, I walk us to my bed, laying her down so her head is resting on the pillows and covering her body with mine. I can feel her heart pounding as she tries to recover from her orgasm and every beat feels like proof that she's here. That she's mine. That we belong to each other. The emotion of it threatens to take me under. Needing a second to get myself under control, I stand, stripping off my jeans and boxers in one move. Seeing the way her eyes slide hungrily up and down my body has my cock twitching against my stomach, and I stand there, letting her look her fill.

"Come here." Julie's command is low and sultry and has my body moving before my brain engages. I slide back over her, and she parts her legs wider, letting me settle between them. My cock slides right against her hot core, still soaking wet from her orgasm, and when I glide against her clit, she hisses and tangles her hands in my hair. Pressing my forehead to hers, I roll my hips, moving my cock back and forth against her wet slit, coating myself in her while she writhes beneath me. Julie drops her hand from my hair and reaches between our bodies, wrapping her hand around me, gripping me tightly while she slides her hand up and down my shaft. When she rubs her thumb over my tip, collecting the bead of moisture there, I almost lose it.

"Juliette, I need to be inside you, right now."

"Well then what the fuck are you waiting for? Get inside me. Right now."

Supporting my weight on one arm, I reach between us and cover her hand with mine, lining myself up at her entrance and sliding just the tip of me inside her. Taking her hand away, I press our intertwined hands to the mattress above her head and fill her with a single flex of my hips. Our moans join together, hot breaths mingling as I take her mouth in a slow, sultry kiss while I tip my hips against hers, sliding even deeper inside her in a way that has us both gasping. When I'm as deep inside her as I can get, I pull out all the way to the tip and thrust back in, feeling her walls clench around me.

With one of my hands still intertwined with Julie's and my weight on my other forearm, I drop my head to her breast, sucking her nipple into my mouth and laving it with my tongue while I roll my hips against her. The salty taste of her skin makes me feral for more, and I suck harder, rolling her nipple with my tongue. She lets out a strangled moan and palms the back of my head, holding me to her while her hips rise up to meet mine. I switch sides, capturing her other nipple in my mouth and sucking gently while I angle my hips so I hit her clit every time I move back inside her.

"Oh my god," she moans, as I pick up my pace. "I'm so close."

"You want it, Juliette? You want to come again?"

"Yes, god, yes. I need it. Please," she groans.

The sight of her beneath me, face flushed with pleasure, eyes dark, and blonde hair spread over my pillow like a halo makes my wide-open heart crack open even wider, spilling out love for her.

"Look at you," I rasp, keeping my thrusts steady, holding her right on the edge. "Spread out under me, telling me what you need. I want to give you everything. Wrap those gorgeous legs around me, pretty girl, and let me give it to you." Her eyes flash and she does what I say, locking her heels behind my back and bucking up against me, meeting me thrust for thrust until she comes on a long, low moan, dropping her head back on the pillow and closing her eyes as the pleasure washes over her.

"Open those eyes, Juliette. Look at me."

When she does, I lean down, capturing her mouth in a long, slow kiss, still feeling her clench around me with the aftershocks of her orgasm. "I'm so proud of you for coming twice for me. You did so well, baby. You're going to give me one more before we're done," I say, grinding my hips against hers right over her clit.

"Asher, I can't," she gasps, lifting her hips to meet mine.

Her body's response to mine has me feral for more. "You can and you will. Trust me, Juliette. We're coming together."

Pulling out of her, I flip her over onto her stomach, kissing my way up her back, sucking gently on the soft points of her spine and down again before I grip her hips and pull them up so she's on her knees, then sliding inside her from behind.

"*Asher*," she whispers, urgently. "Fuck. You're so deep. I can feel you everywhere."

I pull out and thrust back inside her, and the feel of her pussy gripping me has pleasure shooting up my limbs. "That's what I want, Juliette. I want you to feel me everywhere. I want your body to memorize what it feels like when I'm inside you. No one else will ever make you feel this way. Only me."

"Only you," she moans, arching her back and pushing her hips to meet mine as I rock into her, staring down, mesmerized at the sight of my dick sliding in and out of her. Marking her. I drop wet kisses to her shoulder while I reach around and palm her breasts, rolling her nipples between my fingers, and her breath quickens.

"It's so good, Ash. Oh my god," she gasps out.

I pull out and slam back inside her at the same time I pinch both her nipples. The hottest fucking sound I have ever heard comes from her chest, and suddenly it's not enough to hear her sounds. I want to feel every single one of them. Wrapping an arm around her chest, I pull her up so we're both kneeling on the bed, Julie's back against my chest, her head against my shoulder, and her hot breath in my ear.

"I need you, Ash. I've never needed anyone, but I need you. Make me yours. Please. I'm yours."

The pleading words and raw openness from this strong, fiercely independent, and often guarded woman are gasoline poured on the fire licking through my veins. My entire body ignites. I slide one hand up to grip her throat and move the other down to her clit, rubbing circles as I start to move inside her again. The sound she makes has my rock-hard cock hardening even more and my strokes speeding up, deepening, so she feels every inch of me inside her, and I feel every inch of her as she grips my dick. I fucking love it. I'm addicted to the way her pussy hugs my cock, like we were made to fit together. Two parts of a whole. Julie turns her head so our gazes meet, and what I see in her eyes has my heart thrashing in my chest.

"Kiss me, Ash."

I crash my mouth to hers in a kiss that is hot and wet and completely fucking filthy. My tongue slides against hers while I press harder against her clit, loving how she gasps into my mouth while our bodies move together. She reaches up, locking an arm around my neck, pressing us together even closer before rasping "Harder, Ash" into my ear.

"Anything, Juliette," I grit out, before pulling out and slamming back into her, over and over again, tightening my hand around her neck and sliding her clit between two fingers, strumming it in time with my thrusts.

Her breath quickens, and I feel her walls start to flutter around me. Electricity zips up my spine and I know I won't be able to hold on much longer, but I'll be goddamned if she doesn't come again before I do. I am all pleasure and sensation and wide-open heart, so when I open my mouth, the words tumble out in a stream of feelings and emotion that I have no way to control and wouldn't even if I could. Julie Parker owns me, mind, body, and soul. It's enormous and wild and absolutely inevitable.

"I love you. My hearts beats for you. I fucking *breathe* for you. Come for me, Juliette. You're mine. Come for me and take me with you. Make me yours."

"I love you, Ash. I'm yours. You'll always be mine."

Her words burrow right into my soul and have me immediately, desperately, on the edge. I angle my hips, so I hit her g-spot when I thrust back in and pinch her clit at the same time. She explodes around me, screaming my name and clenching around my dick so tightly it only takes two more thrusts before pleasure takes over my body and my vision blurs around the edges. I come harder than I have ever come in my life, groaning into her neck and spilling inside her as my hips jerk against hers before slowing, rolling gently as we both come down.

When the pleasure ebbs, we collapse down onto the bed. I reach out and pull Julie to me, her back to my front, wrapping both arms around her, needing to keep her close, feeling emotionally wrung out by what just happened. She must feel the same because she presses closer, wrapping both her arms around mine and snuggling deeper into me.

"So, that was..." her voice is a little shaky, and it trails off before she finishes her sentence.

I press a kiss to her shoulder, her neck, and finally to the side of her head, tightening my arms around her. "I know, baby. For me too."

"I know you know this, but I feel like I have to say it again. It's never been like this for me. Never. You make me feel... everything."

My chest tightens with emotion at her vulnerability. It will never not feel like a gift when she opens herself up to me. "It's never been like this for me either. You make me feel everything too."

"I love you," she whispers. "So, so much."

I rest my forehead against her shoulder, breathing her in, feeling my heartrate calm. "I love you too, Juliette."

Her breathing starts to slow, and I know she's close to sleep. I reach down and drag the comforter over both of us then tangle us back together, laying one of my legs over hers. With my arms securely around her, and our bodies as close as they can be, I follow her into a deep, dreamless sleep.

Chapter Forty
Asher

I know I'm alone in bed before I even open my eyes. After weeks of waking up wrapped around a soft body, it's Julie's absence that rouses me. I roll over and peer at the bathroom, but it's empty and dark. Then I hear it. Her murmured voice, the clanging of a pan, the refrigerator door opening and closing. I smile into the dim morning light, enjoying the sounds of her moving around my house. It sounds like home.

Pushing myself out of bed, I stretch and wince at the ache in my shoulder. The stab of pain is a cattle prod to my brain, and I immediately remember what today is. My appointment with the team doctor. Almost certainly an MRI of my shoulder. The day all the unknowns become known. Or at least less unknown. The day that will, almost certainly, determine the future of my career. Or possibly the end of it. After last night, I thought I was prepared, but the anxiety churning in my gut tells me that I was wrong.

Needing to not be alone with my thoughts, I use the bathroom and brush my teeth before pulling on a pair of joggers and heading downstairs to see what my girl is up to. When I get to the kitchen, she's standing at the stove with her back to me, a spatula in one hand and a dish towel in the other, a pan full of vegetables sitting on the unlit stove. Her phone is pressed between her ear and her shoulder, and one of my t-shirts skims her thighs. The sight of her in my kitchen, wearing my clothes and doing...whatever it is she's doing with the vegetables that look like someone took a hatchet to them chases away my morning angst and has warmth spreading right through me.

"Wait, how long do these vegetables need to cook before I pour in the eggs?" She pauses, listening to whoever is on the other end of the phone.

"Fuck off, Ben. *Until they're done* isn't helpful. Give it to me in minutes. You know I don't work well in abstractions." I snicker and walk to her, wrapping my arms around her waist from behind and bending to kiss her neck. She relaxes back into me at the same time she lets out an exasperated sigh.

"Well, I would like to thank you for being absolutely no help at all. Don't come to me the next time you need help figuring out a contract for the bar. Your days of free legal advice are over." She hits the screen to end the call and tosses the phone onto the counter before turning around in my arms. With her hair piled up on her head and her face scrubbed clean, she looks so damn cute that I lean in and kiss her nose.

"Whatcha doing, Juliette?"

She looks a little embarrassed. "Trying to make breakfast."

"But you hate cooking."

"I know, but I remember you telling me about your lucky game day breakfast your mom used to make for you when you were in high school and how you make it for yourself now. I know it's not a game day, but it is a pretty important day where you could use a little luck, so I thought I would try and make it for you. Except when I got down here, I remembered I hate cooking because I suck at it. And I hate sucking at things. So, I called Ben who is, like, the breakfast king, and he was no help even though he makes omelets for Hallie every damn morning. Why is it so hard to tell me how long to cook a pepper for?"

I chuckle, then cup her neck with one hand and tip her head up, bringing my mouth to hers in a long, slow, dizzying kiss. When we break apart, Julie looks marginally less disgruntled.

"Okay, I mean, I don't think I deserve a reward when I can't even make breakfast like a regular human, but there are worse ways than that to start a morning."

I wink at her, taking the spatula from her hand, setting it on the counter, and slinging the dish towel over my bare shoulder.

"So damn hot," Julie mumbles.

Grinning, I guide her to one of the barstools that line the kitchen island, sit her down on it, and rest my hands on the island on either side of her, caging her in. "I can think of about ten better ways to start a morning than that, but they all involve you being naked in my bed and, sadly, we don't have time for that just now. But we do have time for breakfast, which I'll make. Ben isn't the only breakfast king."

Julie's face brightens. "Does that mean you'll make me breakfast every morning like Ben does for Hallie? That smug queen comes waltzing into the office every morning, caffeinated and well fed and totally sexed up and it's beneath me to be jealous of that, but you know what?"

I grin at her, loving morning, playful Julie. "You're jealous of that?"

She points a finger right at my chest. "Bet your ass I am."

"Juliette, I will keep you so caffeinated, well fed, and sexed up that even Hallie herself will be green with envy."

"If this is what having a boyfriend is like, I should have gotten one forever ago."

"Fuck no you shouldn't have. No boyfriends unless they're me."

She gives me a sly smile. "I love it when you talk jealous to me."

"I'll give you jealous." I lean in and kiss her neck, before latching on with my teeth, biting gently and growling into her skin, relishing the warmth and smell of her.

"Okay!" she laughs. "I think I was promised breakfast."

"At your service," I say, "but I'll caffeinate you first."

"Oh, I figured that out myself." She points to a half full coffee mug I missed. "Googled the instructions to the espresso machine when I woke up."

"You figured out that monstrosity but had to call Ben to ask how to cook a pepper?"

She shrugs. "Yeah, so?"

I just look at her, awed by all of her complexities and contradictions, hoping that I get to learn something new about her every day. "I adore you."

"Yeah, yeah, I adore you too, but you need your lucky breakfast, and I'm starving too."

"I'm a slave for you, Juliette."

I pull back and give her one last kiss on the forehead before I circle the island. I flick on the burner under the pan then open a cabinet, grabbing a glass and filling it with ice before pressing it against the Dr. Pepper dispenser. Then I open the drawer with her peppermint Hershey Kisses in them and toss her a couple, which she catches handily and with a smile. I grab a handful of gummy worms from the drawer below for myself.

She studies me as she unwraps the candy. "Are you nervous about today? That's probably a stupid question—of course you're nervous about today. But I want to give you the space to talk about it if you want to."

I lean against the island opposite her and absently trace circles around her wrist while I consider what she said and decide to give her the full truth of it. "I'm not nervous. I'm fucking terrified." She nods, like she expected this answer, but doesn't say anything, giving me the time to collect my thoughts.

"They could tell me my playing days are over."

She rests a hand over mine. "They could."

Somehow, her frank agreement does more to calm my nerves than if she had tried to slap a happy face on this and tell me everything is going to be okay.

"I don't know how it's going to go or what they'll find, and it's the unknown that's getting to me. I wish I could fast forward time to tonight when I'll at least know one way or another."

"Well, I can't fast forward time, but I can come back here after work, if you want that."

"I want," I say immediately. "I don't know what's going to happen today, but what I do know for sure is I want you here at the end of it, no matter what it is."

"Then I'll be here."

"Thank you," I lift her hand, kissing her palm before standing to check the stove.

"Ash," she says, before I can turn all the way around.

I lean back down against the counter, and she takes my hand in hers. "Whatever happens, I'm here, okay?"

I wonder if she can see the hearts shooting out of my eyes. "Juliette, I love you madly."

"I love you too," she says, reaching over and stealing one of my gummy worms.

"I love you so much I won't even be salty that you took my last red one."

She smirks at me. "It was right there and it's the best flavor; what do you expect?"

"Baby, you can eat all my red gummy worms from now until eternity."

"You really do love me."

I lift her hand, kissing her knuckles this time. "You honestly have no idea."

This time I do turn back to the stove with a lightness in my chest that wasn't there five minutes ago, and I owe every ounce of it to her.

"Sorry it took so long, Asher."

I'm sitting in Doc's office, my knee bouncing up and down. My palms are sweating, and my heart is beating so fast I'm legitimately afraid it might break a rib. I'm sure my blood pressure is high enough that there's a non-zero chance I'll stroke out right here on the floor and then it won't matter whether my shoulder is fucked or not.

"No problem. I appreciate you coming in today," I say, amazed at how calm my voice sounds when I am freaking the fuck out on the inside.

"It's no problem at all," he says, his face giving nothing away as he sits down, waking up his computer and typing in his password. He clicks around, pulling up an image and spinning the monitor around to face me. I've been around the league long enough to sort of know what I'm looking at. It's an MRI of my shoulder, but that's the extent of my understanding. I suddenly wish fervently that radiology had been a part of pre-med.

"Okay, so this is the MRI we did of your shoulder this

morning." He uses his pen to point to a spot on the image. "This is your joint. Now, in a healthy joint, we typically see what looks almost like a cushion between the bones. That's cartilage, and it helps the parts of your bone move easily against each other. What we see on your MRI here is that the cushion is completely gone, which means your bones are essentially grinding against each other every time you move your shoulder, causing substantial inflammation and, likely, a lot of your pain."

He points to another part of the image. "And here you have a number of bone spurs, leading to joint swelling. What we are looking at here is extremely advanced arthritis. You mentioned earlier that you have been in pain since the hit you took in the last playoff game, but what I'm seeing on this MRI, and the results of the range-of-motion tests you did earlier, leads me to believe that you have been in pain for a great deal longer than that. Am I correct?"

His eyes are kind, and I don't have it in me to lie, so I nod. "Yes," I say, my voice gravelly.

He nods in understanding and doesn't ask me exactly how long I've been in pain. I can see he already knows, based on the MRI, and my stomach sinks.

He turns the screen back around and leans forward, resting his arms on his desk. "Asher, I have been working with professional athletes for a very long time and rarely, in all my years, have I seen a player with a greater love for the game than you. You are one of the most dedicated athletes I have ever had the privilege to know, and I wish more than anything I could tell you that you have a long career ahead of you. But based on these scan results and the results of your physical..."

"Just tell me," I interrupt him, not able to sit still much longer without knowing the full truth of it. Then I take a deep breath, scrubbing my shaking hands over my face. "Sorry. I'm so sorry, Doc. I didn't mean to snap. I just need to know."

"Asher, your playing days are over."

I feel the force of his words like a full body impact. My breath wheezes out of my lungs, and I struggle to take in oxygen. Dropping my head forward between my shoulders, I squeeze my eyes shut, trying to get my body under control, forcing myself to stay seated when my ears ring and my fight or flight instinct screams at me to get up and flee. To outrun this bombshell until it ceases to exist. I wish fervently that I was still in my kitchen laughing while Julie tries to steal my gummy worms instead of sitting in this office while the death knell of the career that has been the driving force for most of my life reverberates off the walls.

I take a jagged breath and force words up my throat. "There's no chance I can play again?"

"Asher I'm honestly surprised you're not in agonizing, debilitating pain all day every day. Your shoulder is a mess, and your range-of-motion is limited enough that I'm shocked you threw as well as you did in your final game."

Final game. I have played my final football game. I can't grasp the enormity of that fact.

"Without the repetitive motion of constantly throwing a football, and with physical therapy, you should get your range of motion back and limit your pain. But it's likely that at some point in the future you are going to need surgery on your shoulder. Potentially a full joint replacement. I can't clear you to play in this condition. No doctor would. And unfortunately, arthritis, while manageable, is irreversible. I'm so sorry, son. I wish I had better news."

I sit there, harsh, ragged breaths tearing out of me, my head spinning from the news and, likely, from lack of oxygen. The ringing in my ears gets louder and louder until I have a full-blown fire alarm blaring in my head. Sweat drips down my back and my heart pounds and it suddenly feels like the walls are closing in, squeezing me on all sides. I stand quickly, wavering a bit before I get my balance.

"Thanks, Doc," I manage. "I'll be in touch about the PT and all that."

Then I rush out of his office, blindly making my way out of the stadium, praying to a god I don't even believe in to take me anywhere but here.

Chapter Forty-One
Julie

"Jules," Molly squeals when I walk through the front door of the office. "Hallie, Em, she's here," Molly yells up the stairs before throwing her arms around me and squeezing. She hasn't let go yet when Hallie and Emma come barreling down the stairs, joining our hug so that all four of us are wrapped together in the entryway of the office. In the circle of my friends' familiar arms, it hits me how much I missed them, and how grateful I am that I have this to return to. I have anchors all around me, I realize suddenly. It's long past time I start using them.

"Missed you," Hallie whispers.

"Missed you more," I whisper back. She leans her head on my shoulder, and I am really, truly home.

We all pull apart and Molly studies my face carefully, her hands on my shoulders.

"You look happy, Jules," she says. "Really, really happy."

Her voice is quiet, a little serious. It's uncharacteristic of her, and a little jarring that my happiness is the first thing she commented on instead of demanding the details about all the sex I'm having.

"I am happy," I say simply, because it's the absolute truth.

"I'm really glad." There is something in her eyes, an expression on her face I don't quite understand. For as close as we all are, and as outgoing as she is, there's a part of Molly that stays walled off from us. A tiny piece of her she protects. Once, early in our first year of law school and soon after the four of us became friends, we all got drunk on tequila at some random dive bar, and Molly let it slip that she was still heartbroken over her college boyfriend who broke up with her late in their senior year. I will never forget the haunted look in her eyes when she mentioned his name. That was the only time she ever voluntarily brought him up, and the few times one of us has asked about him over the years, she clams up immediately and gets that same look in her eyes. She never talks about it, and she also never dates seriously, and it doesn't take a genius to realize that those two things are linked.

Emma must see what I see because she slips an arm around Molly's waist and gives her a squeeze before we all migrate to the kitchen, taking our usual spots around the island, Hallie next to me on one side and Emma and Molly on the other. Donuts and coffee are already laid out. Looks like they were serious about a breakfast story and, for probably the first time in my entire adult life, I'm not anxious or antsy about getting to work or making a list of all the things I need to accomplish on my first day back in the office in two weeks. All I want to do is sit here with my friends and eat donuts and talk.

"Heads up, Hal." Molly tosses a bag at Hallie, no doubt with a maple donut inside. Hallie loves them, and we hate how they make every other donut taste like maple, so she gets hers in a separate bag. Just one of a million tiny details that make up the tapestry of our years-long friendship.

"Jules." Molly gestures to me with a chocolate donut in her hand. "I think you have some things to tell us."

"Yeah, no shit," Emma says. "Spill it, Jules."

"Hold on." Hallie speaks through a mouthful of maple cream. "First, I think we need to have a moment of acknowledgement and appreciation for the fact that Julie has been in this office for five minutes already and is now sitting at the table, eating a donut, and has not asked about work one single time. She spent two weeks away and hasn't demanded a progress report on her clients or asked what any of us are working on. That has to be some kind of record."

I shrug a shoulder. "There's time for that later." And I know there will be. I haven't turned into an entirely different person. Work will always be important to me, and it will always be important to me to be good at it. To give my clients the best service I'm capable of. I love being a lawyer, and it's a big part of who I am. But what I understand now that I didn't two weeks ago is that I don't have to give it *all* of me. And that's the most critical difference. Sitting here on a Monday morning having donuts with my friends instead of downing my fourth cup of coffee while I work, my entire body humming with anxiety, feels like a revelation. "You guys seem to have held it all together while I was gone."

"And we did it with style." Molly points at me. "Now spill, Jules."

I wonder for a second where to begin and decide to just tell the whole truth of it. "I think it was the best two weeks of my entire life."

All three of them stare at me.

"Better than the day you found out you got an Elle Woods level score on your LSATs?" Hallie asks.

I open my mouth to answer but Emma interrupts. "Better than when you posted that picture on Instagram of your scarily perfect handwritten law school notes that went weirdly viral and that company sent you a lifetime supply of notebooks and pens?"

Molly jumps in again before I have a chance to respond to that. "Better than the day you found out you beat that asshole Joe Thompson's GPA by less than a tenth of a point and edged him out for valedictorian of our law school class?"

"Yes," I laugh. "Better than all of those things. It was..." I pause, not sure what to say next. "He is..." I try again. Then I think, fuck it. "He's everything."

"You love him." Molly says it matter of factly, like she's telling us the sky is blue.

"Are you psychic or something?" asks Hallie. "I remember another conversation about six months ago that went a whole lot like this."

Molly shrugs. "I see what I see. You love him, don't you?"

Fuck it, I think. These are my most important people. "I do."

Hallie reaches over and squeezes my hand, and I give her a smile, grateful for the support.

"He's one of the best people I have ever known. He's kind and patient and funny and really, really fun. He loves his family and bakes cookies and cried when he met his new nephew. And he gets me. Like, really, really gets me, all the way through. He understands things about me that I didn't even understand about myself, and I think he has since the first time we met at the gala in July. It seems weird to say because I didn't think I believed in shit like this, but it feels like he was made just for me. Knowing him for two days or two decades wouldn't matter. He's meant to be mine."

"Fuck, Jules." Molly sniffles and wipes her eyes with a napkin. "I definitely didn't have cry at Julie's love confession on my to do list today."

"It's not weird." Emma speaks with conviction. "Like I told Hallie months ago, love and feelings come when they come. And some people are just meant for us. I understand how it would be harder for you to accept it, though. You love spreadsheets and logic and to-do lists and plans. Feelings are chaos."

I huff out a laugh. "They sure are. But I think I might be getting better at learning to live with a little chaos. I'll never get rid of my spreadsheets because, spreadsheets, yum. But I think maybe I'm a little more okay with everything not lining up in perfect columns. And actually, there's something I need to tell you all before I lose my nerve. The actual reason I went on Asher's road trip."

"Finally!" Hallie says. "I thought we would have to get you drunk to get it out of you."

I take a deep breath and tell them everything about the panic attack and Asher finding me on the floor of my office and suggesting the road trip.

"That was my first panic attack, but I'm anxious, like, all the time. I worry about everything and pretend I don't. And I try and control everything because if I do, then I don't have to worry about something going wrong. I hate half my clothes because they're too perfect to sit in. I hate my house because I tried to make it so perfect that I forgot to make it comfortable. And, until Asher, I never even had an actual orgasm I didn't give myself because I couldn't relax enough with another person to let it happen. I'm basically a mess, and, well, I just thought you should know."

There's a pause, and then Hallie wraps me in a one-armed side hug.

"Thank you for telling us," Hallie says. "It must have been really exhausting for you to put on that façade all these years. I'm sorry I never noticed when you were having a hard time."

I take another deep breath, and this time, when I let it out, it feels like I breathe out a weight I've been carrying for years. "It really has. But don't be sorry. There was no way for you to know. I papered over it with color coded spreadsheets and a perfect wardrobe."

"It's a relief, you know," Molly chimes in. "That you're normal. We're all kind of a mess, Jules. We all hide it to varying degrees, some better than others. I think it keeps us interesting."

"And tell us, okay?" Emma reaches across the island and lays a hand over mine. "When you're struggling. When you need one of us to carry some of your weight. We did it when you went away, and everything was fine. We're a team in this office, and we're friends always."

"I will. I think sometimes it served me. Like, I did really well in law school and was always at the top of my associate class. But, somewhere in there, I got the idea that I had to do everything perfectly, and the whole thing kind of took on a life of its own. But the last two weeks..." I trail off, wondering how I can possibly summarize the last two weeks and do them justice.

"They were kind of a revelation. Asher had a plan, but it changed all the time. We would see a billboard for something ridiculous, and then next thing I knew, we were driving fifty miles out of the way to see a cow made of butter or a giant ball of rubber bands. We played road trip games and ate a million pounds of peppermint Hershey Kisses and gummy candy, and I literally howled at the moon. And after the first day, I barely even thought about work. It was like once I powered down my brain, it was too overworked and exhausted to come back online and it ended up being exactly what I needed. He is exactly what I needed."

Emma squeezes my hand. "I'm really happy for you, Jules."

"So, what happens now that you're back?" Molly asks.

"Now we're going to be together for real, every day, not just on the road making stops to see giant barbershop poles and the world's largest taco. I went to his house when we got back and you're never going to believe this, but he lives five houses down from my parents."

Hallie laughs. "That's a weird coincidence. That's your favorite street in the city."

"It is. And his house is amazing. It's big, but it's comfortable and happy. You can feel it the second you walk in the door. I loved it."

"What about the fame thing?" Emma looks concerned when she asks. "I'm sure no one cared who he was on the road, but here he's, like, the most recognizable face in the city. Maybe it's not as bad in the offseason, but when pre-season starts this summer, he'll be back in the spotlight."

My stomach tightens, thinking of Asher at the stadium, wondering what's going on and whether he will, in fact, be playing come pre-season. I wish I could talk to my friends about it, but it's not mine to tell.

"He actually got recognized the second we got off the plane. It was sweet; a little boy asked him to take a picture. After that, there were cameras pointed at us everywhere and he panicked for a second thinking that I would freak and run, but it turns out I actually don't care about that at all. He's the same guy whether the cameras are pointed at him or not. So, to prove it, I made out with him in the airport. The pictures are probably all over the internet right now."

I've barely stopped speaking when all three of my friends whip out their phones and start typing madly.

"Holy shit, Jules." Molly gapes at her screen. "You look amazing, and it looks like that man can *kiss*."

"Yes, he is very talented in that area. And...other areas."

Hallie snorts out a laugh. "I just bet he is. I bet he's another guy whose mouth could win awards."

"Yes, he and Ben seem to have that in common," I say dryly, still icked out I have that information about my twin brother.

"I could use an award-winning mouth on me," mutters Emma. "It's been too fucking long."

Molly slides her a look. "I can think of a certain ex-hockey player who I'm sure would volunteer as tribute. I bet his mouth can do amazing things."

"Oh, it can," mumbles Emma, her voice so low I'm not sure I heard her right.

Molly seems to have heard just fine because she gapes at Emma. "Is there something you'd like to share with the class, Emma, love?"

Emma looks startled, like she didn't realize she said that out loud. "Definitely not."

There's an air of finality to her voice, and I think we all tacitly agree not to press her, even though I'm curious as fuck.

"Okay, well if Emma isn't sharing, Jules, it looks like you're still in the hot seat." Hallie grins. "We are going to need so many more details. Like, what was your safe word? Tell us more about the head off the bed situation."

"Yeah, I really need to know about the mechanics of that," says Emma, looking relieved to be off the hook.

"It's the best way to give a blow job. Really opens up the throat." I think she's joking, but when I look at Molly, she's dead ass serious and it makes me laugh.

With laughter in the room and my best friends by my side, I settle in for story time, happy to be home.

Chapter Forty-Two
Julie

My phone pings, stealing my attention away from the documents I'm reviewing. I glance at the clock on my computer and see that it's already after four. Picking up my phone, I smile when I see the message is from Asher.

The text bubbles start jumping again as if he's typing something else, but then they disappear. *Shit.* My stomach sinks and my fingers start tapping out a rhythm on my leg. It's not until this moment that I realize there is a big part of me that was optimistic the doctor would tell Asher his shoulder is fixable, even though every logical instinct I have told me otherwise. I have trusts to review, and I've only been through half of the emails I missed while I was away, but nothing feels more urgent than getting to Asher.

ME

I'm leaving the office now. I'll be there soon.

ASHER

Don't rush.

But I do rush. I shove some files into my bag, grab my laptop from my desk, and am out of my office thirty seconds later. I stop in the entry way to grab my coat from the closet and am shoving my arms into the sleeves when Hallie trots down the stairs.

"You're leaving already? You really have changed."

"I'm going to Asher's. He had a rough day and I want to be there."

Hallie's face immediately turns sympathetic. "I hope everything is okay."

I want to tell her everything. About Asher's appointment with the doctor and the likelihood that he has played his last NFL game, and how the uncertainty of it all is making my stomach churn with an anxiety that has been largely absent for the past week or so. But none of this is mine to tell.

"I hope so too, Hal. I'm worried about him, and I don't want him to be alone."

Hallie puts her arms around me. "He's lucky to have you, Jules."

"Fuck yes, he is. I'm lucky too. He's one of the best people I know."

"I like seeing you like this. You're still you, but you shine brighter."

"He makes me feel like I can do anything. You understand, right?"

Hallie smiles, glancing down at the ring on her finger, and I know she's thinking of Ben. "I do."

I give her another quick hug before picking my bag up from where I dumped it on the floor. "I have to go."

"Text me later, okay? Just tell me how everything is."

"I will," I say, heading out and closing the door behind me.

Fifteen minutes later I'm pulling into Asher's driveway. As I make my way to the house, I wonder if I should knock on the door or walk right in. Knocking feels weird but walking right in also doesn't feel quite right and what a ridiculous thing to think about, but I guess I am who I am no matter what and there's a kind of comfort in that. Asher saves me the trouble of deciding when he opens the door just as I'm approaching.

We stand there looking at each other for a beat. He looks exhausted, and I see immediately that it's his eyes where his pain lies. His gorgeous sky-blue eyes are shattered and devastated, and there's something else in them too that I don't quite understand, and it breaks my heart to see him this way. This kind, funny, loving, laid-back man should never look this broken. I take two steps forward and put my arms around him right in the doorway of his house. He wraps his arms around my waist and holds tight, burying his face in my neck. I hear his rasping, shuddery breaths in my ear and his back heaves like he is trying desperately to hold himself together.

"Let it go, Ash," I whisper in his ear. "It's okay."

As quickly as he grasped onto me, he pulls away, shaking his head. "I can't. Not right now."

He turns on his heel and walks back to the kitchen. I freeze for a second at his uncharacteristic withdrawal but then follow him. In the kitchen, he grabs a glass and fills it with ice, pressing against the Dr. Pepper dispenser. Lost in thought, he doesn't notice the glass is full until it's overflowing onto the counter.

"Shit," he mutters, staring at the puddle that's starting to stream onto the floor. Walking over to him, I gently grasp his arm, tugging him away from the mess. He comes willingly. I take him to the sunroom off the kitchen, guiding him to the couch.

"Sit, Ash, okay? I'll handle the kitchen."

I turn to walk back to the kitchen, but he grabs my hand to stop me, pulling me back towards him. He lifts my hand to his mouth and presses a kiss to my knuckles, looking up at me through his lashes.

"Thank you," he whispers, his voice gravelly, as if just pushing those words up through his throat is painful. I lean down and cup his face in my hands, kissing his forehead and both of his cheeks before smoothing his hair away from his face like my mom used to do to Ben and me when we were sad. It's a gesture of comfort that seems to have the desired effect when Asher leans into my hands, closing his eyes and taking a deep breath.

"Always. Anything. I'll be right back, okay?"

He nods, and I go back to the kitchen, cleaning up the spilled soda and filling a new glass. I carry it back to the sunroom and hand it to him before sitting sideways on the couch so I can face him, my legs tucked under me. He takes a long sip and sets the glass on the coffee table, turning so he can face me too, one leg on the floor and the other bent against the cushions. He's not ready to break; I can see that. I understand that better than anyone. I'll be here when he is, but for now, I ask him the question I would want someone to ask me if I had just been given life-altering news and wasn't ready to deal with the emotional part of it.

"Do you want to tell me what happened?" I keep my voice even, matter of fact, and I know it's the right move because he takes a deep breath, dropping his head down, and starts to talk without making eye contact.

"There were so many tests. Blood work, range-of-motion, other ones I don't know the names of. I met with a physical therapist, a trainer, the doctor, and my coach. When you're a starting quarterback saying words like *pain in my throwing arm*, it makes everyone nervous, so they check everything. Then they brought me down for an MRI. There is actually an MRI machine right in the stadium. Makes for easier scans and results to diagnose injuries during and right after games. I went from the MRI right to the team doctor's office, and even though I probably only had to wait for a few minutes, it felt like hours. When he came in, he started talking about how I was one of the most dedicated athletes he has ever known, and I couldn't listen to any of that. I knew what was coming next and listening to everything he was saying to try and cushion the blow was fucking torture. I snapped at him. I hate that I did that. I never snap at anyone, but I felt like I was about to jump out of my skin. I told him to just say it. So, he did. He said..."

Asher cuts himself off suddenly, breathing hard. It kills me to see him like this, so I reach over and take his hand in mine, and he grips it like a lifeline, looking up at me for the first time since he started talking. His eyes are a little wild, panicky, like saying out loud what he is about to say will make it true. Make it real.

I nod at him, squeezing his hand. "Just say it fast."

"I have arthritis in my shoulder. It's bad. Really bad, and it's not going to get better. I can't play anymore. My football career is over."

His words tumble out in a rush and then he sucks in a breath and rubs his free hand over his heart, as if speaking those words out loud broke it in half. And I understand now the look in his eyes when he met me at the door. Grief. Asher is grieving and he probably doesn't even know it. And I didn't know until this minute that it was possible to actually feel another person's pain as if it were my own. Asher's grief is a living, breathing thing, sitting right in this room with us.

In the face of this enormous shift, my lawyer brain is doing the thing it does when I get complicated information. Parsing through it. Breaking it down into its parts. Making a mental list of missing facts. Finding a solution. Making a plan. It's habit. Instinct. As natural to me as breathing. Which is why my next words come out without me considering them first.

"So, what happens now?"

I know immediately it's the absolute wrong thing to say. Asher looks at me blankly for a few seconds, then drops my hand and pushes up from the couch, pacing the length of the sunroom with his hands clasped behind his head. After a few lengths of the floor, he turns back to me.

"I don't know. I have no idea what to do next. We didn't get that far. As soon as the doctor told me I was done playing, I just left. I couldn't be there anymore. I don't know what I'm supposed to do now. No one told me. I didn't stick around long enough. My phone has been ringing a lot." He gestures over to the kitchen island where I can see his phone lighting up with a call.

"I haven't looked at it though. I guess I need to talk to my coach. And tell the team. Unless someone will do that for me. I don't want to do it. Or maybe I do. I don't fucking know. I need to tell..." He trails off, eyes glossing over.

"I need to tell my family." His voice cracks on the last word and his breath hitches. He drops his head, pressing his thumb and forefinger to the bridge of his nose, no doubt to stem the flood of emotion trying to pour out of him.

"I can't," he says, shaking his head.

"You can't what?" I ask gently, trying to break him out of his spiral.

"I can't do this now. I'm not ready. I know you want to talk about what happens now, what the plan is. You're so fucking good at making a plan, Juliette. But I can't. Not yet. I'm not ready for a plan. I think..." He stops, collecting his thoughts.

"I think I need to be alone. I'm not good company tonight and I just...I think it would be better if I was by myself right now. The last thing I would ever want to do would be to snap at you like I snapped at the doctor or say or do anything to upset you. This is my worst nightmare, Juliette. I've been trying to avoid this exact thing for four years and now that it's here..." He trails off again, face contorted in pain.

"I've never been here before. I don't know what it's going to look like while I process this. It's not a good idea for anyone to be around me. Nobody could possibly understand how I feel right now. I barely understand how I feel right now." His tone is exasperated. Lonely. He is all alone on this island of pain and grief without a single person who can relate.

"I need time to get myself right, and I want to protect you from that. Please." He looks at me, his eyes pleading with me to understand.

I can feel my anxiety creep in at his withdrawal. My stomach clenching, my heart rate speeding up, my fingers reaching over to scratch at my wrist. But I take a deep breath of my own, determined to shove it down because I do understand. This isn't personal. This doesn't have anything to do with me, or Asher and me. He got the most devastating news of his life today, and he needs to deal with that in whatever way feels right to him. And if he needs a little space to do that, I'm going to give it to him. I'll give him whatever he needs to get to the other side of this, to help him navigate it and figure out what comes next.

"Okay," I say, standing from the couch and going to him, wrapping my arms around his waist and holding tight. His arms go around me too, and I feel him press a kiss to the side of my head. It's a small gesture, but the relief it gives me is enormous. He's going to be okay. I'll make fucking sure of it.

"I love you, Hot Shot. You call me when you're ready to talk."

"I love you too, Juliette. So, so much."

With a final squeeze of his waist I let him go, walking to the front door. He follows me, kissing my forehead before I walk out the door. When I get to my car, I turn around and see him still standing there in the doorway, backlit by the glow of the entryway light. He looks so alone framed in the doorway, his big house all around him. It feels wrong to leave him when every instinct I have is screaming at me that he needs company. And then I get an idea.

He might think there's no one who could possibly understand what he's going through, but that's not actually true. He might not want my company right now, but I know someone who has been where Asher is. If Asher really wants to be alone, he can kick him out, but I suspect Asher doesn't really want to be alone at all. He wants to be with someone who understands. And I don't understand. Not really. Not the way he needs. But I can deliver him someone who does.

As soon as I slide into the car, I pull out my phone and bring up Jeremy's contact. The phone starts ringing as I pull out of Asher's driveway, and Jeremy picks up on the second ring.

"Hey Jules, what's up?"

"Jer, I need your help."

"Name it and I'm there."

Chapter Forty-Three
Julie

I probably should have gone home, but after spending a night at Asher's comfortable, cozy home, the thought of going to my all-white house with uncomfortable furniture and nothing personal is less than appealing. I only live a ten-minute drive away, but I don't want to be that far away from Asher. He needs the space, but I like the idea of being close by, even if he doesn't know I'm there. So, instead of going home, I drive down the street, and thirty seconds later I'm pulling into my parents' driveway. I use my key to unlock the door, and as soon as I open it, I hear my dad's voice in the kitchen and my mom's answering laughter. The sounds of home are a warm blanket over my humming nerves. I was right to come here.

"Jules!" My mom says, when I walk through the kitchen door. "What are you doing here?"

"What? I can't just come over and say hi to my parents?"

"You can, but you rarely come here without some kind of reason. So, what's the reason?"

"Can't you be a normal mom for like five minutes and just be happy I'm here?"

"Honey girl, if you want a normal mom, you'll have to find someone different. I am who I am, and who I am knows there's something going on with you to have you showing up at my house at six o'clock on a weeknight when everyone knows you're never not at the office at six o'clock on a weeknight."

I huff out a breath, dropping down at the kitchen table next to my dad. He leans over and catches me in a hug, and I feel my entire body relax. Steven Parker gives A-plus hugs.

"You know Mom, you should try not knowing everything all the time. It must get exhausting."

"It would be more exhausting pretending I don't know everything all the time. Are you staying for dinner? Dad made lasagna."

"Then absolutely I am." My dad's lasagna is legendary, and I suddenly realize the last thing I ate today was the donut I had at nine this morning and I'm starving.

"Good. He put it in the oven right before you got here, which means you have plenty of time to tell us what's on your mind."

I did decide last night to talk to my parents, and since I'm right here, now seems as good a time as any. I consider how much to tell them about Asher's diagnosis. I don't love the idea of telling his secret, but at the same time, I want him to have all the support I can possibly give him, and there is no better support team than Rachel and Steven Parker. If he wants to be mad at me for telling my parents, he can be, but I suspect he'll be okay with it.

"I was at Asher's house. He got some bad news today, so I left the office to come be with him."

"What kind of bad news?" my dad asks, a concerned look on his face.

"The worst kind of bad news. He has been having some pretty bad shoulder pain since the hit he took in that last playoff game. He got evaluated today, and I think the scan was pretty much as bad as it gets. He has very advanced arthritis in his throwing shoulder, and the long and short of it is that his playing days are over. He didn't say the word retirement to me, but I assume that's where this is headed."

My dad frowns, his eyes radiating sympathy. "I'm sorry to hear that. This must be devastating for him."

"It is. I know he just got the news a few hours ago, but I could already see the grief all over him."

"So why are you here talking to us and not over there giving him the support he obviously needs right now?" Leave it to my mom to cut right to the heart of the matter.

I take a deep breath and blow it out. "He wanted to be alone. I was there long enough for him to tell me what happened. He was devastated but wouldn't let himself break down. At least not yet, and not in front of me. And he didn't want to talk about what happens next. He needed some space, and I gave it to him. So here I am."

My mom eyes me consideringly. "And do you think being alone is what he really wants?"

"I don't. But I don't think I'm what he needs. I think he needs someone who understands what he's going through. So, I called Jeremy. He's on his way over to Asher's now."

"Good." My mom reaches across the table and pats my hand.

"He said he wanted to protect me from whatever it was going to look like when he breaks down. He's a happy guy and one of the kindest people I know. I don't think he could ever not be that, even when the worst happens, but I didn't want to give him anything more to be worried about. I want to help him get through it."

"You love him." Like when Asher's mom and Molly said it, the words are matter of fact. A statement, not a question.

"What, are all my feelings just painted right on my face? Asher's mom and Molly said the exact same thing. Besides, you knew that already."

"I didn't know that. I know he told me last night that he loves you, but you didn't say anything. But I know now. It's written all over you, Jules. I've never seen you talk this way about anyone. I always wondered who your match would be. I'm glad it's him. He's perfect for you."

"Why do you say that?" I know he is, but I'm curious why my mom thinks so. If she sees what I see.

"He sees you, honey, straight through to that very big heart of yours that you don't let show nearly often enough. He knew last night you needed to talk to Ben, and he offered to help in the kitchen and then happily baked a cake with me to give you the time you needed. And then started over when I forgot how much flour I added and had to toss the first one." She gives me a sly grin.

"You did that on purpose." I point at my mom, putting the pieces together pretty quickly.

"Of course I did. That cake takes fifteen minutes, tops, to get into the oven, and you needed more time than that to spill your guts to Ben about how hard it's been on you since he and Hallie got together."

"You knew?"

Of course she knew.

"Of course I knew. Like I told Ben last summer, I know everything that goes on with my children."

"How come you never said anything?"

My mom sighs, reaching across the table and taking my hand. "It's hard sometimes, as a parent, to know when to intervene with your children and when to let them work things out on their own. With you, I found that to be an even bigger challenge. Ever since you were a kid, you have always been so sure of yourself, Jules. So sure of your path, and what you wanted. You made your plans and you stuck to them and you rarely wavered. When you came across an obstacle, you found a way to work it out or shove through it until you got to the other side, and you were almost always successful. When you were eight, there was a group of boys who wouldn't let you and Hallie play on the swings at the park. You came to the park the very next day with a written schedule and a stopwatch so you could time everyone's turns on the swings and damned if those boys didn't listen to you. That's how it always was with you. You solved your own problems and everyone else's too."

She stops then and takes a deep breath, looking more uncertain than I have ever seen her before. "I sometimes wonder if maybe I did you a disservice by not intervening more. If by letting you solve all your own problems, it made you feel like you couldn't ask for help when you needed it. Watching you these past six months has made me sure of it. You never know, as a parent, whether you're making the right decisions at the time, and sometimes you only figure it out years later. I'm sorry for that, Jules. I should have done it differently."

Emotion clogs my throat as I listen to my mom explain this to me, because it's the truth and also not. My mind drifts to Asher helping me through a panic attack on my office floor because of an obstacle I very much did not have a handle on.

I turn my hand over under my mom's, linking our fingers together. My dad sits silently, watching us, letting us have this moment. It occurs to me for the first time how much Asher is like my dad and like Ben. Good men who have a sixth sense about when to speak up and when to sit back. Who have a way of offering their quiet support just by being present.

"It's not your fault, Mom. The older I got, the better I got at pretending all I wanted was to handle everything on my own. And to some extent, I did want to handle things on my own. It was hard for me to tell you if I was struggling. I wanted you both to be proud of me."

My dad does speak up then. "Julie, I'm going to tell you the same thing that I told Ben when he came to me last summer about that deal he turned down. All your mom and I have ever wanted for you both was to find something that made you happy. You have achieved some incredible things, but as long as you're happy, we're proud. We have been proud of you every single day of your life just because you exist and you're ours. You are a good person, Jules. A good daughter, a caring sister, the best friend that anyone could ask for. We would never, ever think less of you because you ask for help. We want you to come to us when you need it. That's what we're here for. Parenting doesn't stop because you and Ben are adults. We'll always be here to help."

"Thanks, Dad," I say, my voice a little thick, tears pricking at the back of my eyes. I decide since I'm in this deep, I might as well get it all out.

"The past six months have been really hard for me. Ever since Hallie and Ben got together, I've felt kind of lost. Like maybe I don't have a place with them anymore now that they're building a life together. The way they love each other is so enormous and consuming, and for a while, I felt like maybe that love didn't leave any room for me."

"But you don't feel that way anymore?" My mom looks at me appraisingly, like she knows what I'm about to say before I say it. And let's be honest, she probably does.

"I don't."

"What happened to change how you feel?"

"Asher happened." I shrug a shoulder as if it's no big deal when, in fact, it's everything. "I didn't expect him. He snuck up on me, and even when I tried to shove him away, he just stuck."

"The best ones do," my mom says, looking at my dad with love shining in her eyes. For the first time in my life, I understand that look.

"I didn't make it easy for him." I laugh a little, thinking of the last month or so. "But no matter what I said or did, he just rolled with it. He's..." I pause, thinking of the right word to describe Asher. "Solid. He's solid. And he makes me feel safe. Like I can tell him anything, show him any part of myself and he'll love it no matter what. I mean, he saw me sitting on the floor having a panic attack over a mistake I made with one of my clients and he just sat right down, got me through it, and then asked me if I wanted to take a road trip with him."

"You had a panic attack?" My mom's gaze sharpens, fixes directly on me like she used to do when I was a teenager and did something stupid. It's the *I know everything there is to know about you so don't you dare even bother lying to me* look.

Shit.

"Yeah. The thing is, I have pretty bad anxiety, actually. Like, all the time. It's why I work so much and why my house looks like a museum and why my closet is organized by color and none of my clothes are comfortable. I've always thought that if I look perfect on the outside and do everything right, then maybe no one will realize I'm mostly a mess on the inside. But it turns out when you meet someone who sees you all the way through, you can't hide any part of yourself. And when that person seems to like what they see, it makes you wonder why you bothered hiding it all for so long in the first place. That's part of what I talked to Ben about, and I told Hallie and the girls about it this morning."

"How did that make you feel?" asks my dad.

"Free. It made me feel free. Like maybe I'm the most myself that I have ever been, and I like this version of me. I haven't said anything to Asher yet about this, but I also think I'm going to look for a therapist. Someone who has experience working with high achieving professionals with anxiety because they try to be perfect and control everything all the time. There seem to be a lot of us. I think it could be helpful to talk to someone."

My mom stands up from her chair then, walking around the table to stand behind me and put her arms around me, holding tight. "Julie Parker, there is nothing in this world you could achieve or accomplish that would make me prouder of you than I am right now. I'm so sorry that I didn't see how much you were struggling, and I hope you won't hide it from me anymore. But I think, maybe, everything worked out the way it was supposed to."

"I think maybe you're right. And I do. Love him I mean. It happened so fast it still gives me whiplash, but I don't have a single doubt that he is it for me. He makes me feel everything. And thinking about him just down the street, in pain over the end of a career he hoped would last at least a few years longer, is making me want to burn the world down for him."

My mom sniffles, and when I crane my neck to look at her, she has tears in her eyes dangerously close to spilling over.

"Um, why are you crying?"

My mom swats me on the back of the head. "I'm entitled to a few tears when my only daughter tells me she's in love. Especially since the man she's in love with is one I'm happy to have in my family." She sits down in the chair next to me so I'm sandwiched between my parents.

"You know your dad and I would have loved anyone you and your brother brought home. But it's an extraordinary thing to also like the people your children choose as their partners. I'm happy for both of you, and I'm feeling smug about my parenting skills right now since obviously I had to have done something right for you both to have found such excellent people to settle down with."

I give my mom a look. "Didn't we just finish a conversation about how you didn't realize I've been an anxious mess for all of my adult life?"

My mom just shrugs. "Seems to have served you well enough, and you're working through it now, aren't you?"

I just laugh because she's definitely not wrong. Again.

"Seriously, Jules, for what it's worth, I think you're doing the right thing now for Asher. Part of being a good partner is knowing when your person needs something you can't provide and helping them find it. You sending Jeremy over there is doing exactly that for Asher. Jer has been where Asher is now and can give him a perspective you can't. Help him get over the shock of it all and understand what comes next. Asher will come find you when he's ready."

"I know he will." And I do. I still feel the low-level anxiety that comes with the unknown of this whole experience. But if there's one thing I'm confident in, it's that Asher won't stay away for long. And when he comes back, I'll be ready to give him whatever support he needs. The oven timer dings, and my dad jumps up from his seat.

"Now that we're all done spilling our guts, should we eat dinner?" my dad asks, slipping on my mom's neon pink oven mitts to take the lasagna out of the oven.

"God, yes. I'm starving," I say, getting up and opening a cabinet to take out plates to set the table.

"Excellent," my mom says, leaning back in her chair and letting my dad and me get dinner to the table. "And while we eat, you can tell us more about your road trip. I think last night you left off at the world's biggest taco and something about you kicking Asher's ass at skee-ball. And I'm going to need to hear all about the four sisters because that is a lot of sisters."

"You have no idea," I laugh. "I love them all."

My dad sets the lasagna on the table, and, confident that Asher is getting what he needs right now, and feeling lighter than I have all night, I sit down with my parents and tell them everything.

Chapter Forty-Four
Asher

The knock on the door startles me out of my misery.

I'm sitting on the sunroom couch, laying back against the cushions. The ice in the Dr. Pepper Julie brought me when she was here has long since melted, and the cup now sits in a puddle of condensation that's probably ruining my coffee table but I can't make myself care. Every time I turn my head, I catch Julie's scent from where she was leaning back against the cushions next to me, compounding my misery.

I shouldn't have asked her for space. Space from her is the last thing I want right now, but I also didn't want her to be around for whatever was going to happen tonight. It occurred to me when she walked through the door earlier that the worst thing has never happened to me before and now that it has, I have no idea how to react. I'm angry and sad and so many other things I can't name, and I don't know how to feel all of this at once. Especially the anger. I'm never angry. Every time I opened my mouth, I had no idea what would come out, and that scared the shit out of me. I would die before I hurt her, so I asked her to leave when what I really want more than anything is for her to be here right now. I want her and her arms around me and her plans and her spreadsheets and her organized brain to counteract my chaos.

I'm a fucking disaster.

I haul myself up off the couch to answer the door. My body feels like it weighs a million pounds, and the only thing propelling me to the door is the thought that maybe it's Julie on the other side. I throw open the door, ready to wrap myself around her and beg her to never leave again, a fucked-up thought since I was the one who asked her to leave in the first place, but I can't be logical right now.

But it's not her.

"We heard you're wallowing."

Jeremy strolls into my house, followed by Ben and Jordan, each of them holding a six-pack of beer and what looks like a take-out bag, and they head straight back to the kitchen. I follow them, wondering for a second how they knew to come here and then it hits me. *Julie.* She somehow knew I didn't actually want to be alone, so she made sure I wasn't. My love for her cuts through the misery like a knife.

"She sent you, didn't she?"

Ben sets his beer and bag on the counter and hugs me. An actual two-armed hug that immediately lowers my blood pressure and has me taking what feels like my first deep breath since I left the stadium earlier today.

"She did. Well, she actually called him." He gestures to Jeremy, who is busy unpacking what looks like a hundred different take-out containers. "She thought maybe it would help to talk to someone who knows what it's like to leave the game because of an injury. He called us because he thought you could use some extra friends."

"And we brought food because I'm assuming you haven't eaten all day," Jordan says, while opening all my cabinets looking for plates. "We didn't know what you would want so we brought everything. There's Chinese, burgers, and Mexican. There's beer too, obviously, but you're not allowed to drink until you eat. I deal with enough puke in my day job. I don't want to deal with yours."

I stand there, a little bewildered at the three men making themselves at home in my kitchen. I'm an extrovert. I love people. But aside from the times my family has been in town, I think this is the most people who have ever been in my house at one time since I moved in nine years ago. That, combined with my current angsty state, has me frozen in place, not sure what to do.

"Come sit with me." Jeremy's voice is gentle, and he presses a bottle of water into my hand before pushing me towards the same sunroom couch I've made my home on today. I sit down and take a long sip of the water, realizing that it's the first thing I've had to drink all day. I'm a mess.

"I won't even ask if you want to talk about it because of course you don't, but you're going to, okay?"

"How do you know I don't want to talk about it?"

"Do you?"

"Well, no, not exactly." I sigh, coherent enough to know that what I want and what's best for me probably aren't the same thing. "But I think talking about it will help."

"It will, even if it feels like you're slicing yourself open and pulling your guts out."

I give Jeremy a deadpan look. "Thank you so much for that delightful visual."

He shrugs, taking a sip of the beer he brought in with him. "I've been where you are. I know how it feels." His delivery is matter of fact, but I can hear the emotion trembling beneath his words. It should probably depress me that he is more than a decade out from his abrupt retirement and is still emotional about it, but for some weird reason it makes me feel better. Like the careers we loved mattered enough to still be mourning their loss in some way.

"I don't know what to think. I don't know what happens next. I left the stadium before I could talk to anyone, and I haven't answered my phone."

"It's February. You don't need to know what happens next yet."

"I kind of do though. If I can't play, they're going to need a quarterback, and that will change their draft considerations. And the combine is coming up, so if they need a quarterback that's going to change who they're watching, and I should tell them so they can plan what to do. If I have to leave, I want to leave the team in the best place I can and to do that I have to know what to do so I can tell them so they can decide what to do and..." I break off, my chest heaving and my heart pounding as I try to take in air after spilling out all those words in one giant rush.

Jeremy puts a hand on my back and waits for me to catch my breath. I scrub over my face with shaking hands.

"I'm a mess, Jeremy," I admit. "I don't know what to do."

"Right now, what you should do is eat." Jordan walks into the sunroom and puts a plate down in front of me. Ben follows with an armload of beers, which he hands out to everyone except for me.

"Eat," he orders. "Then you can drink."

I look down at the plate Jordan delivered and laugh for the first time all day. "Why tacos and french fries?"

"Chinese food and even burgers can be eaten cold," Jordan explains. "But tortillas get soggy and french fries are terrible cold and even worse when you reheat them, so we're starting with those."

"Don't argue with him," Ben advises. "Jordan takes food very seriously."

"Listen asshole, I'm saving you from having to decide between cold fries and reheated fries, and both of those are gross fries."

While they bicker, I pick up a taco and take a bite because it turns out I'm starving. I chew, and I wonder if I'll ever be able to eat a taco again without thinking of Julie and eating tacos with her in every city between Pittsburgh and Boulder, and her hysterical laughter when I took her to see the sixteen foot taco in Casey, Illinois. While I think about her, something hits the side of my face and falls to the floor.

"What the fuck?"

I look down and there are ketchup packets scattered at my feet. When I lift my head Jordan is smirking at me. "Thought you might need ketchup."

"You couldn't just hand it to me like an adult?"

He shrugs. "I just finished a twenty-four hour shift at the hospital, and I'm tired. I didn't want to get up."

"So why are you here instead of at home sleeping?"

"Because you needed us," Ben says.

My throat swells with emotion at his simple statement and I look down, trying to compose myself so I don't lose it completely.

"I don't know what to do." I quietly repeat my words from earlier, putting my taco down and pushing my plate away, appetite suddenly gone.

"It helps to talk about what you know," Jeremy says. "So, what do you know? Just facts. No feelings."

I take a deep breath and shove my feelings aside for now. "I have arthritis in my throwing shoulder. It's about as bad as it can get, and it's not going to get better."

Jeremy nods. "What else?"

"The doctor won't clear me to play. Now or ever. I need to do PT to help with the pain. I'll probably need surgery down the road. A complete shoulder replacement isn't out of the question."

"Anything else?"

"I can't..." I stop, not able to force out the words.

"Just say it fast," Jeremy advises, echoing Julie's words from earlier.

"I can't play football anymore. That playoff game was my last game." I clench my hands into fists, digging my fingernails into my palms to distract myself from the pain lancing through my chest at those words.

"No, you can't," says Jeremy. "And it's completely fucking unfair to have your sport taken away from you instead of being able to leave on your own terms." He rubs at his knee in that unconscious gesture of his, and I know he's thinking of his own experience being forced out of hockey before his time. "But it gets better. You can't see that now. But it does. You'll find your place."

"Have you found yours?" I ask, curious about his answer.

He blows out a breath. "I have my place at the bar and with these two idiots." He gestures to Ben and Jordan. "And you're one of us now, so don't even try and fight it."

My chest warms at his words, because I would never try and fight it. Most things are horrible right now, but I have my girl, and she gave me all of her people too. I love my sisters and never really wished for brothers, but it seems like maybe I found some right here.

"I have my place at the foundation too, which I love, so I guess I have a lot of places."

"You know, if you tell Emma straight-up that you like her instead of dancing around it all the time, you could really find your place." At first, I think Ben is joking, but when I look at his face, it's deadly serious. It's the first time I've heard one of them refer to Jeremy's feelings for Emma in such a direct way.

"It's complicated," Jeremy mutters.

"So be an adult and uncomplicate it." Jordan takes the last swig of his beer and puts the empty bottle on the coffee table, picking up another full one.

"I fucked it up too badly."

"You know, if you ever tell us what it is that you fucked up, we could help you," Ben says.

"No." The single word is final, and Jeremy turns back to me.

"Real talk, Ash. I'm not going to put a silver lining on this, because that's not what you want and there really isn't one. At least not right now. Leaving in this way is fucking painful, and it will be for a while, especially while you sort through all the logistics, and especially once the public gets involved and you have to see it over and over again in the media and talk about it a million times a day with fans. But having a plan for what to do next makes it a little easier, and taking it one step at a time, one day at a time, is the only thing that will keep you from going insane. So, what are you going to do first?"

Somehow, having him lay it all out like that steadies me, and I can think clearly for the first time all day. I open my mouth to tell him I need to call my coach, but instead what comes out is, "I need to talk to Julie."

"That is...not what I thought you would say," Jeremy says.

"Makes sense though," Ben says.

"How could that possibly make sense?"

"Because she's his person. Right?" Jordan looks at me.

I nod at him. "She is. I thought I needed space from her tonight to work this through and maybe I did a little, but I need her. It doesn't feel right talking about my future—even what happens in the next couple of weeks—without talking to her first."

Even the thought of sitting down next to her and having this conversation has all my angst and nerves quieting. As long as I have her, I can get through anything.

Ben lifts his beer bottle in a toast. "You know, you're not at all who I pictured whenever I thought about who my sister would end up with, but I'm really glad it's you."

"Same," Jordan says. "Some of those guys she used to bring around?" He shudders dramatically. "None of them would ever sit around on a weeknight and eat tacos and french fries, that's for damn sure."

"Yeah, I'm going to need details about those guys," I say, realizing for the first time that we never really had the *who did you used to date* conversation beyond Julie telling me that they sucked in bed, leaving me feeling superior because I unequivocally *do not* suck in bed.

"Fuck no," Jordan and Jeremy say at the same time.

"You think I want to incur Julie Parker's wrath for spilling her dating history to you?" Jordan shakes his head. "You want to know, you ask her yourself."

"You know what, I don't even want to know. It doesn't matter. I've got her now."

"You sure do," Ben says. "I've never seen her with anyone the way she is with you. She's happier. Lighter. There's no one who deserves that more than Julie."

I'm not sure how a conversation about the abrupt end to my football career turned into this, but I'm feeling a little better so I'm willing to roll with it.

"I'll be good to her. No one will ever love her the way I do. She's safe with me. She's my whole fucking world."

Ben tosses me a beer, which I catch one-handed. "Well then welcome to the family, brother. Happy to have you."

"I wasn't going to say this tonight because tonight is for wallowing, not decision making. And that whole one step at a time thing. But when you're ready to decide on what to do next, consider working with me." Jeremy has an earnest look I'm not used to seeing on the cocky, confident former hockey player.

"I'm already working with you."

"In the offseason, sure. But..." Jeremy stops abruptly, probably realizing what he was about to say. "Fuck, sorry. I shouldn't have brought it up. We can talk about it another time."

"No, it's fine." I realize it is fine. Or, maybe not fine, but at least, in this moment, not gut wrenchingly terrible. "You can say it."

"You sure?"

"I'm not sure about anything, but I won't fall apart, if that's what you're asking."

"You could fall apart, you know," Jeremy says.

"I might. Probably will. But not right now." I can only think of one person I want to fall apart in front of, and she isn't in this room.

"Good enough. Well, if you find yourself in a position where you're looking for something to do full time, come work with me at the foundation. Emma keeps telling me I can't run the sports camps solo. She says I need a full-time program director, and she's usually right about this kind of thing."

"Usually?" Jordan smirks at Jeremy.

"Always, dude. She keeps your ass in line." Ben leans back in his chair and kicks his feet out in front of him.

"I fucking wish," Jeremy mutters.

Jordan tosses a beer cap that hits Jeremy square in the chest. "If you're not planning on sharing with the class, you should probably stop muttering like that. It's making you look pathetic."

"Fuck off. I'm talking to Asher now." He turns to me, his face serious. "It's simple, really. I need someone to run the sports camps full-time. With all my other responsibilities at the foundation and at the bar, I can't give them the time and attention they deserve, and there's no one I trust to run them more than you. You're incredible with kids, and you have a really good head for this work. There's no rush; I'm not filling the position until you tell me you definitely don't want it. Take all the time you need."

I consider what he said, and my first thought is standing on a frozen high school football field in Boulder teaching a freshman third string quarterback a new way to throw a football and the smile that lit up his face when he finally got it. I don't hate the idea.

"I'll think about it," is all I say. My brain is too jumbled to offer much beyond that, and I don't want to think about anything else until I hug my girl.

"Good enough." Jeremy salutes me with his beer as Jordan gets up to grab the rest of the takeout from the kitchen. My football career is over, and there are going to be some big decisions and hard days ahead while I work out how to end it officially and what's next for me. Today was a fucking disaster, but sitting here with these three guys, beers, and an eclectic mix of takeout isn't such a terrible way to end it. I take a sip of my beer and then set it on the coffee table, knowing that I'm going to be driving later. Because there is no way I'm ending this day without finding Julie. I want to be wherever she is, and hopefully we can figure out all of these next steps together.

Chapter Forty-Five
Asher

The knowledge that she stayed here, right on my street, because I might need her, has love bursting in my chest, making my heart feel like it's too big for my body. My arms literally ache to get around her, and suddenly the five houses between us is an unacceptable distance.

I peer out the window and see that the flurries I noticed when the guys left a little while ago have turned into a real snowfall.

ME

Stay put. It's snowing. I'm on my way.

JULIETTE

If you insist.

I absolutely do.

Less than a minute later, I'm walking out my front door. I consider getting in the car, but the crisp, snowy February air draws me in, so I set off on foot, my boots leaving the first footprints on the snowy sidewalk.

Rachel Parker opens the front door just as I'm raising my hand to knock. I know immediately that she must know about today because Rachel says nothing, just takes a step forward and wraps me in a hug that settles my nervous system in a way that only a mom hug can. After a minute or so, she pulls away just enough to cup my face in her hands, kissing my forehead and both of my cheeks, before smoothing my hair away from my forehead. I realize that must be the Parker gesture of comfort, and I feel both a wave of longing for my own family and gratitude that it seems like maybe I have a family here too.

"Come inside, Asher—it's freezing out here." Rachel leads me into the light and warmth of their entry way. I start peeling off my jacket, but she holds out a hand to stop me. "You're probably going to want to hang on to that."

I briefly wonder why she thinks I'm going to need my jacket inside her house, but she is looking at me with a face so full of sympathy that I should probably hate it, but I don't because it's so damn comforting. The jacket stays on.

"Julie told Steven and me what's going on. I'm so sorry you're hurting, Asher."

I swallow hard, the frank sympathy a blow to the very questionable grip I have on my emotional control.

"I told you yesterday that if you ever needed anything you could come here, and I meant it. You mean everything to Julie, and that means you're important to Steven and me too."

"Thank you," I force out then clear my throat, trying to maintain some semblance of calm.

Rachel looks at me with understanding. "This is the worst day of your life."

I appreciate that it's a statement and not a question.

"Yes."

"Well, on the worst day of your life, what you need is your people. I know Jules sent you one of your people earlier today."

"Three of them, actually."

Rachel nods, smiling. "Those boys have always run in a pack. And have you spoken to your family yet?"

I shake my head slowly. "I haven't. I didn't...I mean I can't..." I blow out a breath, shaking my head before trying again. "I wasn't ready to tell them yet. I needed to get it straight in my head and work out what comes next for me before I try and explain it to them. Especially over the phone. This is one of those times when it's really hard to be so far away."

"You take however long you need, Asher. This is an earthquake right in the middle of your life. It's going to take some time to get your feet steady under you. Now I love seeing your face, but I know it's not me you're here to see. She's out back. She's always liked sitting outside when it snows."

I smile a little at that. "We have that in common."

Rachel leads me through the kitchen, and when I get to the sliding glass door to the back yard, I see Julie on the covered deck curled up on a couch in front of an outdoor fireplace, staring out at the snow. Even just seeing her from the back, her blonde waves spilling over her shoulders, has my entire body relaxing. My shoulders drift down from where they were hovering somewhere close to my ears, and my jaw unclenches. My fingers stop digging into my palm and my breathing slows.

"Love looks good on you," Rachel says quietly. "On both of you. I'm glad you found each other. You go ahead out, honey. She's been waiting for you, and I think you've been waiting for her too."

With that, Rachel pats me on the cheek and leaves the kitchen while I slide open the glass door and step outside.

Julie

I turn as soon as I hear the door slide open. Asher stands in the doorway, and for a few heartbeats we look at each other. His face is sad, but the love in his gaze steals my breath.

"Juliette." He steps outside and is across the deck and around the outdoor couch where I'm sitting in a few long strides. He doesn't join me on the couch, but kneels down in front of me, his hands pushing under the blanket I have tossed over my lap to bracket my hips. I lean forward, sliding my hands around his neck, my thumbs drifting over his jaw. He kisses me, soft and gentle, before resting his forehead against mine. We stay that way, breaths mingling in the cold air, bodies warmed by the outdoor fireplace that roars in front of the couch.

"You didn't go home." His voice is low, laced with both pain and gratitude, and I'm fascinated by the way I can pick out the separate emotions in his voice. Yes, I know this man. Every single inch of him. There is a remarkable sort of comfort in that thought, and it settles me down to my core. Right here is the steady, rock-solid kind of love that lasts lifetimes. And it's mine.

"I couldn't. The thought of going to my house after spending time in yours wasn't appealing, and I hated being that far away. Even if you didn't need me, I liked knowing I was right down the street in case you did. I wanted to stay close to you."

I've barely finished my sentence before Asher's breath hitches. His eyes slam shut. I can feel his body start to shake with the effort of holding himself together, and watching him try so hard not to break has my own heart breaking.

"I'm going to...I need...I can't." His breath is coming in fast pants, and I can feel his heart pounding. Without looking at me, he stands from his crouch to sit next to me on the couch, and I lift up the blanket so he can scoot in closer. I slide an arm around his back and put my other hand on his cheek to turn his face towards me. When our eyes meet, his are covered in a sheen of tears.

"I'm ready fall apart now," he manages. "I can't hold it in anymore."

"You don't have to hold it in anymore, Asher. You can fall apart right here. It's just you and me out here, and I'm not going anywhere. You're safe with me too."

That's when he breaks. Tears flood his eyes and spill down his cheeks, and he leans forward, a gut-wrenching sob coming straight from his chest. I guide him sideways, so his head is on my lap, and I hold onto him while he cries. His shoulders shake and his chest heaves as his grief pours out of him. My own eyes water as my strong, funny, always cheerful man cries out his heartbreak at the untimely loss of the game that has meant so much to him and the uncertain future ahead.

I keep one arm locked around him and I stroke my other hand through his hair while he cries, whispering things like, "I've got you," and "let it out." I don't know how long we stay like that, Asher's head on my lap, his tears falling onto the blanket while the snow swirls beyond the deck and the fireplace warms us. Eventually Asher's sobs quiet and his breathing slows. When he sits up, swinging one leg up on the couch so we can face each other, his eyes are red-rimmed and exhausted. He weaves our fingers together, picking one of my hands up to press a kiss to my knuckles.

"Thank you."

"You don't have to thank me, Asher. This is part of the deal."

His mouth quirks up on one side, like he's trying to smile but can't quite get there. "Part of what deal?"

"You know, the relationship deal. You sat with me and held me through a panic attack on my office floor when you barely knew me. You helped me face some demons that have haunted me for my entire life. There is nothing I wouldn't do to help you when you need it. It's not all road trips and gummy worms and Big Gulps and giant barbershop polls in small town America. Sometimes everything goes to shit and you're sitting on your office floor thinking you're going to die or crying your eyes out in the freezing cold in the middle of a snowstorm."

"If I have to cry my eyes out, I guess doing it outside during a perfect snowfall isn't the worst way."

I smile, thinking about that day in my office when he used the snow to distract me from my panic. "I love being outside during the snow. My family thinks I'm crazy, but I've been sitting in this exact place watching the snow since I was a kid. It's the reason my parents covered the porch when I was eight or nine—to give me a place to watch the snow and stay dry. It always makes me feel better, even when things are shit."

"I love it too. And everything has definitely gone to shit," he says, with a tiny bit of amusement in his voice. Then he takes a breath and blows it out slowly. "I'm ready to talk about it now."

"Tell me," I say, drawing our joined hands into my lap.

"First of all, I'm sorry for telling you to leave. It was a mistake. I needed you. I always need you. But I was scared. I didn't mean to push you away or make you feel like I didn't want you with me."

"You didn't. Was there a part of me that was anxious about it? Sure. I'm an anxious person, and I probably always will be. But I get it. Seriously, I do. You need to navigate this however feels right to you."

"It never feels right when you're not there."

"Well obviously," I deadpan. "I'm fantastic. But it's also okay to need someone who isn't me. That's why I sent you Jeremy."

"Thanks for that. I didn't realize how much I needed to talk to someone who has been where I am. And probably worse off, since I played for double the amount of time he did. And he brought friends."

I laugh a little. "I thought he might. I'm glad he did. Those three can make anyone feel better about anything. Did they bring food? I told Jeremy to bring food."

"They did. I think they brought every takeout that's available in the city. I've never eaten tacos and french fries together before, but it doesn't suck."

I nod, knowingly. "Because you can't reheat tacos, and french fries suck when they're cold and are worse when you heat them up."

Asher chuckles. "That's what they said."

"Yeah, I've eaten a lot of takeout with them in my day. I know the drill."

"Eating was good. And so was Jeremy forcing me to talk

about it but just stick to the facts. You know them. Bad arthritis. Extremely fucked shoulder. I need tons of PT and probably surgery at some point. Maybe a complete shoulder replacement. I won't ever play in the NFL again."

I can see his eyes glaze over a little at that, but he seems steadier.

"But I didn't talk to them about what comes next. It didn't feel right to talk to them about it first. I want to talk to you. You're my person."

It lights me up when he says that. I'm lucky to have a lot of people, but I've never had a person before, the way my parents have each other or Ben has Hallie. But now I do. And he is the very best person.

"So, tell me, Hot Shot. What comes next?"

He takes a deep breath and lets it out, and then another one. "Retirement. I'm retiring. I haven't said that word yet. I didn't want to say it first to anyone but you."

"How does it feel to say it?" I ask, hoping it's the right question.

He seems to really consider it. "Not as scary as I thought it would feel, actually. I don't know what any of the details are. I still haven't checked my phone, but I'm sure I have a million missed calls from everyone from my coach to the PR people for the team wondering what the fuck I'm going to do. And I still have to talk to my agent, and I haven't even told my parents yet, so I'm sure it will be some time before the actual announcement but yeah. I'm retiring. It's fucking weird to retire when I'm only thirty-one, but I guess now I can buy a sports car and play golf and do all those retirement things."

I laugh at that. "Do you want to buy a sports car and play golf?"

"Fuck no. Golf is boring as shit, and I love my Range Rover. Those just feel like retirement things."

"I think whatever things you decide to do are retirement things. And I kind of have a confession to make. It's embarrassing."

"Juliette, sweetheart, I just cried all over you for half an hour. You can tell me anything."

I cringe a little, but decide to just let it out. "Okay, so after dinner with my parents, I was trying to decide what to do with myself. You obviously know this, but I don't do well with uncertain things. And for pretty much my whole adult life when things are uncertain, I do research and make lists and spreadsheets. And, well, it might make more sense for you to see it." I grab my phone from the cushion next to me and unlock it before handing it to him.

He scans it before looking back up at me, his face a little incredulous. "Is this..."

"A spreadsheet of what the most successful retired football players are doing in their retirement? Yes."

"It's color coded." His voice is filled with awe, but I still kind of want to hide under the couch.

He locks the phone and sets it down on the couch. "You made me a spreadsheet for my post-retirement career options?"

I nod, thinking that maybe I should have white knuckled it through the anxiety of it all while I was waiting to hear from him. But then Asher picks me up and sits me down on his lap, crushing me to his chest in a hug and burying his face in my hair.

"Fuck, I love you," he says into my neck. "I love your brilliant, gorgeous brain that now knows what every retired NFL player went on to do with their careers, and I'm so fucking lucky that you get to be mine."

He pulls back and with his hands tangling in my hair, he presses his mouth to mine in a kiss that is full of passion and fire. He glides his tongue along the seam of my lips, and I open for him. Sucking my bottom lip into his mouth, he nips it with his teeth and the tiny prink of pain sends a jolt of arousal right between my legs. When he finally slides his tongue inside my mouth to glide against mine, he tastes every part of me until butterflies are rioting in my stomach and a groan rumbles through his chest. Reaching down to my waist, he pushes under my sweatshirt and his hands are so cold that I gasp against his mouth, and start to laugh a little, ruining the moment.

He pulls away looking a little sheepish. "I guess here's probably not the best place anyway."

I grin at him. "You mean you don't want to get naked outside in thirty-degree weather while my parents are inside?"

He grips my chin and kisses me again, hard and quick. "Juliette, I would happily get naked with you anywhere, anytime. But I have one more thing to tell you."

I put a hand on his chest. "I have one more thing to tell you too. Can I go first?"

"Absolutely you can."

"Okay. I realized something earlier while I was making that list for you."

He leans in and kisses my neck, tightening his arms around my waist. "By list, you mean color-coded spreadsheet separated by team, age, post-retirement career path, and endorsement deals?"

His voice is full of amusement, and I huff out a breath. "Yes. That one. It's not finished. I stopped halfway through because I realized that I didn't want to help you figure this out on a spreadsheet. For the first time, probably in my entire adult life, I realized that I was actually okay to wait for you to come to me. To talk about how you feel and what you think without trying to fix everything for you. It's in my nature to try and fix everything with facts and logic, but this time, I just wanted to know how you felt, and I wanted to help you carry that, not try to fix it."

I stare down at my hands, embarrassed by how ground-breaking it is for me to be able to sit in uncertainty. It's probably something I should have figured out years ago.

"Juliette, look at me." Asher's voice is gentle, and when I don't look up, he hooks a finger under my chin and tips my chin up so I'm staring up at him.

"I'm proud of you, sweetheart. And just the fact that you exist, and are sitting here with me on this couch outside in the middle of this perfect snowfall, makes everything easier. You make everything easier. When I'm with you, my whole world makes sense. I think maybe we were meant to find each other now. To do this, whatever comes next, together. I don't know what's going to happen tomorrow or the next day, but I do know that I want you with me for all of it."

At that, I wrap my arms around Asher and melt into his body. His heart beats against mine and his warm breath flutters against my ear. Love for him flows through me. When our gazes lock, the connection that zings between us is true and steady and strong.

"I'll be there for all of it. Every single minute."

He smiles and kisses my nose. "I'm counting on it. And when I said I didn't know what's going to happen, I meant more in the logistical, all the things I need to do to actually retire part of it." He breaks off and swallows hard, like the word retire is still too enormous to say.

Shaking his head, he starts again. "I think I might know what I'm going to do with all the free time I'm about to have in my schedule."

I smirk at him. "Make me breakfast every day because I suck at it?"

"Definitely that. And when I'm done making you breakfast,

I think I'm going to work with Jeremy. He wants me to be in charge of the camps he's starting. The actual position is program director, or something like that. But really, it's running the sports camps and working with the kids. Maybe the actual day I find out I can't play anymore is too soon to make a decision about what comes next for me, but I don't know. When he mentioned it, it just felt right."

I smile at him because it feels right to me too. "I think it sounds perfect."

He lets out a relieved breath and tugs me against him so that I'm leaning back against his chest, his arms wrapped around me as we both stare out at the still falling snow.

"Hey Juliette?"

"Yeah?"

"As much as I'd like to sit like this forever, the fire is dying and it's fucking freezing. I think it's time to go inside."

I snuggle back into him, so comfortable I don't want to move, even though I can't feel my toes anymore. "Okay, but do you want to stay here tonight? I'm exhausted and your bed is so far away. I have one right upstairs." I turn my head and grin at him a little wickedly. "And my parents sleep at the other end of the house."

Asher lets out a faux gasp. "Julie Parker, are you telling me you want to have sex, with me, in your childhood bedroom, under the same roof as your parents?"

I sit up and turn in his lap so I'm facing him. "That is exactly what I'm telling you, Hot Shot, and I'd like it to happen as soon as possible."

I've barely finished my sentence when he stands straight up, taking me with him.

"Wait, no," I laugh. "Put me down. You can't carry me all the way upstairs. Your shoulder."

He shrugs a shoulder. His bad shoulder. "My shoulder is

fine. I mean, it's obviously super not fine, but I'm not a football player anymore, so I can carry you everywhere if I want to."

"I think my clients might have a thing or two to say about that."

"They'll just have to get used to it because I plan on spending a whole lot of time with you in my arms. Wrap those gorgeous legs around me, baby. We have places to be."

I wrap my legs around his waist and my arms around his neck and he brings our mouths together, kissing me deeply and with all the promise of a dark winter night and a perfect snowfall.

Chapter Forty-Six
Asher

Julie's lips drift down my jaw and over my neck as I carry her into her room and shut the door. I have the fleeting thought that I want to look around, to explore the younger versions of Julie that exist inside these four walls. But then the current version of Julie grazes her teeth over my throat while she grinds down on me, the warmth of her pussy surrounding my cock beneath my sweatpants, and every thought in my head falls away except the one where I fuck her right here in this room until we can't breathe.

Sitting down on the edge of the bed with Julie straddling my lap, I wrap my hands around her neck, tangling them in her hair while I crash my mouth against hers. When I nip at her bottom lip, she lets out a moan and opens for me, sealing our mouths together in a kiss that is slow and deliberate, all passion and pleasure. I slick my tongue against hers, and the taste of her makes me light-headed, and my already hard cock hardens even more. Pulling back, I grasp the bottom of her sweatshirt and pull it up over her head, taking her t-shirt with it. I toss it to the ground and my eyes drift down to her perfect tits, completely bare for me.

"Fuck, Juliette, no bra?"

"Didn't feel like it."

I let out a groan and dip my head down, capturing one nipple in my mouth, rolling it around with my tongue and tugging on the other one with my fingers. Julie's head drops back on a moan, and I switch sides, circling my tongue over the other nipple before I bite it softly and lick to sooth the spot. When I start sucking on it and rubbing my thumb over the other nipple, Julie shifts her hips forward, but before she can make contact, I grip her hips to stop her, and she lets out an impatient gasp.

"You want something, baby?"

Her eyes flash and she leans forward, running her nose up my jaw before capturing my mouth with hers. The way she takes charge of the kiss makes me want to tear off every single barrier between us and slide inside her as soon as humanly possible. She pulls back and looks at me, lust and desire painted all over her face.

"I want you to make me come. Right. Fucking. Now."

Arousal arrows through me but I keep my expression neutral, quirking a brow at her. "And how would you like me to do that?"

One side of her mouth rises in a devilish half grin.

"Dealer's choice."

Motherfucker.

I grip her hips and lift her off my lap so she's standing in front of me. I tear my own shirt over my head and then peel her leggings off her body, taking her underwear with them. She kicks them away while I lean in and press open mouthed kisses to her stomach and slide my tongue along one hip bone, then the other. She rocks her hips forward, but I hold them steady. The scent of her arousal is a heady thing, but I can't resist teasing her a little.

Moving my hands around her back, I glide them down over her ass, almost but not quite grazing over her tight hole in a move that has her blowing out a breath that ends in a moan. *Interesting.*

"You like me touching you there, Juliette?" I don't wait for her to respond before I keep talking. "I think you do. I bet no one has ever touched you there before. One day I will, and I'll be the only one who ever does. I'll slide my thumb into that tight hole while I fuck your pussy from behind and rub your clit until you come so hard you'll feel me for days."

The sound she lets out is deep and raspy and has my cock straining to break free from my sweatpants.

"What will I find if I slide my fingers into your tight cunt right now, Juliette? Are you wet? Are you dripping for me baby?"

"Asher. Please. Fuck." Her voice is pleading. Almost a whimper.

I grip her hips again and pull her back down on my lap to straddle me, widening my legs to spread her open for me. In a single movement, I sink two fingers inside her, and my groan mingles with hers. She is so wet for me that there is no resistance at all. With my thumb rubbing circles on her clit in the way I know she likes, I fuck my fingers in and out of her, pressing deep to hit the spot that makes her moan and writhe on my lap. Pulling my fingers out, I press back in with a third, relishing the feel of her stretching around me, grinding down on my fingers to get them deeper, to increase the pressure on her clit.

"I'm so close," she gasps.

"You gonna come all over my fingers, Juliette? Drip down my hand until I'm soaked in your cum? Do it baby, and then I'll lick them clean. I fucking love the way you taste when you come for me."

I lean forward and crush my mouth to hers, thrusting my tongue into her mouth at the same time as I thrust my fingers up into her. I curl them up and flick my thumb over her clit until she comes on my hand, rocking her hips into me as I swallow her cries with my mouth, a wild satisfaction washing over me at the sounds of the pleasure I gave her. I keep stroking her until she comes down, pulling her mouth from mine, panting a little as her body recovers. I pull my hand out of her, and without breaking eye contact, I slide my fingers into my mouth, licking them clean just like I told her I would.

Her eyes haze with lust as she watches me. "Why is that so hot?"

"I don't know, baby, but it fucking is. You taste amazing. And now I need to be inside you. So fucking badly, Juliette."

She slams her mouth to mine in a wet, filthy kiss before pulling away, eyes glinting.

"Then fucking do it, Hot Shot."

I stand up, holding onto her with one hand and shoving my sweatpants and boxers down with the other. Sitting back down, I kick them away and spin Julie around so her back is pressed to my chest, my cock sliding along her wet slit, soaking me in her arousal. Sliding my hands up her torso to cup her breasts and rub my thumbs over her nipples, I whisper, "Look up, baby," my breath grazing the shell of her ear and making her whole body shiver. She does, looking right into the mirror hung on the inside of her open closet door.

She gasps at the visual, and when our eyes meet in the mirror, I almost come on the spot at the way we look, bodies tangled together, my hands on her tits and her pussy sliding over me.

"Shit, we're so damn hot," she says, her eyes glued to the mirror.

"Bet your ass we are," I say, pinching her nipples hard enough to have her moaning and sliding her pussy over me. "Stand up a little."

I help guide her up just enough to notch my cock at her entrance, a groan rumbling out of my chest as she sinks down on me slowly until she is sitting in my lap, my cock buried inside her. She clenches her inner muscles, and our moans mingle together in the air that is rapidly heating around us.

"Nothing feels as right as you wrapped around my cock. Ride me, Juliette, and keep your eyes on me while you do."

She starts to move, grinding her body down on me as she glides back and forth on my lap, moaning every time she pushes back, and I rub along her inner walls in a way I know makes her go insane. With my eyes still locked on her, I kiss down her throat while she rides me, grazing my teeth along her shoulder and tweaking her nipples harder, making her cry out and ride me faster. The feel of her so tight around me and the view of us in the mirror and the noises Julie is making have me riding the edge so quickly I have to clench every muscle in my body to keep from coming.

"Asher, I need more," Julie says urgently, riding me faster, harder.

"Anything you want, baby," I say in her ear, sliding one hand down to rub her clit in the firm circles I know she likes and thrusting my hips to fuck up into her every time she grinds down on me.

"Fuck. Yes. Don't stop."

"Never," I rasp, bringing one hand up to grip her throat

while I fuck her faster, rub her harder. I can feel her tightening around me, getting close to the edge, and the feeling drives me wild.

"Watch us, Juliette." I grit into her ear. "Watch how we look together. Watch yourself soak my cock and watch me come inside you."

"Asher, shit, yes," she gasps out, as her legs start to shake, and her hips lose their rhythm. Increasing the pressure of my hand on her throat, I slide two fingers along her clit while I thrust up hard and she comes on a cry, her eyes glued to mine in the mirror. The view of Julie falling apart around me has pleasure licking up my spine, my balls drawing up tight before I come on a groan, my teeth sinking into her neck and my arms holding her tightly to me while I fill her up. I have to fight to keep my eyes open, and it feels like we both come forever, the pleasure so intense that it's almost a relief when it ebbs, her body curling into me and her head falling back on my shoulder. I wrap both my arms around her and hold her tight against me as our hearts pound and both of our chests heave with the effort of taking in oxygen.

"It gets better every time," Julie manages, rolling her head on my shoulder to press a kiss to my cheek. The casual gesture after such an intimate moment has emotion rising in my chest, burning in my eyes.

"It will always get better every time, Juliette. We are fire together."

She laughs a little, bringing her arms up to cover mine, stroking a hand along my forearm, and tangled together like this, I feel our heartrates slowly return to normal. As my body relaxes and I come back down to earth, exhaustion suddenly covers me like a weighted blanket, and I think Julie notices because she unwraps my arms from around her and stands. She leans down and kisses me softly, whispering, "Stay here," against my lips. Too tired to do anything except appreciate the view of a naked Julie, ass swaying as she walks away, I do exactly what she says. I hear the shower go on and then Julie comes back, taking both my hands and pulling me up, guiding me into the bathroom and straight into the shower.

"Sit, Ash," she says, gesturing to the built in shower bench. "Let me take care of you." She unhooks the detachable shower head and leans my head back, wetting my hair. Then she reaches for the shampoo and, with gentle hands, she washes my hair for me. Overcome with a tangle of emotions I'm too tired to separate, I lean forward, closing my eyes and resting my forehead against her chest. I feel her kiss the top of my head and then finish working the shampoo through my hair. By the time she rinses my hair and washes my body for me, I am a puddle.

And when she leans down and brushes a kiss over my injured shoulder, lingering there, lips against the place where I'm broken, my heart cracks open all over again. Tears of relief for what I've gained and lingering grief for what I've lost pour down my face, mixing with the shower water and swirling down the drain. My sobs are quiet but Julie sees. She sees all of me. She sticks with me through the tears, whispering words of comfort and love, picking up my shattered pieces to safeguard until I'm strong enough to put them back together. When I'm all cried out again, she makes quick work of her own shower then shuts off the water. She wraps herself in a towel and then grabs a second one, drying me off right where I sit.

"Come on, Hot Shot, let's get you into bed."

I'm so tired my brain can't even form words. I just follow Julie back into her room and slide into bed when she pulls back the covers. She gets in behind me, fitting her body to mine and sliding an arm around me. I'm a big guy, and I don't think I've ever been the small spoon, but the comfort of Julie wrapped around me at the end of this day that has felt like forever is so immense it has tears blurring my vision all over again. I take a deep breath and sink further into her hold, and I feel her arm tightening around me, her lips against my back.

"Sleep now, Ash. I've got you."

And with the knowledge that she does, and the confidence that she always will, I close my eyes and drop into sleep.

Chapter Forty-Seven
Julie

When I wake up in the morning, I'm still pressed against Asher, my arm around him, my hand pressed low on his belly. When he shifts in his sleep, my fingers graze his hard cock, and he moans into his pillow.

"Do it again," he rasps, his voice thick with sleep and so fucking sexy I feel that rasp through my entire body and my clit throbs, as if I didn't have the best sex of my life less than six hours ago. We fell into bed naked last night, so there's nothing between us as I wrap my hand around him and stroke him long and slow.

"Fuck, baby, I need you right now." His raspy morning voice turns urgent as he rolls over, wrapping his arms around me and kissing me deeply, exploring every inch of my mouth until we're both gasping.

"I want my mouth on you," I say, pulling back to watch his eyes go feral, exactly what I was hoping would happen.

"Then do it, Juliette." Asher settles on his back and laces

his fingers behind his head, leaving his body open for me to explore. Knowing that we're on borrowed time and that at some point one of my parents is going to come looking for us for breakfast, I get right to it. Shifting my body to kneel next to him, I grip the base of his cock and swirl my tongue around the head before I swallow him right down. When I slide my mouth back up, grazing the underside with my tongue and sliding my finger back to rub along the sensitive skin behind his balls, his hips shoot up and the garbled sound he lets out is barely human.

I don't have time to be amused by that because suddenly he sits up, wrapping his arms around my legs and swinging me around so I'm laying on top of his body, my thighs bracketing his face.

"Hold on tight and bring your A-game Juliette. First one to make the other come wins."

I don't have time to process his words before Asher grips my hips and pulls me closer to him, sealing his mouth over my clit and sucking so hard my vision blurs. Barely coherent but hating to lose at anything, I grip his cock at the base, sucking at his head while I move my hand up and down, stroking firmly.

He groans against me, and I feel the vibration through my entire body as his tongue laps at my clit, and his flavor explodes in my mouth. I keep my mouth on him as my body coils tighter and tighter, desperate for release at his delicious suction on my clit as his tongue works me. Wanting him to come, *needing* him to come with a desperation that borders on manic, I cup his balls and slide my fingers back to that sensitive spot, making his hips jerk again.

He chuckles darkly against me, and I hear his thoughts as if he's speaking them out loud.

Game on Juliette.

With his mouth sucking me harder, his tongue moving faster, he grips my ass, pulling my cheeks apart and pressing his thumb against my tight hole, the place no one but him has ever touched. The filthy move has pleasure shooting through me, a deep moan rising from my chest. I double my efforts, increasing the pressure of my hand moving in tandem with my mouth. The combination of Asher's mouth suctioned to my clit and his thumb tracing slow circles has me two seconds from exploding, so with my last rational thought I graze my teeth along the underside of his cock at the same time as he flutters his tongue along my clit and presses in with his thumb, and my entire body bursts in a supernova of pleasure while his cum floods my mouth and his deep groan rumbles against me. My legs are trembling against Asher's face as he wrings every drop of pleasure out of me, and I swallow down every drop of him.

When we're both finally wrung dry, I roll off him, collapsing onto the bed, my head at his feet.

"I guess it was a tie." I pant out a laugh, trying to take in oxygen as my heart gallops.

"Jesus Christ, you're good at that," Asher gasps, trying to catch his breath.

"You know how I like to be the best at things. And you've turned me into some kind of sex crazed maniac, I swear." I fling an arm out and wrap it around his leg, my fingers grazing absently along the back of his knee.

"It's just that I'm so good at sex." He lifts his head to grin down at me.

"Well, at least you're confident in your abilities," I say with a smirk, my hand still stroking along his knee. He brings his hand down to cover mine, blowing out a breath and moving it away from him.

"If you keep stroking my knee like that, I'll have no choice but to show you again just how confident I am. But I'm starving, and I hear voices in the kitchen, so I think we're going to have to save round two for later."

"Sad but true," I say, sitting up and laying right on top of him, leaning on my elbows and bracketing his face with my hands. Looking down into his gorgeous face, love runs through me, warm and true and absolutely sure.

"I love you, Ash."

He grins at me, and his face lights up at my words. "I love you too, Juliette."

Asher

If I wasn't so sex drunk and focused on Julie's ass as she walked down the stairs in front of me, it probably would have registered that there was way too much noise in the kitchen for it to be only Julie's parents in there. But it didn't, so when I walk into the kitchen, I stop dead in my tracks, staring at the table where Rachel and Steven Parker sit chatting with my parents, coffee mugs in front of all of them. Julie is already rounding the table to hug my mom and dad and sit down before she notices that I haven't moved from the kitchen doorway.

"Coming, Hot Shot?" she asks, a grin on her face.

"What are you doing here?" I ask. "And why don't you seem surprised to see them?" I direct that question to Julie as five sets of eyes settle on me.

"You'll have to excuse my son, Rachel. He usually has better manners than this," my mom says, giving me the mom look that still shrivels my balls even though I am a grown-ass man.

"Oh, don't worry about that." Rachel waves away my mom's concern, getting up from the table and crossing to the oven, stopping in front of me to pat my cheek. "I have some experience with ill-mannered children." She lets out a dramatic sigh that has me choking out a laugh before she opens the oven and takes out a pan of cinnamon buns.

"Asher, honey, come sit down," my mom says, pulling out the chair next to her that Julie left vacant. I walk over and hug her and then my dad, taking the seat in between her and Julie.

"So now can you tell me what you're doing here, having coffee in my girlfriend's kitchen in Pittsburgh when you live in Boulder and I saw you three days ago?"

"I called them," Julie says next to me.

I turn to her, confused. "When?"

"When I left your house yesterday. I called Jeremy and then I called your parents. I didn't think you would want to tell them over the phone, and I wanted you to have all your people with you. They got on a red eye as soon as we hung up." She shrugs a shoulder, as if it's nothing that she got my parents here and sitting next to me twelve hours after I got my career-ending news. After I've been agonizing over how to tell them. I wrap an arm around her and bury my face in her hair.

"Thank you," I whisper.

"Anything for you, Hot Shot," she whispers back. When I pull away, both sets of parents are grinning maniacally at us.

"Can you all stop it? It's fucking creepy."

Rachel pins me with a stern look. "Asher Hansley you may be a grown man, but you will not say fuck in my kitchen."

I give her a sheepish look as Julie snorts out a laugh next to me. "She's messing with you, Asher. No one appreciates a well-placed fuck like Rachel Parker."

"Be that as it may, watch your mouth, pal of mine." My mom elbows me in the side, and I toss an arm around her.

"So," my dad says, leaning around to look at me. "It seems like maybe you have some news for us."

I take a deep breath, checking in with myself. I'm surprised to find that I'm not anxious about telling my parents. I'm just glad they're here. I don't know what shifted my perspective so fast. But then I get a flash of Julie moving over me, my dick buried inside her, and I realize it's probably that.

"Why are you grinning like you're thinking about me naked?" Julie hisses at me.

I grin at her. "Because I am."

"Jesus Christ," she mutters. "Shut it the fuck down, Asher."

"I love it when your claws come out in the morning. Scratch me, baby."

"You are a toddler."

"Something you'd like to share with the group?" Steven Parker's voice breaks us out of our whispered banter.

"Nothing, Dad. Just Asher forgetting for a minute that he's an adult." Julie smiles sweetly at me, and I chuckle back at her.

"I apologize for my son," my mom says to Julie's parents. "I tried housebreaking him and was almost successful."

"I have an almost housebroken son of my own," Rachel says. "I know how it goes."

"So, Asher, talk." My dad's voice is gentle but firm.

I wonder where to start and then take a deep breath and jump right in. "I'm retiring." It doesn't feel as scary to say it this time as it did last night. "I had the physical with the team yesterday, and my MRI was about as bad as it gets." My parents don't react, just wait for me to continue, so I do. I tell them everything about the appointment, my talk with the guys last night, Jeremy's job offer, and my talk with Julie.

"I'm sorry I didn't call you right away," I say, when I finish.

"It took me a minute to get my arms around it. I would have called you today. Probably."

"How do you feel, Asher?" asks my dad.

"I feel...okay I think. I mean, I hate it and I wish it wasn't happening, but I hate it a little less today than I did yesterday."

My mom leans over and pulls me into a hug, her arms around me, settling me the same way Rachel's did last night.

"We're proud of you, Asher."

"You are?"

"Of course we are," my dad says. "You're making the hardest decision of your career and being smart about it. You're surrounding yourself with good people who are going to help you through this, and you're already thinking about your future."

I get a little choked up at that. Julie covers my hand with hers under the table, and I turn mine over, lacing our fingers together, so fucking grateful for her.

"And you," my mom turns to Julie. "Thank you for making our boy so happy, and for helping him through this. I'm proud of both of you."

"Well Susan, it's a real travesty, having to hang around him all the time, but he has a never-ending pipeline to my favorite seasonal candy, and he put Diet Pepsi in his soda fountain, so what was I supposed to do, really?"

I sling an arm around Julie, pressing a kiss to the side of her head, to the delight of the four parents sitting around the table. "Juliette, you're my favorite human."

"Yeah, yeah, I like you too," she says, squeezing my hand again under the table and tucking herself more securely against my side in a gesture that has my heart exploding.

"Well, now that we've gotten the business out of the way, let's have breakfast and get to know each other, yeah?" Rachel looks around the table like she's daring anyone to disagree with her and then gets up, followed by Steven. He starts cooking while Rachel puts a latte in front of Julie and a giant cup of soda in front of me. "Dr. Pepper," she says, winking at me and taking her seat. And in the bright kitchen with my arm around Julie and our parents chattering away like they've been friends forever, I think maybe, despite everything, this is exactly where I am meant to be.

Chapter Forty-Eight
Asher

"Asher, are you ready yet?" Julie's voice filters up the stairs and into the bedroom where I'm still trying to decide on a tie. A tie for fuck's sake. I fucking hate ties, unless I'm using them to tie Julie's hands to the headboard like I did that one time. Jesus fuck, it was so damn hot.

Focus, Asher.

My mom texted me this morning and told me that I better wear a tie so I don't embarrass her and my entire family today at the press conference. And I may be thirty-one years old, but when Susan Hansley issues an order, I follow it. So here I stand, in front of my mirror, a blue tie in one hand and a green one in the other, with no clue which one to put on.

"Wear the blue one." I turn at Julie's voice. Like it always does, my heart speeds up a little when I see her. I think it will always be that way. At least, I hope it will.

"You sure?" I stare down at both ties again as if they contain the secrets to the entire universe. She doesn't answer, just walks to me and takes both ties out of my hand, tossing the green one on the bed and threading the blue one through my collar, tying it herself.

"You know how to tie a tie?"

"Who doesn't?" She looks at me with a *duh* expression on her face.

"Um, a lot of people."

"Well, I do." She finishes up, flipping down my collar and smoothing the material with her hands. When she glides her hands down my torso, I flinch and hiss out a breath at the sting.

"What was that?"

"What was what?" I play dumb, knowing it's not going to work.

"You flinched when I touched your rib cage. What's wrong?"

"I didn't flinch. It was electric. I always feel electric when you touch me. We're lightning, baby."

She eyes me with a narrowed gaze. "Don't bullshit me, Asher. Show me." She starts to tug my shirt out of my waistband, but I stop her with my hands on hers.

"Okay, look. I was going to wait to show you, but I should have known I can't hide anything from you."

"You're just figuring this out now?"

I chuckle, tugging my shirt the rest of the way out of my waist band and lifting it to expose the bandage on my rib cage.

Julie runs her fingers over it. "When did you do this?"

"Yesterday, when you thought I was at the gym with the guys."

I peel off the bandage to show her the fresh ink; *Juliette* is added to the list of names I have tattooed there. At the top of the list.

Her breath stutters out and her eyes fill as she rests her fingers beside her name. "You tattooed me on your body?"

I grasp her chin, lifting her head so she's looking at me. "In the list of my most important people, you are the most important of all."

She takes a deep breath and lets it out slowly, trying to pull herself together. "I fucking love you, Hot Shot."

I kiss her softly. "I fucking love you right back."

She looks at the ink for a few more seconds before putting the bandage back in place and pulling down my shirt. As she helps me tuck it back in, she snorts out a laugh.

"What?" I ask her.

"Charlie is going to be so pissed that you tattooed my name above hers."

"Charlie will get over it. You're my number one girl now. Besides, she loves you. You're basically the fifth Hansley sister they never had."

"Damn right I am. I even have the Hansley sister group chat to prove it." She brushes a wrinkle out of my shirt and then rests her hands on my shoulders, studying me.

"How do you feel?"

"I feel okay I think. I mean, I don't love that I have to do a whole press conference, and I still don't understand why I can't just issue a statement or something, but I'm ready."

In the month since I found out about my shoulder, I've done nothing but get ready. The first week was a whirlwind of meetings with my coach and the team owners and phone calls with my agent to get everything in order. It wasn't the easiest week of my life, and by the end of it, I was exhausted. So once my part in the planning process was over, Julie and I took a long weekend at the Parkers' lake house with her friends and all the guys. The weekend skiing, building a bonfire on the lake shore in the freezing cold, and spending time inside by the fire was just what I needed to get my head back on straight, and when we came back, I started going into Jeremy's foundation office a couple of times a week to figure out what my new position is going to look like. I'm not going to officially start for another month or so, but I realized pretty fast that sitting around and doing nothing wasn't for me. I need a project, and the sports camps are perfect.

And my favorite part of the last month is that Julie moved in with me. She hadn't spent a single night at her house since she got back from Boulder, and a lot of her stuff had migrated over here. So, when we got back from the lake, she hired movers and we made it official. I love going to sleep with her at night and waking up with her in the morning knowing that this is her home too. My house never feels lonely or empty when she's in it. She has filled my entire world with so much light and joy, and I am just so damn grateful for it. No one on earth could convince me that we weren't made for each other.

Julie studies me and seems satisfied with what she sees. "I think you are. Come on, Hot Shot. We better go now so we get there in time."

She turns to leave the bedroom, but I grab her wrist, spinning her back to me. "What's the rush, Juliette? We have plenty of time."

I slide an arm around her waist and tug her against me. I cup her cheek with my other hand and kiss her, pouring everything I have into it, the taste of her invading my senses until I have half a mind to toss her onto the bed and skip the press conference entirely. As always, she knows what I'm thinking because she pulls away and puts a hand on my chest.

"There's no time. But when we get home later, we can do that thing with the ties again." She grins at me wickedly, then glances over at where the green tie lays on the bed and then back at the tie around my neck, and I immediately get hard.

"It was so hot, right?"

"Bet your ass it was. This time do my legs too," she says, before sauntering out of the room as if she didn't just put the sexiest visual of all time into my head. Fuck, I'm obsessed with her.

A hard on in snug suit pants is not ideal, but I'll have to roll with it because by the time I make my way downstairs, Julie is putting on her coat.

"What's the rush, Juliette? We have a whole bunch of time."

She mutters something about traffic and then grabs my hand, pulling me outside with her where I pause because there, right in my driveway, is a black car that's not exactly a bus, but bigger than a van, with blacked out windows and a yellow stripe along the side.

"Juliette, why is that thing in my driveway?"

She smiles at me, shrugging a shoulder. "Why don't you go over and see?"

As I approach the bus, the door opens, and noise spills out. When I get to the top of the steps I freeze, and emotion clogs my chest because crowded inside are all the people I love most in the world. Hallie and Ben, Jordan and Allie, Jeremy, Emma, and Molly sit along one side with Steven and Rachel Parker. And along the other side are Charlie, Annie, Kyla, and Lucy with their husbands and my parents. Five of my nieces are spinning around the poles that line the center of the bus, and the three babies are strapped into car seats.

Julie comes up behind me, wrapping an arm around my waist and kissing my cheek. "Surprise."

"What are you all doing here?" I knew my parents were in town and would be coming to the press conference with Julie, but everyone else is a surprise.

"What, you think we would let you do this alone?" Jeremy stands and tosses an arm around my shoulder. "No way dude. No one in this group does anything alone."

"What he said," says Ben. "If there's one day you need your people, it's today."

My people. God, I am so fucking lucky.

I put a hand on Julie's face, turning her to face me before kissing her breathless right there in front of everyone. "Thanks." I grin at her and the way her eyes go a little hazy when I pull away.

"I wish I could take credit for it, but this is a Hansley girl operation." Julie smiles over at my sisters.

The words are barely out of her mouth before I'm attacked by my sisters on all sides, and then my nieces abandon the poles to throw themselves at me, and by the time we pull out of my driveway, it really does feel more like a party, and far less like what it is, which is the official end of my football career.

Julie

"Wow, there are...a lot more of you than I was expecting." The head of PR for the Renegades stands outside the press room, staring at all of us. "Some of you are going to have to wait out here and watch on the TVs." She points at the TVs mounted on the hallway walls. "I'm not sure we'll have room for everyone."

Asher opens his mouth to talk but I put a hand on his shoulder and step in front of him. "So make room. Asher has been the starting quarterback for this team for eight seasons and he is retiring today. He gets to have his family with him when he does that. They're all coming in."

"Fucking right, we are," I hear Molly say behind me.

Asher slides an arm around my waist and tugs me back into his chest. I don't have to look back at him to know he's grinning at the PR rep.

"What she said."

The PR rep lets out a long-suffering sigh and rolls her eyes. "Athletes," she mutters as she turns and walks into the press room to, presumably, do some rearranging.

"I love when you go all lawyer mode," Asher says into my ear. "It's so damn hot, Juliette. Makes me want to go sneak into the locker room for a quickie."

"Keep it in your pants, Hot Shot."

"I just can't do that. You know what being around you does to me." I do know, and I hope it will never change. But before I have a chance to respond, the press room doors open, and we're ushered inside. There are seats right in front for Asher's parents and sisters, and the rest of us gather along the wall at the side of the room. When Asher's coach walks up to the podium at the front of the room, I hear Asher's breath hitch a little, and I take his hand in both of mine. Leaning into him, I speak into his ear.

"It's going to be okay. Just take some deep breaths, and if you need a break, look at me while you're talking. I'll be right here, and as soon as you're finished, we'll go home, okay?"

His body relaxes at the word *home* like I knew it would. For a man who loves people as much as he does, he also loves being at home and is fiercely protective of the time we spend together. He takes a couple of deep breaths and squares his shoulders.

"Okay. I'm ready."

It's just in time because his coach finishes up and calls Asher to the podium. He takes my face in his hands, kissing me and whispering "I love you," against my lips before heading up to take the microphone. He pauses for a minute before starting to speak, glancing around the room, eyes lingering on me and our friends and then his family in the front row. All the familiar faces seem to steel him for what he is about to do because when he starts to speak, his voice is strong.

"Thank you to everyone for being here today. As you all know, I am here today to announce my retirement from professional football. An MRI of my shoulder about a month ago showed substantial damage, leading to a diagnosis of severe arthritis, making it impossible for me to continue playing."

He pauses, taking another deep breath to steady himself before continuing. "Playing for the Renegades for the past eight seasons has been a dream come true and the joy of my life. I loved every second I spent in this stadium, with this team. But it's time for new dreams now, and I'm looking forward to what comes next."

He glances over at me, and I keep my eyes steady on his, sending him whatever strength he needs to get through the rest of his statement.

"I want to thank the team and the entire Renegades organization for the opportunity to spend my career here, and my teammates for being the best group of guys I could have ever hoped to play with. And to the city of Pittsburgh, you didn't know anything about me when I got the starting job, but you rallied around me, a kid from Boulder who dreamed of playing in the NFL, and your support has been everything to me over the years. I'm a Colorado boy, but I love the city of Pittsburgh with my whole heart and will be making it my permanent home.

"I always thought I would go back to Colorado when I retired, to be with my family. But last year, I met a girl."

Asher glances over at me and grins slyly, and I know two things immediately. He's about to go off script, and whatever he's going to say will be embarrassing.

"The first time we met she refused to give me her phone number, and it was six months before I saw her again and finally convinced her to give me a chance. It took a little luck and unwavering persistence, but I've got her now, and she is, without a doubt, the very best thing to ever happen to me."

The look he gives me is full of so much love that it has tears filling my eyes and spilling down my cheeks. Hallie links her arm through mine on one side and Molly on the other, Emma putting her hand on my shoulder as Asher continues, his eyes never leaving mine.

"Juliette, I love you fiercely. Thank you for sticking with me through this past month, and helping me see all the goodness that is waiting for us on the other side. Thank you all."

With that, he stands up, ignoring the reporters shouting questions at him, and walks straight to me, eyes laser focused on mine. He kisses me and pulls me into a hug. His body is shaking a little, and his heart is pounding with the adrenaline of making that speech, so I wrap my arms tightly around him, rubbing my hand up and down his back until he starts to calm.

"I'm so fucking glad that's over," he mutters.

"I love you," I whisper in his ear so only he can hear. "I'm so proud of you, even though you did embarrass me in front of a room full of reporters."

My words have the desired effect because he chuckles, his chest moving against mine. "I just wanted to love you out loud, Juliette."

"Okay, but maybe love me just a little quieter next time."

"No can do baby. This love is too big to contain."

And how fucking lucky am I that it is. We pull apart, and I glance around the emptying press room, the reporters leaving to file their stories and our friends and family drifting out to the hall. I hold out a hand to him, and he takes it, winding our fingers together and pulling me closer to him, kissing my forehead and lingering there for a minute before leaning back and tucking my hair behind my ear with his free hand. I look at him and am happy to see that his eyes are clear and calm, happiness dancing in the blue.

"Ready for what comes next, Hot Shot?"

"Juliette, with you, I'm ready for anything."

Epilogue

Asher

Five Months Later

"Do we really need that many cookies?"

I glance over at Julie as she pads barefoot into the kitchen and takes a seat at the kitchen island. She's gorgeous, her hair loose, her face freshly washed, and with tiny sleep short clad legs that I'd like to wind around my waist right here in the kitchen.

"Are you doubting my baking prowess?" I ask, as I slide the latte I made for her across the island, picking up her left hand and running my thumb over the diamond on her ring finger. We got engaged a week after my retirement press conference. I bought the ring a few days after I made the decision to retire and was just waiting for the right moment. When a freak March snowstorm blew through the week after the press conference, I took it as a sign and proposed right here in the back yard in the middle of the storm. After I slid the ring on her finger and kissed the breath out of her, we collapsed back into the snow and laid there, holding hands, watching the snow fall from the darkened sky. It was just the two of us and a perfect snowfall, and it was the best moment of my entire life.

She smiles gratefully, taking the first sip. "I mean, no? I'm just wondering if twelve dozen cookies might be too many cookies considering it's just our friends and family coming over."

I sigh dramatically, mainly for effect. "We've been over this, Juliette. We need everyone's favorites. Hansley family tradition. And since all the Hansleys are coming over today, it had to be done."

She smiles. "I know. I'm just fucking with you. I love when you make all the cookies. You look super hot all busy in the kitchen."

"Hot, huh? Tell me more." I saunter around the island until I'm crowded up between Julie's legs. I slide my hands into her hair and tip her head up, taking her mouth in the kind of kiss that belongs in a dark bedroom and not a bright kitchen at seven thirty in the morning with the sun streaming through the windows. But I can't help myself. I never can around her.

"That's a hell of a way to start a morning," Julie says, a little breathlessly, when we pull apart.

"The best way." I wink at her and walk back around the island to grab the last tray of cookies from the oven.

"So, we're all set for today," she says, leaning her elbows on the island and propping her chin on her hands. "The food is coming at ten, and I told everyone to be here at ten thirty. Charlie already texted Sand told me they might be a little early because the girls woke them up at five and she is, and I quote, "so over parenting and ready to dump the kids on us and have a mimosa."

I laugh, knowing that I'm about to spend at least a part of the morning in the pool entertaining kids while Charlie drapes herself over a lounge chair with a drink in her hand. She's a whole entire mood.

"Works for me. It'll be good practice."

"Practice for what?"

"For when we have our own. I'm thinking at least four, with the option for five."

Julie narrows her eyes at me. "Two, with the option for three."

I scoff at her. "Two isn't enough. Can't play a good football game with just two kids."

"Here's a thought. What if your kids don't want to play football? What if they want to, I don't know, dance. Or do art. Or sit on the couch and read a book."

"They'll want to play football. It'll be in their genes."

"I don't think you understand how genetics works."

"You know what? I don't really care how many of them we have or what activities they like. They'll be awesome no matter what."

"Oh yeah? What makes you so sure?"

"Because you'll be their mom."

Her breath stutters out at that, and I watch her eyes get misty. I round the island again and pull her up from her stool, wrapping myself around her. When I feel her arms go around my waist, I am one hundred percent sure no one in the world has ever felt as happy as I feel right now. It's just not possible.

"I love you, Juliette. You are my whole entire world."

"I love you too, Ash. It's a good life we're making here."

"The best."

I kiss the top of her head, closing my eyes and breathing in her honey vanilla scent, thanking whatever god is listening for bringing this woman into my life. For giving us to each other to love.

When we break apart, we look at each other for a beat, and

twin grins spread across our faces. I know what she's thinking, and I'm thinking the same.

"I should go get dressed," she says, taking a step away. I pull her back for one last kiss before releasing her. She walks towards the stairs while I start putting the now cooled cookies onto the platters I have waiting. She pauses for a minute, like she always does, when she passes the gallery wall of pictures from our road trip. When she moved in, the first thing she did was go through our shared album and choose pictures to frame and hang. I don't even know if she realizes she does it, but I love seeing the soft smile that always takes over her face when she looks at the memories of the two weeks that changed both of our lives.

"Hey, Juliette?" I call as she turns away from the wall and heads up the stairs.

She turns back. "Yeah, Hot Shot?"

"You ready?"

"I'm so ready." She flashes me a bright smile and disappears up the stairs.

Julie

The backyard is full of people. Kids splash in the pool, Asher is chatting with the guys, my parents and Asher's parents are sitting around a table laughing together, and I'm crowded around the buffet table with Hallie, Emma, Molly, and Allie. Tonight is the Kids Play gala, and Asher is giving a big speech detailing all the progress they have made on the sports camps since the foundation kicked off the capital campaign at last year's gala. His whole family is in town, so we invited everyone over for a pre-gala brunch.

"Jules, this taco bar fucking rocks," Molly says, a plate of tacos in one hand and her second margarita in the other.

"Seriously. You guys really outdid yourself on the food." Allie studies the platters laid out on the buffet and grabs a chicken taco, taking a huge bite. "This is amazing."

"I'm more impressed by the cookie table. There must be like, eight dozen cookies," Hallie says, peering over at the impressively decorated cookie buffet with Asher's meticulously labeled signs.

"Twelve," I mumble, my mouth full.

"And he made them all?" Emma looks incredulous.

I swallow my last bite, taking a sip of my drink before answering. "He needed to make everyone's favorite. It's a whole Hansley thing."

"Well, it's a thing I can get behind," Hallie says. "Can steal some to take home later?"

"Ask Asher. I'm sure he'll be thrilled."

"Ask Asher what?" The man in question comes up behind me, wrapping his arms around my waist and leaning down to kiss my neck.

"Hallie wants a doggie bag of cookies for the road."

"It would be my greatest pleasure."

"Asher Hansley, I've always liked you."

He winks at her. "Everyone likes me, Hal. It's a gift. Okay if I steal my girl away for a few minutes?"

I thought I would be nervous when it was time, but nerves are the last thing I feel. Instead, I feel a shimmer of excitement, knowing what's about to happen.

"Go for it," Molly says. "We were finished with her anyway."

I stick my tongue out at her as Asher leads me towards the

center of the yard. On the way, I catch Ben's eye and nod to him. He breaks away from Jeremy and Jordan and makes his way towards Asher and me.

"Hey, can I have everyone's attention for a minute?" The backyard quiets as everyone turns at the sound of Asher's voice.

"Thanks so much for coming. We really appreciate you all being here." Asher takes my hand and smiles down at me and my heart speeds up, electricity sparking in my veins. "Okay, so we kept the real reason behind this little get together a secret mainly because I love a surprise. And even though my girl here does *not* love a surprise, she loves me, so she went with it. The reason you're all here is that we're getting married. Today."

The backyard is completely silent for a minute before everyone starts talking at once, shouting out questions so fast I can't grab hold of any of them. I glance over at Asher, and he's grinning at me. He wraps an arm around me and pulls me into his side, pressing a kiss to my temple.

"Told you this would be fun."

The truth is, it is a little fun. After we got engaged, I started thinking about wedding planning, and it took about ten minutes for my anxiety to spike at the thought of the perfect dress and the perfect food and hair and makeup and having everyone's eyes on me. When Asher saw what was going on, he sat me down and asked me what I really wanted. Not what I thought everyone expected, but what I really, truly wanted. One of the things I've been talking to my therapist a lot about over the last few months is making sure that when I do something, it's because I want to do it, and not because I think it will look good, or because it's what I think people will expect of me. And when I thought about it, I realized all I wanted was to be married to Asher. I didn't care about the wedding at all. In fact, all it did was stress me out and suck the joy right out of being engaged and starting this life together.

So, we concocted this plan to get married in our backyard, surrounded by our family and closest friends, wearing absolutely nothing special, and not to tell anyone about it until the day of. And we picked the day of the gala because it's the one-year anniversary of the day we first met, and we both liked that symbolism of getting married on this day and then going to dance at the gala. The Julie of a year ago would never have imagined getting married this way, but I like the person I am now. The person I found when I opened myself up to Asher and let him see all of me.

"I guess you were kind of right."

"Juliette, you are so sexy when you tell me I'm right."

I laugh a little, leaning further into Asher, feeling his arm wrap more tightly around me. I watch as his sisters grab their kids from the pool and bundle them into towels, and laugh again at the visual of us getting married surrounded by kids in bathing suits and my best friends half drunk on margaritas.

"You okay?" Asher asks me quietly.

I kiss his cheek and lean my head on his shoulder. "I'm perfect."

The backyard quiets and everyone forms a semi-circle around us. When I glance around, a bubble of emotion rises in my chest seeing everyone I love the most in one place, and I know with a bone deep certainty that no perfect dress or immaculately catered wedding would beat this moment, right now.

"You guys ready?" Ben asks from his place next to us. When I said we didn't tell anyone, what I meant was we didn't tell anyone except for Ben. I let him in on the secret a few days ago, because we asked him to marry us.

Asher faces me and takes both of my hands. When our eyes meet, he winks, and every part of me lights right up.

"I was ready a year ago. Took Juliette here awhile to catch up, but she's here now."

I sure am.

Ben grins at that. "She always has been a meticulous decision maker."

I scowl at him. "Don't you have a job to do?"

"Only my children would find a way to fight at my daughter's surprise wedding. That's happening now. That no one told me about." My mom narrows her eyes at me, and both Asher and I burst out laughing.

"Told you she would hate being out of the loop," he says.

"It's good for her. Keeps her honest. Can we get this show on the road?"

Ben pulls me into a side hug, whispering in my ear, "Love you. I'm proud of you, Jules."

My eyes burn with tears at that. And when I glance around, I see my friends and Asher's sisters with huge grins and misty eyes. It should be illegal to be this happy.

"Okay," Ben says, stepping back. "I'm going to skip the 'we are gathered here today' and all that because I literally got ordained on the internet three days ago. I'm so happy for you guys. I love you so much, and I'm glad that you found each other. You are the best people I know, and you deserve all the happiness in the world. I know you both have things you want to say to each other, so have at it."

"Talk to me, Juliette." Asher squeezes my hands in encouragement. I told him last night that I was nervous about spilling all my feelings in front of everyone Brind all he said was, *just talk to me.* Butterflies swarm my stomach at his reminder. There is no better man on the planet than him.

"I used to think no one would ever see all of me and want to stick around. I didn't feel safe enough to show anyone the parts of myself I thought were broken. I was getting through every day, but I wasn't really living, I don't think. But then I met you, and I didn't have to show you anything, because you just saw every part of me right from the first dance. You took me on a road trip and showed me what it was like to live. You brought me happiness and joy and so much fun. You did carpool karaoke to Taylor Swift and made me howl with wolves, and you took me to see a sixteen-foot taco and laughed when I beat you at skee-ball six times in a row. You exploded my world, and if I had to make one wish, it would be for more of this. More of you and me and this life that we are building together right here in this house. I love you, Asher. You are the best thing that has ever happened to me, and every day, I'm grateful that you're mine, and that I get to be yours."

My voice breaks on the last word, and I lose it a little, a tear slipping out and rolling down my cheek. Asher reaches up, his hand cupping my face as his thumb swipes away the tear. His own eyes are glassy as he starts to talk, his hand never leaving my face.

"Juliette, you are my favorite everything. You knocked the breath from my lungs the first time I saw you. I only had to hear your voice to start falling for you, and I have fallen more every single day since then. I want to go to sleep with you every night and wake up next to you every morning. I want to make you lattes and buy you all the peppermint Hershey Kisses you can eat and sit outside during perfect snowfalls and make you breakfast before you go to work. I want to watch you slay all the dragons and then come home at night where it's just you and me and this life I love so fucking much. I want to hear all your secrets and tell you mine, and I want us to always be safe with each other. You are my whole world, Juliette. I will love you every second of my life and on into eternity because a love this big can't be anything except for forever."

My tears are falling freely now, and so are Asher's. But

somehow, even though everything else is a blur, I see him clearly. I am focused so intently on Asher that I barely notice the rest of the ceremony. Ben says things, and we say I do, and we slip rings on each other's fingers, and our eyes stay locked the entire time. And when it's over, Asher kisses me so thoroughly and deeply that my head spins and everyone bursts into applause, but I don't hear any of it. All I hear is Asher's voice in my ear as his arms wrap around me and hold me tight against him like we are the only two people in the world because in this moment, we are.

"I love you, Juliette. Forever, okay?"

"I love you, too, Hot Shot. Forever."

Acknowledgments

To my readers, it still blows my mind every day that you read my first book and are now here for book two. Thank you, a million times, for every edit, review, tag, and message. Talking about books is my absolute favorite thing to do, and talking to all of you about my book has been the joy of my life. Thank you for loving Hallie and Ben, and your enthusiasm over Julie and Asher and the whole Laws of You crew. I can't wait to bring you Emma's and Molly's stories.

Mom and Dad, never have there ever been two parents who are more supportive of one of their children than you are of me. You have always been on my side, and cheered me on every step of the way, no matter where my life has taken me. I had the courage to do the thing and write the books because I always knew that you were standing behind me. I am the luckiest.

Katie and Lou, never has anyone had better sisters than the two of you. Thank you for being the greatest cheerleaders of my author life, for reading my books, for loving them, and for delivering paperbacks to all your neighborhood friends. You are both my favorites, and Lou, even though you now live across an ocean, the Julie and Asher paperback is already in the mail.

My White Plains girls, thank you so much for being so supportive of my brand new author life. For reading the books and telling your friends, and throwing me the absolute best book release party any girl could ask for. I love the life that we have built together in this place, and am so grateful for all of you. I couldn't have asked for better friends.

Ruth, my OG author bestie. Trading alpha reads, voice notes, and WhatsApp messages full of plotting and daily details is such a joy. It's hard to believe that it hasn't even been a year since that first message. I am so grateful for your friendship, and couldn't do any of this without you.

Brittany, what do I even say? Getting to know you has been the absolute joy of my year. I love our daily messages, our book doppelganger bestie brains, and sharing little life tidbits with you. I can't wait to find a time to meet IRL because squeezing you in person is an absolute must. Thank you so much for all your Asher and Julie love, and for being the world's best cheerleader.

Sariah, my love. You are the OG Julie-stan and I am so freaking grateful for you. Thank you for answering my "can you just read this one little thing" messages when I was up late writing, for your absolutely contagious enthusiasm for all things Asher and Julie, and for once again being the queen of the beta doc comments. I love you endlessly and your friendship means the world to me.

Grayce, Ginsa, and Jess, I have no idea what I would do without you. Our group chat is my favorite place, and our writing sprints are the best part of my week. Thank you so much for being the best friends I could ever have asked for, and for being there for all the highs and lows of indie author life. I am so grateful that we found each other, and am looking forward to all the books we're going to write together.

My Betas, Britt, Sariah, Taylor, and Shann, the When I'm With You beta doc is my favorite place on earth. Thank you all for your Julie and Asher love, for the amazing and hilarious comments, and for being the best support system I could ever have asked for. I couldn't have done this without you, and I hope you are all ready to beta read my books forever and ever, because I'm never letting any of you go.

The Goddesses of War Group Chat, thank you so much for being the most supportive friends in the world, for my favorite group chat of all time, for introducing me to dark romance (and holding my virtual hand while I read it), and for being the inspiration behind Chapter 30, IYKYK. Love you all, and can't wait to squeeze you IRL next year.

Tina, thank you for all the things. For the book chats, for opining on model covers with me, for adding to my TBR on the daily, for never steering me wrong when it comes to book recs, and for being the best editor I could have asked for. Thank you for being so supportive of me and my books, and I am so sorry about all the em-dashes, and the fact that I sometimes forget how to use a comma. You are officially stuck with me forever.

Lemmy, I could never do any of this without you. Thank you so much for your friendship, your PR and marketing genius, and being an all-around amazing human. I am so happy to know you and so proud to work with you and with Luna, and I am so proud of you for all you have accomplished. Love you so big.

Mudge, my favorite Pittsburgh girl. I am the absolute luckiest to have met you. Thank you so much for all your Ben and Hallie and Julie and Asher love. I appreciate you so much, and I can't wait for everything we have coming up next year. December and our big Pittsburgh meetup can't come soon enough!

Andi, your support means the world. Thank you for your reel-making prowess, your friendship, for reading early copies of my books, and for letting me be unhinged about the Langfield men and the Boston Bolts/Revs in your DMs. You are absolutely the best, and I am so grateful to have met you on this wild ride.

David, Will, and Bella, none of my author dreams would be possible without you. I love you all to the moon.

Books by Samantha Brinn

The Laws of You Series

Because of You

(Hallie & Ben's story)

When I'm With You

(Julie and Asher's story)

Anything for You

(Emma's story)

Coming early 2025

About the Author

Samantha Brinn (Sam to everyone who knows her) is an author of sweet, spicy, and swoony contemporary romance novels. A Pittsburgh girl currently living in the suburbs of NYC, Sam stole her first romance novel off of her mom's bookshelf at age thirteen and has read pretty much nothing but romance ever since. Her Kindle is basically an extension of her hand at this point.

A lawyer by day and author by night, Sam can most often be found in bed with her laptop and writing desk late into the night, having the time of her life writing words and weaving stories and grinning at her characters' hijinks.

Aside from being a reader and a writer, Sam is a lover of French fries, Reese's peanut butter cups, and diet Pepsi, and much like her debut FMC, she rarely makes her coffee the same way twice. A mom of two, Sam cosplays as an organized human, but at her core, she's mostly chaos and prefers it that way, and is loving every second of this wild indie author ride.

www.ingramcontent.com/pod-product-compliance
Lightning Source LLC
Chambersburg PA
CBHW031830310726
48972CB00005B/1236